# Honour
# Bound

Alaric Bond

Honour Bound

Copyright © 2017 by Alaric Bond

Published by Old Salt Press LLC

ISBN 978-1-943404-14-8 e.book
978-1-943404-15-5 paperback

The cover shows a detail from *Off Barbados* by James Edward Buttersworth (died 1894).

Publisher's Note: This is a work of historical fiction. Certain characters and their actions may have been inspired by historical individuals and events. The characters in the novel, however, represent the work of the author's imagination. Any resemblance to actual persons, living or dead, is entirely coincidental. Published by Old Salt Press. Old Salt Press, LLC is based in Jersey City, New Jersey with an affiliate in New Zealand. For more information about our titles go to www.oldsaltpress.com

For R&L

(The Railway People)

By the same author

## The Fighting Sail Series:

# CONTENTS

# Honour Bound

## Chapter One

Of all the occasions when King had sat in Sir Alexander Ball's office, this was the first time he noticed a chill in the air. But there was nothing so very surprising in that; November had become firmly established and, despite its latitude and the broiling hot summer just past, Malta was still heading towards winter. The coolness was more ethereal than physical though, which certainly was unusual. Ball might be a good deal older and, as a senior Royal Navy captain, considerably outranked a newly promoted commander such as King, while his position as Civil Commissioner effectively made him the Governor of a pivotal British outpost. But a measure of empathy had always existed between the two, yet now it was very obviously absent.

"Your manning problems must wait; I assume *Kestrel* is ready to return to sea without delay?" The question had interrupted King in the midst of a lengthy explanation and sounded unusually sharp.

"Yes, sir." The reply was automatic and neither spoke again as Ball's attention returned to the paper in front of him. King tried to remember a previous occasion when the Civil Commissioner had been quite so aloof, but failed. The closest he came was when Ball asked him to conduct his only son on the first stage of a journey back to Britain. But King had sensed then that any awkwardness was simply to disguise a father's reluctance to send his child into danger. And he had looked after the boy well enough, even to the point of releasing his first lieutenant to see him safely to the end of the journey.

The great man was still apparently immersed in his reading, and King's eyes began to roam about the room. It held one of the few fireplaces in the large building, but wood was a precious

1

commodity on such a barren island and the temperature had yet to drop to the extent that a fire need be lit. Above, on the marble mantle, a white-faced clock dolefully rang out the hour. It was twelve noon; he had already been with the Civil Commissioner for thirty minutes, which was a long time for nothing to have been revealed or resolved. King was still uncertain if he were to face some form of censure: *Kestrel* had been at sea for the last few weeks, and any amount of mischief might have been made in his absence.

There had been the unpleasant incident of the murder of a prominent civilian, someone who also happened to have been one of King's closest friends. It was a matter that undoubtedly contained wrongdoing and, strangely, was also linked to Ball's son returning to England. But King had long ago convinced himself that no blame for any part of the event could be placed at his door.

And then there was the recent court martial for mutiny – a rare charge, when brought by a post captain against his own first lieutenant. But that had closed before *Kestrel* sailed and the eventual verdict of not guilty for the accused, followed by a less public retirement for the captain, must surely have settled the issue. In fact, so brief had the proceedings been, King was not required to give evidence and, when such a lot of whitewash was used to keep the finer details quiet, he doubted anyone would dig deeper now.

Ball finished reading and moved the paper away, although his tired eyes remained lowered for several seconds longer. Then they rose to meet King's, and a measure of warmth returned.

"You are to be transferred," the older man informed him with a further softening in his expression. But there was no humour: even as King watched it became a look of sadness and, in a flash of empathy, he knew the mighty Alexander Ball was sincerely sorry King would be leaving.

As he was himself, for this represented nothing short of a disaster. King had been on the Malta station for less than a year, yet that time had seen him plucked from a mundane job on the beach, welcomed back into the Royal Navy proper, then promoted and given a spirited little sloop to command. *Kestrel* had come in that morning and currently lay not half a mile from Ball's offices in the *Auberge d'Italie*. Despite being fifteen able men down, King had entered the room full of hopes that he might take her to sea

2

again without undue delay, but to sail from Malta with no certainty of ever seeing the island's warm brown visage again was another matter entirely.

However, it wasn't the thought of leaving that concerned him; he had taken to the place for sure, but losing the influence of Sir Alexander Ball was far more important. King was a man with few friends in high places and the sombre senior captain opposite represented his best chance both of staying in employment and future promotion. He owed his current ship and rank to him, yet where he was going there would be others in command who would also have favourites. And some might not consider a one-armed officer such as himself capable of captaining a sloop, let alone suitable for further responsibility.

"Since you took that Frenchman, it has been relatively peaceful hereabouts," Ball was continuing, his manner easing further now the dreadful news had been delivered. "There have been developments aplenty elsewhere, however, and that is where you are needed."

"Would that be Toulon, sir?" It was a simple question but an obvious one. Nelson had been conducting a loose blockade outside the French port for some while, with repeated attempts to lure out the entrenched enemy fleet within by apparently withdrawing his own forces. Estimates varied, but reports from agents ashore together with the evidence of the blockaders' own eyes indicated up to twelve line-of-battleships were ready to sail immediately while, so desperate was Nelson to bring these to combat in open water, they were often guarded by nothing more than a couple of fifth rate frigates. Such a strategy required good lines of communication if the main bulk of the British fleet was to be alerted in good time, so a ship of *Kestrel*'s particular sailing qualities would be valuable indeed.

"Initially you will be sailing to Gib.," Ball replied. "After that I have no idea, though should be surprised if a ship of *Kestrel*'s capabilities remained on blockade for very long."

That could mean any number of things. For all King knew, Ball may have information that the French had already sailed; Nelson might be searching the wide inland sea for them at this very moment – a caper the Admiral was more than accustomed to after his experiences during the last war. Or developments elsewhere could mean Toulon, or the French south-east coast in general, was losing its importance and *Kestrel* was to be despatched to some other quarter. This was the least probable option, but one that soon proved most likely.

"If I am any judge, we shall be fighting the Dons as well before long," Ball grunted, glancing down at the paper yet again. "In fact we may already be at war and have yet to learn of it."

"Indeed, sir?" It was no secret that Spain lived in fear of a French invasion, her neutral stance being bought by a yearly transfer of over seventy million francs into the *Trésor*. Yet for Spain to declare war on Great Britain would be a major step indeed and one she was unlikely to take as it must surely endanger her many foreign interests. King could only foresee such an outcome following an outright attack on her land or shipping; something that was unthinkable in the delicate times they lived in. Then Ball's next words proved him wrong for the second time that morning.

"The late summer *flota* has been taken," he stated baldly and there was now no trace of sympathy on the Civil Commissioner's face. "Four frigates under the command of Graham Moore. The Spanish were actually carrying more than we anticipated," he continued in the same flat tone. "Over four million gold and silver dollars, as well as several hundred thousand pounds' worth of specie and other goods. Moore intercepted them as they made for Cádiz and offered safe refuge in a British port. Of course they refused, as he would have expected, and when they did he opened fire." He sighed. "It was under orders of course but, as we were not at war, remains a crime nonetheless."

"And were they taken?" King asked. He had met Moore twice after the Battle of Tory Island and could not believe the dedicated young Scott could allow a squadron of Spanish treasure ships to get the better of him.

"Oh, they were taken right enough," Ball confirmed. "One blew up and went straight to the bottom, but there was still a good deal of cargo aboard the other three, which is now on its way to Gosport."

"So we are at war," King replied, too shocked to fully comprehend what had actually taken place. The sudden injection of up to a million pounds might please the government's quill drivers but, as a sea officer, he could predict immediate trouble and on a

4

far more personal level.

"If so, it has not been confirmed to me," Ball replied. "Though I think we both know it is merely a question of time. And I need not remind you how this weakens our own position, both here and in European waters." He paused. "And throughout the whole damned world, if the truth be known."

That was undeniable; the larger Spanish ports were of immense value to British shipping. Without access to their water, supplies and repair facilities it might become impossible to maintain ships in the Mediterranean, while even regular communication with London would become a thing of the past. But King felt the major consideration must lie in actual sea power, and clearly he was not alone.

"The Spanish might not make the best seamen, but they can certainly build ships," Ball continued, relaxing once more. "At present Britain would be lucky to raise more than eighty third rates and now the Dons are involved, we will be facing over a hundred: such things are hard to keep secret. They are also well placed with Guarnizo and Ferrol being a couple of day's sail from our coast; if Boney truly intends to invade, this will be his best chance to date. Put a sensible man in command, and he should have no trouble in securing the Channel for the six hours he claims to need – or six weeks, if it came to it."

There was little that could be said to such a statement and King remained silent.

"To my mind, the whole thing was appallingly handled," Ball added bluntly and King was mildly surprised at his candour. "I hate to criticise my superiors and understand better than most the reasons that can lie behind such an action. It is likely Admiral Cornwallis was obeying orders every bit as much as Moore, but to send an equal force to do the work was surely asking for trouble..."

Ball's glance had now fallen back to the desk and, so immersed was he in his thoughts, he might have been talking to himself.

"Had a couple of liners been spared from blockade they might have surrendered without losing face. As it was, the Spanish were given little option other than to fight. And a good many died, including civilians, so any loss of honour was entirely on our side. Boney is bound to make much of Britain sending warships to attack a neutral convoy but, however it be served, this is hardly a dish that will go down well with potential allies."

Ball said nothing more for a while, and King began to feel awkward. Then the older man finally looked up from his desk and seemed surprised to see him there.

"So, Mr King, I think we can assume that war with Spain is inevitable," he said. Then, after a moment's thought, added, "And you would look to be heading straight into the heart of the action."

* * *

The words remained with King as he made his way out of the *Auberge d'Italie* and down towards the Customs House where his gig would be waiting to take him back to *Kestrel*. They had found her berth with the last of the moon, so the ship would be in the mild state of confusion expected when returning from a trip. But he had no doubts that all would soon be under control; James Timothy was a fine second in command, and one who performed his duties with a casual ease that King secretly envied. Although several years older, and with considerably more sea time than his captain, Timothy had never shown any resentment at King's rank or position, and neither did he offer advice or opinions, unless they were specifically requested.

The rest of *Kestrel*'s officers were equally satisfactory. In Brehaut he had a first-rate sailing master and even Adams, a senior midshipman who, despite failing his board, was making a reasonable fist of acting as second lieutenant. How any of them would take to learning they were to be transferred from Malta was a different matter, however, and it was a change that would affect the lower deck as much as any of the officers.

On an island station, shore leave was granted with relative generosity and the majority of regular hands had established personal connections ashore. Two marriages had already taken place during *Kestrel*'s short deployment and he was quite sure a good many less formal relationships formed. Indeed, King could only think of one man who would welcome the move and, even in his case, could not be certain if it would turn out to be a good one.

He had sailed with Robert Manning for many years and both knew the other better than most. As a surgeon, King considered him without peer, while, in a life that offered little continuity, Manning had remained dependable as both friend and shipmate. When King was a newly appointed midshipman, Manning had been mixing drafts as a loblolly boy and together they had progressed to their current positions. King wondered if the change of station, which would inevitably bring them closer to England, might see the end of their relationship.

Post had been delivered at first light and, even before King had left to call on the Civil Commissioner, Manning had burst into his cabin with news that his wife hoped to be adding to their small family. Considering when he had last seen her, and the inordinate time it took for private messages to reach the outpost, the child could be expected quite shortly; probably before the end of the year. It was a harsh service, but surgeons were not considered as other officers, and might request leave at any time. If *Kestrel* were to be sent to home waters, King doubted that Manning could resist the temptation to be with her.

Despite the time of year, there was a decidedly floral scent to the air as he turned off the main street and began to stride down the wide steps of the *Triq l-Arcisqof* before making for the Lower Barrakka Gardens. From below came the sound of raised voices that he guessed to be coming from the Customs House Wharf. He looked down to see a dark-haired, dusky-skinned fisherman who stood out from a crowd of other seamen as he complained loudly about some injustice or other, although the soft, rounded vowels of the Maltese language made even a harsh complaint sound lyrical. Turning, King skipped down a series of steps and increased his pace as he headed along the *Xatt il-Barriera*, while the protests faded amidst an outburst of unexpected laughter and the aroma changed to that of the nearby fish market. Boldly painted *dgħajsas* were criss-crossing Grand Harbour and brightly coloured shades had appeared at some of the small, square windows, for even in late autumn the midday sun could be strong. And all the while there was the ever-present clatter of church bells that seemed to sound without reference to time or services. It all seemed so vibrant and alive; the tiny island might hold a fair amount of sadness for him – one of his best friends had been killed in the most distressing of circumstances, while there was another he would never see again – yet King already knew how much he would miss both the place and the life he had made there.

But now he could also see *Kestrel* lying in wait with a collection of other Navy ships, although none could compete with the elegance and style of her French design. And she was his true home, one he would not be leaving behind, while aboard her were those that meant more to him than any he could name on land.

His gig was waiting by the wharf with her crew, if not as decoratively dressed as some captains required, apparently alert and sober. They sat more upright as he approached and King had to repress a smile as Summers, the newly appointed midshipman, shot up and delivered an over elaborate salute that made the small boat wobble alarmingly. He stepped aboard, the gig pushed off with the barest hint of an order and was soon fighting its way through the crowded harbour.

*Kestrel's* first stop would be Gibraltar. She might remain there for some time or be immediately transferred to one of several blockading squadrons currently cruising off French ports. Or, if Ball's prediction of war with Spain was born out, they might find themselves despatched to a totally new station. But wherever they were sent, King was confident of his ability to carry out a workmanlike job. He had held his current rank for long enough to be sure of both himself and the ship, in fact never before could he recall a time when he had felt so expectant of the future, with only the slightest of doubts to remind him that few things at sea could truly be depended upon.

\* \* \*

Lovemore scraped his bowl clean with his spoon before slowly luxuriating in the last mouthful of plum duff. His portion had contained an inordinate number of raisins and now sat atop the pusser's pound of boiled pork and pease pudding that had preceded it, while all was soaking pleasantly in the midday issue of blackstrap. He sighed, and brushed back the thick mane of curly hair that was just too short for a queue, a truly contented man. Along with every other lower deck hand, Lovemore had worked hard since Up Hammocks, putting to rights the minor defects that had been postponed until *Kestrel* reached harbour, and now was inwardly certain there would be a period of rest.

There was nothing prophetic in his thinking so, as Lovemore was quick to reassure himself; plain cold hard logic dictated it. The ship had been in harbour for less than a day and it would be another, at least, before the first of the stores appeared, while shore leave could not be expected until all was safely stowed. Besides, there was no hiding the fact that three sacks of post had been taken aboard almost as soon as the ship came in, so it would be strange if a Make and Mend were not called for that afternoon.

But some of his thoughts did seem unusual, and not so easily explained. Nothing had been said by anyone in authority, and the notion was not even a subject for discussion in galley gossip, yet still Lovemore remained strangely confident their stay in harbour would be brief. And more: he was equally convinced that, once she left, *Kestrel* would not be coming back for a good while, if ever.

He came from a travelling family so never expected letters from home, but his sensitivity extended to those of his fellow men, and Lovemore enjoyed the atmosphere of well-being that usually prevailed when mail was opened. The general discussion of news from a distant England always raised morale, and made an overseas posting seem less remote.

The expected pipe came when the last remains of their meal had been cleared away. Lovemore headed away from his bench on the berth deck and down towards the aft companionway that led to the orlop. Even as he went, men were starting to roust out various pieces of work from their ditty bags – clothing that was half made or needed repair, or perhaps a piece of bone or tooth that was steadily being turned into something that, if not beautiful, at least contained a measure of naïve charm. Lovemore was not skilled in that direction, and neither could he cut hair, pen verse or indulge in the new fashion for *crochet* that seemed to be sweeping the lower deck of every British ship in service. But he had other talents and, after a considerable period of abstinence, there was one Lovemore was positively itching to indulge himself in once more.

He stood in a line of men waiting for access to their sea chests and, when his turn came, opened the heavy wooden lid of his own. Inside was a stiff leather pouch resting on a pile of linen and he smiled to himself briefly before collecting it. Lovemore had not touched the thing since *Kestrel* set sail, and was keen to put some of the ideas into action that had subsequently formed during quiet watches or before sleep came to claim him in his hammock.

"'Avin' a bit of an hop, are we, Curly?" Cranston, who shared his mess, enquired as he made his way up the companionway once more. Lovemore considered the prospect seriously; that was not out of the question, but first they would have a song and it would be the one he had heard in a Floriana tap house during his last shore leave. He thought he had the melody about right, but would play it over until certain, or at least for as long as those about him did not complain too hard. But Lovemore was confident of mastering the tune before then, and being able to enter it into his repertoire where it would rest amidst the many already learned by heart.

When he reached it, the forecastle was crowded, although a small section of deck remained free next to the bitts. Lovemore quickly claimed it before opening the pouch. The rosewood German flute within was about two feet in length and came in three sections, with yellowed bone rings protecting the joints and eight silver keys that were actually set between metal posts, rather than slotted into the body as in older or inferior models. His instrument also featured a metal lip plate that made playing for any length of time more comfortable, as well as protecting the all important hole that gave both pitch and tone. Lovemore had bought the flute in Gibraltar several commissions past when his pockets were well filled and, despite the lean times since, had never let it go.

He eased the instrument's body into the foot joint, being careful not to crush the keys that could be bent out of line so easily, then inserted the head, turning the warm wood until it felt comfortable against his lower lip. His fingers rippled over the holes and keys for a couple of seconds, then he took the thing away and wiped at his mouth before addressing himself once more and blowing cautiously.

Nearby a group of men was listening with rapt attention as one of their number read aloud from a pile of letters, and further away an old shellback was patiently explaining the process of making a Turk's Head to some youngsters. Several solitary seamen were engaged in more private crafts; some turned to glance briefly at Lovemore, but even when he started to play the opening of his tune their interest lapsed. He frowned to himself; he had the basic melody, but it was not quite right – far too bright, with none of the sadness remembered and he wondered if it actually opened on a fourth rather than a fifth. He played it again and more slowly, taming the odd note with either keys or cross fingering until it was pretty much as he recalled. On the fifteenth run-through all felt fully established, and he tried it twice more before the occasional grunt of protest threatened to turn into something more vocal.

The ship's bell sounded and Lovemore realised he must have been playing for almost an hour, which probably was enough for one piece. He glanced round to see what his fellows were about and sensed most were becoming bored with their tasks. The group that had been reading were running low on material and had begun the pile again, despite several letters remaining unopened. These would be addressed to shipmates who had died earlier in the commission and were bound to be ignored and eventually discarded, even though some might contain rare messages from wives or sweethearts. Other men appeared content enough in their work, but Lovemore knew they would respond, if he could be bothered to rouse them. Then he saw Raymond, the fiddler, on the half-deck and guessed Philby, their marine drummer, would be near enough to hear.

He raised the flute to his lips once more and drew breath. The opening bars of *The Morpeth Rant* flowed freely and were quickly followed by a general murmur of approval from all about. This spread as a seaman sprang to his feet to begin tracing out the steps of a hornpipe and, by the time the first verse was finished, there were four dancing. Soon the treble strains of Raymond's fiddle came to join him, while the figure of the marine, oddly scruffy in open shirt and duck trousers, could be seen hurrying along the starboard gangway with his second best side drum under one arm.

The ship was at rest, and some of the dancers shouted with unaccustomed freedom as their steps grew more nimble. Philby's drum caught them on the second time through, the staccato rhythm sending a compelling call throughout the ship, and when they struck up *Soldier's Joy* the groups of dancers had spread almost as far as the break of the quarterdeck.

Lovemore looked back over the crowded waist and noted the number responding to his music with private satisfaction. Some he liked a lot, others less so, but all were under his control and had been drawn together by the shared enjoyment of sound and

11

movement. He even noted a bunch of midshipmen looking down from the quarterdeck and tapping their feet openly to the compelling beat. There had been no permission sought before setting to partners, but *Kestrel*'s officers were a sound bunch and most would have preferred the men to exercise on deck, rather than indulge in far riskier games aloft.

"*Fisher*'s!" Raymond, the fiddler, announced as the last notes died away and Lovemore drew breath once more. He had long since ceased calling the tunes and was more than content to play whatever was asked of him. As a hand, Lovemore had been rated ordinary with little likelihood of progression. But though he might be clumsy aloft and not too handy with a marline-spike, he could predict a wind or judge the run of a tide with the best of them. And there were other talents: the same fingers that found knots and splices so very taxing were a wonder when given eight metal keys and a series of holes to control.

*Kestrel* was a good ship, with considerate officers, so Lovemore's musical skills were recognised and allowed him a measure of respect far beyond his lowly status. And on a clear November afternoon in Grand Harbour, his talent had been the catalyst necessary to lift the spirits of the lower deck, most of whom would far rather have been on shore leave. But a natural ear for music and an understanding of his shipmates' needs were not Lovemore's only attributes; he had another which was equally valuable.

It was also something Lovemore determinedly kept private, even though a little of its power had already been guessed at by a few of his closer acquaintances. In reality, the very existence of the gift worried him, to the extent that he had been trying to deny, suppress or ignore it for most of his life. But despite this rejection, the talent remained. And, if properly recognised, could easily have made him the most important person in the entire ship.

# Chapter Two

Much was accomplished over the next three days. *Kestrel's* last voyage had been brief; a convoy duty that lasted little more than a month and was without action. During that time she had only fired her guns in exercise or warning and, on returning to Valletta, her main need was for consumable provisions: mainly biscuit, meat and water. The latter was traditionally taken aboard just before sailing, and *Kestrel's* first lieutenant, James Timothy, had been lucky in obtaining most other requirements almost immediately. Now these were safely stowed there was only an order of slop clothing outstanding. So when he was summoned to the captain's cabin he had a clear conscience, at least as far as the ship's requirements were concerned.

For Timothy's personal needs went a little deeper. He enjoyed service life, and being *Kestrel's* executive officer especially. However, there were times when he guessed his previous position as junior lieutenant aboard *Maidstone*, a particularly active frigate, might have held a better chance of promotion. Admittedly he was second in command of *Kestrel*, and a successful action was likely to see him promoted. But he had only been one step away from the same position in *Maidstone*, with a greater chance of both action and victory.

But *Maidstone* was not officially stationed at Malta, and he found the place a particularly hospitable posting. Many of the residents extended open invitations for officers such as himself to become house guests while their ship was in harbour. And twice the offers had extended beyond simple hospitality; a good few of the English residents, either members of the military, civil service or independent traders, had daughters. These were young women, often extremely attractive, who they were particularly keen to see married off to a suitable candidate and, as a commissioned sea officer on active service, Timothy found himself in that category.

Long before the Malta posting he had dismissed the possibility of marriage. Admittedly some serving officers were fortunate in finding wives, but he was not amongst them. There had been a few close shaves, but any potential mate had eventually been put off by his choice of career. And who could blame them? Who would want to be left ashore, probably with a veritable tribe of children to control – Timothy had no aversion to large families – while he gallivanted about the high seas in pursuit of wealth and position?

Those he had met on Malta were of a different cut, however. There had been one false start with a child more interested in testing his feelings than satisfying them, but since then Timothy had met with several potential partners, and was currently embarrassed by the luxury of choosing between two who were particularly determined. Both came from military families so were accustomed to travel, along with the many other constraints of a service career, and each seemed equally set on both marrying into the Navy and securing one sea officer in particular.

This last fact had not been discovered by any questioning on Timothy's part: the information was readily available and, in one instance, almost the first thing learned of the young woman. As a man fast approaching forty and fully aware that the riches of youth were steadily eroding, Timothy was more than usually encouraged, and actually hoped the forthcoming interview would provide him with the opportunity to request a spell ashore, when the matter might finally be settled.

But even if the captain proved compliant, Timothy was secretly aware that one or two evenings' leave would not be sufficient, as there was so little to choose between them. Both were hardly in their first bloom, but attractive enough, in a maternal sort of way. And each knew their own mind – an important consideration when they would be representing their husband's interests while he was at sea. Neither offered much in the way of romance, however; there was no sharing of verse – poetry being one of Timothy's principle interests besides the sea – and nor did either seem particularly attracted to him as a man. But Timothy as a naval officer was a different matter, and this aspect was heightened further by the father of each repeatedly intimating their ability to see him made commander following a successful union with his daughter.

Timothy was currently serving a captain several years younger than himself, and one who had been a midshipman when he already held his current rank of lieutenant, so the idea of shipping a swab on his own left shoulder was almost as attractive as securing a bride. Although if anything the offers only made any decision more difficult. They seemed to emphasise the fact that each were looking for position as much as a husband, with the person beneath the uniform mattering very little. It was not an attitude he could argue with, as Timothy was undeniably in search of a wife, although he would have preferred it if a little more attention were paid to his personal qualities.

But as soon as he was announced by the marine sentry and entered the captain's day cabin, he could tell there was to be no long stay in harbour and all thoughts of extended shore leave would have to wait. Commander King was not at his desk but had been pacing about the small space and turned to meet him with an unusually alert expression that spoke of imminent action.

"How is the ship, James? Are we ready to sail?"

They were not questions that would normally have caught him on the hop; a first lieutenant must always be aware of his vessel's condition and every sea officer knew immediate departure was a prerequisite of any warship on active service.

"A-a day, sir – two at the most," he stammered, his thoughts still set on finer prospects and it was only when he realised an immediate departure must see their postponement that Timothy began to focus his mind properly.

"What do we await?" King demanded.

"Water, sir – there is usually a twenty-four hour delay, unless special measures are taken."

"We have just received orders for Gib." Timothy's eyes now took in the piece of paper King was holding. "We're taking a small convoy that was to have fallen to *Childers*, though she has yet to return from the Adriatic."

*Childers* was another sloop, though slightly smaller than *Kestrel* and of only two masts. Timothy knew her well, as he did her captain who, although a nephew of Nelson, lacked the energy and initiative of his uncle.

"She might still return, sir." He regretted the words as soon as they were spoken. If *Kestrel* had been detailed, there was no room for argument and Timothy should have known better. But King did not seem particularly concerned.

"There's more to it than that, I'm afraid," he said, indicating a chair and seating himself behind his desk. "We were to be leaving the Malta station at any rate: this just brings matters closer."

Leaving Malta. Professional or not, for several seconds Timothy could only think of his personal repercussions to the news. He had hardly ventured ashore since the ship's return to Valletta and no formal proposal had been made to either woman, although he grudgingly accepted that each had every right to expect one. Both had won his heart in differing ways and it would have been hard to turn either down, but to abandon the pair was going to be devastating. And he was equally aware he would be walking away from a chance that might never occur again.

"When are we ordered to sail?" he asked.

"There has been no date, as yet," King grunted as he read the paper once more. "The convoy is all but ready, and waiting in Marsamxett Harbour; they have one more of their number to complete lading, another is making minor repairs, but all should be done by the end of the week."

That was three days – for a moment a flicker of hope rose in Timothy's breast. It was unusual for an executive officer to be granted shore leave when his ship was under orders to sail, but not impossible. He might squeeze one evening, although such a period was not long enough to see both women, and could make the situation, and his sudden departure, worse.

"You can organise the water by then?"

"Oh yes, sir," he found himself replying automatically. "And there is a small amount of powder and shot." Like water, munitions were also traditionally taken on at the end of a stay, although the Valletta armoury was far more organised and would have no problem in delivering *Kestrel*'s moderate requirements. "But we are also awaiting slops, sir, and they may take considerably longer." This was not another attempt to prevaricate: the fact had genuinely slipped his mind.

"We shall sail without, if need be," King replied lightly. "And may even find better in Gib."

"Will we be there long, sir?" Timothy asked.

"Impossible to say." King sighed. "There are political developments that I am unable to discuss, but guess we shall be staying to the west, for the time being at least."

16

The west; not even the Western Mediterranean. Timothy pursed his lips as a number of dreadful thoughts presented themselves. For all he knew, *Kestrel* might be sent to England, and could even be paid off. Then, rather than an active lieutenant with a ship, he would be just another half-pay officer pestering the Admiralty for employment; a poor proposition for any potential bride, and just when he was finding the prospect of married life so very agreeable. Something of this must have shown on his face, as he noticed his captain regarding him with concern.

"Have you a worry, James?" he asked.

"No, sir." Again the reply was automatic. To Timothy's mind first officers did not have personal lives. Or if they did, they should not admit to them.

"I'm not saying we shall never return to Malta," King continued, "but if you were making plans for the near future, I suggest they be postponed."

\* \* \*

King's estimation of three days proved remarkably accurate and the time was not wasted. Further and less vital repairs were addressed, along with the never-ending maintenance necessary aboard any wooden sailing ship. There was the scent of linseed in the air as the upper stem, beakheads, and much of *Kestrel's* bows were coated with additional layers of marine paint, while much of her accessible bare woodwork was heavily payed and left sticky with oil. But however sound the ship, a discontented crew still made her a liability, and King made sure attention was given in that direction as well. *Kestrel* had barely been in commission six months, which was exactly the period a cautious Admiralty held back wages, so no pay was due to the men. And with departure imminent and numbers already down, neither could they be allowed shore leave, although he was able to provide for them in another way.

Before taking command of the sloop, King had worked in Valletta as an under secretary in the *Auberge d'Italie*. His position had nothing to do with the payment of prize money, but in such a close society connections could be made and he had shamelessly drawn upon them. In the summer, *Kestrel* was involved in the taking of a French frigate so her people were due a tidy sum in prize money. The vessel currently wallowed at anchor off Manoel Island and was destined to be in the hands of the dockyard a considerable time. She had been assessed at the prize court, but payment would not normally be made until well into the New Year, and by then would have been depleted by at least one set of agents' fees. However, King had been able to rush matters through, and now each lower deck man was richer by at least six guineas, while some of the petty officers had fourteen or more burning holes in their pockets.

But though this was undoubtedly appreciated, the sudden access to money could actually have worsened the average man's lot, and made the absence of shore leave even more distressing. Consequently, King spoke with Timothy who arranged for a market to be opened aboard the ship herself.

And so it was that, immediately after breakfast on the morning before *Kestrel* was due to leave, King emerged from his quarters to see the first of the bumboats heading across Grand Harbour. The hands knew they had a little over three hours to complete their transactions, then there would be Up Spirits, dinner and the rest of the day would be spent taking on water and powder – the small amount of shot required having been loaded the afternoon before.

The forecastle lookout was bellowing out a challenge to the first boat as King came on deck and he looked on with approval as Sergeant Black called the line of marine privates standing on the starboard gangway to attention. The men, who were half the NCO's force, went through the evolution as one, and might have been considered an unnecessary precaution for a morning's civilised dealing. But all knew what could happen when naïve seamen were confronted by professional tradesmen; it would only need one lower deck man to perceive himself at the bad end of a bargain for all to end in riot. The rest of the Royal Marine contingent had been given liberty to barter for half the time, and would then replace their colleagues. For no one was to miss out on this opportunity for commerce.

The first of the traders appeared at the larboard entry port shortly afterwards and were taken in hand by Kyle, the master's mate who had the anchor watch. Each was allocated a position on the main deck between cannon that had already been stripped of all moveable equipment. They carried large canvas bags lined with oil cloth, which were a better alternative to wooden chests when carried aboard small boats. Each was bound with leather straps or hoops of iron and secured by padlocks. On being granted their pitch, the traders laid out their ware under the watchful gaze of *Kestrel*'s men. These could be anything from looking glasses to legs of fresh mutton and each revelation evoked a low rumble of interest from the spectators.

But there was no actual trading at this stage, or even open discussion. The merchants were fully aware they were not trusted, while the seamen equally acknowledged their innocence when exposed to commercial trade. So a tense atmosphere hung over the ship as each party viewed the other with equal suspicion while the feelings of mutual uncertainty were magnified greatly by the presence of women.

For some of the visitors came with assistants; these were invariably female and none of *Kestrel*'s officers had any doubt of the dangers they represented. Despite gaudy cosmetics and come-hither smiles they could be carrying any number of exotic and intimate infections, while a superficial rummage through the clothing of one had already revealed three bladders filled with illicit drink that could have blinded an unsuspecting customer. Orders were given that no man was to take a woman below on the pain of a flogging, although all were aware of the average seaman's ingenuity, and knew the next few hours would see the rule broken, or at least severely tested, on several occasions. And this was despite the common knowledge that a dose of the pox was likely to be far more damaging and permanent than a dozen strokes from the cat.

The morning was cold, King's breath almost condensed in the still air, and the leather waistcoat he wore beneath his uniform tunic was especially welcome. He watched as the men began to trade, at first hesitantly, then with more enthusiasm as their confidence grew. Nearly all his adult life had been spent as an officer and afloat, mostly aboard warships, but *Kestrel* was his only official command and the men before him now his first permanent crew. His eyes switched from one to another, noting those he had served with in other vessels as well as some he barely knew by name. But they were all part of the ship and of one family; that much was apparent by the way the seamen remained in tight groups as they bartered. And they were *his* family, he supposed. None would regard him as a father figure, but he was undeniably their captain and King was quietly confident he had earned their respect. All were now aware they would be leaving Malta for good and, as he had predicted, the news had not been universally welcomed. Even this treat of an on-board market was regarded as little more than a sop, and small compensation for not being able to say proper goodbyes to the friends they had made ashore.

But that was a seaman's lot and at least they were likely to be going somewhere nearer to home. *Kestrel* might even be sent into a British port for her next refit, while a decisive victory at sea could spell the end of any threat of invasion and ultimately the war itself. In which case the ship would be paid off, with many of those before him now finally given the chance of returning to their homes and families. It was a pleasant thought although, if what he knew of the average British tar was correct, King guessed few would be comfortable with a land-based existence.

*Kestrel's* people contained an unusually high proportion of professional seamen; trained hands for whom a life afloat was the only one they knew. And probably the only one they could tolerate, he decided smugly, before realising that he himself fell into exactly the same category.

\* \* \*

"How much you askin' for the tatler then, matey?" Cranston enquired. The slight, dark-skinned man looked down at the brightly polished watch, then back and into the seaman's eyes, assessing him as if he himself were potential stock.

"It can be yours for three guineas," he said thickly, adding a brown-toothed smile for good measure.

Cranston shook his head in mock disgust. "Na, I can't give that, not for what's likely to be bilge."

The trader took the comment with apparent offence. "Nothing I sell can be described so, it is of the utmost quality and at a very low price." He sighed theatrically. "But if you have such little faith I shall add this," he added, suddenly holding up a short glistening watch chain which had apparently appeared from nowhere.

"So it's three yellow boys for the watch," Cranston pondered, his eyes fixed on the length of golden metal that was uncommonly bright in the morning's sun. "And with a cable and pit thrown in?" He turned to another seaman standing nearby. "What d'you think of that then, Curly?"

Lovemore, who had been searching for a fife, found himself drawn into Cranston's negotiation instead and reluctantly examined the watch.

"I should not touch it," he said, his tone unusually authoritative. "It may last the week, but will be useless after." Cranston nodded knowledgeably as Lovemore turned the timepiece in his hand. "And even while it works, no one would think of giving much more than half what you're being asked."

"There you go, matey," the seaman announced turning back to the merchant in triumph, and tossing the watch back in his direction. "Lovemore here says it's trumpery, an' he knows what's about."

The trader caught the watch expertly, and placed it back down with exaggerated care before setting his attention on Lovemore. For a moment their eyes met, then the smaller man seemed to back down. It was as if he had noticed something surprising in the seaman, and it was a reaction that did not gratify Lovemore one bit.

"Then you may prefer this," the trader said, keeping his eyes on Cranston's friend as he delved beneath his oil cloth and finally produced another watch. This one he handed straight to Lovemore, and did so with a measure of respect.

The seaman glanced at it briefly, before passing it over. "That one will be fine," he told Cranston. "Though I should not pay more than two guineas for it."

"Fine, you say?" the seaman questioned. "Looks just the same as the other."

"It will not work in salt water," Lovemore replied patiently. "And you can lose or break it as easily as any. But if cared for, that watch will run for several years, of that I am quite certain."

"I will take your two guineas, and include the most valuable chain," the trader confirmed, although again he spoke to Lovemore, rather than Cranston.

"Then two it is," Cranston chirped, flipping a pair of gold

coins across and snatching at his purchase before heading off into the crowd. But Lovemore remained, and the merchant addressed him once more.

"That is a good watch," he said. "Your friend will be very happy with it." For a moment he looked imploringly into the seaman's eyes.

Lovemore returned the gaze steadily and with a rare steely glint. "I know," he replied.

\* \* \*

King's earlier thought had been correct; they might be in the minority, but there were definitely some aboard *Kestrel* who would welcome a posting nearer home and her surgeon was certainly one. But Robert Manning was not the only officer pleased to leave the Malta station.

Holby, the purser, had been an English man of business living in Valletta who had taken up his duties some while after *Kestrel* first commissioned. He came with a splendid recommendation from someone her captain trusted more than most, and seemed ideal. Until then, King himself had been acting as purser and was eager to shift the responsibilities of running the only business aboard a man-of-war, so the slightly portly, middle-aged man was signed on without delay.

And it did seem that Holby was right for the post. He immediately took charge of the ship's books, accepting his captain's somewhat erratic accounting without comment, and set all to rights remarkably quickly. In fact King was extremely happy with his services, as were all aboard the sloop, and Holby's genial smile became a popular sight in *Kestrel*'s tiny gun room. Even that small affability was a bonus, as it was not an attribute commonly associated with the position of purser.

Amongst all the officers, he was the only one expected to run a business, and his duties naturally brought him into conflict with those of every station. But Holby carried out his work with both competence and understanding. He seemed to make a point of not asking outrageously high prices for slops, or any of the seamen's personal requisites, and went out of his way to see every store *Kestrel* took on was the best that might be expected. Holby also made intelligent substitutes: when raisins were in short supply, he had obtained a shipment of currants which, although not the seamen's regular fare, were grudgingly accepted.

It was generally known that *Kestrel* was his first posting as purser, but to all outward appearances Holby had been born to the position, and the captain mentioned on more than one occasion how pleased he was to have chanced upon someone so ideally suited to the task. But now, as the noise of the market on deck filtered down to his tiny office on the orlop, Holby did not seem quite so assured.

Jack Dusty, his steward, had been given leave to visit the market and he sat quite alone as he pored over the pile of open ledgers before him. These were both ship's books and his own personal journals, and they did not make good reading.

Of course the problem really came from the captain's impatience. If Commander King had only gone through the correct channels, all would be straight. Holby knew a number of people ashore and had been anticipating a tidy sum in commission from the prize and head money recently paid out. But with Sir Richard-bleeding-Banks taking charge, he had been unable to touch a penny – worse, others were equally disappointed and now looked to him for compensation.

That part did not worry him greatly; he need only stay in the ship to remain relatively safe. Creditors were only allowed on board Royal Navy vessels to pursue legal debts above twenty pounds. The amount he supposedly owed was in excess of that, but the way in which it had been accrued fell well outside the law, so Holby knew himself protected on that count at least.

But not on others. He also had liabilities that were totally legal and could not be avoided. The Lesro family were important men of business on the island: he owed them over nine hundred pounds for previous services and a concern like theirs was not used to being tipped the double. Holby guessed they were searching for him now and probably had been for some while; should it come to light he was aboard *Kestrel*, the bailiffs would be despatched for sure. Then the glowing recommendation Commander King received from the office of Lesro's son would be revealed as a forgery, as was the bond Holby had passed across when accepting *Kestrel*'s general stores. He would be hauled off the ship in a most undignified manner and probably sent straight to prison, without even a spell in the sponging house. Once so confined there could be no chance of getting out of debt, while his position would be wildely known to anyone who cared to ask. Those who had recently lost money must still be angry and it would be little trouble for them to send in a couple of rampers to settle his account for good.

But Holby was not completely discouraged. *Kestrel* had been in Grand Harbour for several days and he was still alive. Admittedly the stores recently taken aboard had not been so carefully checked so may be below his usual standard, and he had been unable to prise even a few pounds' worth of slop clothing from any source. But worse had been weathered in the past; he only need keep his head down a little longer and they would sail, and it was fortunate for him that it would be a permanent departure. Not every debt would be left in their wake, but a good few could be written off, and a change of location must surely make the work of the more diligent catchpoles harder.

Besides, Holby had already discovered the duties of a purser to be ideally suited to supplementing his income. Some he had tried already, and there were plenty more that should prove equally successful. With luck, his time aboard *Kestrel* would allow him to amass a reasonable sum and, as soon as she reached a British port, Holby would have no hesitation in running.

Then the problem of the forged bond would come up, and the captain might not take too kindly to finding himself saddled with a considerable debt, but Holby would be many miles away and probably living under yet another false name. Besides, the bold Commander King would be only one more in what was already a long line; Holby had managed to avoid them all so far and, however much he might worry about his immediate problems, felt he could continue to do so for some while to come.

\* \* \*

And so they sailed, and did so at the break of dawn, six days after gaining harbour. It took just over an hour for the nine ships they must escort to be tempted out of the adjoining bay, but by mid-morning, under an iron grey sky, *Kestrel* was taking up position to windward of the small fleet, and setting her stem towards the west

24

and the distant outpost of Gibraltar.

The quarterdeck had been full, as was to be expected when a convoy formed, although those not officially on duty soon drifted away once all began to settle until the only officers remaining were Acting Lieutenant Adams, who had the watch, along with Summers, the duty midshipman. The watch below had been stood down, leaving the running of the ship to their colleagues. Only a few off-duty men remained gathered in the waist, and were bothering to look back at the sandy landmass fast disappearing off their larboard quarter.

One of these was Lovemore. He stood amid a group of men that had special reasons for missing the place, and all were silent as they watched what had become their home port steadily fade into the distance. Lovemore was now inwardly sure that, for most aboard the sloop, it was the last they would see of Malta. A few might come back, but not for some considerable time and then it would be aboard a different ship. For he was equally certain that *Kestrel* was never to return.

# Chapter Three

It was the seventh day of the voyage and Adams had the watch once more when they made the sighting.

"She's showin' lateen sails," Hobbs, at the main masthead, reported. "I can only see two at present, but reckon there'll be a mizzen lurkin' about there somewheres."

Adams had already sent Summers to notify the captain and was calming himself by staring out in the general direction, even though there was no chance of spotting anything from the deck. But if the lookout was correct, the sighting must be somewhere off their larboard quarter and, with the wind as it was, probably coming up fast. Hobbs' description was vague in the extreme; there were vessels aplenty that could have answered it, with only a small proportion being ships of war. But the course was not that of a merchant making a port-hopping journey along the coast, and could easily be the classic angle of attack used by Barbary Pirates.

King appeared shortly afterwards when there was a little more to learn from the masthead.

"Sighting's holdin' her course, an' gaining; she'll be hull up in no time," Hobbs reported in his customary doleful tone. "There's a mizzen for sure, an' I'd say she must have seen us by now, even without regular fightin' tops."

"What looks to be a xebec in sight on the larboard quarter," Adams muttered to the first lieutenant as he appeared on the quarterdeck.

"Would that be a corsair, sir?" Timothy asked, approaching the captain.

"Too soon to say," King's tone was level and unexcited, although Timothy noted he was working the stump of his left arm, which was generally accepted as a sign of agitation, if not concern.

Adams stepped away from the binnacle to give his betters more space. The watch was halfway through and had been uneventful to that point, but now all could gauge the tension.

If she was indeed a xebec there were at least eight hours of daylight left; time enough to deal with such an enemy. All knew she would be fast, well armed, and likely to be carrying a crew large enough to swamp a Royal Navy frigate, let alone an unrated sloop, were King foolish enough to allow such a thing. But then *Kestrel* carried eighteen-pound carronades: heavy guns that could do a deal of damage to a xebec's fragile frame. And, though her opponent would be larger, she should be more than capable of dealing with any ship of that nature.

"I have her!" Summers' voice rang out in the silence and all eyes turned first to him, then the object he pointed to on the horizon. There was a flicker of light that came and went, but soon it settled into something more solid that gradually began to take shape. It was a xebec right enough and, as Hobbs had stated, travelling fast; she would be up with them in no time. The lookout was also correct in guessing *Kestrel*, and the convoy she escorted, would have been in sight for some time. Compared to a square rig, a xebec's tophamper was strange in the extreme. Most of the height came from massive yards that carried huge triangular sails, with the masts themselves being relatively short. But even a lookout placed at such a low vantage point would have had them in view for a while.

"Deck there, I've somethin' else." Hobbs clearly had more words of wisdom to impart, and all remained silent as he did. "There's another just the same and close on her tail."

* * *

Two hours later *Kestrel* was cleared for action and all had accepted the first issue of blackstrap would be postponed for as long as it took to see off the enemy. Some ceremonies were considered more important however and this included the regular noon sight. There might be two potentially deadly warships a couple of miles off the larboard beam but, even in the Mediterranean where a ship's position could often be fixed by a shore bearing, the measurement of latitude remained sacrosanct. Consequently, the sailing master stood next to the binnacle with sextant in hand, while he waited for the appropriate moment.

A respectful hush descended over the quarterdeck as Brehaut finally raised the instrument and set it towards the sun. Then his slender fingers began to adjust the mirrors and lenses until he gave out a small grunt of satisfaction.

"Thirty-eight degrees, seventeen minutes, north." His voice was reassuringly positive and Kyle, the master's mate, made a mark on the traverse board, before repeating Brehaut's words to the retiring officer of the watch.

Adams duly turned to the captain, saluted and gave the latitude yet again, even though it was the third time of hearing for all present.

"Very good." King's tone was no less formal. "Make it so."

"Make it twelve," Adams instructed and the master's mate called for eight bells.

Parker, the weather-beaten old quartermaster, then muttered, "Turn the glass and strike the bell," and the new navigational day could begin.

The event would have usually been followed by the hands trooping off for their midday meal, but that, too, had been suspended and a more uneasy silence fell as *Kestrel* continued at the convoy speed of just over three knots.

"What do you make of it, James?" King asked softly, although all close by could hear every word.

"They're obviously biding their time," Timothy replied, as both men considered the enemy. Neither ship flew the customary red flag that positively identified them as pirates, and it was possible they were sailing without the official blessing of the Barbary States. But there could be little doubt what they had in mind, and that *Kestrel* would have to perform a few clever tricks if she wished to keep the convoy, and herself, safe.

"We have a fair wind," King muttered and Timothy was quick to agree. On her current heading the sloop could add several knots to her speed and with such an experienced crew, few ships of her size would be quite so manoeuvrable. There was only one of her, however, and should the enemy attempt a two-pronged attack, it would be difficult to see off both without the loss of at least one merchant.

Thinking of their charges naturally made King turn to the convoy, currently sailing innocently enough a mile off their starboard beam. Some had increased speed on sighting the raiders, only to draw back on realising the act only made them more vulnerable. And now all were holding station better than at any time during the journey.

King's attention returned to the pirates that seemed content to keep pace with their prey. Like lions stalking a herd, they would be looking for the chance to move in and seize one, probably the weakest, then haul it away, while avoiding the bothersome guard that stood between them. It was possible they would work as a team, with one xebec making for *Kestrel* and attempting to occupy her, while the other had their way with the convoy, although King thought not: Barbary Pirates were not known for collaborative attacks. The fact they were operating together was all the cooperation that could be expected, which may be a point in his favour. For, were the two xebec frigates to truly work in concert, they would be an impossible force for an eighteen-gun sloop to tackle.

But there was also a downside; should he be lucky enough to disable one of the craft, the other would not break off their own attack to go to its aid. If King were truly to defend the convoy, he had to take both, and take them decisively.

* * *

*Kestrel*'s main armament comprised of carronades: short-barrelled weapons that were lighter than conventional long guns yet still capable of firing an eighteen-pound load almost as far as their more conventional cousins. Carronades also required a smaller measure of powder and had the additional advantage of being less demanding on manpower; only five men were needed to tend each piece and they could be worked with less in an emergency. Consequently, each pair of cannon effectively had three crews, with the third detailed to move between the two pieces, depending on which battery was in use.

Wherever possible, the gun crews aboard *Kestrel* were made up of men from the same mess, as the first lieutenant regarded familiarity and close association to be an aid when working as a team. And on one particular pair of guns, something of the captain's thoughts were being mirrored by the servers. They were currently formed up at the larboard piece, the gun most likely to see action and, in the absence of food or drink, had been filling the

29

time by chatting quietly amongst themselves as they regarded the nearby enemy with ostentatiously nonchalant ease.

"Ask me, that's a reasonable enough force for the barky to take on," Cranston remarked, after signalling his contempt with an elaborate yawn.

"Don't know why the captain's even botherin'," Harris, one of the guns' transient crew, snorted. "Never met a merchant master yet who didn't try to bob me of my pay. To my mind they can look after theirselves."

Lovemore, the curly-haired musician who handled the sponge and rammer on both guns, remained silent. He was as interested as any in what was about to happen, although for him the battle had suddenly become far more personal.

"Well there are captains a plenty who would simply call it a day and split the convoy," Cranston agreed. "If they all added canvas an' altered course, not even a pair of xebecs would be able to take the lot."

"I can just see that bunch sailing off on different headings," Harris scoffed. "They've done little else so far this cruise."

There was a rumble of laughter from most, but Lovemore did not join them; his focus remained fixed on Harris' face, which seemed to draw him with a mixture of fascination and horror. Harris was a north country man, gangling in frame, and with a coarse, reddish skin which might have been the product of an earlier illness. That was not what had caught Lovemore's attention, though; it was something far more ethereal... and deadly.

"But won't they catch us an' all?" Roberts, the lad who served both guns with powder, asked, while wondering vaguely why he appeared to be the only one taking the matter seriously.

"Na," Beeney, a loader, snorted. "Pirates won't choose to meddle with a Navy ship. Not when there's rich pickings to be had elsewhere."

"You said they was frigates," the boy persisted. "And they seem to be well enough armed."

"They're what they *call* frigates," Cranston corrected, "but no match for even one of our Jackass tubs, nor a sloop like *Kestrel* neither, not if she's handled right."

"But there are two of them," Roberts sighed.

"Then we get twice the payout when they're sunk!" Harris

countered with a triumphant grin. Most had just received a goodly share of prize money from the recently taken French frigate, so the subject was a particular favourite.

Lovemore finally tore his attention from his shipmate's face and looked down at the deck instead. For most of his life he had been a sensitive soul, which probably accounted for his ability in music. And he had already acquired a reputation amongst the men when it came to sensing when land could be expected, whether a stay in harbour would be short, or judging such things as the quality of a watch. But this was an entirely new experience, something far more subtle than simple intuition, and he had to admit to being frightened by it.

Of late, Lovemore had noticed his talent for premonitions to be improving and this was just such an example; what he could see in Harris' face concerned him greatly, as did the fact that no one else apparently noticed.

"Aye, and you can forget about their cannon," Cranston was adding blithely. "They might be heavy beasts, but won't have no range."

"And it'll be more wind than shot if they do get close in," Harris agreed.

"So we got nothing to worry about?" Roberts asked with cautious relief.

"Well I wouldn't be saying that," Kenton, who had recently been promoted captain of the larboard gun, replied. "Them xebecs might be made of little more than daub and kindling, but they carry large enough crews."

"You're right there," Cranston reluctantly agreed. "And I'd say the captain's going to have to play this one carefully. Let them board and we'll be overrun; then you can say goodbye to Gibraltar, England, or any god-fearing place, and look forward to spending the rest o' your lives as slaves."

\* \* \*

King had no intention of being a slave and neither did he wish to abandon the convoy. If the pirates were content to simply keep pace, that was fine by him, and he was certainly not going to be drawn into anything so foolish as turning into the wind to attack.

The ship's bell rang out twice, it was one o'clock in the afternoon, so still plenty of time for action. He supposed the enemy might wish to stretch things out until dark, when a night attack would be harder to defend and, if they were intending to simply destroy the convoy, was probably the better option. Two fast xebecs carefully handled would wreak havoc amongst the heavily laden transports. There would be no moon to speak of, so the pirates could play a game of hide and seek amongst the slow moving shipping. It would take little more than a broadside to sink or burn any one and, if no prizes were carried off, they could account for all before morning, while still avoiding *Kestrel*'s attempts to stop them.

Destroying the merchants was not their intent, however; the pirates were looking for profit, and that only came when ships were taken, not sunk. Besides, if the stories he had heard about corsairs were correct, a long patient wait played no part in their thinking or fighting tactics.

Despite the ship being at quarters, Adams had quit the gun deck, which was his battle station, and was deep in conversation with the first lieutenant. King had no idea what they were talking about and did not greatly care; they were both professional officers and could sort most problems on their own. If intervention from him was called for he would soon know about it, and it was at that moment, as he was considering taking a few paces along the crowded deck, that the enemy finally reacted.

With a flicker of white from her canvas, the sternmost xebec turned savagely to starboard, and was soon heading for the rear of the convoy with a plume of spray that could almost be steam streaming from her bows. For perhaps a second the beauty of a craft so ideally suited to such conditions triggered something close to appreciation in King's seaman's brain, but such thoughts were instantly dismissed as his eyes switched to the leading pirate. Sure enough, she too had changed course, although not quite so dramatically, and was heading for the merchants' van. There was a muttering from the officers about him which he ignored, and neither did he wish to discuss the situation with anyone. This would be a fast action; he must rely entirely on his own instincts and opinions if they were to win.

"Take us to starboard and add t'gallants," King snapped, adding, "Man the starboard battery – Mr Adams you will oblige

32

me by returning to your guns and seeing they are run out to that side."

Adams gave a hasty salute as he made for the quarterdeck ladder, and Brehaut began to bellow out a stream of orders that would see them close-hauled on the starboard tack. *Kestrel* turned, perhaps not so gracefully as the first xebec, but it was a serviceable manoeuvre and seemed to have caught the enemy by surprise. The aft xebec to the east had already travelled a considerable distance towards the last of the traders, one of which had actually veered from her own course at the sight of what bore down upon her. But the pirate may not have been expecting King to apparently ignore the more westerly attacker, and could well have noted the stubby barrels of *Kestrel*'s deadly eighteen-pounders as they were hauled into the firing position.

The guns were already loaded with round shot, which was not ideal as King would have preferred to simply disable his opponent, although equally he had no wish to draw close and receive too much fire. Behind him, the westerly xebec would be nearing the convoy; he dare not look but knew he was cutting it fine in dealing with the stern attacker, while still allowing time to settle the other's hash.

"Mr Adams, you will fire upon my order," he bellowed to the young man, now back in his position in the waist. "And target the hull: the hull, do you understand?"

Adams touched his hat in acknowledgement and King could see him speaking to Summers, the midshipman supporting him. All the servers would have heard their captain's orders, but still they were repeated, and some of the gun captains began to adjust the heavy elevation screws as they prepared to size up their target.

For it would not be long; King could see that, and the tension steadily mounted with the only sound being the wind in the lines as *Kestrel*'s stem ripped through the calm water. The enemy was barely a point or so off her starboard bow, and they were closing at speed, although King was well aware that every yard they gained would have to be won back when they turned to take on the other attacker.

The easterly pirate was almost dead ahead when they finally reached the range he required. This was the dangerous time: the distance was less than a mile and King felt confident of scoring at least one substantial hit on the frail craft's hull, although *Kestrel* was also sailing headlong towards a battery of cannon that were probably heavier than her own. At the bows, Crabbe, the gunner, was standing ready by the twin chasers and, at a wave from King, both guns spat jets of flame and smoke that were instantly whipped away by the breeze. There was no telling where the shots had fallen and King had too much on his mind to even enquire. The enemy was also still to fire, but all King's attention was on the timing for their turn, which must be absolutely right.

Then, just when he gave the order and the ship begun to buck as her helm was put across, the first sign of activity was seen from the pirate. It could hardly have been called a broadside – there was at least a second's delay between each shot – and neither was it the measured pace of deliberate shooting. But by the time *Kestrel* had settled on her new course and with the xebec comfortably within the arc and range of her own starboard battery, the last of the enemy's shots had been fired, and King was pleased to see all had fallen short.

"Ready men," he cautioned. Then, raising his good arm high to give emphasis. "Fire!"

The sloop gave a lurch as her starboard guns roared out almost simultaneously, and immediately her servers began to attend their weapons. King was hoping the job would be done by the first broadside, and actually felt a distinct pain in his jaw whilst waiting for the shots to land.

When they did, he noticed with relief that the guns had been well laid. At least three balls struck the pirate squarely, although it might have been four as there was considerable damage near the xebec's stern. But whatever the number, it was clear sufficient iron had been delivered to penetrate the frail hull, forcing the xebec to veer off course, her bows coming round unwillingly to face her tormentor. What had been a graceful and elegant vessel now seemed ungainly; she began to wallow almost immediately and King would have liked to have stayed to finish her off, if matters elsewhere had not demanded his attention.

And he may already have left it too late. As he ordered *Kestrel* further to larboard, he finally allowed himself to look upon the westerly xebec and realised they would be hard-pushed to reach her before at least one of the merchants was taken. Even now he could see individual puffs of smoke that told how the pirate was trying to intimidate the nearest into spilling her wind.

"Will she take any more canvas, Mr Brehaut?" he asked.

The sailing master glanced up briefly, before shaking his head. "I should not wish to chance it, sir," he replied.

"Very well." King had suspected as much, and knew it would do no good to increase speed at the risk of losing a spar or springing a mast. *Kestrel* was making a fair pace, but it was anyone's guess if it would be sufficient. He had already anticipated the pirate's probable line of attack: they would fire on at least three merchants, leaving them damaged, possibly ablaze and probably sinking, then seize a third and carry it away. King would be forced to look to the injured ships, and must reconcile the certain capture of one, to the potential loss of many.

He sighed, and found himself gritting his teeth once more as he glared at the hated xebec. That might be the pirates' intention, but it was up to him to see they did not.

# Chapter Four

It was generally accepted that, when firing a cannon, the only members of its crew who did not tie neckerchiefs about their heads were those who were already deaf. But despite precautions, the despatch of that single broadside had left a faint ringing in the ears of all on the main deck. Lovemore was no exception, although he had been less affected; as a musician he valued his hearing, so always used a strip of thick canvas heavily stuffed with oakum to cover his ears. There were times when he wished his other, less public, abilities could be as easily suppressed and this was just such an occasion.

For even as *Kestrel* cut through the placid waters, racing to meet a potentially deadly enemy, what he had noticed on Harris' face was the only thing on Lovemore's mind. It was broadly similar to that seen in the past: a yellowed death's head skull that seemed to glow with an inner radiance. And on each occasion the image had appeared when they were going into battle.

But this time the effect was greater and more gruesome in its detail. It now completely enveloped his shipmate's head and was as plain to him as the faces of any other man on deck. But just to him; Lovemore silently accepted that he was the only one who could see anything out of the usual, and the only one who knew exactly what it meant.

"You lot stayin' with this gun, or movin' over to join Kenton?" Potter, the captain of the starboard piece, bellowed.

"Blowed if we knows," Cranston shouted in reply. "Pirates are still a mile out of range: it all depends on how we approaches 'em."

"I'd say it'll be starboard," Harris added cheerfully as he removed the cloth from about his ears, and Lovemore could hardly conceal his wonder at the man's relaxed attitude.

"Aye, more'n likes," Cranston agreed as he also slipped his neckerchief down to its rightful place. The warm gun had been loaded once more and there was little for any of them to do, other than wait for a chance to fire it. The sound of pipes and shouted orders from the quarterdeck made them turn, and soon a flurry of topmen were swarming up the larboard shrouds at a pace that would have done credit to a pack of monkeys.

"Captain's orderin' the royals," Potter said, with a hint of respect. "An' in this breeze'n all."

"Belike he don't want to be late," Harris snorted, and drew a few smiles from his mates.

"Pirates have already damaged the poleacre," Cranston pointed out as *Kestrel*'s speed increased further and they began to pass the nearest merchant. The vessel had indeed been hit, and was clearly afire, although both masts were still intact and the only damage to the hull appeared well above the waterline.

"Ask me, they'll rough up a few more," Cranston stated with authority. "Then grab one, and we'll be too busy savin' the others to do anything about it."

"Unless we can get to 'em first," Harris again, and Lovemore had to force his eyes away, so firm had the vision now become. "And frankly it can't come fast enough for me – I'm just in the mood for a scrap."

* * *

The order to add royals had not come easily to King and contravened both the advice of his sailing master as well as his own instincts. But if *Kestrel* did not show more speed the enemy would succeed in their plans, and he would rather risk damage to the tophamper than be forced to watch while a pirate ran off with one of his charges.

As it was, one of the merchants was already afire, a lucky shot having started a blaze in the poleacre. By rights, he should be slowing and transferring men, and probably their fire engine, to tackle the problem. The xebec had moved on and obviously intended engaging others; if they were similarly treated he may be forced into defending the bulk of his ships allowing the leader – a smart little red brig that had been in the van throughout – to be captured. But first he would have a crack at seeing the attacker off.

The extra canvas was starting to tell and they were fairly skimming across the water. On *Kestrel*'s quarterdeck no one spoke; the only sound was the scream of wind in her lines, water hissing at the bows and the occasional groan of protest from their tophamper. Nevertheless, the effort was not being made in vain; the British were drawing noticeably closer with every breath and, as the pirates fired on yet another merchant, King was reasonably certain of being able to engage them before they were given the chance to move deeper into the convoy.

And so it proved: *Kestrel* came into extreme range just as the xebec was about to close on the fourth in line. Instead, she turned away, but it was not soon enough to avoid the wrath of the British warship. The sloop's broadside roared out and neatly bracketed the enemy vessel; there was no telling what damage had actually been done, although little significant could be expected at such a distance. The message had been delivered, however, and the pirate ship continued her turn to the west, clearly hoping to make a final attempt for the convoy's leader.

The red brig had sensibly broken out of line and was steering to the south-west in an attempt to put as much distance between her and the enemy, while still allowing *Kestrel* to intervene. King nodded approvingly as he ordered the helm across, to allow his ship to effectively split the distance between the two. It would mean holding fire from his own broadside guns until he was almost up with the xebec, but was the best course of action if he wished to protect the leading ship. And he should, King told himself firmly; with luck the xebec could even be chased away, otherwise a few choice broadsides would finish her for sure. They might take a hit in return, but *Kestrel* was a stout ship for her size, and would withstand it well enough. In fact King was quietly confident of victory... providing, that is, his tophamper held out.

* * *

On the gun deck, Acting Lieutenant Adams was not unduly worried about *Kestrel*'s masts: his concern lay elsewhere. The young man was barely in his twenties and had already failed one attempt to reach the heights of commissioned rank. But if there was one thing service life had taught him, it was patience. He was now back to his previous rank of acting lieutenant, and would get another chance at a board in time. Besides, he was officially *Kestrel*'s gunnery officer, with overall charge of her cannon, so he

38

could rightly reassure himself that there would be no difference in his actual duties were he to have been commissioned.

And he was reasonably happy with his department's performance thus far. There had been no misfires, and one enemy vessel was disabled as a result. But when *Kestrel* next engaged it would be at far closer range, and Adams was aware of the difference between firing at a distant target, when there was little chance of receiving a shot in reply, and engaging a dangerous enemy close up.

On their current heading, *Kestrel* looked likely to all but run aboard the xebec, something he was sure the captain would avoid at all costs, but still he wondered if a tight action might shake some of the less experienced hands. And even outdated artillery, such as might be expected aboard a Barbary Pirate, could cause problems when tasted at close range. He took a pace or two across the crowded deck and gave a nod to Summers, stationed further forward. The two first met less than a year before, yet had gone through so much together since that there was a strong bond between them. The midshipman treated Adams to a boyish grin that was hardly appropriate when directed at a superior officer.

"Never seen the old girl travel so fast," he said, his gaze rising briefly to the taut canvas above their heads.

"And you are unlikely to do so again, Mr Summers," Adams replied more formally. "Captain's playing it pretty close to the mark, though it will be worth it if we can see that prigger off."

His statement was punctuated by the double report of *Kestrel's* twin bow chasers, which had been keeping up a regular fire for some while. The range was closing fast, but no one expected much from the six-pound round shot, although possibly the sound of rescue was reassuring to those aboard the red brig.

"Will we be taking her to starboard?" Summers asked, as the pair drew closer. Adams pursed his lips.

"I should say so, and would frankly prefer it. The pieces are warm, even if they have been loaded at speed."

The lad glanced over his shoulder, clearly keen to keep an eye on the enemy. Despite the xebec's sleek lines, *Kestrel* was taking the wind more favourably and definitely gaining on her. Before so very long they would have the pirates in range of their broadside.

"Surely we could reach her now, were we to yaw," he said,

turning aft once more. "Let off a long range barrage, and see how they likes it."

This time Adams could not hide a smile. Even in the brief time they had known each other he had seen the lad grow from a timid volunteer to the devil-may-care midshipman he saw before him.

"We might," he agreed. "But it would slow us considerably to do so. And that could be all they need to either take the merchant, or escape. Nothing's for certain at sea." He continued, "We may still shake a spar, or the enemy might suddenly take flight. But if she stays as she is for much longer we will have her for sure. And if you're serious about a naval career," his eyes now fixed the midshipman's in a kindly stare, "you'll discover patience to be a valuable asset."

* * *

And nearby, at one of the starboard carronades, Lovemore had no objection to waiting. His team were totally absorbed in the chase, with most simply itching to bring their weapon to bear. But Lovemore was hoping for the exact opposite. There was still time and sea room a plenty for the xebec to escape; all the enemy need do was turn a few points to starboard and make a run for it: *Kestrel* would never abandon the rest of the convoy to follow. But however hard he may wish, he remained inwardly certain there was to be no anticlimax. Harris stood nearby and, although Lovemore tried to avoid looking at his face, whenever he did that same diabolical image was just as strong. He had no idea if the forthcoming action would be successful or not, or any detail of how the battle was going to pan out. But *Kestrel* would be taking at least one hit, of that Lovemore was quite sure. And in the same way, there was no doubt in his mind that the lanky northerner that stood so close to him was about to meet his death.

* * *

"Ready starboard battery!"

The waiting was almost over and *Kestrel*'s tophamper had stood up manfully. Now King eyed the angle between the xebec on their starboard bow and the brig, that was listing slightly, to larboard. The merchant had already received one broadside from the xebec, which was as clear an indication as any that the pirates were abandoning any attempts to capture her. And there was still a chance they might escape without receiving a shot from *Kestrel*. But King thought not, he knew little of his counterpart aboard the enemy vessel, but sensed he would not run meekly from a sloop without raising at least a token defence.

On *Kestrel's* main deck, all the starboard guns were trained as far forward as possible, and he could see Adams by the forecastle with Crabbe, the gunner, waiting for the time when they could open fire. It was even possible *Kestrel* could get her shots away without receiving any in return although, again, King thought not. The Barbary Pirates might make their living from preying on poorly armed merchants but, when the need arose, were not frightened of fighting a proper warship. And *Kestrel* was about as small as such things came.

"Enemy's altering course!"

The call came from Timothy, and King's attention immediately returned to the xebec. There was no doubt she had yawed slightly and he watched as the brightly painted hull continued to turn, until her slender broadside was bringing *Kestrel* into her own arc of fire.

"Hard a larboard!" King ordered. So be it; if his opponent wanted a stand up fight, he would not deny it.

Even as they made the sudden turn, Adams was raising his hand and, as the first signs of fire were seen from the xebec's cannon, *Kestrel's* own broadside spat back.

For a moment there was confusion. The pirate's fire was not so defined or concentrated, water erupted all about the British sloop and long after her own shots had been despatched in a crisp and solid barrage, individual cannon continued to speak from the slender vessel's hull. But it was the thrashings of a wounded animal. *Kestrel's* guns had been fired with cool precision, and carried out their work most effectively. The enemy's tiny mizzen mast was taken down, and her foresail flew free, robbed of support from its sheets, although the vessel's hull suffered the most damage.

In two places, holes had appeared amongst the intricate decoration while another, larger and further forward, may have been the result of two shots landing in close proximity.

"And again, Mr Adams. You have control!"

The young officer raised a hand briefly to King's words, even though it was clear his attention lay elsewhere. His gun crews were throwing themselves into reloading their pieces, and already the procedure was halfway completed.

*Kestrel* had also been struck, but King sensed her damage to be slight. The starboard cathead was awry, and one of the anchors appeared adrift. There might also be casualties amongst the men although all spars remained intact and there had been no sickening thuds that ran throughout the frame and told of a heavy shot striking below the waterline.

"Fire!" Adams roared as soon as the last gun captain's hand was raised, and once more the starboard battery erupted in a broadside that neatly covered the xebec's ornate hull. This time there was no return fire; the enemy ship seemed stunned into silence and inactivity, only a faint scream carried against the wind and told of the havoc *Kestrel* had wreaked about her decks.

King watched grimly; it was as he expected – as he had hoped, even if seeing an enemy destroyed so brought him little actual pleasure. But he would hardly have had it any other way and, on contemplation, had to admit to a degree of satisfaction.

\* \* \*

Lovemore had neither time nor space for such thoughts; so totally caught up was he in serving the carronade that even concerns for Harris, and that vile image, had been pushed to one side. The enemy were yet to fire a second broadside, while he and his team were preparing for their third. But when the work was done, when all were stood clear and Potter's hand was held high, Lovemore did draw breath and finally risked a glance at his shipmate.

The image was the same, as he knew it would be; if anything the fearsome skull seemed even clearer than before. Then the order came to fire; *Kestrel*'s starboard broadside was released and once more spat vengeance on the pirate ship that lay at point blank range across the dark water. Once more, the discharge made their ears ring, while the smoke was blown down on the enemy ship. But Lovemore had no time for that either, as he and the other servers threw themselves into the work of reloading the gun. And so wrapped up were they in their work, that no one noticed when the xebec eventually fired a final spasm of erratic shots in reply.

* * *

That third broadside from *Kestrel* had done the business. Some shots struck the xebec's hull, while others merely added further confusion to the mess of her rigging. The ship was by no means destroyed but, even with a large crew, there would be enough to do in simply keeping her afloat, without putting any effort into further fighting. King turned to his first lieutenant.

"A good job well done, Mr Timothy; thank you for your very able assistance."

"Thank you, sir," Timothy replied, with equal formality. "We have an able crew and a happy ship."

King was pleased to note that Timothy was taking the compliment in the right spirit, it being to the ship that he managed rather than any personal quality.

"Shall we finish her off, sir?"

"No." It was a bald answer, but one King had no hesitation in giving. There was little fight left in the xebec and already he could see men swarming over the damaged areas, while her helm had been put across and she was gamely heading away from her tormentor. When Brehaut had taken the noon sighting – and could it really have been so recently? – they had been roughly a hundred miles from the nearest coast. The pirates would do well to see their vessel to safety, in fact King was quietly positive they would not. But to give chase and invite surrender would be dangerous indeed. Even if such a thing were offered, King would have more than double his own crew as prisoners, and he did not relish the prospect of seeing that many to safety in Gibraltar.

"No," he repeated. "The enemy cannot be salvaged and the people will see a healthy return in head money as it is – let them be, I say. Better we reassemble the convoy and continue."

Timothy nodded in agreement. He too had been wondering quite how such a number of hostile barbarians could be contained aboard their tiny sloop. The carpenter was approaching with a midshipman apparently in tow: King turned to them.

"No damage to the 'ull, sir." The older man carried more important news than any youngster in a fancy uniform, and spoke first. "There's some work to be done on the bows, but my mates can see to that."

"Very good, Mr Vasey." King acknowledged the carpenter's knuckled salute with a touch of his own hat. The midshipman was next.

"Message from Mr Adams, sir. Little material damage, an' nothin' that cannot be fixed. Two men down from number four cannon, an' a hand fell from the larboard gangway. All have gone below to Mr Manning, sir."

"Thank you, Mr Bremner."

As a butcher's bill that was light, considering two enemy warships had been all but destroyed. But there were still the merchants to attend to; King could see the smoke of one as she burned steadily astern and, as they drew closer to the red brig, she no longer appeared quite so pristine.

"Very well, Mr Timothy, you may clear away the boats; we have a measure of work ahead of us."

* * *

Two hands were certainly down from number four cannon. One was Potter, who had been struck in the right thigh by a chunk of wood ripped from the ship's side, and the other Harris, hit squarely by the same shot that had caused the splinter. As the midshipman reported, both were now below with the surgeon although – had they been in the thick of action – Harris' body would have been neatly despatched over the side with no further thought. For there was no question in anyone's mind that he was dead; the fact was unavoidable.

However, for Lovemore, standing by the damaged bulwark and wholly exhausted by the day's activities, there was a modicum of consolation. The northerner had been hit squarely in the belly and would have died instantly, although his head was left completely untouched. And when Kenton, his tie mate, formally took possession of the body, Lovemore noticed the dead seaman's face lacked any trace of the vile image that had previously tainted it. Instead there was an attitude of peace about him and, had it not been for the terrible injury, he might even be thought asleep.

# Chapter Five

King pulled his greatcoat tight against him and shivered as he stared back over *Kestrel*'s stern and into the dark wake that flowed steadily from below her counter. The Atlantic breeze was quite different to that of the Mediterranean. Far more brackish and with a chilling bite, while the novelty of snow filling the air and catching what light there was from the slender moon made the sun-kissed stone of Malta seem a long way off indeed. They had reached Gibraltar ten days after dealing with the pirates and, following minor repairs, spent the next two months awaiting employment. During that time – a period when Spain declared war on England, Napoleon crowned himself Emperor of the French and all the world seemed to be gathering for a concerted attack on Britain's shores – *Kestrel* had stagnated, apparently forgotten.

The sense of abandonment was made worse as matters were hotting up back in their old station. Even *Childers*, the sloop with which they had shared so many convoy duties, was starting to make a name for herself, having chanced upon a dozen Algerian warships gathered in the mouth of the Adriatic. Meanwhile, *Kestrel*'s size and lack of importance was seemingly emphasised by the tremendous rock that towered overhead, as well as the numerous commissioned warships that came and went with true purpose and annoying regularity.

December had brought winter and rain; Christmas was the wettest known for years and, through the misery of a damp ship in harbour, many of *Kestrel*'s officers and some of her hands remembered the previous year when they had fought for their lives and lost a good many friends on the southern coast of France. And then on St. Stephen's day, when half his people were plaguing the taphouses ashore with the rest aboard ship recovering from their own excursions, King had finally received orders to join Admiral Graves and his blockading force off Rochefort.

It was a posting none of them expected and few desired, while the sudden urgency that betrayed many weeks of rotting at anchor did little to raise the morale of men for whom intense physical work had become a novelty. And the officers were equally affected; it was a station slightly nearer to Britain admittedly, though not actually in home waters. They might get news and post more regularly but leave would be almost unheard of and there would be no more nights spent ashore as honoured house guests or potential suitors.

It was probably a measure of general discontent that the disappointment spread as far as King, who had more to gain from being attached to a fleet than anyone. But then, he had served under Jervis, Duncan, Nelson and, most recently, Ball: powerful men who commanded respect. So he was sceptical about the little known Graves. He consoled himself with the knowledge that the man came from a naval family and had been present at the Battle of the Saints, as well as Copenhagen, so might not be a total keep space. But if the rumours circulating Gibraltar were correct, Graves himself was currently on sick leave in England, with Nesham, a post captain of less than three years' seniority, carrying his flag.

However, King was forced to acknowledge the past few days' active service had already blown some of the cobwebs from his own mind, as well as those of his people, and readily accepted that even the monotony of blockade would be preferable to lying in harbour without pennant or goal. As the smallest ship on station, *Kestrel* was bound to be given the more dangerous jobs of closing with the enemy to check on shipping or shore emplacements, which would be preferable to the monotonous back and forth of the patrolling battleships. And he was equally sure that if there was action – if, by some gift of providence, the French were to break out or be joined by another force from either their own country or Spain – there might be a glorious battle indeed. One that, if not settling the course of the war must certainly alter it, and would be well worth being part of, if only in a saucy little sloop.

And he was just starting to think of the possible ramifications such an action would bring when the noise of someone's approach caught his attention. He turned to see a figure looming up in the darkness. It was Brehaut, equally trussed up in watchcoat and sou'wester, and eyes half closed against the sting of driving snow.

"All well, Mr Brehaut?" he asked. It was an unnecessary

question: if the sailing master had any concerns, King knew he would have been advised of them long ago.

"As well as I can say, sir," the Jerseyman replied in his customary laconic manner. "Yesterday's noon sights put us properly on course for Rochefort, but none were possible today. Dead reckoning places us almost a hundred miles west of the French coast, which gives a wide enough margin for error, though I would be happier if there were at least a star or two in sight."

Both men glanced up at the sky; the glimmer of the moon was just about evident, but all other celestial bodies were blanked by a heavy layer of cloud, as well as the blizzard that currently ranged all about. And there was no better visibility on deck; King could make out the foremast and some of *Kestrel*'s bowsprit, but beyond that lay only mystery. And so it came as a mild surprise when the voice of Hobbs, patiently on station at the main masthead, chose that moment to break into their thoughts. But when he did, it was not the customary confident bellow: Hobbs' tone was almost apologetic.

"Sail in sight off the starboard bow," he called, adding, "An' maybe one to larboard, but I couldn't be sure."

King's eyes caught those of Bremner, the duty midshipman sheltering in the lee of the binnacle. "To the maintop with you," he hissed, "and I should like Mr Soames on deck, if you please."

The lad took off at once, pausing only to grab the night glass, while the call went out for the midshipman in charge of *Kestrel*'s signals.

Hobbs' announcement suggested a fleet, or at least a small flotilla, and King had to suppress a momentary panic when he realised that, despite her speed and manoeuvrability, it would take little for an enemy force to snap up his tiny command on such a night. Reason soon took hold, however; they were further offshore than expected, but it seemed far more likely *Kestrel* had merely run across the blockading squadron. With an inexperienced captain in charge, it would have been understandable for the main force to withdraw, while the wind, fluctuating as it had been between north and north-west, would naturally force them further south. But he needed to be certain, which required more information and Hobbs was being annoyingly vague.

"What do you see there?" It was proof of his concern that he

48

used the speaking trumpet; usually King spurned such instruments, but it was not impossible that an enemy lurked nearby undetected and the short brass horn directed the voice more reliably than an all out bellow.

"Can't say for certain, sir," the seaman replied hesitantly, and there was something in his reticence that increased King's concern. "I only caught her for a moment: she were less than a mile off, and looked to be heading west. But there could be no doubting her size: she were a thumper right enough – a liner or somethin' similar."

King took Hobbs' estimation of size with the proverbial pinch of salt; he had known many instances when lookouts fooled themselves into thinking they could see whole fleets of warships only to discover them to be nothing more than fishers distorted by the aberrations of weather.

"What sail was she showing?"

"I caught tops'ls an' a forecourse, sir," Hobbs replied. "Might have been more but, as I say, it were only for a second."

King had rarely been aloft since the loss of his arm, and only then with the indignity of a man rope, but he could still remember the difficulties of lookout duty. Hobbs may well have been debating with himself for some while before sounding the alert, and was now probably regretting having caused so much fuss. But if what he said was correct, it was hardly the action of British ships. King would have expected an offshore squadron to be lying hove to and, if they had been heading in any direction at all, it would not have been west. Others were not of the same opinion, however.

"Belike that'll be one of Admiral Graves' ships," Brehaut murmured and, even in the poor light, King thought he could detect relief on the sailing master's face. That was quite understandable, after all, it was Brehaut's duty to see they made a safe rendezvous with the blockading force and, with the weather being so, to find he had apparently succeeded must have come like a blessing from heaven.

"Heard the call, sir!" Timothy, the first lieutenant, was clambering up the aft companionway and looking strangely exposed in his frock tunic. He gained the deck and made straight for the traverse board, a steward carrying his watchcoat in hot pursuit.

"We've sighted a ship – maybe more than one," King confirmed as he also turned for the binnacle. "Bremner is up there now: we're awaiting further news."

"Admiral Grave's squadron?" Timothy asked, while being helped into his coat. "It would seem a mite soon, surely?"

"And too far to the west," King agreed. "Which is also where they appear to be heading."

"I have her!" It was the voice of Bremner, and doubly reassuring as it carried a measure of certainty. "She's a liner right enough, an' carrying t'gallants, though no lights that I can see."

"Bearing and heading if you please, Mr Bremner," Timothy directed sternly.

"Sorry, sir. She's a couple of points off our starboard bow and a mile or so away; steering west, as near as I can say. Lost her again for a moment then, but now she's back."

"Any sign of more?" King asked.

"No, sir," Bremner reported. "But it's precious difficult to see anything much."

King totally accepted that; the snow was actually falling harder while any estimation of distance in the current conditions could never be trusted: even an experienced hand could make a pig's ear of such things without a known point to judge by. But there seemed little doubt the sighting was heading west, while her size and position made her likely to be a warship.

"That still might be one of Admiral Grave's force," Brehaut insisted, although his tone was now less certain. "Sure, a Frenchman wanting to head across the Atlantic would be heading south-east, to pick up the current."

King pondered for a moment. If they were at peace, the sailing master may well have been right. But at war, and with British ships in the vicinity, a group of escaping French warships would hardly invite trouble by seeking out the Gulf Stream. Certainly if King had been in command he would have tried to put as much distance between his own force and the enemy as possible.

"There's another to larboard!" It was Bremner's voice again, and carried a note of what might have been panic. "She's much nearer, an' must have been covered by a squall."

"How close, Mr Bremner?" Timothy demanded.

"Less than a mile, I'd say," the lad replied. "An' another liner,

50

that's for certain."

"Douse all lights!" King's response was automatic and, as the cry of darken ship began to echo about the small vessel, he could feel the tension rising.

"Clear for action, sir?" This was Timothy, and King had to bite back a curt response.

"No," he replied, with studied control. "Though you may call back the watch below and see the topmen are properly awake and ready."

Were *Kestrel* to be truly heading towards a fleet of enemy liners, clearing for action would serve little purpose and might even reveal her position. Far better to have every hand primed and at their sailing stations.

"Another: dead ahead!" Hobbs once more, and his voice had risen further.

Now there was no doubt in King's mind. "Take us to larboard," he snapped, and Brehaut immediately ordered the helm across. *Kestrel* had been close-hauled under topsails and topgallants; but she would be faster than any lumbering battle-wagon and a further order reduced her to topsails alone. King's certainty that they had found an escaping French fleet was growing all the time, and he was not unaware of the fact that *Kestrel* 's importance had effectively risen from the obscurity of an unrated warship to something approaching that of an entire battle squadron.

For, if they really had happened upon an enemy fleet, it was valuable information indeed, and King's duty was now to shadow them wherever they may go. *Kestrel* must be ready to signal their presence to any British force capable of engaging, as well as warning potential targets on whatever side of the Atlantic they lay. But to do so would mean sailing near enough to monitor the enemy's every move and, in the present conditions, that meant very close indeed. It was one thing to shadow a hostile fleet in broad daylight and clement weather, quite another to do so on a snowy winter's night. And all the while he was equally conscious that, were he to lose them, all *Kestrel*'s value would instantly vanish. Just as it would if he took matters too close, and found himself taken.

King took a turn about the deck; only the binnacle light was left burning and the weather appeared worse than ever. With all officers summoned the quarterdeck was crowded, yet the figures gathered about had become little more than vague apparitions that could only be picked out by their snow-covered clothes. As he paced, he felt he might be the one living soul left aboard a ghost ship, which was actually quite appropriate. For whether they stayed in contact and shadowed the enemy's progress, or lost them in the night, forcing *Kestrel* to go running back with news of what had got away, much, if not all, would ultimately depend on him.

\* \* \*

Lovemore woke in his hammock and blinked for a moment in the darkness. Something had interrupted his sleep, yet there was nothing unusual in the shipboard sounds and *Kestrel* seemed to be sailing sweetly enough. He snuggled himself down; his watch would be on deck again before long, so it was particularly galling to have been woken for no reason.

And then he saw Harris.

The man was standing over him and appeared to be looking down, which was strange as Lovemore's hammock was hung especially high against the deckhead. He could also see the face quite clearly, which was doubly odd, with the only lamp burning being many feet away.

"What cheer, Curly?" Harris asked. "I were in action, but then you knows all about that," the seaman continued confidently.

Lovemore blinked in momentary confusion; they had been in harbour for so long that the details of their last engagement did not come readily to his sleep-filled mind. Then he remembered everything, including Harris' fate.

"An' I were all but cut in two by a round shot," the vision added cheerfully enough.

"I'm sorry," Lovemore whispered softly, although his words seemed to echo about the darkened deck and were spoken far louder than his visitor's.

"Oh, it weren't so bad," Harris gave a wry smile. "Never saw it coming – though you may have," he added with a questioning look.

This time Lovemore did not reply.

"Not that I blames you," the vision continued. "Probably

would have done the same myself. But I wanted you to know I were aware."

"I see," Lovemore was whispering still, but this time drew a groan of protest from Cranston in the next hammock.

"An' I wanted you to know somethin' else," Harris continued. He was speaking as loudly as before, yet there was no reaction from anyone else. "You're going to be in action again soon, an' it will be a sad one."

"Sad?" Lovemore barely mouthed the word.

"Aye, about as sad as it can get," Harris assured him. "But you don't want to worry, no one will be snabbled."

No deaths, yet the action was to be sad; Lovemore's bewildered mind could not unravel such a conundrum.

Another sound broke the spell; it was the scream of boatswain's calls summoning all hands, and soon the entire deck seemed to be erupting in a mass of bodies as men struggled to free themselves from their hammocks. But Lovemore remained: he was transfixed. And Harris stayed with him.

"So you'll be all right, Curly," the vision told him. "You an' all your mess – for now at least."

Lovemore went to nod although, as he was still resting on his pillow, the action was stunted. But Harris, it seemed, understood.

"Keep your nose clean, and don't do nothing foolish, an' you've nowt to worry about," he continued. There was chaos on every side by now; men were shouting and the sound of bare feet drumming on the wooden deck above his head told how the ship was preparing to manoeuvre. But Harris' words still came through clearly, and Lovemore remained transfixed.

For a moment a knowing expression spread across Harris' face, then he gave a wink, before disappearing completely.

A heavy jolt to Lovemore's shoulder broke him from the trance.

"Here, we're being called on deck," Cranston told him roughly.

Lovemore knew that well enough, but for a moment it was as if his limbs had lost all ability to move. That had definitely been Harris, sure as a gun, yet the man had been dead these long months. He swallowed; was this how matters were to progress? From faint inklings about the future, through images seen on men's faces, then finally visitations from their spirits? If so, he wanted none of it.

But how did one opt out of such a situation; turn off a power that was steadily growing inside and seemed likely to take him over? Lovemore did not have a clue; the only thing he knew with any certainty was how frightening the whole thing had become.

Cranston's face had replaced Harris' now, although it lacked the luminosity. "Hey, Curly, you got to shake a leg," it told him firmly, and Lovemore finally began to stir. His mate disappeared far more clumsily than Harris had and, for a moment, Lovemore was left alone with his thoughts.

"Spend much longer in your hammock, an' they'll start stitching you up in it," a boatswain's mate grumbled near by, and Lovemore finally moved. But even when he had made the deck, and was following his fellows up the main companionway, his mind was somewhere else entirely.

* * *

By the end of the middle watch, King, and most of the officers aboard *Kestrel*, had been up and on deck for over eight hours. Throughout that time there had been little to see of the enemy and, so regular had been their course and speed, even the occasional glimpses of their sterns had become common place. With nothing else to do, and the first light of dawn not due until the end of the new watch, King was finding it hard to keep his mind focused. The snow was lessening, but still fell without a break, while the wind had actually increased. He could hear the murmur of quiet conversation from the afterguard, and at one point thought there might have been a hastily interrupted snore. But even that was understandable; he had stood down the watch below several hours before, and it was typical of the average British seaman's arrogance that he should proclaim himself bored when so close to the enemy.

For if their quarry truly was the Rochefort fleet, they must be following several powerful liners, as well as whatever small stuff the French had been able to cobble together to send with them. Yet despite this power, his tiny eighteen-gun sloop was able to keep pace at their rear, apparently invisible to their lookouts.

And the monotonous night had granted them one major

benefit; King was now convinced all his enemies were before him, while equally knowing he had canvas in hand if *Kestrel* were spotted. Should the alarm be given, it would take little to turn to larboard and add sail. He had no real idea of the size of the ships he was shadowing, but there were few vessels afloat capable of catching *Kestrel* who could do her significant damage if they did. His only true fear was to be trapped.

The muted call that replaced sounding the ship's bell had clearly stirred the stewards into action, and there was a murmur of approval from those around him as hot drinks began to be handed out. King had long since abandoned tea or coffee in favour of the rich, dark chocolate he had grown so fond of in Malta, and accepted a mug of the stuff from Thompson, his servant. Sipping the thick, hot liquid cautiously, he glanced down at the glimmer of light from the binnacle. The compass still showed their course as westerly; at their current speed, *Kestrel* must have been following the enemy for over forty miles, and would cover a few more yet before dawn broke to reveal her presence. Then there might be a touch of excitement and, following the unslept night, he would have to be especially alert. He proposed to drop back when daylight became imminent and await developments but, with *Kestrel* in top form, remained confident she would out-sail any Frenchman that tried to take her. Then they would continue through the next day, keeping a good distance and the fleet under observation, until dusk came to herald another sleepless night. If they truly were heading to cross the Atlantic, there would be many more to come, and they would be made more dangerous by an enemy fully aware of their presence.

In which case he would have to sleep during the day, and make sure his officers did the same. Then, just as he was contemplating this and exactly how he would while away the next couple of hours, the masthead lookout called out once more.

"Deck there. Another sail in sight, an' this one's to larboard!"

The bald words of the midshipman were barely audible yet still they broke into the minds of all on the quarterdeck, and many beyond. An enemy to larboard was bad news indeed, and meant their first avenue for escape had been effectively blocked. King was about to demand a course and distance when the lad continued.

55

"Mile or less off our larboard beam and on our heading, but coming up fast. She's a frigate, or something the likes of – single deck, and showing topsail's, forecourse, stay's and jibs."

King's mind began to race. It was conceivable that this new sighting was not part of the French fleet at all, but a British ship sent to intercept. Conceivable, but unlikely – even if Graves' squadron knew they had missed the escaping ships, it would have been all but impossible for any sent to catch them to be successful. Far more probable the newcomer was another Frenchman, perhaps one that had left port later and been chasing the fleet throughout the night. Then King realised that there was an alternative, even if it were too terrible to contemplate: despite his recent certainty he had to admit it possible that *Kestrel* was not sailing at the rear of the fleet after all but amid it, and there were further enemy ships to her stern.

It was a terrible thought but, even if it were the case, he still had to react to the immediate problem. A known threat lay to larboard, and appropriate action must be taken.

"Luff up to starboard, Mr Brehaut." It would do no good to appear hasty and King gave the command in as steady a tone as he could muster. "And summon the watch below once more, if you please."

Despite the sudden emergency, he still felt they were not in any great danger, but the men would hardly have settled into their hammocks, and it was probably wise to take all precautions.

The ship turned into the wind, and her canvas began to snap noisily as she lost way. All was silent on the quarterdeck, although most could not resist the temptation to stare out in the direction of the new sighting. But however close she might lie, nothing could be seen, either on deck, or aloft and *Kestrel* began to roll slightly in the swell. King knew he would have to take her under control shortly, but considered it worth allowing the enemy to gain a lead if it meant staying out of sight of the mystery frigate. And then there came another call from the masthead: it was one that he had been secretly dreading, and the excited voice of the midshipman sent a chill deep into his soul.

* * *

Holby knew about the watch below being called. He had heard the news from the comfort of his cot in the tiny shuttered cabin off the gun room. A midshipman, bursting in with the grace and tact of an elephant, had advised all present of an enemy squadron and there was a flurry of activity from the other officers as sword belts were buckled and watchcoats demanded. But *Kestrel*'s purser had simply snuggled deeper into in his bed and resigned himself to sleep. The ship was not clearing for action, and neither had the men been sent to quarters, so he had no intention of stirring himself unnecessarily. Holby had a battle station, it was in the orlop where he was designated to assist the surgeon. But he was sure such an eminent medical man as Robert Manning could manage without advice from him.

Besides, Holby had just spent the most nerve-racking two months of his life. Hardly a week had passed without several vessels arriving from countries where he was a wanted felon and now he simply felt pleased to be at sea, and free from the fear of imminent arrest. At one point during their stay a smart little American schooner had come into harbour. The other officers had discussed her at length as she lay nearby and he soon learnt she was to take on supplies before heading for her home port across the Atlantic.

For all the time she lay at the mole, Holby considered her, while the idea of a new life on the other side of the world steadily grew on him. Finally he had taken the plunge, invented an excuse, and clambered aboard the next liberty boat. There were few captains who would not welcome an extra hand, even if they had no need for a clerk or a purser and Holby also had the foresight to equip himself with a dozen guineas from the officers' victualling fund, so could have paid his passage in full if need be.

But he never got as far as actually approaching the marine guard standing sentinel at the short boarding plank, and even now wondered why seeing the group of seamen had made him veer off at the last moment.

They were from *Kestrel* and there was one amongst them that he knew relatively well. He had dark curly hair and played the flute; several times the man had enquired of the chance that Holby might persuade the captain to issue him with a fife. It was something the purser was considering as he should make a fair sum from the transaction, but so far had come to naught. The seaman caught his eye, and Holby remembered almost withering under his gaze.

"On a spree, are you, Mr Holby?" he had enquired and Holby muttered something neutral in reply. But the man was not to be put off and, even now and in the warmth of his bed, the words still chilled him.

"Only I should be careful where you goes. This may seem a friendly place, but there's danger aplenty, even if you don't go looking for it."

Holby, who had been about to explain his business to the uniformed guard at the gangplank, stopped. The seaman moved on, leaving him standing in thought, and then *Kestrel*'s own captain, together with her first lieutenant and surgeon, appeared at the American vessel's entry port.

The three had obviously been dining aboard, and dined well – at least Holby was not spotted as he slunk off into the confusion of a busy dockyard. But if any of the officers had seen him it might have been awkward indeed, and the entire incident was enough to cure him of any notions of stretching his luck further. And he certainly had no intention of rousing himself now, even if they were in the midst of an enemy squadron, he would remain safe and warm in his bed.

* * *

"Sail in sight, to starboard, less than a couple of cables off and comin' up fast!"

The midshipman's voice cracked with excitement, and King felt a surge of energy sweep though his body.

"Bring her back to the wind!" His order owed more to instinct than considered thought although, in the circumstances, there could be no other. Brehaut let loose a stream of orders and the ship was suddenly charged with the buzz of activity. But *Kestrel* had been wallowing with her bows to the wind and, whatever they did, it would take time to see her underway again.

"My word, that's her!" This time the cry did not come from the masthead but Soames, the signal midshipman, on the quarterdeck. All turned to look and there, indisputably, was the prow of a heavy battleship, already impossibly close and steadily bearing down upon them.

*Kestrel* would soon be taking up speed, but it would be a standing start.

"Set t'gallants!" The order came from Brehaut and had not been instigated by King, although the time for niceties had long since passed. The topmen made for the weather shrouds and soon began to fly up the ratlines, despite the ice that probably saturated the untarred hemp.

"To larboard!" King ordered, his voice still as measured as he could make it. But however much he might try to play the confident captain, an inner feeling told him the situation was fast becoming hopeless.

Having just escaped a blockading squadron, the enemy would already be cleared for action and, with the menacing bulk of a battleship closing on their stern, it simply didn't seem possible to keep his ship safe.

"There're lights aboard the Frenchman!" That was Timothy and, looking back, King could see he was correct. The oncoming liner had been sailing in pitch darkness, but now the glint of lanterns told of activity on her decks. *Kestrel* had come round and was taking the wind, but the Frenchman remained in plain sight off their quarter, and was steadily closing in for the kill.

King glanced at Timothy and both understood their predicament; were they to turn and run with the wind, *Kestrel's* stern would still be in point blank range for some time. No sloop could recover from a raking by a ship of the line; even if the French gunners were not up to scratch, she could hardly avoid being both dismasted and holed, while a single broadside would probably account for at least a third of her people.

"It'll be close," Timothy gasped. The Frenchman was now in a position to open fire, although her captain appeared to be waiting for the ideal time; when *Kestrel* would be directly under his guns and must suffer the worst damage.

"Too close," King replied. Even as he watched he could see further lights appearing as the liner's ports were opened. Her guns were being run out, and *Kestrel* would be a target even a fool could not fail to hit.

"Deck there!" That was the masthead once more, and for a

moment King wondered what extra devilment the midshipman was about to announce.

"Sail fine on the larboard bow – it's the frigate we saw earlier, she must have come about."

And then King could see her too, appearing out of the darkness like a woken monster emerging from a cave. She could only have been a thirty-two, but remained considerably more powerful than *Kestrel*, and was sweeping in as close to the wind as she could manage. He wondered for a moment if her presence would dissuade the liner from opening fire, only to decide it unlikely. They were closer to the two decker, and there was little chance of even the wildest of shots hitting the frigate, while the lighter ship was perfectly placed to block *Kestrel*'s last chance of escape.

King swallowed dryly – it hardly seemed possible that less than fifteen minutes before he had been contemplating a chase across the Atlantic, yet now had to accept the likelihood of his ship being sunk or taken.

To avoid either he would have to act fast; even now the liner was moving into position for the perfect broadside. It would be a barrage *Kestrel* could not avoid even if she turned further to larboard, while the frigate was heading to take her if she did.

"It's no good," he murmured to Timothy. "See to it that the signals book and all confidential papers are jettisoned." The first lieutenant nodded once before hurrying off leaving King strangely alone on what was still a crowded quarterdeck. The orders that were sending him to rendezvous with Admiral Graves held nothing of value to the enemy, and *Kestrel* had not been charged with mail or despatches. No ensign was flying, which made the business of surrender a little more complicated, although he doubted if such a subtle signal would have been noticed anyway. Besides, there was a far simpler way to strike which he hoped would be understood by all. Then, with a final glance about the ship, King raised his voice and bellowed the last order he would issue as captain of HMS *Kestrel*:

"Let go the sheets."

# Chapter Six

There was something unreal and utterly humiliating about being ushered into what had once been his cabin. And the feeling only increased when King noticed the smart, moustachioed officer who had so recently accepted their surrender seated comfortably behind his own desk. The man had obviously been through King's personal papers, as many still lay out and in disorder, and was now examining the pistol Nik Lesro had given to him with obvious interest.

"Ah, Commander King, do please be seated," he said, without standing or properly looking up. King hesitated for a moment, then lowered himself into the small, hard chair that had once been reserved for his visitors.

"Fascinating piece," the man informed him as he brought the hammer back. "You have excellent taste in weapons." He spoke in good English with little trace of an accent, and seemed extremely comfortable in his present position; a fact that only annoyed King further.

"It was a gift," he explained grudgingly.

"Then your friends have taste." The hammer fell with a loud click that made King jump visibly, and he found it hard not to curse the smug face opposite.

"You will forgive me, we have apparently got off to a bad start." The officer looked up and appeared genuinely contrite. "I will introduce myself properly and we shall begin again, maybe? I am *Lieutenant de Vaisseau* Coombes," he continued after King had made no response, "and now have charge of your fine ship." He regarded King with interest before continuing with a slight smile, "Though I think I may be correct in saying she was never truly yours, Commander; perhaps history will regard her as merely having been on loan?"

King made no attempt to unbend, even though Coombes was undoubtedly right. *Kestrel* had begun life as a French national warship – a corvette that he himself had helped capture. And now she would return to her country of origin, although the young *lieutenant* was wrong on one point. She had been King's once, and he would always consider her so.

"Where are you heading?" he found himself asking, and the man's smile returned.

"I, or the fleet? To be honest with you, Commander, I do not know exact details; you and I are but small cogs in a large machine."

King bristled once more; a few hours ago he had captained of one of His Majesty's warships, and was not used to being brought down to the status of a lieutenant.

"You were heading west," he countered, "to cross the Atlantic, maybe?"

"Maybe," Coombes shrugged. "It will do little harm revealing our plans in general – you are hardly in a position to benefit from such knowledge. And besides, the entire world shall be aware within a month. But while you may wish for idle conversation, it is not something I enjoy."

King consciously held his tongue and told himself that if Coombes did not wish to talk that was of no concern to him, although he actually sensed the opposite and was soon proved correct.

"Though I will say this," the Frenchman continued after a suitable silence, "we are due to meet with another fleet."

"Another?" King asked, despite himself.

"Oh yes," the officer confirmed. "And one that is even now preparing to burst through one of your famous blockades."

The implications were immense and, despite the circumstances, King felt his brain begin to race. Breaking a blockade was not so very hard as had already been demonstrated. He guessed his captors had taken advantage of either the bad weather or inattention from whoever commanded the British to make their escape: possibly both. And if one squadron could do it, others might be equally successful. There were even admirals who placed only a token blockade in the hope the warships they guarded might be tempted out to fight. Several French fleets were currently contained so, as well as a couple of Spanish, and some comprised up to of fifteen line-of-battle ships. There were far less in the current squadron, yet they need only meet with another of the same size to make a considerable force. Then they might visit each major French port in turn, overwhelm the blockading squadron by sheer numbers, and release every captive warship within until a truly massive armada were assembled. It would be a fleet capable of annihilating any the British might send to meet it, and still be strong enough to hold the Channel for a French invasion.

"And is this ship to join that fleet?" King asked, his tone as dispassionate as he could manage.

Coombes smiled. "No, Commander, I fear we shall be returning to France."

King felt his heartbeat increase further, to return meant abandoning the main body and travelling independently. *Kestrel* was only a sloop, so may still be recaptured by a wandering British warship and, if not, must surely pass through a blockading force before reaching harbour.

"But you need not gather hopes that your ship will be retaken," Coombes continued, the smile ever present. "We shall not be heading for Rochefort, or any of the ports where your fleets are so persistently vigilant. And I would say this, if any British warship was to find us in the current weather, you will truly deserve to have your vessel returned."

* * *

Lovemore had known all along the mystery fleet was French, as he had that *Kestrel* would be taken. And now, as he sat on the crowded orlop with most of the lower deck hands pressed hard into one apparent block of humanity, he also knew they were heading for France. To either end of the airless space a line of uniformed Frenchmen were holding their muskets at the ready. Lovemore had no idea if they were soldiers or marines and did not care greatly either way. But when he and the rest of the seamen had been herded below, a smart officer had told them they would be fed and well treated. At the time most had not believed him and, as light was starting to show at the gratings, the promise must now be several hours old.

"I'll pay a guinea for some scran an' a wet," Beeney's offer rose above the generic muttering of quiet conversation and received no takers. It was repeated until someone told him to shut up, but the appeal seemed to focus the men in some way.

"There's bread an' mash near enough, if we wants it," another proclaimed.

"Aye, an' grog – no jollies guardin' the spirit room – just got to take down these jokers an' we can drink our fill."

"Belay that!" It was Curry, the master-at-arms who, although of warrant rank, had opted to remain with his men. Another began to call out "scran!" in a regular chant and soon the entire deck was quivering to the sound of strong men bellowing in unison. One of the guards tried to shout over the noise but made little progress, then the darkness was temporarily lit by the flash of a musket shot and, as the report echoed about the suitably muted crowd, Lovemore thought he could hear the sound of far off sobbing.

"Anyone hurt?" Curry enquired levelly, and again there was no response. Then a slim figure could be seen skipping nimbly down the aft companionway and all eyes turned to him.

It was the officer with a moustache who had sent them below and promised food. He stood next to one of the two lanterns that lit the dismal scene, and stared out over the sea of closely packed bodies.

"When everything is calm and in good order you will be fed," he said, after gathering his thoughts for a moment. "But if there is any further disturbance I shall order my men to open fire – is that clear?"

"We've no water," Curry announced from deep within the crowd. "And some of us are needing air."

"Water will be supplied," the man replied. "And food; soon both will be arranged. There is still the snow outside; when it stops I shall also see that all are given exercise, but you must understand that nothing can happen immediately."

There was an expectant pause, and Lovemore could sense the officer assessing his audience.

"You are sailors and must know our problems; we have to care for the ship and need the space to do so."

"An' there are more of us than you!" a grim voice added from the throng to an accompanying growl of menacing laughter.

"That I cannot deny," the Frenchman replied instantly. "Though I will promise it to be the worse for any who try to retake this ship. And you must recall that we are also holding your officers."

"That's all right, matey," the same voice retorted. "You can keep 'em!"

This time the laughter held a greater measure of humour, and the Frenchman acknowledged this with a faint smile.

"Maybe so, but I shall send water now, the food will come soon. And it is not so very late: I am sure the English are not so governed by their stomachs as some might say." The officer paused, as if gauging the crowd once more, then continued, "and soon we will be reaching land, when I can promise you all will be well cared for."

"All very fine making promises; they has to be carried out," Cranston, who was on Lovemore's immediate right, grumbled. "From what I hears, you frogs treat prisoners worse than criminals. Make 'em row in the galleys and the like."

"There'll be none of that," Lovemore hissed without thinking. "And he has every intention of seeing us fed. We'll be getting a bite of breakfast within an hour, and hot food by the afternoon watch."

"That right is it?" another seaman asked.

"Aye," one of the afterguard added with a sneer. "Frogs keeping you informed, are they, Curly?"

"If he says so, you can depend on it," Cranston stated with absolute certainty. "Lovemore's about the only one round here you can trust."

* * *

*Kestrel*'s gun room was also more crowded than usual. In addition to the two armed French marines who stood sentry at the door, it held all those accustomed to calling the mess home, as well as most of the ship's junior and petty officers who rarely came near the place. And for this last group, the splendour of what in larger ships would be referred to as the wardroom was novelty indeed. The senior men had naturally gravitated to the long table that ran down the centre of the space where they were used to being fed, and the absence of their usual choice of refreshments had made some a little tetchy. But at least there was water as well as soft tack

65

brought from Gibraltar which *Lieutenant* Coombes had agreed they might share. And in the main they could be seated; there were enough of the hard, upright dining chairs to accommodate most of the quarterdeck officers, while the boatswain, carpenter and other warranted men crouched less comfortably on the deck.

"Captain seems a reasonable enough cove," Timothy was saying as he helped himself to a chunk of the bread that was far from stale. "Comes from your neck of the woods, I believes," he added, looking across at Brehaut.

"He's a Channel Islander sure enough," the sailing master allowed. "From Sark, though I'd wager he's not been that way for many a year."

"Did he say anything of our destination?" This was from Adams. The young acting lieutenant rarely took part in gun room discussions although with so many junior men present the atmosphere was more casual than usual.

"Nothing to me," Timothy admitted, but the captain is with him now, he may discover more."

"Far be it from me to steal Mr King's thunder, but I would suggest we are heading for France." All eyes turned on Brehaut as he spoke before switching, somewhat guiltily, to the two uniformed guards standing mute at the door. The marines stared back blankly, clearly unaware of what was being said and the sailing master continued. "I chanced to overhear a conversation between the two younger officers," he explained quickly. "Neither had any idea I knew their language and spoke freely. They seemed disappointed to be missing out on what proposes to be a major voyage, with potentially an action to match."

"But the French have no more than a handful of liners," Midshipman Summers pointed out.

"Aye," another agreed. "Hardly enough to stage anything major."

"But now they are free, more can be raised easily enough," Adams mused. "There are French warships ready to sail in any number of ports nearby."

"And Spanish," Brehaut added in little more than a whisper.

"Even a few liners coming from seaward should be enough to draw out a blockading squadron," Timothy agreed. "And give those within chance to escape."

A noise from outside drew everyone's attention, and the marine sentries stepped to one side as King was shown into the gun room by an adolescent French officer in a smart blue uniform.

"It seems I shall be sharing your quarters, gentlemen," the captain announced, approaching the table as the boy slipped silently out. "And apologise for the inconvenience that might cause."

"You will be a welcome guest, sir," Timothy confirmed as he and the other officers stood awkwardly under the gun room's low deckhead. "Though there are more of us than usual, so you may find it rather overcrowded."

"Well, it should not be for long," King replied, taking the chair that one of the midshipmen had speedily vacated. "*Lieutenant* Coombes informs me we shall be separating from the main French fleet shortly, and heading for the French coast."

"Rochefort?" Timothy asked as King was seated. The senior man shook his head.

"Further to the north – our host was most forthcoming, and why should he not be?" he added with a half smile. "Place called Royan, do you know of it, Master?"

"Town on the north side of the Gironde estuary," Brehaut answered quickly as everyone looked to him.

"I don't recall anything there worth blockading," Timothy added.

"So we should be able to slip in without detection." King's tone was flat as he accepted a mug of water from Adams. In his heart he had never held up much hope of running in with a British ship, but announcing this turn of events seemed to make the prospect even less likely and he found it hard to hide his disappointment.

"And what will happen to us after that?" Adams asked, as no one else seemed to be saying much.

"After that, we shall doubtlessly be imprisoned," Timothy replied.

"But up for exchange, surely?" Adams persisted.

"I think not." King's words seemed especially cold, even in such depressing circumstances. "Prisoner exchange is a mite too civilised for the new Emperor of France," he continued, while casting a guilty glance at the two mute sentries. "There have been no major examples so far in this war, and I cannot say that any appear likely."

"And when it all began once more, did he not seize every British subject in France?" Timothy reminded them. "Whether they be serving officers or not?"

"I believe so," King agreed. "The men needed only to be of military age, and even that requirement was greatly stretched."

"*And* he took their wives, *and* their children," Brehaut added. "Whole families were imprisoned as I remember, and most remain so."

"Servants as well, I hears," Timothy agreed.

"It does seem that *Monsieur* Bonaparte is set to play this war to his own rules." King once more. "And those in our position are likely to suffer."

"But the last went on almost ten years!" Adams exclaimed indignantly. "The next may be longer – we cannot spend all that time as prisoners!"

"Well if you have any other ideas, Mr Adams," King sighed, "we would be glad to hear of them."

* * *

*Kestrel* left the French fleet two hours later. By then snow had ceased to fall, but the sky was still covered by grey, leaden cloud and there was no sign of any shipping, British or otherwise. Lovemore had been allowed on deck along with nineteen of his fellows and together they stood at the larboard bulwark of the ship they had so recently considered their own.

"Fore tops'l could do with being taken in," Cranston grumbled. "And they've made a proper pig's ear of settin' that jib."

Some nodded in silence, although most seemed to have lost the energy to criticise, while a few inwardly accepted that the French had a scratch crew aboard. They might not be up to everyone's exacting standards, but it was no easy task to take over from another set of hands, and were actually carrying out their job well enough.

"So how long will it take us to raise land then?" Cranston asked, turning to his friend, but Lovemore looked away.

There had been no official announcement to the men, but

earlier he had inadvertently let slip his belief that they would not be continuing with the main fleet, something that had been instantly accepted by all. And now he was proved correct, no psychic powers were required to realise he was firmly established as the source of all knowledge amongst the men.

"I wouldn't care to say," he muttered, and that was indeed the truth.

"Well, will it be France?" Cranston asked, hoping for a compromise.

"It's possible," Lovemore agreed.

"Come on, Curly!" a heavyset seaman with dark tattoos demanded. "Don't play the innocent maid – you know more'n you're tellin'."

"I'd say we're probably bound for France, but other than that..." Lovemore left the sentence unfinished and was silently relieved when the men let it be.

The snow might have stopped but it was still devilishly cold although even the chill of a January day was preferable to the airless orlop they had just left. Some began to pace the deck, enjoying the chance to move about, but Lovemore was not amongst them. Instead, he found a sheltered place on his own under the starboard gangway, and assumed roughly the same position he had held for the last few hours below.

His joints complained, but that was actually a welcome distraction as he had a far greater pain to bear. For, whatever he had told the men, and however much he might not wish for it, he actually had a fair idea of what they might expect. The knowledge was still vague in places and, like a faded memory, gave only an impression, much of which was bad. But not all, and the presence of at least some good encouraged him as he tried to concentrate on that alone. No attempt to alter the images was successful however, whatever tactic Lovemore tried they were still presented to him like the writing on a page, and one he had no option other than to read. Even as he sat on the deck of his former ship the facts became clearer and when the French officer bellowed for all to reform and return below, he felt he knew their immediate future in reasonable detail.

First, and probably most importantly, he was sure *Kestrel*'s lower deck men would remain together and be relatively safe, but after that more disquieting images appeared to trouble him. For he would not be amongst them; his path seemed to be leaving theirs and heading for a destination that remained unclear. And when he tried to look further it became even more disconcerting. He could see himself amongst officers, which was strange indeed. Some he already knew, others he did not. And there would be bright lights, music and at least one other ship that looked as if it was to become important. There was also a tremendous feeling of release that he welcomed but could not explain, while any pleasure that evoked was immediately outweighed by a far more immediate account of who amongst *Kestrel*'s crew would survive and who perish. This was already being made plain to him, even as he watched his fellows as they formed up in an orderly huddle at the mouth of the fore hatchway.

He rose to join them, trying hard to let the pain in his stiff joints distract him from the knowledge he had of their destinies. But there was no ignoring some; their fates appeared set, and Lovemore could see them all too clearly on their faces.

# Chapter Seven

"There will be no luggage train as such; we only have that cart for our dunnage," Brehaut told them through half closed lips. "Anything that can't be shipped aboard must stay behind."

King, and the rest of his officers glanced across at the two-wheeled wagon that stood nearby with a brindled mule waiting patiently in its traces. Of all those assembled he probably had the most possessions but, even if each limited themselves to one sea chest apiece they would more than fill the small cart. Brehaut had just emerged from a stone building that seemed to act as a combination of customs house and base for the civil authorities. He had been inside for more than half an hour, and King was hoping for more news of the journey ahead rather than the arrangements for moving their luggage.

"Is there word of the people?" he asked. Despite the dramatic change of circumstances, he could not regard himself as anything other than *Kestrel's* captain, so the men that had recently made up her crew remained his responsibility.

"As far as I gather, they left earlier this morning," Brehaut replied. The sailing master was the only officer with a proper command of French and, in the brief time they had been ashore, had become their natural liaison with the authorities.

"And where might they be bound?" Timothy asked.

Brehaut shrugged. "I'm afraid I have no idea," he admitted, adding, "though I rather suspect it to be the same general destination as ourselves."

King looked away to hide his frustration. The land was low and featureless and, in the clear morning air, he could still plainly see *Kestrel* moored to the quay no more than a mile away. A tricolour was flying jauntily over her British ensign which, either through ignorance or insult, the French had hoisted upside down and his eyes did not remain on her for long. Beyond, the estuary was devoid of any significant shipping and the other square, stone buildings that made up much of the port appeared abandoned.

"There was another matter," Brehaut continued. "Before we undertake any journey, we shall be asked to swear not to escape."

"Escape?" Timothy exclaimed aghast. "We know well enough that exchange might not be immediate, but surely none of us will feel the urge to desert?"

"If the chance arose, I should find no hesitation," Manning, the surgeon, informed them calmly. "My child is to be born in but a few days, and I have no intention of awaiting the whims of a madman who chooses to call himself Emperor."

"Then I fear you will make any journey in chains," Brehaut told him firmly. "Though doubt if it be worth the bother as they will be sending us under escort. Besides, in such a godforsaken land, I doubt any attempt would be successful."

For a moment there was silence as the group considered this. They were mostly *Kestrel*'s senior men, with a few of her warrant officers and midshipmen: the rest, including master's mates as well as standing and petty officers, had been judged inferior and grouped with the lower deck hands. King took the opportunity to consider those that were left; Timothy and Adams, who were his lieutenants, even though the latter only carried an acting warrant, Brehaut, the sailing master and Manning, the surgeon who was also his best friend. Then there was Holby, the purser, and the three remaining midshipmen although he could not expect much from these, and feared the youngsters might become a liability. All appeared unusually shabby after several days in the same clothes and he could sense the prospect of a long march was the last thing any wanted. But King knew them well enough to detect an element of spirit and, as long as that existed, there could be hope for the future.

"Well, little can be served by standing about," he said, summoning an enthusiasm he did not feel. "What say we start consolidating our baggage? How long do we have, Master?"

"The officer I spoke with was not particularly forthcoming," Brehaut admitted, "and I gather *Kestrel*'s appearance was unexpected. We may have to wait for whatever escort they are proposing to provide."

"Then we had better be ready for them when they do arrive," King replied briskly, before making for the untidy pile of chests and bags that had been unceremoniously dumped by the side of the track. Thompson, his steward, had been taken with the regular hands but he was quite used to caring for himself. The other officers joined him, and soon all were sorting through their uniforms, linen and books, as well as the small and often foolish personal items that had made life aboard ship more pleasant. They were less than halfway through when a cloud of dust signalled the arrival of five horsemen that came up the road at a brisk trot. These were headed by a sallow man with a short beard who rode the largest mount. When they drew near, he raised his right hand and called the detachment to a halt.

"I look for Commander King," he told them, after swiftly dismounting and passing the care of his horse to one of his men. The officer was dressed smartly in a dark uniform that appeared military, although King had no idea of the regiment.

"My name is King," he announced, and the Frenchman sniffed slightly as he regarded him.

"*Capitaine de la Gendarmerie* Fabron," he muttered, removing his gloves but not offering to shake King's hand. "I shall be conducting you for the first stage of your journey."

"I am delighted to hear it *Capitaine*," King replied. The man spoke reasonable English and it was a relief to be able to conduct negotiations himself; the first time he had been allowed such a luxury since bidding farewell to *Lieutenant* Coombes. "Perhaps you will be so kind as to inform us as to our destination?"

"You are bound for Verdun," Fabron told them briskly. "And indeed, must count yourself fortunate in being so. I hear it is a splendid place, and one where you should be able to sit out this war in peace and comfort. My men and I expect to accompany you as far as Saintes, where my division ends. It is in the *Charente-Inférieure* and more than thirty kilometres away, so I suggest we begin forthwith."

"That is a considerable distance," King replied as he eyed the heavy horses of the *gendarmes*. "Are we expected to walk?"

"Indeed so, Commander," the officer snorted. "Unless you have alternative transport that I am unaware of. With luck we shall arrive not so long after dark, and you will be given an adequate place to rest."

"But thirty kilometres..." King began, before sensing further complaint would be considered a weakness.

"Thirty kilometres is perhaps the optimistic estimation," Fabron told him stiffly. "Some may say it is closer to forty. But that will seem like nothing when you finally reach your destination."

"And how far is that?" King guessed Fabron would be keen to tell him, but still could not resist the question.

"Much would depend on the route," the officer replied with a considerate smile. "But it will not be a short journey. I would suggest you prepare yourselves for a walk of considerably more than seven hundred kilometres."

* * *

Lovemore, Cranston and the rest of *Kestrel*'s lower deck men were already on the road, and had been for some hours. They, too, were walking and, though the mounted escort that surrounded them was considerably larger than that allocated the officers, only three carts of a similar size had been provided for their possessions. Consequently, most were carrying anything of particular value and, walking to the rear of the column, Lovemore needed no supernatural powers to predict the piles of seamen's chests and ditty bags currently being carried must soon be abandoned to allow those suffering from blisters or twisted ankles to be borne in their place.

But he had been able to secure his flute, which currently nestled between his shirt and round jacket, while he also had the straw hat bought in Gibraltar, as well as an additional pair of socks and some linens that were stuffed into a bedding roll secured to his back. And surprisingly he also had money; the French had been unexpectedly honourable in that department. Despite the fact he had chosen to hide the instrument, he was forced to concede that nothing of value had actually been taken from any of them, and at no time had they been properly searched. Even his pusser's dirk, the clasp knife that is an essential tool for any seaman, still hung about his neck, while the boatswain had been allowed to retain his rattan. There was still a reassuringly heavy purse in his jacket pocket and he had two more shirts and a pair of trousers bound up in a blanket that, for the time being at least, was bouncing along behind in one of the carts.

"What cheer, Lovemore?" The voice came from behind, and he turned to see Cranston, who had increased his step and was coming alongside.

"Fair as it might be," Lovemore replied. "Though I've a stone in my shoe and would welcome the chance to stop."

Cranston nodded in sympathy; they were marching as a body and, although the mounted guard stationed at either side allowed movement within the group as well as a degree of fraternisation, there had been no pause for over three hours. Even the moderate pace they were maintaining became wearying after such a period and some amongst them were visibly tiring.

"We're a fit enough bunch as a whole," Cranston supposed, "but stoning decks an' heaving lines ain't the same as this continual walking, and there's those not so well provided for in the way of shoes."

Lovemore muttered a cautious agreement and no more was said for several paces, although he sensed his mate was eager for something and feared it might be information.

"Belike we shall stop for a bite of scran afore long?" Cranston finally suggested, and the curly-haired seaman knew he had been correct.

"Well, maybe we will, an' maybe we won't," he replied enigmatically. Lovemore actually had an uncanny feeling there would be no pause for some time, but Cranston was one of many who had smoked his particular abilities, and he had no intention of encouraging him further. "Either ways, we'll sleep well in our beds tonight."

"So we'll be sleeping in beds?" Cranston asked hopefully, and Lovemore glanced at him sidelong.

"Maybe we will," he repeated, "an' maybe we won't."

\* \* \*

By late afternoon the officers had also started the march and, as the sun began to dip relentlessly towards the low western horizon, it became clear it would be dark long before they reached their goal. King, wearing his short boots, was walking easily between Timothy and Brehaut when he noticed the mounted Fabron was becoming agitated. Twice men had been sent to spy out the road ahead and on the return of the second the *Capitaine* brought his horse alongside and slickly dismounted.

"You are not making the speed we expected," Fabron informed him as he walked stiffly next to him. "There is still eighteen kilometres to cover, and only two hours to darkness."

"We were late setting off," King responded flatly, "what with that nonsense about signing papers. And it is your men that set the pace, not mine."

"It was necessary for the *Parole d'Honneur* to be acknowledged," Fabron replied. "If some of your officers had not wasted time in arguing, we would be nearer a safe rest. As it is, we shall have to find shelter in the next village and I promise you, it will not be so comfortable."

"It makes little difference to us." King's tone remained defiant. "One *auberge* is very much as another, and we are in no rush to clear your sector and reach Verdun." He looked directly at the officer. "Even if you are."

Fabron met the gaze, but it was clear their late arrival would not be popular.

"Well, perhaps it will not be an *auberge*, Commander," he sneered. "Perhaps, if we do not make Saintes, you shall have to be placed in the nearest village prison?"

"Then you will find yourself in a deal of trouble," King snapped back. "We are prisoners of war; treat us as criminals and it will be the worse for you and anyone responsible for your actions."

As he spoke, King noticed the Frenchman's face blanch slightly but he was determined not to back down. This was the first time he had been able to exert any authority since *Kestrel* was taken and, even though annoying his gaoler might not be the best course of action, he knew right to be on his side.

"I am also aware that an allowance must be paid to us while we are partaking of your hospitality," he continued. "I believe the amount is the equivalent of three shillings a day for myself, as well as a pound and a half of bread."

"Such an amount is for a captain," Fabron scoffed. "You are merely a commander, and not entitled to so much."

"I was the captain of HMS *Kestrel*," King retorted, "and should be victualled accordingly. My officers also have their rights; rights that have been agreed by your Emperor, and I

76

demand they be honoured."

"Demand?" Fabron all but spat the word out. Then he considered for a moment before continuing in a more even tone. "You may ask, Commander, and perhaps a small concession might be allowed, but you are in no position to demand."

"I understand a letter to your Minister of War would not be well received," King replied, his voice as level as ever. "If you will not grant the right for me to contact him, someone else shall, and it will be the worse for you when I do."

The officer said nothing for several seconds, although he did look towards King, and even opened his mouth to speak. But no words came, and he finally turned away, only to stumble slightly as he went to remount his horse.

"An angry man," Timothy commented after the *Capitaine* had ridden to the front of the small column.

"Angry indeed," King replied as he watched the officer berating one of his men for some minor misdemeanour. He was quietly sure of his facts; the Admiralty issued pamphlet giving advice to captured officers was unequivocal, and had been one of the few items he had access to while being held prisoner in *Kestrel*'s gun room. It now sat safely in his tunic pocket although, after being read so often, it must surely have been learned by heart. Whether or not he had been wise to assert himself so was another matter, but of one thing King was determined; he and his officers would not be spending that night in a common prison.

* * *

Lovemore, Cranston and the rest were not so fortunate. They had begun their journey earlier and been set a faster pace, so reached the outskirts of Saintes just as the sun was about to set. The small town had been expecting their arrival; a group of unmounted *gendarmes* came out to meet them and the exhausted seamen were silently ushered towards their place of rest, which turned out to be anything other than a pleasant inn.

France's Revolution had taken place many years before and much of the country's class system had subsequently been either destroyed or altered beyond all recognition. But despite this, the concept of a gentleman still persisted, if only in the minds of those in authority. This appeared to be an almost mythical being whose word was unbreakable and, in a country that was testing the depths of extortion and corruption, someone who could be ultimately trusted. By definition, all senior officers were considered so, and simple signatures or even verbal affirmations were regarded as sufficient to secure them every bit as firmly as any prison cell. But despite claims for liberty, fraternity and equality, seamen were viewed differently; they were commoners, and deservedly despised for the fact. Such a low state of humanity could never be expected to attain anything like the moral standards of their betters.

And so it was that those who had populated *Kestrel*'s lower deck found themselves shown into the capacious nave of a ruined church set to the north of the town. It was a clammy, dismal place where no fire greeted them and the only acknowledgement to their comfort was several bales of straw that looked as if they might have been assembled from the sweepings of a stable.

"This is hardly Fiddler's Green," Curry, the master-at-arms, grumbled as they were led into the vast, damp space. "Least they could do is light a brazier or two, Lord knows, they ain't in no need of a chimney!"

"A few lanterns wouldn't come amiss, neither," one of his corporals agreed.

"There's a box of candles under here," a seaman exclaimed as he heaved a small wooden crate from under a pew and into the open. "You want for us to light 'em?"

Curry looked over to the grey-uniformed officer who was in charge of the guards.

"What do you say, matey?" he asked, but received nothing but a blank look in reply. "Aye, go ahead," he called back to the man. "If it ain't approved, we'll soon learn of it."

A light was called for and soon the men were able to view the accommodation in its full glory. Enough wooden pews remained to provide beds for roughly half their number; the rest would have to use the straw, which hardly looked welcoming. And, as Curry had intimated, even the largest of fires would not have smoked them out; the remains of the roof only covered half of the building and most of that was missing tiles.

"We'll know all about it if it rains," someone commented, looking up, but Curry was quick to distract their attention.

78

"That's as maybe, but the important thing is to get ourselves set. Farmer, Abbot and Robinson; your messes can attend that straw, and see if any is fit to sleep on. An' Mr Sylvester, perhaps you and your team could take a tout about for something in the way of covering, in case the heavens do decide to open? The rest of you can grab at a swab and bring this place back to somewhere fit for decent people to live in."

They went about their tasks, grateful to have been given something constructive to do, and there was the occasional comment and laugh to show their spirits were a long way from broken. Being of Farmer's mess, Lovemore, Cranston and Hobbs began to sift through one of the stacks of straw, while the sailmaker and his men set to, dragging out what appeared to be an ancient tarpaulin and rigging it above the central section of roof where it might at least dissuade the morning dew. Their guards seemed to have regarded them as relatively safe within the ruined building, and left them to their own devices.

"So what sort of a lark is this?" one of the cook's mates asked when they could finally speak at ease. "We've been walking all day and half the night, and not a crumb's been offered."

"Aye, what's the chance of some scran?" another agreed, and all eyes fell on the master-at-arms, who had become their natural leader.

"All in good time," Curry told them. "We've still to get this place shipshape." He was equally at a loss with regard to their next meal and every bit as hungry. But many years' service had taught him that busy men were less likely to complain, although the concept was lost on some of Farmer's mess.

"As I hears it, we got a whole load more marchin' to do," Hobbs grumbled as they sorted through the long strands of yellowed straw. "And every step of it's takin' us further from the sea."

"Why should that bother you?" Lovemore asked, although he felt he already knew the answer.

"Stands to reason," Hobbs replied. "Even if the officers get themselves exchanged, we're not likely to. The previous war lasted the best part of ten years, I don't intend to spend such a spell cooped up with a bunch of Frenchmen. And the longer we leave it, the harder it will be."

"The longer we leave what?" Cranston asked.

"Why, escaping, of course," Hobbs replied.

* * *

King's prediction turned out to be remarkably accurate. He and the other officers had started some way behind the men and, even though Fabron reluctantly agreed to an earlier stop, it was still quite dark by the time they found shelter. This was in a village a good way short of their intended destination but, when they reached it, their accommodation was better than anything the ordinary seamen had been offered.

Rather than an empty ruin, they were billeted in a warm and welcoming inn, one that boasted several good fires, the scent of cooking and even a trio of young women who were happy to see to their needs. The one downside to the arrangement was that the British were expected to pay *Capitaine* Fabron's costs, as well those of his NCO and *gendarmes*, together with their mounts. King naturally objected to such an arrangement but, as there was nothing to contradict it in his Admiralty pamphlet, and the alternative might easily be for them to continue marching into the night, he was forced to back down. He had slightly more than twenty-two guineas in his purse and hoped the others would be able to raise a similar amount between them. Accommodation for the entire party could cost no more than fifteen shillings, so they could continue to live in such luxury for some while, even without the statutory pay they were entitled to. He had no notion of how his men were being treated but, after the events of the last few days, King felt he and his brother officers might benefit from a degree of comfort.

And as they sat at the large wooden table devouring the last of the soft, white cheese that seemed to be particular to the area, he decided it had been a wise choice. They all had a considerable walk ahead of them, but as there was the promise of warm beds, clean sheets and a hearty breakfast, he supposed things might be worse.

* * *

The morning, for *Kestrel*'s ordinary seamen, was very different to that of their officers', yet also not as bad as it might have been. Despite their surroundings, most slept remarkably well; a draught-ridden stone ruin being little different to conditions inside a warship once the lights were extinguished. There was even a modicum of rain from an overnight shower that made it past the sailmaker's precautions to complete the illusion. Hard pews, or even beds made on the best of the straw, were no substitute for a comfy hammock, however, and they also missed the airless fug of a crowded berth deck. But a pile of blankets had materialised just before they turned in, so most had been warm at least.

These were delivered along with three large pots of a vegetable stew by a group headed by the mayor of the town, who seemed particularly pleased to see his visitors and asked for nothing other than a chance to practice his antiquated English on the bemused seamen. Bottles of a rough, red wine were then brought by a wizened old lady whose grandsons carried her wares. These were offered for a *sous* each, although four British pennies were accepted without comment, and the warrant officers had to use all their authority to ensure no man bought more than one.

The *gendarme* officer who would be guarding them for the next stage of their journey appeared as they were rising. He had little English, but it was gathered the man had in some way been responsible for their food of the previous night. He was older than his predecessor and, though he carried an almost permanently sour expression on his slightly podgy face, apparently held a good deal more compassion for his charges; something that extended to a reasonable breakfast of soft white bread and cow's milk that was provided a little later. But as they gathered to eat in small groups that roughly represented the messes of their lost ship, there was no change in the attitude of some.

"I reckons we'll get the chance today," Hobbs told his mates as they ate their meal. "Give it a couple of hours, then arrange to ask for a visit to the heads," he continued, thinking as he spoke. "If enough go at once, they'll have to either stop or split the guard."

"That's assuming anyone listens," Cranston reminded him soberly. "The cove we had yesterday weren't taking no chances; we could have pissed ourselves for all he cared."

"Well, it looks like we got a better option today," Hobbs said.

He had just noticed a *gendarme* pouring milk for a seaman and he indicated this with the heel of his loaf.

"You've precious little idea where you are, and none of how to get anywhere else," Lovemore told him. "And though this lot might show a bit more kindness, they're still carrying weapons and they ain't for show. And they won't be taking no chances; if someone don't come back when called, the first they'll know of it is when a ball hits them in the back of the head."

"They might not know we're gone," Hobbs replied.

"They'll do a count," Cranston sighed. "They always do."

"Aye," Hobbs agreed. "That's exactly what I'm depending on." And he popped the last of the bread into his mouth with a grin.

# Chapter Eight

King, Timothy, Brehaut and Manning, who had shared one of the two rooms allocated to the British, were woken by a shirt-sleeved *gendarme* just before dawn. King was the first at the washstand; he picked up the enamelled pitcher and carefully measured out slightly less than a quarter of its contents into a tin bowl before finally plunging his face into the water's cold embrace.

It soaked into his five day growth of beard and dripped on the tiled top as he rubbed his face with a towel, while more fell onto the bare floorboards as he addressed the rest of his body with a sponge. While he worked, King caught sight of himself in the mirror and decided it was probably time for a shave. It was something normally attempted every day, even when at sea and in the heights of a storm, although strangely he had not felt the need since *Kestrel* was captured.

Little lather could be gained from the soap provided but, even as he began to brush it into the stubble that was fast claiming his chin, King began to feel better. The blade swept smoothly across his jaw, wiping the hairs away while leaving white, clear skin in their place. And when the last stroke was done and he could look without shame at a clean, if slightly foam-streaked, face, he knew he was coming to terms with captivity and actually beginning to fight back.

"Rain seems to have cleared," Manning said, as he turned away from the window. "With luck we'll make Saintes, and meet up with the men."

"If they haven't gone on before," Timothy grunted from the depths of his bed. "There's a way to go, and I can't see the French wasting any time in getting us there."

"I was wondering about securing a carriage." All eyes turned to Brehaut who had made the suggestion, and King paused in washing his face once more. But the sailing master continued, unabashed. "It would make sense; there are nine of us, counting the youngsters. If some rode aloft, we might all squeeze into one and make twice the speed, maybe more."

"Nine would be pushing matters slightly," Manning replied.

"Unless one were also the driver," King added, through his towel. "Though it must come at a cost."

"And you'd have to be sure of finding fresh horses," Manning agreed.

"Horses are not a problem," Brehaut told them blithely. "There are hackney posts throughout France and what is spent on transport would be saved on accommodation; with luck we should be there in twice the time."

King considered the prospect as he continued to dry his face. What the sailing master said made sense: they must be able to raise a fair sum between them and had already learned that much could be obtained in France, providing it were paid for. And, despite their status as prisoners of war, the prospect of hired transport was not so very fanciful; it need not be anything grand, even a small cart might suffice. Nevertheless, there remained something vaguely dishonest about riding when his men would be consigned to walk and, as King moved away from the washstand, he decided the subject needed further consideration.

First he had lost the ship and now, effectively, the command of his people. But although those who had inhabited *Kestrel*'s lower deck might be several miles away, they still remained his responsibility and he could not deny a feeling of guilt for not doing more for their welfare. He had no intention of abandoning them completely, but was equally at a loss as to how best to provide for them at a distance. His pamphlet said much about what a captain might do for his crew in such circumstances; there were certain rights with regard to victualling, shelter and allowances that had been agreed between the two countries and might need to be enforced. But however helpful the Admiralty guidelines, they assumed the two would not be separated. So the idea of a carriage might still be a good one, if only to allow him to catch up with the rest of his men.

"Ready for some breakfast?" he asked Manning, who was just finishing at the washstand.

"I could certainly eat," his friend confirmed while pulling on a shirt, adding, "and it might be an idea to enquire about laundry arrangements," as he buttoned it up. King nodded, the idea had crossed his mind, although he had thought to delay until reaching the end of his clean clothes, when some sort of routine for the journey should have become established.

"You are intending to stay with us a mite longer then?" he asked, as he followed the surgeon to the other side of the room. Brehaut now stood at the washstand and Timothy was still abed, but there were no guards about, so it was a good opportunity to talk.

"I have heard nothing from Kate for several weeks." Manning's tone was devoid of expression although King knew he was controlling deep emotion. "You understand as well as I what a time she has had with childbirth in the past. I should be with her – I want to be with her, so yes, if a chance occurs, I shall take it."

"But you have given your word," King's voice might have been low, but his protest was no less strong.

"Ah yes, Tom, my word," Manning agreed as he looked directly at his friend. "And a gentleman never breaks such things, nor tells a lie. Anything of the sort would be contrary to his honour. Ain't that the case?"

King found himself physically taking a step back. He had known Manning many years, with most being spent aboard the same ship. Yet here was a different side to him, and one he never expected to encounter. The man seemed unusually defiant, and there might even have been a hint of anger in his expression.

"You cannot deny such things are important," he suggested cautiously.

"Indeed not," the surgeon agreed, although there was no softening in his look. "Perhaps we should speak more on the subject on another occasion?"

* * *

The room next door was shared by Acting Lieutenant Adams, Holby, the purser and the three remaining mids., and there things were not quite so ordered. The same *gendarme* woke them, and a similarly sized pitcher was set on their washstand, although the midshipmen were harder to shift from their beds, and Holby, the oldest present, was quick to take much of the water for his own use. Noticing this, Adams had left the room in search of more, leaving the three lads to share the little that was left. Bremner fancied himself with a razor and used more than half the remaining stock, yet his face remained as hairless as when he started, and Soames was just remarking on the fact, while preparing himself for the inevitable argument, when the purser spoke.

"We shall have to address the matter of paying for our accommodation," he said, "and I feel it prudent for us to pool our resources."

Summers, who had no illusions about needing to shave and had been waiting patiently for the chance to simply wash his face, was the first to speak.

"How do you mean, Mr Holby?"

"Why, we cannot allow the captain to cover all our costs," the purser continued casually, while putting the final adjustment to one of the white cotton cravats he commonly favoured. "And I am sure you lads have a little remaining from what was paid out at Malta."

"That were prize money," Bremner was quick to point out. "Me an' Soames weren't entitled to any, not being present at the French frigate's capture."

"No?" Holby was surprised but not dissuaded. "Though I am sure Mr Summers qualified for some. And there would be your usual pay or allowances. I understand tonight's bill will be nearer two guineas than one – I should say five shillings from each of you would meet your obligations well enough."

"Five shillings?" Soames exclaimed in what might have been pain. "A whole beastly crown?"

"Aye, and for what?" Bremner agreed. "Sharing a room and the joy of listening to an old man's snores?"

"There's no call to be rude," Holby told them primly. "And you should not just be thinking of yourselves. The captain has to meet the costs of our escort, as well as his officers – did you not hear his discussing it with the French *Capitaine*? I am sure an offer would be appreciated, and probably relieve him from having to ask you directly. Such forethought will be remembered and look well when it comes to future boards."

"It's not right that we have to pay for our gaolers," Bremner sulked. "Besides, what do we do when the money runs out?"

"The frogs will all go home, so we can as well!" Summer piped up brightly, although the situation was fast passing the point

86

where humour was acceptable.

"Come now, I am only asking for what is your due," Holby insisted. "If you do not give the money willingly, perhaps you would prefer to argue it out directly with Commander King? And remember," he added with a flash of inspiration, "the Lord loves a cheerful giver."

\* \* \*

It was five hours later when King and his men had long since passed through Saintes, and were continuing along the open road to Cognac, that they sighted the small group in the far distance. For some while their features were hidden in the mist but, as the officers plodded relentlessly closer, they gradually became discernible. There were five in all; that was the first thing any were certain of, with three horses standing patiently nearby, although steaming slightly, as if they had recently been ridden heavily. And, as they drew nearer, it became obvious two were seamen and probably British. Then they were recognised properly.

"How is it with you, Cranston?" King asked, when they finally met up with the men, and they were unceremoniously forced into the column with their betters. There was a babble of French from one of the seamen's guards and what sounded like an argument between him and the officer in charge of King's group, but soon all was settled and the three waiting *gendarmes* rode off ahead amid a cloud of dust.

"Seems we have acquired a couple more for our party," Brehaut murmured softly. The *Capitaine* is none too happy, though has little choice."

King turned to Cranston as the column moved off.

"So?" he persisted. "I am waiting for an explanation."

"We must have got lost, sir," the seaman told him as he fell in with the officers' step. King could see there was a livid red mark across the man's forehead and his companion, the curly-haired hand whose name temporarily escaped him, seemed to be limping.

"Lost?" King questioned.

"Aye, sir," Cranston continued with heavy innocence. "Missed our group, so we did."

It was such an absurd concept for men under guard that King

chose not to honour it with a further comment. Then Cranston spoke up.

"We tried to escape, sir," he confessed.

"What happened?" King had turned his attention to the other man, who he thought might be called Lovemore and could only be a better source of information.

"Hobbs had a plan," the second seaman told him more succinctly. "We was to hide three of our number for the morning's count. Then, if we got the chance to run later, it would have been harder for the frogs to realise anyone were missing."

King said nothing. From what he had learned of French efficiency when it came to guarding prisoners, it was a plan doomed to failure.

"Everything went well enough at first, your honour," Lovemore continued. "Me, Cranston and Hobbs took shelter under the altar of the church where we was billeted, and they counted up all fine and dandy, with no one realising they were any short. Not until we were on the road, that is. As soon as we could, we made a break for it, but were spotted."

The other officers were quiet as Lovemore related his tale, and remained so when he paused.

"Them three horsemen were sent to bring us back," he finally admitted. "And in this country, there's not a lot of places to hide."

It was what King and the others had suspected, though none said so.

"They ran us down," Lovemore continued. "Cranston got a whack with the side of a cutlass, and I was winged by a ball that skimmed the side of me leg." He pointed down to a small tear to the top of his trousers.

"And Hobbs?" King asked.

"It were all Hobbs' idea," Cranston interrupted. "They knew that, and saved up something special for him."

"What exactly happened?" King demanded, turning back to Lovemore again.

"Hobbs was shot in the head," Lovemore told them coldly.

"Aye," Cranston confirmed. "He was caught and weren't giving no trouble. But they killed him nonetheless."

\* \* \*

Even at so great a distance the sudden contact with death did much to add a sense of seriousness to the small group. King needed no more details; he knew well that the French were inclined to blame the ringleader, or *chef de complot*, in such an incident and inflict punishment on them alone. Instead he switched to asking about the remainder of his former crew, and the mood fell further when he learned more about the conditions they were enduring.

That all were being fed and apparently making the best of it was actually good news, although he still regarded them as his responsibility and was used to being accountable for their welfare. But now he knew himself to be utterly helpless and, as he slowly began to realise, would probably remain so for all their time in captivity.

The British officers were handed over to another troop of *gendarmes* on reaching Saintes when Fabron and his men made a surly departure and King decided to request an interview with their replacement *Capitaine* at the first opportunity. However it turned out the new man had no English and having to use Brehaut as an interpreter once more only increased his annoyance.

"It seems hopeless," the sailing master informed him after an exchange that had been all too brief to King's mind. "It appears their policy is to keep men and officers separated – probably to avoid problems with anyone interfering," he added, his face entirely straight. "And it would seem the men are not even bound for Verdun, but somewhere further on."

King said nothing – it was what he had secretly feared: not only had he lost his ship, but also the men he commanded.

"But the new *Capitaine* seems better than most," Brehaut continued. "His name is de Garmeaux and the "de" is significant."

For anyone's surname to be important was surely ridiculous in the extreme, and King remained sullenly silent.

"It signifies he is of the *Ancien Régime*," Brehaut continued. "Noble stock: a rare thing in these times, but not totally unheard of. The *Capitaine* was probably born a gentleman and certainly understands etiquette – and I would not believe him to be totally unsympathetic to our plight."

"How long will he be with us?"

"For about twenty-five kilometres. France contains many departments, each of which are divided into cantons and, in turn, communes. The guards keep to one canton where possible."

King was already getting used to the divisions that seemed similar to the counties, boroughs and parishes of England.

"I asked also about the possibility of a coach, and he was not so very negative. But such things are expensive, and I would judge that, should we indulge ourselves, it would not be for the best."

"Why so?"

Brehaut pursed his lips for a moment. "In truth it is more a feeling. But, if we did catch up with the men, I doubt we should be allowed to travel together, even if our paths were to coincide. And such an expense might lead the French to thinking we had more money than is the case."

"Very well," King sighed. "Then it appears there is a long walk ahead of us, and I suggest we make the best of it."

\* \* \*

Lovemore was doing exactly that, and had been for some while. He had known for certain the escape attempt was doomed to failure, and only accompanied his mates in the hope his presence might help to avoid bloodshed. That he had failed so singularly to do so only reinforced his growing respect for the psychic powers, even if they became even less attractive as a consequence.

With Hobbs, there had been no repetition of the death's head image seen on Harris' face, but still Lovemore had been reasonably sure that at least one of his friends was to die. And it was ironic that the faith he had in his ability to survive was purely due to the vague inklings that kept appearing to tell of his own future.

He was now amongst officers; something he had certainly foreseen, even though it had seemed totally impossible the day before. And he could now visualise more clearly the bright lights and music that lay before him. In fact Lovemore was forced to concede his future at least appeared moderately rosy. Then there was still that same, undefined promise of release; no further details were being allowed him, but even without specific information, he sensed it to be wholly good. And there were even times when he found himself longing for it, in the same way a young girl might dream of romance.

\* \* \*

King's group made better progress the next day and managed to raise Cognac by late evening, although the inn they were led to was not as sumptuous as the previous night's. The rooms were also smaller, while an additional two prisoners needed to be accommodated, although the new *Capitaine des Gendarmes* did seem more reasonable. Speaking through Brehaut was an inconvenience of course, but the Frenchman did not insist when King refused his request for Cranston and Lovemore to berth in the stables with his men. A further room was booked, and King found himself literally paying for his stance from his own purse.

But he was less successful when it came to providing for the rest of *Kestrel*'s lower deck hands. They had not stopped in the town and neither could he get further news of their whereabouts. But if he was unable to care for all his former crew, King decided he would content himself by seeing those within his control were properly looked after.

And at least he had less to worry about as far as the officers were concerned. *Capitaine* de Garmeaux confirmed that each man's confinement allowance had been approved and the first instalment would be paid at the end of his particular sector. It hardly amounted to much and barely covered their true travel costs, but he and Timothy would also be entitled to their normal half pay as commissioned officers. Brehaut, Manning and Adams were also making a small contribution, and King had not intended asking anyone else, so it came as a pleasant surprise when Holby requested a brief interview during which a handful of silver was passed across.

The money came from Summers, Bremner and Soames, the three youngsters. It was merely a shilling each, although Holby had also added a florin from his own pocket. It might not cover all their costs, but the gesture was appreciated and King was also pleased to note the purser was proving as dependable as ever.

# Chapter Nine

Captain Sir Richard Banks swallowed the last mouthful of toasted bread before dusting the crumbs from the front of his freshly laundered shirt. The coffee pot was empty and what remained in his cup would be cold by now; he considered calling for more, then rejected the idea. It was already gone nine: too long had been spent on the simple matter of eating, and he should continue with the rest of his morning's routine.

It was one that had become established during the four months of living alone in the small house and suited him well, or so he had convinced himself. The elderly woman who lived next door and filled the role of both landlady and housekeeper was currently cleaning his parlour; shortly she would return to clear up the remains of his breakfast and then set the kitchen to rights. By that time he would have walked a little under a mile to the upper town where he might meet up with Brenton, Wolfe, Lee or any of the other senior British officers and gentlemen who lived thereabouts. Then they would doubtless take tea and perhaps some *dragées* – the sugared almonds that were a speciality of the town's confectioners and something Banks knew he was becoming dangerously fond of. Unless anything of importance had emerged over the last twenty-four hours, he would probably dine with at least one of his companions, before returning to find his bed made up for the nap he was accustomed to taking most afternoons.

On that particular day a short sleep might be especially wise: there was to be a reception at a club housed in the Bishop's Palace that evening and Banks already knew it would be a tiresome affair. The proprietor, Mrs Concannon – a middle-aged former actress of slender means but generous proportions – seemed to delight in providing every type of distraction to see her guests remained long past midnight. Such an event would not have bothered him normally, but the weekly meeting with *Général* Wirion, the town Commandant, was scheduled for the following morning, and he preferred to keep a clear head for what could be a difficult couple of hours.

Neither commitment could be refused, however. Despite being about as trustworthy as a rook's promise, Wirion remained an important man and organised social occasions such as Mrs Concannon's had to be attended: it was one of the unwritten rules of the place. Verdun was a strange dichotomy of gaol and home, but one that offered a lifestyle quite unlike any Banks had previously encountered. He was one of several senior British naval officers contained within the town's stone walls and there were far more junior men, as well as a vast number of civilians who had been illegally seized when Britain declared war on France. The latter included women, children – even servants – as well as doctors, priests and members of parliament; positions that were usually considered neutral by even the most belligerent of adversaries. Despite this, all were being held against the word and spirit of international law, with their presence only enforcing the impression of unreality that seemed to saturate the place.

His blue broadcloth tunic had been draped across the only other chair in the small dining room. Slipping it on, Banks walked through to the equally tiny kitchen, and collected the cloak that hung by the plain wooden back door. The house was on the *Rue Chaussée* and cost him a hundred and twenty francs a month, which included domestic services, as well as his basic food. Anything extra could be ordered, and he was sure additional meals would also be available, although at no time during his tenancy had Banks felt the need to entertain.

Of course, he could have afforded a considerably larger place, and one in the fashionable upper town. Such an address would be more suited to a Knight of the Realm and was bound to include a garden, stables and probably room to store a carriage. And it could be managed by quite a large retinue of staff to cover his every requirement, including a woman to tactfully address a solitary gentleman's more intimate needs. But Banks was not an indulgent man and had a wife and family whom he loved. Besides, he actually preferred a modest house in a quiet area where he could properly be alone.

He stepped outside, and paused. The early spring sun was low and bright. Its rays hurt his tender eyes although they soon became accustomed and the features of the town were revealed to him.

Verdun was surely a picturesque place, and he was steadily learning its history which went back as far as the Gauls. The heavy wall that ringed the place was begun some two hundred years before and had yet to be completed, although that was just one of many tasks that remained unfinished. The Prussians had captured the town a few years back and signs of the battle were still obvious on some of the smaller houses, yet positive mansions had been built relatively recently and the town itself boasted far more shops and businesses than was normal for a civil population of ten thousand.

There was also an abundance of trees, as well as a particularly attractive river that gave a feeling of calm as it meandered slowly around the quiet streets, while several small parks and promenades provided more than enough space for recreation. Noticing these once more he remembered it was not impossible for Sarah and the children to join him. Several of his fellow officers had sent for their families; something the French were happy to permit, as a group of people must inject more gold into the hands of the town's administrators than any single man. There was even talk of setting up a small school, and the number of London traders also permitted to establish themselves in the high street was growing almost daily.

Indeed, Verdun was an odd contradiction: a small part of France that the English were apparently borrowing, and one that contained most of the niceties of a gentleman's life while excluding almost all responsibility. None of the residents had a house to maintain, land to manage or positions to keep up, and the lack of external contact meant many of the usual conventions of polite society, such as church attendance, formal dress or entertaining house guests could be conveniently ignored. In fact every inhabitant, from the poorest to the most wealthy, was well provided for and should want for nothing. Except, perhaps, their freedom.

"Good morning, sir."

The voice came from behind and Banks turned to see the smiling face of one of his former lieutenants. Corbett had served with him in *Prometheus,* the seventy-four gun two-decker that Banks had commanded, although in those days the lieutenant would never have dreamt of greeting him with anything other than a serious countenance and a crisp salute. But this was on land, neither were wearing hats and, with both being held prisoner, the rigid strictures of a commissioned line-of-battleship had long since faded. Besides, Corbett had been one of those accompanying Banks on the long and eventful journey to the town; little of a post captain's status could be retained when so much needed to be shared and the experience had even introduced an element of friendship between the two.

"It is a fine one indeed," Banks agreed. "I'm for the Citadel, would you be heading such a way?"

"I'd be glad to accompany you as far as the *Rue Moselle*," Corbett replied affably, and the two men struck out together along the cobbled road.

"I had a package from home," the lieutenant announced when they had travelled a little distance. Banks gave a nod of interest; news from England was not so very common and always welcomed.

"It contained a letter from Lewis," Corbett continued easily, then added, "Lieutenant from the old days. It were sent to my father," when Sir Richard failed to comment.

"Oh, I remember him, right enough," Banks replied after a further pause, and Corbett was conscious of having touched upon a nerve in some way.

"He is well," the younger man continued hesitantly, "and seems to be surviving."

"But I assume no longer in the service," Banks stated coldly.

"Indeed, sir; that is correct," Corbett agreed. "I understand he has found alternative employment."

"Why was he writing to your father?"

"The letter was to me, sir," Corbett explained. "I would chance he did not send it here for fear I might not receive it."

"I should think that likely," Banks grunted. "The French postal system is unreliable at best, but in any case I cannot see messages from the likes of him being allowed through."

Nothing was said for some while, and the lieutenant was thinking of a way to restore the atmosphere when inspiration struck.

"And my father included something else." Corbett felt in the tail pocket of his tunic and produced a newspaper which had obviously been folded tightly for some time. "I shall be taking it to the *Café* Carron, but thought you may be interested in a small section. It is nothing more than we already know, but interesting nonetheless – on the back page," he added, pointing his finger at the relevant place, "under 'Naval Matters'."

Banks took the newspaper and slowed his step slightly while he began to read, then stopped as the piece took his full attention.

"Poor Tom," he sighed, when he had finished. As Corbett had said, there was nothing new in the report; the French press had already made much of a British sloop surrendering to an inferior force, but to read it in the *Morning Chronicle* in some way gave the incident credibility.

"It says nothing of the capturing vessel," Corbett pointed out.

"No it does not," Banks agreed, as they started to walk once more. "But whether it were merely a single brig, or a whole fleet of liners, it hardly alters the fact that *Kestrel* has been captured."

"And Tom King with her," Corbett agreed. "That is, unless he were wounded."

"No loss of life," Banks grunted. "The *Chronicle* would have got much of the detail from the French reports, but that particular point has the ring of truth about it." To his mind, that fact also made the sloop's easy surrender even less likely. Banks had known Tom King for almost ten years, both as friend and brother officer and, until the dreadful news first appeared in the *Moniteur*, his time in Verdun had been enlivened by following the lad's exploits. Under his care, King had progressed from raw midshipman to experienced lieutenant and Banks was quietly confident he would never have given up his first command quite so easily.

To be reminded that King's career had come to an end made him unutterably sad, and it was with effort that he continued making small talk until they reached the main street, when he could once more be alone. But as soon as Corbett went, Banks immediately felt his loss, and cursed himself inwardly. It would have taken little effort from him to persuade the younger man to join him at one of the many clubs or coffee houses. They may even have met up with more former officers from his old ship – there were enough of them living in the town, even if he rarely met with any other than by chance. Banks felt he had already relaxed a little from the stiff, rather crusty officer that had once commanded a

Royal Navy battleship and it wouldn't have done him any harm to unbend slightly more, and enjoy the company of erstwhile shipmates.

The road was starting to rise slightly and he found himself stepping heavily on the cobbles as he strode along. He missed his wife, yet would not send for her, and had taken a house away from his peers, only to complain of being alone. And now he was heading to meet with other curmudgeonly old souls like himself, where he would be given weak tea and be forced to address his mind to mundane matters when he would so much have preferred to drink coffee and yarn with old friends. But then Sarah had told him often enough that he had a perverse nature, and he supposed age was doing nothing to improve it.

* * *

"We're less than forty kilometres away," Brehaut informed them as he returned to the table.

"Will we do it in a day?" King asked, and received a nod from the sailing master.

"I should say so," he told him. "It will be a stiff walk but our new guard is based in Verdun and seems keen to return."

There was silence as the officers digested the news. They had been travelling for the best part of three months during what must surely be the worst time of year for such a journey. And all the while the prospect of Verdun had been like the donkey's carrot; constantly in view, but never reached. Now that their goal was not only close, but actually appeared achievable, it was definitely time for reflection, and King found he was eating the mutton stew before him, a meal that had smelled so appetising, with only abstract attention.

They were in the town of Roches-sur-Meuse, although the residents insisted upon referring to it by the pre-Revolution name of Saint-Mihiel. A pretty, tree-lined place set beside the banks of the Meuse, a winding river that, Brehaut assured him, also passed through their destination. And that night they would have rather splendid quarters in an abandoned monastery, although such luxury had not always been afforded them throughout their journey.

During the eighty-one day odyssey, King and his fellow officers had slept in such a variety of places, and been under the care of almost as many units of guards, that only a few could be recalled in any clarity, the rest having consolidated into a fusion of neutral rooms and bland faces. There were some that did stand out however, such as the times when no commercial accommodation had been available.

On all these occasions it was decided they must be billeted in the local gaol, and at first King had objected vehemently. Twice he was successful, and they found themselves guests of minor dignitaries of the town; men who grudgingly provided poor beds and draughty rooms, then charged more than a good country *auberge* for the privilege. But on the third occasion, when all protests had fallen on the deaf ears of a particularly obstinate *Capitaine des Gendarmes*, they found themselves treated surprisingly well. The cells were at least dry and relatively warm, while the meal the gaoler's wife provided contained a good deal of meat and was followed by a fine, boiled pudding. After that, the occasional night in a local gaol was not so despised. Only once had they been expected to mix with common felons, and that was soon rectified with Brehaut haughtily explaining the difference between criminals and prisoners of war. And they soon realised that such rudimentary accommodation actually carried a distinct advantage: besides having to pay for their food, which was not expensive, there was never any charge for their keep, which was popular with all.

Having to pay their way at all had come as a surprise at first, although they soon grew used to it, and could console themselves in the knowledge that rarely were they charged more than the equivalent in England, and often considerably less. The food offered, which varied in content from region to region, was normally quite palatable and wine, that could be as cheap as a penny a bottle, also plentiful. Coin itself seemed to have more value than in Britain; English money was accepted in many towns and it was generally held that a tuppeny cartwheel could buy at least threepence worth of goods in France. In fact, if what averaged as five days out of every seven had not been spent walking, King guessed some of their number might have grown quite sleek on their diet.

The days when travelling was not required were invariably spent in larger towns, when the British were given access to the services of a washer woman, or at least a usable *blanchisserie*. There would also be the chance to exchange some of their English guineas for smaller French currency, and buy a few essentials. In both of these they were treated with an honesty that surprised them all; King had only a rough idea of the value of gold in France but knew it to be in short supply, yet the goldsmith he approached in Langres had been transparently fair and paid out more than he expected. Some of their personal requirements may have been expensive; King was sure he had been overcharged for a heavy woollen overcoat and three pairs of socks, but guessed a foreigner would have been treated similarly in many English towns. They had also been given the allowance stipulated in King's Admiralty pamphlet, which went some way to offset their costs, while having ready access to either French or British currency pretty much guaranteed a welcome wherever they went.

Which, on balance, they were, and that also came as a surprise. The French had been going through a particularly bloody revolution when war was first declared and the subsequent conflict must have affected all in some measure. Now, after an interval of less than fourteen months, the fight had not only resumed but seemed likely to last every bit as long as before, so it was reasonable to expect the sight of a British uniform would not be universally greeted. Yet that was not the impression King or his officers received. On the days when no travel was required, they became used to walking, unguarded, down the main street of whatever town currently provided for them. The worst any experienced were curious looks and, on one occasion, a rotten apple thrown from the security of an open window, but in general they, and their money, were accepted.

And the fact that all were allowed to wander with no security other than their word was the final revelation. For a country which had so turned against any system of rank or privilege to acknowledge the concept of a gentleman, let alone allow them such a degree of latitude, was almost laughable. Even Cranston and Lovemore were given the same leniency, although King had the uneasy suspicion that the rest of *Kestrel*'s ordinary seamen would not be faring so well.

Repeated requests for information about his former crew had been consistently ignored and neither was it possible to send money or food to aid them, although he had recently discovered a little more of their fate, and the news was reassuring.

It had come through a brief conversation with a fellow Englishman, an elderly cobbler King had taken for French when trying to purchase a fresh pair of boots. It seemed some forty years ago he had been a Royal Navy midshipman, before marrying a French woman. That had been long before the outbreak of the Revolution or subsequent wars, and so entrenched in French society had the old man become that he avoided being swept up with other *détenus*. However, it was clear some vestige of his former life remained; King remembered him staring at his own tattered uniform with a mixture of wonder and perhaps fear, although he still gave more information in the short time they were together than King had been able to obtain elsewhere.

Several hundred prisoners of war had passed through the town eight days before and it seemed likely his men were amongst them. They did not stay, but had been heading for a barracks a few miles further that could take such a number. Their eventual destination was almost certainly Givet, a large fortress to the north-west of Verdun. And King found he need not concern himself too much for their welfare. None would be living the high life but, as the cobbler assured him with a hint of irony, all could expect conditions better than those found on the lower deck of a British warship. Once installed at Givet, the men would be given reasonable accommodation, a regular allowance and possibly even paid work, although nothing like the conditions an officer might expect on reaching Verdun.

This naturally sparked King's interest and he had asked more about the town, at which point the cobbler became quite animated. It would seem Verdun was a contentious point with many traders; the old man had been trying to secure a premises there for a year or more, but even small shops were all but impossible to find, while the rents charged when any did become available were more than ten times that usually paid. But he had not given up, for it also appeared few traders failed in Verdun, and high profits were pretty much there for the taking.

A pair of nearly new boots were then produced and offered for a remarkably low price, providing he remembered him if ever there were a shortage of shoemakers in Verdun. There was no point in refusing, even if King saw little likelihood of being able to help in return. But such an eagerness to set up business in a town that mainly served as a prison had certainly sparked his interest.

And now, with the fortress town a mere day's walk away, King was keener than ever to find out more. He had already spent several months in captivity and was resigned to the fact it would be a good while longer before there could be the slightest chance of gaining his freedom. Apart from his current journey and a brief spell on the Texel, King had little experience of captivity but, from what he had heard, there must be worse locations than Verdun. And if it was to become home for the foreseeable future, he may as well get used to it.

* * *

The two seamen were in the more public part of the *auberge*; a place where rush matting gave way to straw, and wine came in jugs rather than bottles. This was not the first time they had been segregated; even when walking, their usual place was at the rear of the column, while it soon became common for both to be billeted with the *gendarmes* who had accompanied them throughout that day. But neither objected to such arrangements; there had been few overnight stops that offered worse conditions than those expected aboard ship, while Cranston at least preferred being amongst officers during the day. Not only did they eat better and receive more respect from their guards, there was none of the japing and tomfoolery that could be expected when a bunch of Jacks travelled in company.

But spending most evenings with the French had given both men an ear for the language. Cranston had not progressed beyond a few dozen phrases, but Lovemore found he was a natural linguist and, after only a matter of weeks, could communicate reasonably well with even the fastest speaker. And the constant walking meant little to either of them; they soon accustomed themselves to the exercise and had no aversion to fresh air. Besides, it had been a journey not without interest; over the past months they had seen a good deal of the French countryside, so the prospect of a stay in

Verdun was not so very daunting.

They also had met a few memorable people and seen even more remarkable sights. Like at Montluçon where the mules carried wine in skins along with women who rode like men. And at Moulins, when the entire group was accosted by a mother and daughter who turned out to be as British as any of them. The pair were in company with a high-ranking officer of the *gendarmerie* who insisted the entire group should be taken to the ladies' house, where all were treated to fresh cake and real tea. No one enquired how two women could live apparently at ease in a hostile country, although they obviously regarded themselves as perfectly safe.

Then there was the time they had been forced to sleep in a general prison, and the pair found themselves sharing a cell with a group of enemy deserters. One had told Lovemore of the conditions most French soldiers endured. The seaman could sympathise with much, especially the wages which seemed very much on the lines of a British Jack's, where actual payment was often delayed by several years. The food seemed far less plentiful, however; barely a loaf of bread being provided each day, with the understanding that, if more was required, it would have to be scavenged from the local countryside. And victuals were not the only source of complaint; the soldier had finally deserted after being posted to the invasion force gathered at Boulogne. Apparently a missive from the Emperor decreed every member of the famed *Armée d'Angleterre* must prepare for their forthcoming adventure by taking a daily walk into the sea. This had to be done in full uniform and, faced with such a prospect, the man decided to take his chances elsewhere and deserted.

And now the British were reaching what would be the end of the journey for some at least. Verdun was known as a place where officers were accommodated, the ordinary seamen being sent to Givet or Valenciennes. But they had already discovered it was not totally without Jacks, and were silently hoping to also be taken in. In common with the vast majority of lower deck men, the two could turn their hands to most things, and a place where officers vastly outnumbered seamen was likely to prove lucrative for those of their talents.

"Last day or not, sounds like we've got a fair old trek ahead of us," Cranston muttered to his friend, who was rarely the first to strike up any conversation.

"So they say," Lovemore agreed. "But if we leaves early, we should still be there afore dark."

"An' if the stories are true, it's more like a fortress than a town," Cranston continued. "Think perhaps we'll spend tomorrow night in the dungeons?"

"Like as not," Lovemore murmured, although he had no such thoughts. Verdun may be nothing more than a glorified prison, but he had a surprisingly good feeling about the place. He knew it probable they would be shipped out straight away, although still felt such a thing to be unlikely. The pleasant images of lights and music that had come to him in the past remained and, if anything, were growing stronger, as was that final undefined feeling of release. And if a walled town that contained not only officers but gentry were truly to be their destination, the time when his intuitions turned into something more solid did not seem so very far away.

"Dungeons? You don't mean it?" Cranston exclaimed loudly, only to receive a call to pipe down from a pair of midshipmen who happened to be passing on their way to the necessary house.

"Well?" he demanded in whisper when they had gone. "Have we really come all this way, only to be locked up."

"Blowed if I knows," Lovemore replied with elaborate casualness, although he had no illusions about fooling his friend.

"Go on, you know more than you're tellin'," Cranston persisted. "An' don't try with that 'maybe we will, an' maybe we won't' lark."

Lovemore sighed. "I don't think we're bound for no dungeons," he admitted. "That is, not unless you try something especially foolish. And if it's worth a jot, I also don't think this will turn out too bad."

Cranston nodded, completely satisfied. Lovemore's opinion had always carried a great deal of weight with him, but in the last few months he had come to rely on it totally. Of course, he would rather have been aboard ship or, if it had to be land, English soil. But Lovemore felt Verdun was worth a light, and if he thought so, Cranston was prepared to make the best of it.

# Chapter Ten

"My dear Tom, how good it is to see you."

King felt the remembered handshake of his former captain and found he was smiling every bit as much as the older man.

"Good to see you also, sir," he mumbled.

"Though not in these circumstances of course," Banks assured him hurriedly. "Tell me, how was your journey?"

"Well enough, thank you," King replied.

"Come, we cannot stand about here." Banks looked from left to right. The street was crowded and King appeared to be under the charge of a *gendarme* officer that Banks knew vaguely by sight.

"Do you have business with this gentleman?" he asked the guard, before realising his mistake and repeating the question in halting French.

"I am to take him to the Commandant," the young officer replied in far more fluent English.

"But you can wait until we have had the chance to speak," Banks told him. "I have an interview with the *Général* in an hour and can escort Mr King to him personally."

"He has yet to sign his *Parole*," the officer objected.

"Mr King is a British officer and will give his word," Banks countered with a hint of annoyance in his voice. "And if that is not good enough for you, I shall vouch for him myself. You are aware of whom you address, I assume?"

"I am, Sir Richard." The younger man ran Banks' name and title into one word in the French fashion. "And am certain that will be in order. Commander King has no precise appointment, but is expected. If you agree to explain, I shall pass him to your care."

Banks gave a stiff nod and the officer turned away, clearly pleased to be free of his charge, although King wondered if he were equally keen to avoid a meeting with his superior. But the matter was soon forgotten; the pair had far more important matters to concern them.

The last time they were together was on the quarterdeck of

*Prometheus* when Sir Richard was suffering from severe concussion; a state that left him little better than a mumbling fool. Much had obviously healed since; the man looked bright, alert and as healthy as ever, although there was perhaps a shade more grey about his thinning temples. But Banks would appear to have lost none of his ability to command, even if King found seeing him behave in such a high-handed manner to a *gendarme* – an officer who was effectively his gaoler – almost disconcerting.

"That is kind of you," King told him, "but I hope it will not cause future problems."

Banks raised his eyebrows. "Pah, the French only respect authority when it is thrust in their faces. Besides, where *Général* Wirion is concerned, problems can never be avoided." He gave a sudden smile. "But what say we face them together, and later? I was due to meet with the Commandant at ten, but he asked for it to be postponed – a bad case of fat head I should not doubt. But you and I have much to discuss, and there is a tolerable coffee room in the next street. We can take a booth together, exchange a few yarns, and let the dear *Général* wear out his carpet until we are finished."

\* \* \*

For Holby, the journey to *Verdun* had been a bore, but no more. There were a few minor inconveniences and he hadn't enjoyed walking one little bit. But the money made, both from the midshipmen who were still proving as gullible as ever, and by relieving some of his French hosts of a few small items of value, more than made up for any physical effort.

Currently he was more than seven English pounds better off than when he started, and still had three porcelain figurines that must be worth more than the seven francs he had been offered in Saint-Mihiel. And he was feeling safer than he had in years: if there was a better way to truly avoid his creditors he had yet to hear of it. Being a captured officer in enemy territory made him as sound as the Bank of England. Old man Lesro and his cronies could huff and puff all they wished, Holby knew himself to be totally invulnerable, and might continue to lie low, making a bean here and there, while a regular allowance came in from the government that he would do absolutely nothing to earn.

And now, as he walked unescorted around the streets of Verdun, his business senses were truly coming into their own. Seldom had he judged a place to have so much potential; there were more shops than was usual, and all seemed to be buzzing with activity, while those that were artless enough to display prices proved the town was a veritable haven for bloodsuckers.

Just how he was to profit had yet to be seen, but Holby was confident he would. It may mean taking a small business himself – he was not averse to such things if the remuneration were right – or perhaps simply backing one currently in operation, although another, far more lucrative, avenue was occurring to him and that would probably be the one he explored first.

He had hardly been inside the town walls a couple of hours, yet already knew gambling was rife. Apart from cockfighting and other such crude pastimes, casual enquiry had revealed there to be gaming tables at the *Café* Thierry, but something must be amiss as a sign on the door stated the French were banned from using them. Holby guessed what this meant, and it intrigued him. The place boasted the backing of those who governed the town, yet was blatantly dishonest. And for a casino to be anything other than totally square was unnecessary when enough could be made by simply playing by the rules.

So competition was clearly needed; it might not get official permission, and no rogue gambling house could run for long without sanction, but Holby was used to overcoming such difficulties. Something a little more clandestine might work for a while, especially if he changed the location on a regular basis, or there were other ways; he just had to decide which.

If not, he had read in a news sheet of a jockey club being established; this must have official permission as regular race meetings were to be held in the next village. That such a thing should be permitted within what was undoubtedly a gaol made him wonder for a moment, but Holby had never been one to turn away a golden opportunity. There was money to be made for sure and he was determined to see a good deal found its way into his pocket.

But before he started anything, he had to establish a centre of operations for himself, and whoever would assist him. Something simple would be better to begin with; a set of managed rooms or maybe a small house. Holby could work and live there for now, then take a separate place for himself later on. Already he had noticed a few respectable houses on the open market and, once all were properly established and he had a suitable pile to back him, Holby intended renting one. Then he would make the important step into polite society, and he really would have arrived. He had no illusions about the upper classes; few truly knew the value of money, and even those that did could usually be convinced otherwise. He only needed a regular supply of gullible gentry with access to funds and, however the war turned out, Holby was sure to emerge victorious.

* * *

"Well, that is certainly a different report to the one the French published," Banks snorted. "I suppose our press do not know any better."

"The Admiralty must be aware of the circumstances of *Kestrel*'s capture," King replied. "I was able to send my journal and assume it to have been delivered, even if it were read a dozen times before."

"Besides, it is three months since she were taken," Banks agreed. "The French cannot keep secrets for long – why *Amiral* Missiessy and his fleet have been back in France for several weeks, so it is doubly strange the British do not see fit to deny their claim."

"But when all is said, *Kestrel* were only a sloop," King stated firmly. "And, whether it was by a merchant brig or a fleet of liners, there can be little doubt she were taken."

"Though important to you, if no one else," Banks suggested more softly and King was forced to agree.

"So, that is my news, sir; what of yours?" he asked.

"Little to tell, I fear," Banks sighed. "And nothing of such excitement. I may have had a slightly longer journey to Verdun but the trip was no more eventful. Most of *Prometheus*' people are housed in Givet, which is six days' ride from here. I visit them each month and Captain Brenton the same, so we know they are being cared for well enough."

"Brenton?" King questioned; the name was familiar to him, although he could not remember why.

"Jahleel Brenton," Banks told him. "Had *Minerve*, a fifth rate that were lost off Cherbourg last summer."

"I do remember: shore batteries was it not – or am I mistaken?"

"No, shore batteries right enough; that and gunboats. The ship took ground and could not defend herself. He lost a few men and could see no way of bringing her off, so did the honourable thing. It was our luck that he found his way here, though. The fellow's a positive spitfire: if you feel I deal harshly with the French, you should see him when cleared for action. He has just come back from touring the nearby depots and looks to have set quite a few wrongs to right."

"But how can he behave so?" King questioned. "I mean, we are captives, yet seem to hold the whip hand."

Banks smiled. "Aye, it is a strange set of affairs," he admitted. "As you say, we are prisoners of war, but certain rules must still be respected. And respected by all, including this newfangled Emperor, if he wishes to retain any credibility internationally. Officially we are under the care of the Minister of War; a reasonable man by all accounts and a former noble, which is rare enough in these times. He listens to any legitimate protests we have and has shown himself willing to act."

"I had heard he was a viable avenue for complaints, but could hardly believe any would be taken seriously."

"Oh, but they are," Banks assured him.

"So you are in regular contact?"

"We are able to write. The Commandant may slow down our messages, but he would be a fool if he stopped them completely, as that would be an infringement of our rights."

"And he truly takes notice?"

"Usually," Banks allowed. "Though we have to take care not to over-value good connections. There is a measure of misdealing within the depot that we can have no control over; the Commandant may only be a *Général des Gendarmes* so is inferior in rank to me and other senior captains, but still retains a deal of power due to his position which we would be wise not to challenge.

It was a reasonable explanation, even if the idea of prisoners behaving so still felt at odds to King's expectations. "But you are allowed out?" he continued.

"Oh, indeed," Banks confirmed. "Brenton's trip was an official one, though all can come and go pretty much as they please. In truth, you will find life here amazingly lax – or least that is how it might appear," he added. "We are even permitted swords, should we still possess one, and the opportunity to buy another, if not."

"Swords?"

"Oh yes," Banks grinned. "The British propensity for duelling is well known and encouraged at every opportunity."

Now King felt there was little that could shock him more. In the past the very subject of duelling had provoked an angry reaction in Sir Richard, yet now it was as if he were discussing nothing more controversial than the weather. Perhaps it was the absence of professional responsibility; not having a ship and all who served in her relying on his every word. Or maybe there was security of sorts in being held prisoner, but the man who sat across from him now was a distinctly different proposition to the commanding officer he had served under for so many years.

"There can be no doubting a good amount of leeway is allowed," Banks added, "though be warned: sail too close to the wind and you will soon luff up, and find yourself in serious difficulties. There is an *appel* for all each day, you have to present yourself between eight and ten, and again 'twixt two and four, other than that you may go as you please."

"And leave the town?" King asked.

"Indeed; we have passports, which must be left with the gate house. If you do not return, they will know when the next *appel* is not signed, and then come looking."

King nodded. When his group had reached the outskirts of *Verdun* they had been met by several small parties of uniformed British officers wandering outside the town walls with no sign of a guard; after what Banks had told him, this would appear to be quite normal.

"And do many escape?" he asked.

"Escape?" Banks appeared surprised. "Some indeed have deserted but – you will forgive me, Tom – I should not call it escape: such a thing is indeed a novel concept."

"You mean, it is traditional for officers to be exchanged?"

"Traditional, and altogether more civilised," Banks confirmed. "But I see where you are heading, the current regime in France has made its position clear; no such niceties are to continue, though I understand our own government are returning French merchant officers, as well as a few of their military in the hope the procedure might begin once more."

"Then does escape not become an alternative?" King persisted, and Banks frowned.

"I suppose you may see it as so, though hardly a viable one." His reply was notably flat, and the subject clearly affected him in some way. "Some of the mids. have tried it," he continued. "Though few have proved successful. Truth is, Verdun is about as far from the sea as can be in France. Besides, all who sign the *Parole* are bound by their word of honour."

"Ah, our word of honour," King found himself smiling. "Does a revolutionary government still value such things?"

"Oh yes, they take the word of a gentleman very seriously." Banks obviously spoke sincerely and now King was surprised. "Why, you must have experienced it yourself during your journey here?"

"I was accustomed to giving my word," King began hesitantly. "And would have every intention of keeping it. But I wonder that the French do not copy our example?"

"Explain." Banks' face had now lost all humour, and King was starting to feel uncomfortable.

"I understand the French seized a lot of civilians when war was declared," he began.

"The *détenus*?" the captain inclined his head slightly. "You are quite correct. Every man of military age, be they serving officers or not. Their wives and families also; it were known as the *Second Prairial Decree*.

"And was that an honourable act?" King questioned.

"Undoubtedly not," Banks agreed. "And many *détenus* do not consider themselves bound by their *Parole d'Honneur*, even if they have given it. But I fail to see the point you are making. We are both King's officers as well as English gentlemen; however badly the enemy behaves, if we pledge not to escape, our word should be as binding as any prison cell. Otherwise..."

"Otherwise?" It was King's turn to question, and Bank's expression relaxed once more.

"Look, Tom, it has taken an old bird like me some time to come to terms with not being exchanged. And I fear it will be a good while longer before I can even contemplate the concept of breaking my word. But don't think I am alone; there are several senior men of the same opinion, in fact I would say we are in the majority. A few might feel otherwise and some have even attempted to defect, though little good it has done them. Most are swiftly caught, in which case they can expect nothing more than being sent to Bitche – a hell hole if ever there was one. And don't expect those who do make it home to be greeted with open arms. The service has no use for a man who cannot keep his word, and neither are they welcomed by society. Why, even a colleague of ours disgraced himself so – you will recall Lewis: junior lieutenant in *Prometheus*?"

King started visibly. He did indeed remember the man, a former ordinary hand who had made the massive leap from lower deck to wardroom, and one he would have trusted with his own life.

"Lewis?" he asked. "What part has he in this?"

"He was with me and the other officers from *Prometheus* on our way here," Banks explained. "The cove deserted a week into the journey, along with a couple of midshipmen. Oh, I cannot blame the youngsters – they are merely warranted, and have no more responsibility than a common Jack – but thought better of a commissioned man. Though Lewis did begin on the lower deck, and I suppose it merely demonstrates that a gentleman is born, and cannot be created."

King felt himself bristle slightly at Sir Richard's words. Despite a humble beginning, the Lewis he knew was as honourable as any found in a wardroom.

"Did he make it back to England?" he enquired.

"I believe so," Banks replied sharply, before softening slightly. "In fact I am certain of it. Though he did not fare well when the truth came out."

"What happened?"

"He left the service of course," the senior man continued. "And would have had to resign from his club – assuming he were a member of one. I hear there was even talk of returning him to the French."

"Returning him?" Now King could do little to hide his surprise. "After what he must have gone through in escaping? Did they really think to send a British officer back to the enemy?"

"And why not?" Banks retorted. "When a man betrays his honour he is of little use to his country; better by far to give him back to the French, and let them make what they can of him."

\* \* \*

Timothy was the last of *Kestrel*'s senior officers to pay a visit to the Citadel; in fact it was not until late evening, and after he had taken a good look at his new home, that he finally made the long uphill climb to the fortress that dominated the town. But those few hours made an impression on him, and he had to admit to being mildly stunned by the place.

For much of his adult life, Britain had been at war and never had he encountered such a vast array of shops, all seemingly piled high with goods that were almost unheard of in his home country. And other businesses were also prospering; these ranged from clockmakers to confectioners, hairdressers to hatters, while some trades were represented in a number of guises, with tailors specialising in anything from simple outfitting to those exclusively making women's riding habits. The latter was presumably to satisfy the needs of the thrice-weekly hunt that he had noticed publicised on every available hoarding. And many concerns were British; there were grocers and tea dealers from London, a firm of Edinburgh jewellers and several *cafés* that advertised traditional Devon cream teas.

The French were apparently encouraging what was almost a holiday spirit in other ways – Timothy had been surprised at the relative informality of the arrangements even at the Citadel itself. The Commandant was not present, of course – a mere lieutenant

112

hardly warranted such lofty attention – but he had spoken at length with his deputy; a thin-faced *Capitaine des Gendarmes* who had passable English and seemed happy to explain a prisoner's obligations, as well as a little more about the town.

What Timothy learned would have seemed hard to believe if he had not noticed so much since his arrival. Verdun was undoubtedly run on relaxed lines, although his poetic mind quickly saw the inhabitants as being held within a velvet-lined cell, with only their word and the knowledge they were many hundreds of miles from the sea to keep them so contained. But there was no doubt of the heavy stone walls that lay behind that soft lining; the *Capitaine* had hinted that the slightest deviation from what was considered good behaviour would be severely punished, and Timothy did not doubt it.

The illusion was maintained, however, and he had been dismissed from the brief interview with the greatest politeness, after having given nothing more than his name, place of birth and profession, together with a signature on what appeared to be an innocuous piece of paper. And now he was back on the streets and, to all intents, a free man. Timothy had been used to a fair degree of latitude on the journey, and was accustomed to roaming free on days when no travelling was required. But always there had been his lodgings to return to, with the next day spent trudging along the road while guards rode to either side. Now the only French uniforms in sight belonged to the sentries at the *Porte Chaussée*, along with an occasional sentinel within the town, yet there were more than a dozen fellow Royal Navy officers close by, along with maybe forty of what could only be British civilians walking leisurely about the streets. The latter were of both genders and included entire families; they mostly stood out from the locals by virtue of their fine clothes and casual demeanour although, as he looked closer, Timothy found himself noticing something else, something subtle but far more poignant.

They were indeed dressed well, although it was with studied care, as if the act had taken considerable time. And, whether young or old, service or civilian, all before him shared a common attitude that was betrayed in small ways. They walked at an ambling pace, as if with nowhere to actually go or, if standing, appeared to be waiting with little true aim in mind. There was also a general listlessness in the air that not even children's laughter or the barking of a young dog could dispel. Such signs were vague indeed but surely amounted to one thing; Verdun might have been designed to give them everything they wanted and probably more, yet the British all shared the same indelible mark. And it was that of the prisoner, Timothy soberly decided, however decorated their cage.

# Chapter Eleven

It was April, spring was now firmly established and, despite the apparent comfort of his surroundings, King was feeling more restless than ever. Along with Manning, Timothy and Brehaut, he had taken a small house just along the road from his former captain's residence and only marginally larger. With two men each sharing a room and their meals provided by an efficient, if theatrically stern, landlady, he supposed captivity could be a good deal worse. But still the hunger to be free was starting to nag at him and seemed to be increasing.

His first few weeks in Verdun had been spent getting to know the place and, probably more importantly, the main inhabitants, most of whom had impressed him in one way or another. The British Naval prisoners were effectively commanded by a group of senior men that included Banks, although he was by no means the leader. This title fell on Jahleel Brenton, the former frigate captain Sir Richard previously mentioned. Brenton had only been made post four years before so was actually junior to the others of his rank, although that did not stop him from being the most active in seeing to the care of his fellow prisoners.

From running the Verdun Relief Committee to investigating the setting up of a school, Brenton was either in charge or heavily involved although his attentions were not confined to the gaol that was his home. He had just returned from another exhaustive journey to Valenciennes, Givet and Sarrelibre, the principle prisons where ordinary seamen were confined, as well as Bitche, a more local depot and one used as a place of punishment for those of any rank who misbehaved, or were caught in the act of escaping.

This last aspect was one that concerned King the most; he still felt an element of responsibility for *Kestrel*'s former crew and appreciated the work done on the ordinary hands' behalf. Nevertheless, part of him wished a little of their efforts could be directed to the more positive goal of getting men out of captivity and on the road back to England.

When they first met he was surprised Banks had not given the matter more importance, and had since found other senior officers to be equally apathetic. The majority still expected Bonaparte to relent and reintroduce the exchange of prisoners that had been prevalent throughout the last war while, even without the necessity to sign the *Parole d'Honneur,* a few plainly viewed any attempt to escape as being against some subtle code of honour that King knew nothing about. He had no intention of breaking his own word, but was equally sure some way of revoking the agreement could be found. Each fresh issue of the *Moniteur* contained reports of Bonaparte's actions on land, and anyone who had served at sea in the past year must be fully aware a French invasion attempt could be expected at any time. After so long in the service, there were few at home that King held dear, but he had no intention of sitting back and waiting for the event to take place, however comfortable his present conditions may be.

For they were comfortable, there could be no doubt of that. Ignoring the fact that little was required of him, he had reasonable access to money, and plenty of places in which to spend it. But all the well-stocked shops and nightly entertainments paled to nothing if the war was to end with his country being soundly beaten and forced to beg for mercy.

And there was more to trouble him; for so many years Banks had been King's immediate superior, and the idea of going against his wishes was almost abhorrent. But Sir Richard remained against any attempt to escape, and King was coming to the conclusion he would either have to go without him, or not at all. Fortunately others were not so adamant; he knew Robert Manning had been making discrete plans for some time and, as the surgeon entered the small kitchen and placed himself at the table next to Brehaut, King decided it was finally time for him to broach the subject.

\* \* \*

Holby was trying to keep the look of satisfaction from his face. The place was perfect; below ground, admittedly, and there was a distinct smell of damp, but with a few rugs on the earth floor, a decent blaze going in the hearth and lamps and candles scattered about, no one would be any the wiser. Besides, there was room for

116

maybe three hazard tables to be running simultaneously, with up to four smaller set aside for cards. Then there was the discrete entrance that led to a substantial staircase which was perfectly grand enough for what he had in mind.

In addition to the main area where they now stood, there were two smaller: ante-rooms that could easily house more private parties. These were currently filled with all manner of rubbish but, once cleared, would be ideal for the especially rich gamesters who were bound to be the biggest losers.

Besides, his customers should be looking for something different, and not coming to be seen – the very reverse, in fact. Serious gamblers craved anonymity and rarely brought wives or partners – something Holby was happy to encourage as solitary players were more likely to take risks – and felt the underground rooms would give just the right amount of exclusivity. It might take a while for word to get around, although Holby had already mixed with the Verdun gaming crowd, and felt he could encourage enough to give him a reasonable clientele. Once established, he was equally confident they would respect the anonymity he offered by keeping his club discrete.

Of course, it would not last forever, which was another reason why Holby was reluctant to pay too far in advance. He might get some support from those in authority, but could not hope to entertain the entire civil administration. If some took against him he may well face the occasional fine, although Holby was not unduly worried on that score. The British community was rife with rumours about the potential severity of their French hosts, but he preferred to believe the evidence of his own eyes.

On several occasions Holby had found an open bribe to be readily accepted by officials at almost every level, while even the town Commandant was known to be easily squared. With a pessimistic estimated nightly return of over two hundred francs, there should be enough to pay a few substantial dawbs while still showing a profit, and if it all went bad and he was forced to close, Holby would simply open another club; possibly a larger one elsewhere. Or maybe two...

"How much?" he asked the greasy-haired Frenchman who stood before him.

"One hundred francs." The accent was thick, and Holby had to think for a moment before realising what had been said. One hundred was a lot, but not by much, and there might be room to manoeuvre.

"A month?" he chanced.

"A week," the man stated more clearly. "And you must pay me three months in advance."

That would use all Holby had earned on the journey and more, leaving him very little for paint or furnishings, to say nothing of hiring staff.

"That negotiable, is it?" he asked, only to receive a look of non-comprehension from the wiry little man.

"I can pay cash," Holby persisted in a louder voice, while reaching into his pocket and bringing out a handful of *Louis d'ors* that immediately drew the Frenchman's interest. "Four hundred francs for six weeks," he continued, jingling the coins in his hand as he spoke.

"Four hundred?" the Frenchman questioned, only to receive a curt nod in reply. "I was 'oping for more."

"Four hundred," Holby repeated, before making to replace the coins in his pocket and only stopping when the landlord gave a faint moan of protest. Then the money was passed across, and Holby felt a pang of doubt as the warm coins slipped from his fingers. But he looked about again – yes, his earlier assessment had been correct, the place was ideal. And if it cost a bit of gold initially, he need not worry, he was well on the way to making it back; that and a whole heap more.

"You will have to do any painting yourself," the landlord warned. "And I will not be servicing the rooms in any way. In fact you will not see me until the next rent is due."

"No? But you would be welcome," Holby told him with an ingratiating smile. "As well as any friends you may have."

The Frenchman regarded him suspiciously as he pocketed the money. "My son is a *gendarme*; you would like him to come, perhaps?"

"Your son would be treated most kindly." Holby would not be banning any Frenchman from attending; he cared little where the money came from and regular customers who were also members of the *gendarmerie* could only be beneficial to his interests. "Tell me," he added on an impulse, "are you a gambling man?"

"Gambling?" the landlord asked, then shook his head and added, "No, I do not gamble."

"That is a pity," Holby responded with a sympathetic grimace. "For your humble cellar is to be turned into one of the finest gaming rooms in France. The cream of society will be coming for entertainment, and you would be most welcome to join them."

But the Frenchman showed no regret and simply shrugged. "I have no wish to waste my money so," he explained. "Besides, I still enjoy the ladies."

* * *

"So, are you both still game for escape?"

Brehaut dropped his fork and Manning stopped in the act of raising the coffee cup to his lips and looked across at his friend.

"Escape? Tom, are you serious?"

"And why should I not be?" King asked from the other side of the room. The kitchen of their rented house was a place the officers were inclined to treat as a general mess and, now the landlady had gone about her business, the three of them were completely alone.

"Because whenever Robert suggested such a thing in the past, you have hardly been forthcoming." Brehaut had recovered his fork, and was about to address his omelette once more when another thought occurred. "Though I must say your change of heart is encouraging."

King knew he deserved that. Manning had been keen to be gone from the start and steadily worked on both of them to join him. The sailing master relented some while ago; for all he knew, the two may already have made some headway in forming plans. But despite his friends' requests, King had always declined, and knew this had not been well received by either officer.

He supposed that, as their erstwhile captain, it was reasonable for them to expect him to not only join in but actually take the lead in such an enterprise. And it would do little good to admit he in turn had been waiting, hoping, his own previous commander would become involved and so take charge. But Sir Richard Banks was still making it plain that he saw his duty in remaining in Verdun, where he could best ensure the welfare of the ordinary seamen held nearby. It was a course King found hard to accept, and he could not help remembering the dashing frigate captain he had first served under with a measure of regret. When they had last spoken, Banks was even talking of sending for his wife and family to join him.

"Perhaps I were getting used to the place," he explained vaguely, "but now see no reason to linger."

"And your *Parole*?" Manning asked, before taking a hasty sip from his cup.

"Let us set that aside for now," King hedged. "I cannot help but think there to be a way about such an obstacle."

But Manning was not to be put off. "And if not?" he persisted. The surgeon had previously announced it would take more than a simple signature to separate him from his wife. There had been no news of her since Gibraltar; the child should be born by now and his mind was becoming increasingly dominated by concerns for his family's welfare.

"If not, I still say we should go," King stated firmly, even if his thoughts were not quite so set.

"I'm with you in seeking a solution," Brehaut agreed. "Many of those detained illegally see no reason why they should not run, but we are legitimate prisoners of war..."

"Breaking our *Parole* will probably be the least of our difficulties," Manning added quickly. The fact that King was coming round to his way of thinking was to be encouraged, and he had no wish to lose gained ground. "Though getting out of the town should not be one," he added.

"There is talk of the rules of *appel* being relaxed for senior men," Brehaut mused. "But even without, we should be able to make several miles before anyone knows us missing."

"Though then our troubles must surely begin," Manning conceded.

"Aye," Brehaut agreed. "It is nigh on two hundred miles to the western coast, though that is how the crow flies, and I cannot see a bird large enough being interested in such a journey."

"And were we to go east?" King asked.

"The nearest border is closer – not much more than fifty. But that only takes us into Germany. The Germans hate the French, but we would still not be safe and it would be a lengthy trek to reach a truly friendly country."

"That might be the better option," King pondered. "The French people seemed unusually friendly on the trip here, but it's one thing being a captured prisoner of war, quite another to be fugitives."

At that moment a noise from the front of the house made them all stop, and look guiltily at one another before the greatcoated figure of Timothy swept into the room.

"Well, that's a proper turn up," he announced as he shook the rain from his coat. Then he noticed their set faces and added, "Forgive me, was I interrupting?"

"Nothing that cannot wait," King assured him. "What's about, James?"

"I went for coal," Timothy explained, as he accepted a cup of coffee from Manning. "Our previous supplier is becoming devilishly expensive, and I remembered seeing sacks of the stuff outside an ordinary house on the *Rue Neuve*. After a few enquires I met with a Breton family named Silva whose son is in the business. They'll sell it to us and a darn sight cheaper than those Richardson robbers."

"News indeed," Brehaut commented politely.

"No, there's more," Timothy assured them. "They invited me in and gave tea – seems the whole family were in service, caring for Lord and Lady Tweeddale; a couple of British *détenus* who had been living in Brittany. The Silvas followed them here but both have since died, so they are making do by selling their son's coal."

The lieutenant paused and noticed the lack of enthusiasm in his fellow officers. "Have I said something amiss?" he asked innocently.

"Not at all, James," King assured him. "It was just a dramatic turn in the conversation."

"But don't you see?" Timothy demanded. "If we have to stay in this cursed place, we may as well be friendly with the natives. They're holding a family dance tomorrow even', and do so every Tuesday; all the locals go and it's one of the few things the Commandant does not tax. We've been invited, and I said we shall surely be there," he added quickly as all three went to talk. "It is only a *sous* for every set of dances – the whole evening will cost you less than fourpence. And you may get the chance to hold a girl again – or have you forgotten how that feels?"

King certainly hadn't, even though that was mostly down to having a good memory, and it was the main reason he persuaded himself to attend the dance. He had heard about such events of course; the small, domestic gatherings were a tradition amongst the French inhabitants and a popular subject of speculation between younger British officers. They sounded like the very antithesis of the high class affairs hosted by Mrs Concannon at the Bishop's Palace and were usually held in one of the larger houses to the lower end of town. Those who attended came from every social level and some said it was not unheard of for servants to dance with their masters.

The entertainment also sounded uncomplicated, with a minimal band and no fancy steps; the emphasis being on people simply enjoying themselves. Attendance was by word of mouth however, with no advanced publicity, and there had never been any mention of British prisoners of war being invited.

But there turned out to be more to Timothy's question than the lieutenant cared to reveal. Only when they questioned him further did the officers discover that, in addition to their son, the Silva family also possessed daughters. Timothy had actually shaken hands with two of the creatures while a third was also to be present at the dance. And he had made it clear that, even if the remaining lass turned out to be Venus herself, she would be the ugly one of the trio.

Consequently, King had gone to pains to make himself as presentable as possible and was amused to note that, despite their faint protests, the other two had turned out fresh tunics and clean shirts. In fact, as they walked up the short path to the stone house, the British officers looked quite respectable, with even Manning, in the sober uniform of a Naval surgeon, cutting what might be considered a dash.

"I'm not too able at this dancing lark," King sighed as they reached the front door and Timothy rapped soundly with the knocker.

"If you're worrying over your lack of an arm, I should disregard it," Manning told him. "From what James says, they sound a pleasant enough brood and will surely make allowances."

King was not so certain and went to reply when the door

122

swung open, revealing a young woman in her middle twenties.

Her hair was light brown, almost golden, and she had pale skin and a pleasant smile. She was dressed in a simple gown that was obviously home made, although it fitted her perfectly, and had a succession of yellow flowers embroidered onto the light grey cotton. But as he looked on her, his doubts increased; Timothy had been right, it was a long time since he had held a girl, or even seen one as pretty as this. So when her eyes found his and the smile increased, he became full of misgivings.

\* \* \*

Two hours later Timothy was thoroughly enjoying himself, even if it was not quite in the way he had envisaged. The flood of feminine company on Malta had been followed by Gibraltar's absolute drought which, when coupled with the long march through France, had all but quashed his ideas of finding a wife. So he naturally assumed that, as soon as he met with nubile women once more, his previous intentions would be awakened. But it was not to be. There were dancing partners of every age at the party, from a couple of spotty girls that might barely be in their teens to several more mature women, one of whom was paying him particular attention. And the host's two daughters previously met were every bit as appealing as before, while the third comfortably matched them in beauty and elegance, yet Timothy was surprised to find that romance was the last thing on his mind.

Perhaps it was those close shaves at Malta, or maybe he simply needed more time, but somehow the emotions would not be stirred. The older woman was every bit as comely as those he had previously abandoned and spoke a tolerable English while, as an enemy prisoner of war, he could be sure any attraction she felt was not influenced by his position. Still, he felt no urge to encourage her attentions and neither was he particularly interested in the Silva's three daughters. They all danced beautifully and were patience personified when it came to teaching him the steps, but when the music ended and they retired to their chairs he was quite content to remain in the middle of the floor and wait for it to begin again.

Perhaps he was growing old, and his last chance was already

wasted; even Tom King seemed to have made a strong connection with the third sister, despite his painfully awkward gait and the lack of one arm, yet Timothy could feel no regret. If he were truly past the time for romance, then any marriage would be a sham, and it was better he realised that now than later. Besides, he was certainly not unpopular as a guest and, with such dances being relatively common, could be confident of at least some female company for the foreseeable future. And that would probably be enough for him, Timothy decided; at least for all the time he remained a prisoner.

* * *

They were calling for yet another waltz, and Lovemore raised his eyebrows briefly before bringing the flute back to his lips. He really did not mind, however; playing for a simple house party was not the bright lights and loud music he had foreseen, but was a lot better than any other kind of work. The fiddler was an elderly Breton named Petre who spoke quietly and with a thick accent. Fortunately Lovemore's French was improving daily, so the two understood each other well enough although, even if they had not, there was communication to some extent through the universal language of music. Cranston began to beat out a dependable, if uninspiring, rhythm on his side drum and the musicians came in with perfect timing. Many of the French songs were so similar to those Lovemore already knew that changes were unnecessary and he had quickly picked up a few new ones from the old man, while passing on several English melodies in return.

And in general he had settled well to the strange environment; certainly the evenings spent playing were one of the more enjoyable aspects of Lovemore's life in Verdun, although the days were not quite so pleasurable. *Kestrel*'s former purser was setting himself up in business and had recruited him and Cranston to help renovate his new premises. The pair had spent the last few weeks clearing out and painting a damp and stuffy cellar, so Lovemore was especially pleased to be able to earn a little extra doing what he enjoyed most. And, if he had understood Petre correctly, the season for these private dances was only just beginning; often there would be two or three in a week. The old man had also said

124

something about accompanying theatrical performances, although Lovemore was still unsure of the exact details. But even if nothing came of that, he was happy to play on nights such as this; it was what he was used to doing aboard ship, after all, and the sight of men and women laughing and dancing together was far more enjoyable than watching a bunch of thunder-faced Jacks tackle a hornpipe.

Across the crowded room he could see several he knew. Some were senior officers from his last ship who had been surprised to notice him there, and in such a capacity. But any awkwardness soon disappeared in the genial company. And once Lovemore began to play and the officers dance – the latter hesitantly at first, and then with increasing confidence – the difference in rank was soon forgotten.

And now all seemed to be enjoying themselves mightily. Even the surgeon, who was known as a dour old soul, had taken several dances, and was losing the preoccupied expression that had been haunting him of late. While the other men, the true sea officers, had taken on a completely different identity. Gone was any trace of authority or position, instead they simply appeared as lively young men enjoying the company of equally spirited women. He found it a pleasure to play for them, and even Cranston, still pounding away solidly on his drum, was smiling.

Lovemore closed his eyes as they laid into the chorus for the ninth time. It was just a shame that what was such a happy and innocent event should be spoiled so. As in previous instances, nothing had been obvious to anyone else, and he so hoped the evening would end well. Besides, what he had noticed was just a glimmer, the very beginnings of things seen before and best forgotten. But still he could not ignore the image that had been superimposed for the briefest of moments over one of the officer's faces.

It was one he had noticed before, except on that occasion it had been a messmate. And Lovemore knew exactly what it meant.

# Chapter Twelve

Lewis supposed that, even if he had not broken his *Parole*, the odds on him ever obtaining a command in the Royal Navy would have been short. And he could console himself further by remembering few ordinary seamen ever rose as far as commissioned rank; for him to have swapped a lower deck mess for the splendours of the wardroom was an achievement indeed. Then there was the new life he was about to enter; in addition to being a seagoing appointment, it held a promise of wealth far beyond the hopes of all but flag officers. And if any doubts remained, he might only remember the way he had been treated.

For the wounds were still raw, and yet to show even the first sign of healing. He carried them about like any injured warrior and, even though they might not be immediately obvious, thought of them often. And he was the first to admit the fault may be his in not being gentlemanly enough to honour his word, but foolishly honest in admitting the fact. The nett result was the same however: he had little feeling left for either the service, or his country.

For much of his adult life Lewis had been fighting wars he had no part in starting; risking his life in an effort to keep an increasingly distant Britain free. And, while he was doing so, those left behind had either died, married or simply forgotten him. So were he to backslide a little now, turn his back on a country that had effectively turned its back on him, would that be so very dreadful?

And so he had started on a journey that had left his country behind in more ways than one. It had felt strange to cross the sea once more, to return to the continent, a place so recently escaped from. But he was returning in a different role, no longer a fleeing prisoner of war but a man to be respected by anyone he met. And this was not France, but the Batavian Republic, what most in England still referred to as Holland, and a far better prospect, whatever the political situation.

Lewis had arrived in Flushing the night before and was now

standing before a brig that must be the one intended for him. She appeared sound enough and should really be referred to as a langard, as the furled-up mass of canvas beneath her mainyard would be a square sail. Certainly she was the only vessel in sight with any semblance of seaworthiness about her. The rest, though larger, could not have ventured beyond the small harbour entrance in years, and some looked as if they never would again. He began to trudge slowly along the hard; it was good to be able to stretch his legs after so long cooped up in a tiny cabin and, as the details of the vessel became clearer, interest began to stir deep inside him.

For it wasn't as if he was alone in his change of career. Even when young, when the next village was a fair distance and before the wicked French rose up to threaten his family's tidy lives, there had been plenty working hard to feather their own nests at a negligible cost to the nation. His father had regularly bought brandy from the flaskers, a group that included many respected members of local society and was led by the magistrate.

Of course, his current position was a little above that of simple shore-based runners, or even the leader of a gang of enterprising free traders. The vessel before him now was an armed brig – almost a ship of war – and there would be far more than liquor or tobacco in her holds to distribute to an eager population. For it would be two-way traffic; in return for delivering what he could persuade himself to be essential supplies to a war-weary Britain, he would be collecting a cargo in return. Such exports could be anything from wool to gold bullion but, whatever the commodity, of one thing he was certain: his country would be the worse off without it.

And then he remembered that dreadful interview in the offices of the Board of Transport – surely an odd body for the government to choose when it came to interrogating escaped prisoners of war? It had been a smug band of well dressed elite; men who had never raised their heads above a bulwark, or dodged the musket balls of a desperate band of *gendarmes*, yet placed to pass judgement on those who had. And they possessed the total lack of understanding expected of any who would only meet after ten, and expected to be finished by noon.

"The fact that you were able to escape does you some credit, Mr Lewis," one had told him with a sardonic look on his fat face.

127

"But that is cancelled by the act of breaking your word of honour."

Word of honour – Lewis still wondered what kind of world they lived in. Was it honourable when men of business grew wealthy on wars that were principally fought by the poor? How many laurels should a landowner receive for selling oak at inflated prices when his country is crying out for ships?

"We can expect nothing less," another had commented as they peered at his service record. "Why the man was nothing more than an ordinary seaman, a Jack Tar!" he added, beaming at his cronies.

Lewis' career had certainly begun on the lower deck, and it had been no easy matter to haul himself up to the status of a commissioned officer, although now it seemed the act was to work against him. An ordinary seaman would have been simply enlisted into the next available ship and, though he may be left with little more than a host of stories with which to while away a quiet watch, nothing more would have been said. But an ordinary seaman would not have been asked to sign his *Parole* and, even if he had, hardly expected to honour it. Lewis was an officer, and therefore a gentleman. It was a status that came with obligations and no such leniency could be allowed.

"Should he be dismissed the service?" the fat one had enquired, though his hopes were soon dashed.

"Not our decision," another replied. "If the Navy wishes to waste time and money on a court martial it is their concern. Ours ends with filing a report, though I fear it will not make good reading."

Lewis knew he should have been ashamed, his inquisitors clearly expected nothing less. But all he could feel was a hot resentment and the longing to remove the row of supercilious smiles with the back of his hand. But he curbed the temptation; such an action might be expected of a common seaman but not a commissioned officer, and Lewis clearly retained certain standards.

He had not waited for a trial, though; not when the verdict was so predictable and any feeling he had for the service was long faded. And in certain areas he had been lucky: usually when a gentleman was so disgraced the repercussions continued for some while. He would have to resign from every official office and avoid all forms of polite society – that or face the indignity of being publicly cut. Such things did not concern Lewis, although he soon discovered no back pay was owing and even his prize agent, a man who would normally have assessed his account for owed money, refused to have further dealings with him. And then there had come the problems with employment.

His first port of call had been the Honourable East India Company, although he now realised the title should have warned him from the outset. But that was in the days when he had yet to realise the impact a loss of standing could cause, and much had been learned since.

It had meant a three day trip to London, and all the expenses of travel, together with staying in a Clerkenwell lodging house that cost far more than his usual Southsea room. And he needed to call the day before to leave his name, so there was also the cost of an evening meal, as well as the fresh shirt he had so desperately needed. But the expense would have been justified if it meant securing a well paid seagoing post, and he appeared slightly before the appointed time, only to find the John Company staff were already way ahead of him.

Either they had been tipped off, or news of his disgrace must have travelled further than he expected, as Lewis was hardly inside the marble lobby before a white-haired man with gold spectacles came out to intercept him. He was backed by a positive band of blue-coated men, and Lewis knew from the off he had backed a loser.

There had obviously been a mistake; officers from the Royal Navy were usually welcomed, although the Company were not in need of further seagoing personnel at that time. They were still standing in the prestigious hall which was hardly an appropriate place to beg, although Lewis had asked of the possibility of shore-based employment. But one look at the stony face of the old man had been enough, and he turned and left before the blue-coats were given the chance to assist him.

And then he had begun the weary slog around other independent shipping companies, all of whom seemed equally alert to his circumstances. Until then, his only employer had been the Royal Navy, and the manner in which even the smallest merchant concerns cooperated came as a surprise. With unlimited time and funds there might have been an opening for an office clerk, or possibly even a petty officer aboard ship, but Lewis' stock was low, and unlikely to be revived by the sort of position he might secure. So it came about that he found his present posting and, even though taken through desperation, it was not without possibilities.

He had reached the brig now and stood looking at her with eyes that had seen a thousand such vessels. She would be more than a hundred tons, but not significantly so. And behind those ports he could expect to find guns of some description; maybe not a full broadside of nine- or twelve-pounders, but sufficient to see her clear of trouble if the need arose. Two masts made for a different style of rig of course, and he would have to get used to handling that hefty mainsail. But there were plenty of smaller craft flying a commissioning pennant and, though she might not be maintained to the standards of a government vessel, she should certainly suit his purposes.

The crew could prove a problem, both assembling one and enforcing discipline when he had, although his backers had been remarkably glib about that aspect and seemed confident the wages and rewards they offered would be enough to attract men. Once at sea, it would be up to him to tame them, however, and Lewis wondered how much he might depend on his officers, who would have been recruited in much the same manner as himself.

But it remained a seagoing position, and the best he had been offered. The brig could use a little priddying, but basically appeared solid. And even if she might be sailing under a different flag and ultimately serving a country at war with his own, Lewis was already starting to feel an element of pride in his new command.

* * *

"The *Général* will see you now."

Manning collected the leather case that carried what was left of his medical instruments, and followed the *gendarme* through the stone archway into a large and surprisingly light room. It was high up; probably one of the very upper stories in the Citadel and looked out over the walls of Verdun. For a moment he stared at the distant countryside, his thoughts turning to what lay beyond when

130

a cough brought him back to reality.

"If I can have your attention, Doctor: there is not time for the day dreaming."

Manning swung round and noticed a short, slightly sallow man who lay reclined on a *chaise longue* next to one of the windows. He was wearing the dark uniform of a *Brigade Général de la Gendarmerie*, with the red ribbon of the Legion of Honour prominent on his pigeon chest.

"*Général* Wirion?" Manning asked cautiously.

"Indeed," the officer confirmed. "I assume you are the new English doctor?"

Manning had been treating irascible patients for long enough to know there was little to be gained in contradicting them and nodded silently.

"Well, get down to it!" he spat. "I doubt you will be able to do better than those that have come before, but may as least make the effort!"

The surgeon stepped closer and lowered his bag. The *Général* could not have been more than forty but his thinning hair showed a fair amount of white. And though his frame was slight, the man clearly lived well, and had a sizeable double chin. Manning caught his eye for a moment and noted that, despite the anger, there was a trace of fear there, while the forehead and cheek carried a faint sheen of sweat that could equally come from pain or fever.

Manning reminded himself that this was the town Commandant; for all military and civil personnel his word was law, while Wirion was also known for being as corrupt as a Cheapside brothel keeper. And he had also expected the summons as the *Général* was known to make use of any medic amongst his prisoners. They would be expected to treat his ailments without payment, the only encouragement being the knowledge that a failed remedy would buy a one-way trip to Bitche. He knew all that, and had made the appropriate preparations before even setting foot in the Citadel. But now he was actually there, Manning was surprised to note a change in his own attitude.

Maybe it was professional pride, or even honour, but, now he had been consulted, the surgeon found himself prepared to do his best for the Commandant, as he would for anyone under his care.

"What appears to be the trouble?" he asked.

Adams and the three younger midshipmen had also taken a house together, although theirs was far smaller than any of *Kestrel*'s former officers' lodgings, and lay in the shabbiest, cheapest, part of the town. The rent was still inordinately high however, especially considering they could have lived for virtually nothing in the Citadel. But all agreed it better to retain some measure of independence, even if doing so meant cutting back in other areas.

For none were exactly flushed with funds. The British government made regular payments to the French to sustain their prisoners which worked out at twenty-five shillings a month for each lad, or roughly a quarter of that allowed a captain, who could also draw upon his half pay. They might apply to what was commonly referred to as English Lloyd's; the patriotic fund set up in a London coffee house for the welfare of seamen, although Adams, the eldest, was not even allowed that. As he had been serving as an acting lieutenant, the charity expected him to be able to provide for himself from his own half pay; a basic clerical error as the Admiralty refused to consider one of his rank to be anything other than a warrant officer, for whom such luxuries were not permitted.

And so they had all set to supplementing their income from work in the town itself. There were plenty of official ways of making money; the Commandant's staff provided a number of enterprises where men could earn funds from small manufacturing projects. These usually centred on basic crafts such as tailoring or carpentry, although there were other choices. Captain Brenton's Relief Committee, a body headed by captured senior captains, was happy for any prisoner to work as long as it did not aid the French war effort, or take a job from a serving enemy soldier. And there were other ways to make money: those skilled in dancing, music or the arts could take on pupils or sell their talents in other ways. None of the lads were particularly gifted, although they did have access to another avenue, which was provided by a former shipmate.

Holby's casino was taking shape at a remarkable rate. Cranston and Lovemore had done wonders with brooms and paintbrushes; several tables were found, including two ideal for hazard, and the purser had even chanced upon an ancient, but workable, roulette wheel. Reliable staff were needed as croupiers, however, and the four young men seemed ideal.

And so they had spent the past few days playing endless hands of cards and wearing out the dice on an improvised hazard table until each could tell themselves they had a good understanding of their new vocation. Not one of them were particularly enamoured with the prospect, which was nothing more than a means to an end, but working for a British officer and former shipmate was surely better than for the French. Besides, what harm could they come to?

* * *

"Lieutenant Lewis?"

So engrossed had he been in examining the brig's burton tackle, which was totally different to any he had known before, that Lewis failed to respond immediately. And when he did, it was not to correct the older of the two who had apparently crept up behind him. For despite the confident smile that was verging on the brash, there was also something obviously brittle about him, so much so that it encouraged protection rather than correction. Thin lips and high cheek bones gave his face an oddly feminine appearance, while the white skin that held perhaps a tinge of green seemed at odds with the oilskin smock, clothing that was totally unnecessary in the mild weather.

"I'm Lewis," he confirmed. "You are?"

"Reid," the young man announced. "John Conway Reid – that's R. E. I. D." he explained. "Not as some coves would have it."

The brash grin was seemingly pasted on his face as he thrust out a hand that only just appeared beyond the oilskin's sleeve. Lewis took hold, noticing how thin and bony it felt in the grip of his own weathered paw. The tendency for men to sport two Christian names was undoubtedly spreading, although Lewis had never understood the need for it.

"And you?" he asked, directing his gaze to the younger, who appeared barely in his teens.

"M-Masters," the lad stammered.

"We're to join you," Reid stated with assurance. "Mr Crabtree sent us over from Deal."

133

"Did he indeed?" Lewis was surprised.

"I'm to be your negotiator." The smile was now taking on a look of importance as Reid explained: "Liaise with the various men of business on both sides of the water, as well as assisting in command of the ship, of course."

"I assume you have experience?" Lewis instinctively doubted the young man held many skills beyond a pathological belief in himself, but preferred to appear positive.

"Oh yes," Reid replied. "Served at sea since I were fourteen, so am capable enough."

That might make him an adequate second in command, but Lewis was more interested in Reid's negotiating experience.

"And I assume you speak Dutch?"

At this, the brash exterior took a slight dent.

"Not actually Dutch, sir..."

"French then? German? Limburgish? Walloon?"

Now the façade collapsed completely, and Lewis almost felt sorry for the man.

"No, sir, only English."

"When did you arrive?" Lewis was now addressing both, but it was still the older one who replied.

"We left last night," Reid announced. "And came in not half an hour ago. Dreadful trip, I've forgotten how those small luggers can tip. Our possessions are still aboard."

Lewis felt further twinges of doubt. A lugger was certainly the quickest and least conspicuous way to cross from England, but it was strange for one supposedly acquainted with the sea to complain of the motion. And though not every seasoned mariner referred to his personal belongings as dunnage, there remained something decidedly unseamanlike about his visitor.

"What about you," Lewis turned to the younger, and was disconcerted to notice the lad buckle slightly under his gaze. "Masters, isn't it – what's your experience?"

"Volunteer, first class, sir," the lad admitted. "I was assistant to the gunnery lieutenant aboard *Chloe*."

"How long did you serve?" Lewis demanded.

"Seven months," Masters admitted. "But five of them were at sea."

"Did you see action?"

"No, but we cleared three times and beat to quarters twice. Mr Keller said I'd make an excellent midshipman and I were only let go 'cause the ship was called for refit." The boy's confidence increased as his spoke, which was encouraging, while, despite his somewhat hesitant persona, the lad had intelligent eyes and should learn his duties quickly, although Lewis remained surprised that either had been recruited without reference to him. As it was, Crabtree had arranged for both to come across on the assumption they would be given responsible posts; something he hardly felt inclined to do, based on his first impressions.

"How old are you?" he found himself asking the younger. It probably wasn't the most diplomatic of questions, but the first one that occurred and, as Lewis had been appointed the brig's master, he was allowed to be a bit bumptious.

"Seventeen," Masters replied before adding, "come June," with what might have been a blush.

There was an air of honesty about the fellow and he had no doubt the lad spoke the truth. But that was considerably older than Lewis had suspected. He switched his attention back to Reid.

"And you?"

The man seemed taken by surprise by the question, and rolled his eyes slightly as he answered. "Me, sir? I've not long turned twenty."

So one was older than he appeared, and the other a good deal younger; neither could be blamed for either fact, but it remained disconcerting.

"And you propose joining me?" Lewis asked. To that point the only parties to the venture he had met were Crabtree and his fellows: men spoken with in England and likely to remain there. One of the least attractive aspects of his role would be to contact and coordinate with the Dutch side of the team. The brig must also be victualled and maintained, a delicate business and one with which he would have appreciated assistance.

"Indeed, sir," Reid replied, his confidence returning. "Mr Crabtree said your ship would need officers and we were pleased to offer our services."

The brig required a crew of thirty or so hands, and there was no doubt Lewis would need support in commanding them. But they were likely to be the roughest and toughest of seamen who must be closely supervised. Anyone serving as an officer would need an iron will and probably a fist to match; there would be no room for lightweights. Something of this must have shown in his expression, as Reid became quite agitated.

"You've no need to concern yourself, sir; I am highly experienced," he declared with a tinge of arrogance. "Served as a John Company cadet for four years, and temporary fifth officer for one; afore that I were a volunteer."

Now Lewis did begin to have his doubts. For such a brittle specimen to have survived the rigours of long-distance travel hardly rang true.

"What ship and master?" he demanded.

"Thomas Greg," Reid replied smartly. "First in the *Kitty*, then I followed him to *Richmond Hill*. She were a sight bigger than this," he added, while glancing round the vessel.

Lewis knew little of HEIC shipping, and had only vaguely heard of one of the vessels.

"When did *Richmond Hill* pay off?" he asked, and once more Reid's assurance began to fade.

"She didn't, sir," he confessed. "I left her at Bombay and made my own way home. I..."

Lewis raised a hand and stopped him. There was no more to be said: however much Reid wished to tell his story, and however plausible it might sound, Lewis could guess all he needed to know. For a merchant officer to leave mid-way through a commission did not bode well, while seeking employment from the likes of Crabtree only reeked of desperation. But then Lewis remembered his own story might not sound exactly impressive to some, and resigned himself to the fact that another could have been treated equally unfairly.

"And now you wish to become smugglers?" he asked, only to receive hopeful nods from both.

"Mr Crabtree..." Reid began, only to be interrupted yet again.

"I'm not interested in Mr Crabtree," Lewis told him sharply. "He does not command this brig. When we sail, I shall be her master, and she will only be carrying seamen; tell me, can you hand, reef and steer?"

"I – we – thought to be officers," Reid replied, a little bitterly.

"I have no intention of placing any man in charge of hands

unless they can carry out similar duties," Lewis snapped. "In fact, they must be better," he continued, warming to his theme and including both in his glance. "The type of men we will be shipping won't suffer fools; any officer who wishes to serve under me must be wise to their tricks, and one step ahead at all times."

"I can do that, sir," Reid replied in a tone that came dangerously close to a sulk.

"And you must be able to give orders," Lewis added, centring on him. "Ones that bear close inspection, and could entail you risking your own lives, as well as those about you. But before then you will have had to win their trust, then keep it, so those orders are carried out correctly. Can you do that as well?"

"Yes, sir," Reid said, swallowing. "Yes, I think so."

Masters also gave a hesitant nod and Lewis sighed. However misplaced their confidence, in the face of such certainty there was little more he could say. He supposed he would have to give both a chance; let the pair loose amongst a mess of hardened Jacks and see what they made of them. If all turned out as he expected, he would have ample reason to let both go and start again with others.

"Well my first job is to contact the authorities, and it won't be easy," he temporised. "The berth here is paid for until the end of the year, but I have to arrange for repair facilities before they become necessary. And there will be stores and victuals to order, as well as recruiting a crew. I also need to coordinate with Mr Crabtree's contact in the Batavian Republic. You might think we are in Holland, but the political system is very different, and probably fraught with difficulties."

There was a silence as both took this in, then Lewis turned his attention to young Masters.

"And what about you?" he asked. "We won't be under military discipline; the men you command will have as much of a stake in the venture as you do and, with no redress to the cat, it might not be easy."

"Yes, sir," the lad replied hesitantly. "I understand."

"Well, do you think you can do it?" Lewis demanded. "What can you offer that might be of use?"

There was a pause as Masters considered this, then his expression lifted slightly. "I can speak a little Dutch, sir," he announced hopefully.

# Chapter Thirteen

Spring was certainly taking hold, and King was beginning to regret wearing the long, woollen coat he had purchased on his way to Verdun. The warmth had been welcome then, but the sun now shone so hard he was forced to walk with it unbuttoned and open in a way that might be considered too bohemian for a serving sea officer. The garment had one redeeming feature however; its long sleeves and heavy folds might be unsuitable for the time of year, but at least they disguised the loss of his left arm.

Not that his companion was unaware; after having spent most of the previous Tuesday evening dancing together, only a fool could have been ignorant of King's injury, and he had already decided the golden-haired woman with the bright smile and a truly wicked wit was no fool.

But the story behind the loss of his arm was just one of many secrets each had to reveal, although the couple were still a long way from the stage when deep conversation and profound disclosures were called for. For it was a simple matter: they had met, felt a mutual attraction, and were now learning to trust. And though both felt inwardly comfortable with the other and might even have sensed the amount they had to explore, neither were in any rush.

Except in the purely functional manner of leading her in a *gavotte* or a *bourrée*, King had yet to even take her by the hand. This, and so much more, were pleasures to come; for the moment they were content to simply be together, occasionally gaze, perhaps for too long, into the other's eyes, and share a knowing smile.

"Will it be the river, Miss Silva?" he asked, after they had walked a little way from the stone house that was her home.

"The river, yes," she replied. "Though you must not call me Miss Silva."

"Too English?" he asked, remembering a previous conversation.

138

"Too English for sure," she agreed with a slight chuckle. "I told you, I have no time for that accursed country, or its inhabitants."

"You speak its language well enough," he pointed out.

"Maybe, but it is not so very hard; otherwise the English themselves could not manage it."

"Then do you prefer *mademoiselle*?" he asked.

"I prefer Aimée, as you well know."

"I think Miss Silva is more dignified."

"Dignified? Pah!" He loved the way her eyes flashed when they were sparring. "I shall have you know it is the name of a woman who was anything but dignified, though they say she has become important despite this."

"Very well, Aimée, then it will be the river," he conceded. "But can we go beyond the town?"

"Oh indeed yes!" she exclaimed. "Sometimes I feel those horrible stone walls closing in upon me. It is such a sunny day – let us run through the long grass and leave Verdun far behind. You have your passport, I hope?"

King nodded and tapped his pocket. "I have, though cannot stray farther than three miles."

"I don't know how you can accept..." She began to falter.

"Being held prisoner?" King finished for her. "It is not so very difficult, though perhaps when I have been here for longer it will seem so."

"I have lived in the town for less than two years and am already tired of the place. To know I could never truly leave would be unbearable."

They had reached the *Porte Chaussée* and waited behind a group of midshipmen who were apparently leaving to exercise a pack of beagles. When their turn came, King presented his passport which was duly accepted by the bored *gendarme*, then signed his name on a sheet of paper and the two of them were free to walk through the high arch and out into the lush countryside beyond.

"There are times, such as now, when it is hard to believe I truly am a prisoner," he confessed, resuming their previous conversation. "This is a pleasant spot to be sure."

"Oh, I have lived in far worse places," she agreed. "Though we came from Brittany and for me that will always be the nicest."

"Where was worse?" King enquired and Aimée immediately became flustered.

"Pardon me?" she asked.

"Where did you live that was worse?" he repeated more clearly. He had posed the question innocently enough and was surprised to have caused such a reaction. "It was just that I assumed you to have come straight from Brittany to Verdun," he explained.

"Oh, but I did," she claimed, although still appeared uncomfortable; almost as if she was keeping something hidden. "I was just, you know, talking..."

"I know," he agreed, remembering times when he had spoken out of turn. He glanced across; really she was such a wonderful person, how could he even suspect her of hiding anything from him?

"And would you like to go back to Brittany?"

"In the same way as you wish to be in England," she replied. "Though perhaps not so badly. But there is nothing making me stay."

She went to say more, and King waited for several seconds before speaking again. "Nothing to keep you at all?" he finally chanced.

Once more those eyes flashed in his direction, but when she spoke it was of more mundane matters.

"Sometimes I do dream of escaping," she admitted. "My mother and father have no need of help and, even if they did, there are my two younger sisters living at home and they have no desires to wander. But really I have nowhere to go. There is my *grand-mère* in Brittany, but she also is very independent, and at least there is work here that I can do."

She thought for a moment.

"I suppose you are lucky in a way, you have a goal, even though it may never be realised."

Nothing more was said for some time as they continued to walk further away from the stark grey walls of the town. Ahead of them the midshipmen were shouting at their dogs and hurling the occasional stick, which was always ignored, while a solitary man fished in the nearby river.

"My parents are holding another dance soon, did you know

that?" she asked at last.

King shook his head; he was aware such things were a regular occurrence, but had not considered them further. Dancing was not entirely in his line; even before his injury, he barely appreciated most forms of music while attempting to move to it turned him into a clumsy oaf. Meeting with *Aimée* at her parents' party was a wonderful piece of luck; she had been kind and all but shepherded him through, although he had no wish to repeat that part of the experience.

"Will you be there?" he asked.

"I live in the house: there is little choice," she replied, before adding, "unless I find a way to escape," with another flash of eyes.

The word triggered a series of emotions deep within him, and he found himself slowing his pace.

"Escape? In what way?"

She shrugged. "The word has many meanings, and some we may explore together in time. But for now, let us just say that, if someone were to ask me to abandon the dance and go out walking with him instead, then I would not say no." She smiled. "And then we will have escaped together."

* * *

"Ready about, Mr Reid!" Despite the fact that Lewis was holding the brass speaking trumpet tightly enough to turn his knuckles white, his hand still shook slightly. This was the first time his command, the brig that held the unlikely name of *Narcis,* had put to sea and he had chosen a spot clear from all shipping and navigational hazards to run through her paces.

They had assembled a crew without too much trouble. A few were Dutch, which was unsurprising as their berth was deep in the Batavian Republic, although all spoke reasonable English, which had become a requirement as soon as Lewis realised just how prized the places would be. But he had also managed to secure a good many British amongst the twenty-eight bodies he needed. One of these was exceptionally powerful and belonged to Price, a hard man with a bullet-head who currently stood in the waist with a knotted rope's end in his hand. In a former life, Price had served as boatswain's mate aboard a two-decker and was now carrying out similar duties in *Narcis*. The knowledge and confidence learned from his previous position were serving him well, and Lewis considered him the ideal counter to the prickly and excitable Reid. As far as he knew, that starter had yet to be used, and it was obvious Price had already won the respect of the men.

And there lay another surprise; most of the regular hands were nothing like as uncivilised or rebellious as Lewis had expected. All were malcontents of some kind but that hardly made them unusual amongst lower deck men in any navy, and there was nothing overtly disloyal about any of them: none of the English would have been seen dead aboard a French vessel, and even the Dutch had no love for the nation. Lewis had not delved deeply into their motives for joining *Narcis* although suspected most of his fellow countrymen had resigned themselves to their new careers in very much the same way he had. Some, the majority, would be deserters, while the rest might have committed any number of crimes that excluded them from shipping before the mast in a conventional British ship.

Of course, he had no idea how a crew of mixed nationalities would get along. The two countries had been fighting a succession of wars over the last few centuries and Lewis had actually been present when Admiral Duncan all but annihilated the old Dutch fleet at Camperdown. But with Bonaparte's men in control and the Batavian Republic firmly established, this was essentially an occupied country. For much longer than any could remember regular trading had been carried out between the two nations. This was usually on a personal basis, between small businesses that were little more than family concerns. Consequently, inter-marriage was common, as well as close friendships that often withstood the trials of national conflict.

And, unsurprisingly, Lewis' main contact in Flushing was a Dutchman, although he had no need of Masters' linguistic skills as he spoke fluent English. Henry van Gent officially held a minor role in governing the port but, in reality, possessed far greater power. Besides his formal duties, the man ran an empire that controlled the supply of all contraband cargo, as well as victualling and maintaining the vessels that carried it. This extended to specifying what each would carry and when they were to sail; something that Lewis would have found galling had Crabtree not been totally in favour. But even then he remained dubious; van Gent was a large and slightly arrogant man who smoked small cigars and treated his own workers harshly, although he was also surprisingly pro-British, and looked after *Narcis'* needs well. The major continental ports were subject to blockade, but van Gent had many connections and seemed able to summon up even the rarest of requirements without a great deal of effort. Lewis did not know how a Dutch civilian could achieve this, nor did he want to; as the brig's master the only thing that concerned him was his command was well cared for, and there were few complaints on that front.

"Ease down the helm!" They were making good speed and, with the nearest fisher a good two miles off, Lewis now had more than enough room to manoeuvre. He glanced across to the helmsman, a red-haired Welshman named Cross who had jumped ship at Falmouth in protest at being pressed aboard a frigate. The man knew his stuff, and was probably wondering if his new captain was equally savvy.

"Helm's a-lee!" The sheets were released and the brig's motion began to alter. Lewis looked about; the hands were intent on their work and, whatever their origin or motive, seemed as sound as any raw crew he had previously encountered. "Rise tacks and sheets!" The lee tack and weather sheets were shortened efficiently enough while, above Lewis' head, the lee spanker topping lift was tightened, and its opposite number released.

"Haul taught!" Still the evolution was running smoothly, and Lewis even found time to glance at the nearby shoreline while the yards creaked and the brig began to wallow in the gentle breeze. Despite what Bonaparte had named the country, he would always think of it as Holland and its soft outline appeared little different to many parts of the English coast.

The men were responding well, and the manoeuvre continued without a hitch. Being square-rigged, the brig was far hungrier for hands than any schooner or ketch of a similar tonnage, although the extra manpower would come in useful if it came to a fight. And this was most likely to be while at sea; on her trips to England, *Narcis* was intended to remain offshore and be unloaded by boats while, on the rare occasions when she needed to be beached, there should be a considerable gang of land-based runners to see her safe. But when she were making what should become a regular dash between the two countries, she could still protect herself, for *Narcis* was also armed.

The brig's weaponry consisted of ten, six-pounder carriage guns divided between the broadsides. The cannon were British, and probably former service pieces, being of a pattern that was steadily being replaced by carronades or the more efficient Bloomfield long guns. But Lewis was not unduly worried by their apparent obsolescence: Armstrongs had been used in countless actions in the past, with their castings proving as reliable as any. Besides, Crabtree and his cronies were confident they would not be needed, although Lewis had been quick to note that a considerable supply of powder and shot had been allowed in case they were.

Reid, standing on the break of the quarterdeck, had rallied a team to haul the boom to windward, and the brig was turning steadily. He must have felt his captain's eyes upon him as he looked around at that moment and gave a nervous, yet arrogant smile.

"Let go bowlin's, sir?" the young man questioned, and Lewis briefly closed his eyes. Price was seaman enough to look after such details without a direct order and, when he looked once more, found he had done so.

There was no doubting that Reid was still giving him cause for concern, even though some of his initial doubts had been eased. Lewis soon came to realise much of the young man's agitated behaviour was down to nerves; once he began to take up his duties, the fellow had relaxed and become almost likeable. However, he still had the annoying habit of questioning orders; this might be done verbally or, more often, by a look or a sharp intake of breath. It was something Lewis was learning to live with, and doubtless would pass in time, but annoying nevertheless.

And at least Masters was proving better than expected, even if Lewis could still not believe him as old as he claimed. The boy had been a godsend when recruiting foreign hands or dealing with individual suppliers on shore, and the men, who must have served under countless inexperienced young gentlemen in the past, respected him as much as any.

The evolution was almost complete now, and *Narcis* was proving herself weatherly enough, although Lewis did not doubt this would change. The addition of cargo, some of which would, by necessity, be loaded in haste, must alter her trim considerably, and with no long sea voyages to raise the level of her crew, she would always be a challenge to control. But Lewis was not concerned: a tidy sum had been promised for every crossing, and it was one that did not depend on how much or what was carried. Consequently, all he need do was stay alive, and free, to make a considerable pile in under a year. That was all he needed; when enough was accumulated he might invest in his own ship, take any of the officers and crew he felt worthwhile and set up in business for himself, although an alternative already seemed more attractive.

To buy a small cottage, somewhere as far away from the sea as he could manage; a place where no one knew anything of his past. Then while away the rest of his days in anonymity and quiet isolation.

And a year should be enough to accomplish it: in the brief time he had been involved in the smuggling trade, Lewis had learned much. The North Sea crossing allocated to him was probably the easiest. He would be serving the Suffolk coast, which was infinitely preferable to Kent or Sussex; counties that abounded with troops stationed to see off Bonaparte's much threatened invasion. There were also fewer Navy vessels that might catch a brig like *Narcis*, while those that could, the fast but frail revenue cutters, would not fare well against a broadside of six-pounders. And though Britain was at war, *Narcis* would be sailing with the permission and positive encouragement of the French government. Should Bonaparte mount a successful attack on his homeland, Lewis would effectively be on the winning side, and certainly in a far better position than an out of work sea officer who was said to have relinquished his honour.

Then a moment of doubt occurred as he remembered the war his county was fighting, along with that invasion he had so blithely envisaged, which might be made just a little easier by his efforts. In exchange for the spirits, tea and lace he would be carrying to his home, he would be bringing back gold and wool, as well as many other commodities the French were desperate for. Because of this, nothing less than a trip to the gallows could be expected, should he fall into British hands.

The brig had now settled on her new course and was picking

up speed. Lewis took a turn along his tiny quarterdeck and breathed in the rich sea air. But really there was little point in imagining the worst: far better to accept the situation as it was and make the best of it. After all he was employed, and at sea, with the near certainty of making a considerable fortune merely for doing what he did best. Besides, Lewis told himself yet again, when it had come to selecting his new career, there had been very little choice.

* * *

"So there you have it, gentlemen," Banks announced. "Mr Manning would seem to have been caught in a familiar fix."

They had left the town of Verdun and were in the parlour of a pleasant, detached house in the nearby village of Clermont, which Captain Brenton had taken at a cost of four hundred francs a month. Though still a prisoner, Brenton was permitted to live there; such a concession being officially available to any senior officer willing to pay the rent and pledge their word not to escape, although an additional regular payment to the Commandant, something that was decidedly unofficial, was also required.

Both the room, and the house, were the largest available to them, as Brenton had applied for his wife, Isabella, to join him, and the senior men of Verdun often met there. *Général* Wirion had offered quarters for their use within the Citadel, although the British agreed that neither the man, nor his security, could be depended upon.

The house was cared for by servants Brenton had reason to trust; the married couple who cooked and cared for him kept their Royalist affiliations well concealed while even the gardener was a Dutchman, whose son had fought against the imposition of Napoleon's republic on his country. And its position was an additional bonus; despite being in sight of the town walls, the place offered an element of detachment from the prison itself and on occasions over twenty had gathered in its accommodating rooms. There was no need for space on that particular afternoon, however; only Captains Banks and Brenton, along with a vicar, the Reverend Robert Wolfe, were present in addition to the unhappy Manning.

"Can you explain a little more about Wirion's illness?"

Brenton, a well built man with a prominent nose and a mild colonial accent, asked after a pause.

The surgeon was clearly taken aback. "I'm afraid that would not be possible," he replied. "I appreciate your concern, and really have no wish to be awkward, but the *Général* remains my patient, and I..."

"Of course, of course," Brenton assured him. "Forgive me, Mr Manning, I had no wish to pry into his personal details."

"I think Captain Brenton was hoping to learn more of the seriousness of *Général* Wirion's complaint," Wolfe suggested. Manning switched his attention to the vicar; he was one of the *détenus* seized at the outbreak of war and the surgeon had only heard good of him, even if his black clothing seemed out of place and almost sinister amid the more colourful and ornate uniforms of the two post captains.

"It can be controlled but not cured," he answered firmly. "The best I can do is suppress some of the symptoms, in which case the *Général* may live for several years. But he will never be well and, as the ailment – along with the treatment I must prescribe – continues, there may be unpleasant side effects."

"The Commandant has never been easy to deal with," Banks snorted. "So the prospect of him becoming less so is not a pleasant one."

"Yes, I fear he is an evil that is ever with us," Wolfe agreed. "Not that I wish him physical harm, of course."

"Well he can rot in hell for all I care," Brenton drawled. "And the sooner the better. His arbitrary fines have blighted our lives for long enough: it is the least he deserves. Why, following my recent tour of the depots, he presented me with a bill for the *gendarme* escort and their accommodation."

"But surely that was official business?" Wolfe protested.

"Indeed so," the large man agreed with a snort. "You might say I was working on behalf of the French Government. Of course, I did not pay."

"Glad to hear it." Banks again.

"Oh, I offered to," Brenton added with an easy grin. "But insisted on an official receipt in return, and he backed down."

"Like any bully," Banks rumbled. "Ask me, we have a first-rate opportunity to be rid of the beast, providing you are willing, of course?"

Brenton and Banks turned to the surgeon, but once more Wolfe interjected.

"I hope neither of you are suggesting Mr Manning does anything against his principles," he said.

"Of course not," Brenton agreed with a sigh. "It would be totally unethical."

"Besides, Courçelles, his deputy, is every bit as bad," Banks added.

"Gentlemen, I think we are missing the point," Wolfe exclaimed. "Mr Manning is in an unfortunate position, and we must do all we can to assist him."

"Indeed," Brenton cleared his throat and regarded the surgeon again. "Has the *Général* been suffering for long?"

"He says not, though I would gauge it to be a year or more at least," Manning replied. "And I have little doubt other surgeons have prescribed a similar remedy to that I propose."

"So I understand," Wolfe confirmed. "I have been in Verdun longer than any of you, and know of at least three physicians who have been called to attend."

"Can they be consulted?" Manning asked eagerly, and the vicar's expression fell.

"Sadly not," he admitted. "They were all sent to Bitche."

A hush fell on the room at the mention of the place, and Manning began to look even more uncomfortable.

"But we must not allow ourselves to be downhearted," Wolfe announced brightly. "There is always a solution in such cases, it just might take time for us mere mortals to discover it."

"You mentioned being able to treat the condition." Brenton again. "I take it the remedy would not be pleasant?" he added, with what might have been a smile.

"The long term administration of lead," Manning replied baldly. He was now certain the others had guessed Wirion's ailment and, with his own life at risk, saw no reason to conceal the facts further.

"I understand such a thing is rumoured to send men mad," Wolfe observed.

"And in this case, there would appear to be a head start," Banks murmured.

"But is there not a more palliative cure?" Brenton persisted. "Something that might ease the condition, but not place him in as much discomfort?"

"And perhaps hasten his death by just a little?" Banks suggested softly.

"I am no physician and have scant knowledge of the more modern drugs," Manning began, "but even a surgeon is bound by certain professional constraints..."

"Yes, yes of course, Mr Manning," Wolfe assured him, adding, "and, as I have said, none of us expect you to misuse your talents in any way," while delivering a significant look to Banks. "But I think Captain Brenton was suggesting some form of analgesic, perhaps to soften the effect; maybe a mild soporific?"

"It is a consideration, I suppose," Manning replied. "Though if another medic were to hear of my prescription, I might have a deal of explaining to do."

"But at least you would be in Verdun to do it," Wolfe pointed out. "I need not explain the terrors of Bitche – suffice to say it is a torturous place. Those who return are few and much changed."

"Then we must do all we can to see such a fate does not befall Mr Manning," Brenton added quickly.

"It will not be a permanent solution," the surgeon pondered.

"By your own words, there isn't one," Banks pointed out. "At least this might buy us time."

"Which is ironic," Wolfe added with a rare smile, "as time seems to be the one thing most of us have plenty of."

* * *

The brig's lower deck was similar in many ways to that of a Royal Navy vessel, which was hardly surprising, considering the source of most of her hands. They had divided themselves into messes of a sort, with all but one being anything other than exclusively British or Dutch. And, again as in service vessels, each mess had a head. This did not rate as an official posting, and neither was it formally elected; the position simply became filled following the laws of human nature that, when six or seven live and work together, one always emerges as leader.

In *Narcis*, Laidlaw had this distinction, although he was an unlikely choice. Rather than being physically strong, the Cornishman was tall, angular and with an awkward gait that was made worse by the need to stoop lower than most to avoid the brig's deckhead. But what he lacked in raw strength was more than made up for in intelligence, although even that attribute would have been of little use without the wisdom he had accumulated over nearly fifteen years at sea.

Laidlaw's route to the brig had been a simple one; he had been a Royal Navy man for all his seagoing career and would not have considered serving aboard any other vessel than a man-of-war. But luck had seen him posted to a sloop that was dominated by a particularly bitter second in command, an elderly lieutenant whose spiteful ways intimidated all the junior officers, as well as her somewhat weak and inexperienced young captain. Laidlaw was wise enough to know that nothing good would come of such a regime so, when an opportunity came to jump ship, he took it. That had been while the sloop was anchored off Deal and an obliging victualler had smuggled him aboard his tender and seen him safely to the shore, although then Laidlaw had found himself to be at something of a loss.

There were several Navy ships in the anchorage and he could have volunteered for any one of them, although the likelihood of a deserter being identified was strong. There was an alternative, but to ship aboard a merchant was no less risky. With the Royal Navy being so desperately short of men it had become customary to strip homebound traders of their crews, so the chances of being pressed back into the service remained high.

For a while he had considered the American navy; they were fighting the Barbary States in the Mediterranean and steadily adding to their fleet of dedicated warships. He would not be immune to being pressed by the British even then, but the Yankees were getting wise to the fact, and he felt there would be more chance of staying aboard one of their vessels than an Indiaman. There were no suitable ships in Deal, and he had just decided to try another port when he ran in with a couple of old shipmates who were seeking passage across the North Sea to join *Narcis*. She was almost a warship, and would be commanded by British officers, while there was the added incentive of the chance to earn a great deal of money. As an opportunity it was simply too good to pass off, and Laidlaw had joined them in signing on.

Of late he had begun to have doubts, however. On reaching her he found the brig to be a happy one, and he had already settled into the order of command, which was far more relaxed than he was used to. And the money was already starting to roll in, with a generous bounty being paid when he first boarded. But even so early into his time aboard, *Narcis* had already run into the Royal Navy. They had sighted several smaller craft during their working up exercises; all had been a fair distance off, while the captain had kept his nerve, and continued as if he were commanding nothing more suspicious than an innocent neutral. Which they might have been; there being no booty on board. And, even though the brig's relatively large crew would have caused a few raised eyebrows, no actual crime was being committed.

But now all that had changed and *Narcis* was due to sail for her first official trip the following morning; the decks were currently being piled high with crates of contraband, while her holds had already been filled and it would take only the most cursory of inspections to establish her for the runner she was. Stories abounded of successful smugglers; men who had spent years afloat dodging all those sent to catch them, then finally retiring with a pile that would see them in comfort for the rest of their days. But Laidlaw was suspicious of any who had been around long enough to gain a reputation: what of those taken on their first trip, or after only a few months into their career? No one had heard of them, so they were not missed.

He didn't know the chances of being captured, nor could he begin to calculate them, but *Narcis* was scheduled to take a trip a week, so, even if it were as low as one in fifty, it would be less than a year before she was caught. And of all the Navy vessels they had sighted, the most common was his former ship.

*Swift* must be patrolling the area and would be on the lookout for *Narcis* and her like. If she happened to intercept them, many of the brig's crew would get off relatively lightly, although he would find himself in deep water indeed.

It was customary to offer experienced seamen captured whilst smuggling the choice between gaol or the Navy, with the vast majority opting for the latter. But, as a known deserter, Laidlaw would have no such luxury. A summary court martial was the best he could hope for, and there could be only one verdict. For many so caught, the penalty was harsh indeed: a short trip to the foremast yardarm at the head of a halyard, with his former messmates hauling on the tail, and it was not a prospect Laidlaw particularly relished.

"Game of crown an' anchor?" someone asked, and he jolted himself away from the dismal thought and turned his attention to the others at the mess table.

"Aye, Jude, why not?" he agreed.

"We're playin' a penny a point," another informed him, "if that stands well with you?"

Laidlaw nodded. He had money in his pocket and the prospect of a good deal more to come. Besides, they were hardly high odds, not when compared with those he faced elsewhere.

\* \* \*

Holby had been at the casino since first light and now, as night had fallen to the extent that it was worth lighting the brass lanterns mounted to either side of the freshly painted front door, he was almost too tired to be nervous. Other than pasting a proclamation on the Citadel walls, he had done all he could to publicise the place, but there was still a gnawing doubt that no one would turn up. The renovations had cost him most of his funds, and there was still a deal more owing. Some, like the wages for the midshipmen who were to act as croupiers, could wait, and there were several small amounts outstanding with those tradesmen content to allow him credit. But others were already pressing him for money and, however attractive his rooms might appear, nothing more could happen until he actually opened the place and truly discovered its worth.

He walked down the wide stone steps that led to his cavern, and noticed how the air felt unusually thick. Several of the candles were smoking badly and, with a click of his fingers, he summoned one of the lads to attend to them, then swept a critical eye about the rest of the room. In the far corner, beyond the gaming tables, three young women stood beside a dresser covered with bottles and glasses. The wine was one item yet to be paid for, Holby's reasoning being it might be returned should the project fail.

Although he was not anticipating disaster: rather the reverse. For the past few weeks he had been making discrete enquires; it seemed the prospect of an alternative to the state-run casino would definitely be welcomed and he could also expect custom from the French inhabitants.

But such a venture could not avoid notice from the authorities forever, and Holby's last remaining funds had been turned into a store of *Louis d'ors* for just such an emergency. There were few things that bullion would not buy in Verdun, and in his case it would be time. Once the casino became established, and numbered several senior members of the *gendarmerie* amongst its clientele, his course should be set, and everything would run smoothly. Until then, if he had to grease a few palms, so be it; the money could be looked upon as an investment. But now would come the real test – the rooms were prepared, all was in place with verbal invitations given to every likely prospect – the only thing he had to do was wait, and see if his preparations had been worthwhile.

# Chapter Fourteen

It was early evening; *Narcis* had been at sea for almost thirty-six hours, and Lewis knew it would be at least as long again before she found shelter in her berth amid the comfortable waters of the Scheldt. In the brief time they had been based there it was an area he had come to know well and like even better. Known as Vlissingen by the locals, most aboard the brig invariably referred to it by the British name of Flushing; a small town that was home to a mixed community who made their living from the sea.

There were already some amongst them that Lewis was starting to think of as friends, despite their countries officially being at war. And not just the Dutch; he had discovered a substantial English community. Further inland, where the waters were more protected, were berths for over forty small craft: luggers, cutters and the like, that boasted British crews and officers and made regular trips to their homeland. They carried out a similar trade to Lewis and some of the masters had been quite forthcoming and supportive. Most were of the opinion he had drawn the short straw with the brig, however.

She may have been larger than their craft, but *Narcis* was nowhere near fast enough to avoid the attention of the revenue cutters, although it was for other reasons that they believed him the more likely to be caught. Whereas the brig must cruise for long periods within sight of land and await the attention of shore boats sent out to meet her, the luggers were nearly always run up on sheltered beaches where they would be unloaded by large gangs of land-based smugglers. Ostensibly it was the more dangerous course, but the sleek little craft were harder to spot and spent less time in British waters. And it was significant that not one had failed to return in over a year.

This information worried Lewis at first, although he soon came to reconcile his doubts. Most of the others were between thirty and forty tons; it would take many more trips to accumulate the kind of wealth he was envisaging, while the paltry armament they carried was surely hardly worth the bother.

And besides, *Narcis* was proving to be an excellent sea boat. Even with her holds filled with double-proof spirit, and much of the deck space cluttered by crates and packing cases, she kept a weather helm. The only surprise had been when topmasts were set up for the first time; her main had been foreshortened in the past and gave the brig an ungainly and rather lopsided appearance. The lack of height hardly affected her sailing performance, it still being possible to set a full-size topgallant, but made for a distinctive silhouette. This was hardly a good thing, considering the use they were putting the brig to and Lewis had already decided to apply for a conventional topmast. Spars of any description were in desperately short supply however, and he rather doubted even van Gent, with his magical network of suppliers, would be able to conjure one up.

But the crew were settling into a viable body; a few might not be the best of seamen, and there was the expected rivalry between Dutch and British, but Price was keeping everything under control, and Lewis had come to rely upon his orders being carried out with reasonable efficiency. In fact the only drawback to his new life lay in his second in command.

Reid was performing his duties adequately enough, and Lewis had been especially impressed by his aptitude on the occasions he was given leave to handle the brig. The young man could see her out of harbour and through the more basic manoeuvres as well as any and, on this current voyage, had adapted to her change of trim with ease. But there remained something about the fellow's character, something intangible, that Lewis found annoying beyond measure.

Putting it bluntly, he supposed it was the feeling that Reid was constantly looking over his shoulder. Even when giving the most mundane of orders, Lewis could sense him silently questioning his right to command, and there were times when he actually had the audacity to challenge his word.

On such occasions, Lewis had been quick to correct although, despite Reid's brittle appearance, his skin was remarkably thick, with even the strongest rebuke being weathered without visible effect. But there was some consolation in the fact that others found his behaviour every bit as annoying: on several occasions Lewis had heard the boatswain raise his voice in anger when Reid tried to interfere with the management of his precious crew, while Masters, who would normally have looked to the first mate for advice, invariably went to his captain instead. Lewis still hoped that time, and the lad's growing confidence, might see a change and had twice confronted him; openly identifying and addressing the problem in the privacy of his cabin. Neither opportunity had been a success, however, as Reid's attitude was difficult to quantify and harder still to object to. Whatever Lewis said, it came across as belly-aching, while the young man had shown no hesitation in justifying his behaviour, and repeatedly proclaimed his only intention was to be a good second officer.

Yes, he was inclined to ask questions, and though such things may be thought of as criticism, they were merely his way of better learning his craft. And if showing too much enthusiasm were truly a fault, it was one he readily admitted to, although Lewis was quick to note that, whilst doing so, Reid still managed to appear slightly hurt that anyone should feel the need to complain.

But then the lad had been a John Company officer, whereas Lewis was Royal Navy through and through, so much of the problem might stem from the difference between discipline in the two services. He told himself he had no desire for the respect usually attributed to a man-of-war's captain, and accepted that traditions such as piping the side, or diligent saluting were out of place aboard a smuggling brig, although inwardly Lewis knew he still expected them.

With such a lack of understanding between the two, it could only be a question of time before a more public dressing-down were called for. Whether Reid survived such an indignity was in doubt, but it would be a shame if not: he had many good qualities and in some ways Lewis was actually getting to like the fellow. But being in command remained a novel experience for him; he had no sailing master and, though the crossings were not exactly challenging, there was enough to think of in simply navigating the brig. That evening's goal was Orford, a small village on the Suffolk coast, and it was vital they arrived promptly. The arrangements had been made with special attention to tides, sunset, and the stages of the moon; to turn up more than a couple of hours early, or late, would be disaster. Then there was the constant threat of running in with British forces, ensuring order was kept amongst the crew, as well as a myriad more minor irritations that plagued any ship's master. So when he could not issue even the smallest command without an enquiring look or pursed lips from Reid, the annoyance became out of proportion. And now it had grown to the extent that, even so early into the voyage, Lewis found himself privately wishing for harbour, and the security he could never have believed a foreign port would provide.

But *Narcis* would be back there soon enough, and before then he must see her first load safely delivered. If he were able to keep the schedule, all they need do was simply await the boats that would come out to take his cargo off. And that was another strange thing: the Dutch seemed to be showing far more confidence in him than his countrymen.

The brig was currently crammed full of foreign contraband for delivery, while only a dozen crates of an undisclosed cargo were to be taken in return. Lewis supposed a few successful runs might instil a little more faith from the English side of the arrangement, but was not particularly bothered either way. He would be paid even if the brig returned empty and there was consolation in the fact he would not be depriving his homeland of much needed resources.

"I don't like the look of that cutter." Lewis broke from his thoughts to find that Reid had joined him by the brig's binnacle and was having the temerity to address him directly, something that would never have been allowed aboard one of His Majesty's vessels. Now the young man was staring towards the coast of England, apparently ignorant of any offence. "Off the larboard bow," he prompted, while keeping his gaze fixed. "I'd say she were revenue."

Lewis' mind cleared completely on hearing the last word; the lookout had reported the cutter some while back, and he supposed it should have been checked more carefully before then. After looking himself for several seconds, he reached for the deck glass without comment.

The optics were both clouded and scratched and it took a little time to fix the vessel, but he could see enough to tell him she was a cutter right enough. And the bowsprit may well be on the long side; if so, then he was undoubtedly examining a government vessel. He could not be certain though; she was still several miles off, night was starting to fall and most of the detail was lost against the backdrop of a cliff-ridged coast.

"I can't see a pennant," he muttered, temporising.

"Well of course not, she doesn't have to fly one." Reid's reply was almost a reprimand, and Lewis felt his anger build as he took the glass away to consider him. Sensing that he had now become the object of attention, the young man took his eyes off the sighting and turned to his captain. "Pennants need only be flown when a cutter is in chase," he announced primly.

"Indeed?" Lewis' tone was suddenly cold. "You seem uncommonly knowledgable on the subject, Mr Reid."

"I once had a mind to join them," the lad informed him, "and did a deal of reading on the subject."

Lewis raised an eyebrow. It was an avenue he himself had considered, though long before realising how far a bad name could spread.

"Well, let us hope your studies come in useful," Lewis continued, raising the glass once more. "Though not too much so: I intend on keeping as far away from the revenue service as possible."

"I declined, of course," Reid continued absent-mindedly. "In truth, they are nothing less than a bunch of sapheads."

"That's your opinion, is it?" Lewis asked tartly, lowering the glass again. "All revenue officers are fools, simply because they refused to offer you employment?"

Reid's expression had changed from one of justified resentment to frank surprise. Masters was by the binnacle and there were two regular hands next to the helmsman, but Lewis was beyond caring. "And to them do we add anyone who does not meet with your exacting standards?" This had gone on for long enough and, cutter or no, he was suddenly determined to finish it. "Tell me, Mr Reid," he continued in a savage whisper, "have you considered for a moment that the fault may lie with you? You and your airy-fairy, kiss my boots arrogance?"

Reid remained silent for a moment. Then he turned to him and lowered his head.

"I am sorry, sir – I spoke out of turn, and know such things can annoy."

Lewis, who could never resist an apology sincerely offered, nodded briefly in acknowledgement although Reid, it seemed, had more to say.

"I do appreciate that you have been tolerant with me." The words were all but whispered. "Indeed, I have never yet encountered anyone quite so patient. And suppose you will have guessed by now that I was dismissed from my previous post," he added, drawing closer.

"It seemed likely," Lewis grunted while wondering what exactly could be coming next.

"It were a misunderstanding," the lad told him. "I were suspected of squirrelling goods: signing an indent for a consignment of soap that turned out not to exist."

"Then why did you?"

"I did not," Reid replied sadly, then repeated the phrase once more and with an added 'sir,' that was barely audible.

"Someone forged my signature," he continued in a stronger tone. "I'm not sure who, though have my suspicions. But nothing could be proven and no one would speak on my behalf."

Lewis said nothing; the last point did not surprise him greatly, although it was probably not the right time to say so.

"And I do know how I might appear, sir." Once more his voice was barely audible. "However hard I try, people do not take to me. Though I never expected my unpopularity to be so great."

Again, there was nothing Lewis could add to the conversation, despite knowing he was listening to what must be a major revelation.

"And, of course, I had to protest," Reid sighed. "If I'd said nothing, I might have come away with a simple reprimand, but it seemed of the utmost importance that I clear my name. First I took the matter to the captain and, when he failed to listen, the company agent in Bombay: demanded an official enquiry, and generally made a nuisance of myself." He smiled suddenly in the privacy of the dying light and Lewis wondered if he should really hear any more. But Reid, it appeared, was determined to tell all.

"I soon learned there are more ways than one to solve a nuisance, and the easiest is simply to dispose of it. I was put off the ship and forced to beg my way home aboard a Portuguese tartan."

For a moment Lewis was conscious of a wave of empathy

between himself and this strange young man. There was no doubting the story was true, and almost comforting to learn he was not the only one to bristle at the lad's unfortunate personality – something that probably explained the reason for him to be singled out for the fraud in the first place. And Lewis could well imagine Reid making any amount of fuss, until those in authority could only see one way to both shut him up, and rid themselves of future problems. As a former commissioned Navy officer, Lewis had found a seagoing berth difficult to find, how much harder would it have been for an unpleasant junior mate with a history of theft?

"Sounds a rum deal," Lewis told him gently.

"It were, sir," Reid agreed, then added, "but probably only what I deserved."

* * *

"If escape is really what you have in mind, I think we may be able to help."

It had been an unusually pleasant meal. Aimée's invitation to eat at her home had been casual and, when he arrived, King was surprised to note not only were all her immediate family assembled in his honour, but there were also two members he had yet to meet. These were a frail but remarkably vocal old woman who was introduced as an aunt, and Antoine, Aimée's brother, a man of about his age who had excellent English which he was obviously keen to use.

"It is something we have done on a number of occasions," the man was explaining now. "In the past it has been for money, but in your particular case..."

King blinked in the gentle light from the candles. He had no idea what story Aimée had told her family, but they plainly regarded him as special, and wished he had forgone the second glass of wine Aimée's father had pressed upon him.

"Verdun is a long way from anywhere," he found himself temporising. "How exactly would you be able to assist?"

"Well, first you will have to make your way to Valenciennes," Antoine said. "It is about two hundred kilometres from here and the place of another large prison depot, although not one where you can live in such luxury as Verdun." The man gave a gentle

160

smile which King returned; it was strange how there were some people he naturally felt comfortable with. "You will understand the reasons why I cannot help before then," Antoine went on to explain. "It would be too easy to trace me back to my family; as it is, every one of us shall be taking a considerable risk."

That was undoubtedly the case. Luxurious or not, all were aware the lifestyle shared by both prisoners and civilians in Verdun was built on fragile foundations. There had been four occasions during King's short stay when the *gendarmes* had foiled escape attempts and on all but one, every civilian suspected of assisting was also hauled in. Their entire families were then removed and, on the last two occasions, the head of the household had been summarily executed in the market square.

"But once you are in Valenciennes you will be safe."

That sounded unlikely: the town must still be a considerable distance from the sea and, even though close to the French border, the neighbouring countries were under Bonaparte's rule.

"I have a small business carrying coal to the Low Countries," Antoine continued. "From certain ports you will find a boat willing to take you to England."

"Indeed?" The way it had been presented, escape suddenly seemed almost within his grasp, although inwardly King still could not believe such a thing possible. "Is such a thing so very easy?"

"Not easy, perhaps, but there are ways," the man assured him gently. "But before we discuss these, we must know how many will be coming with you."

"I-I really had not considered the matter," King began. He had, of course, and knew for sure there were others besides Manning, Timothy and Brehaut willing to join in any feasible plan. But until that point none of them had thought further than getting away from Verdun. Antoine's help was appearing like a gift from heaven although, even as vague as it was, he began to see flaws.

First, there were those two hundred kilometres between them and Valenciennes; such a journey must take several days and for all that time they would be hunted men. And even when they reached the safety of Antoine's barges, there must still be a considerable distance to cover to the coast, while a regular service must surely be constantly inspected by the authorities.

And last of all there was that final sticking point – their

*Parole*. Manning, he knew, was prepared to flout it, and Brehaut and Timothy would probably do the same, although he was still not comfortable with the idea himself. But Antoine had risked much in even offering him the chance, and it would have been foolish to voice objections at that point.

"Four, possibly five in total," he said at last.

"I assume they will be naval officers," Antoine continued casually. "So will require civilian clothing."

That was a point King certainly had considered. To travel through France in anything other than their naval uniforms would make them spies, and liable to be shot on capture.

"Some we can help with here," Antoine smiled at his mother, who nodded eagerly. "But you would do well to find what you can in the village. Do not buy all at once, and avoid paying too much for any of the items – that is assuming such a thing is possible in Verdun," he added, to mutual laughter. "Try to provide yourselves with at least one overcoat, as well as a couple of suits, shirts and appropriate linen."

King knew that would not be difficult; with the number of *détenus* in the town, there were any number of tailors willing to make civilian clothing, as well as general outfitters for the less wealthy. They must be sure of who they bought from though; the French authorities lived by bribes and were not above paying them out for valuable information.

"My parents can advise you on who you should approach," Antoine, who had obviously been following King's thoughts, continued. "I merely wanted to check on numbers so the final arrangements can be made. Five, you said?"

"For now," King agreed. "But you will forgive me, this has all come as rather a surprise."

"Of course, I suspect you were not expecting to go for some while," Antoine laughed. "And it may take some time yet, though it is best we make our plans early; after all, you are not the only ones concerned in this matter."

King looked at him doubtfully.

"Well others will have to make arrangements also," he explained. "Aimée has responsibilities in the town, and it is important her disappearance is not immediately noticed.

"Aimée?" King asked hesitantly.

"Why, yes." Antoine appeared confused. "Were you not aware? My sister intends to be escaping with you."

\* \* \*

It was a shout from Price that alerted Lewis to the danger; the revenue cutter must have been travelling faster than he had thought, and was coming up on their larboard bow. She remained a good two miles off, but closer than he would have liked, especially as the seas about them were now otherwise empty. The sun was almost set and, though the moon would be full and bright, it was not due to rise for several hours. In less than an hour they might be hidden, but the darkness would be too late to conceal them when it mattered.

"Take her three points to starboard!" He gave the order in a steady voice, despite the fact that his heart had begun to pound so noticeably. Reid also seemed to have awakened to the danger and drew hastily away while his voice rose by several notes as he ordered the yards round to keep the sails tight. The wind was now coming nearer to the larboard quarter, and *Narcis'* bows dug deep into the waves as she picked up speed.

"Only just in time," the lad snorted. "But at least we should be able to put some distance between us." The remark would normally have caused Lewis' hackles to rise, but now it simply washed over him. The only important matter was the danger close by. Their turn might have been obvious – if he had any wit at all, it should have been more gentle, and begun a while before. But three points was hardly savage, although any vessel manoeuvring so with no apparent reason might still draw the attention of an alert revenue officer.

"Masthead, what do you see there?"

His bellowed question was probably unnecessary. The lookout was a seasoned hand who had served aboard three men-of-war and would alert him to any danger in good time.

"Nothin' of note, sir," came the measured response. "A couple of doggers way off to larboard; them an' that cruiser."

Mention of the revenue vessel made Lewis turn back to her, and he noted with a slight intake of breath that she was also altering course.

163

"Cutter's coming round to give chase," Reid reported dolefully. "She appears to be making for us, what would you say?"

Lewis felt a surge of anger, and opened his mouth to deliver a reproof when he noticed Reid's expression alter.

"Forgive me, sir." The lad spoke in a softer tone, and clearly meant every word. "I spoke out of turn."

"Very good, Mr Reid," Lewis told him, and the two men's eyes met in a moment of understanding.

* * *

Holby could not imagine what he had been worried about. It was nine o'clock – early evening in gaming circles, yet already the place was heaving. Across the forest of bodies he could see players vying for a place at the hazard tables, while roulette, whist and *vingt-et-un* were equally oversubscribed. In between it all the girls were hard at work, threading their way with trays of drink, and exchanging banter with customers as if they were old friends. Which some might well be; the waiting staff had been easy enough to obtain and were employed on the basis they earned their money solely through gratuities. Some would supplement this by personal trade, which did not bother Holby in the slightest, in fact he was secretly wondering if it might not be a service he could add to others offered at the casino. The midshipmen also seemed to be settling well. The younger ones had looked almost comical in the dark suits he had acquired for next to nothing. However much they mixed and matched, all were far too large, but their naval uniforms were smart enough and the lads seemed to be making a fair fist of running the tables.

The atmosphere was thick with the scent of cigar smoke, cheap perfume and hot candles while the sound of rolling dice, excited shouts and the constant clatter of chips on slate echoed all about. But much of this passed unnoticed; all Holby could hear was the chink of coin as it entered his deep and accommodating pockets.

There had been a little trouble earlier on when a bunch of off-duty *gendarmes* had attempted to gain access. They had been drunk and were turned away efficiently enough without him needing to touch his store of bribe money. He tapped the filled purse in his breast pocket as he remembered and for a moment experienced doubts. Perhaps he had been a little high-handed; the French were welcome to use his facilities after all, and it might not have been a good move to upset even minor officials. But soon his natural optimism took over and he relaxed; the money would be better spent on more important intruders, although none had shown up and he quickly dismissed the incident.

"All well with you, Commander?" he asked suddenly as an elderly naval officer rose from one of the card tables. The man was known as a prolific gambler, although not for his ability to win.

"Capital, Holby, capital," the Commander assured him. "Can't tell you what a pleasure it is to play a straight game after all those months of losing money to those priggers at the *Café* Thierry. Guard my seat, will you? I have to pump ship."

Holby dutifully stood to one side before lowering himself onto the empty chair. It was *vingt-et-un*, a game he knew little of other than the odds, and Soames was in charge. The young man offered to deal him in, but Holby shook his head. Next to him, the commander's glass was half empty: he turned in his seat and beckoned to one of the women who came across with a bottle in each hand and topped it to the rim. The others at the table all seemed too intent on their cards to want for anything else, which pleased Holby all the more, and the woman left in a flurry of petticoats.

Yes, it was all going extremely well and he might consider rewarding himself. Holby had hardly touched a crumb of food all day and it would be little effort to break off now to find a bite to eat; there were staff enough on hand who would continue earning money for him. And then he noticed the first warnings of potential trouble.

There was a shout – not loud enough to silence the constant murmur for long, but very different from the sound of exuberant players. Holby was instantly alert: he exchanged a glance with Soames before shooting up from his seat and almost knocking over the elderly naval officer who was returning to claim it. Looking across the sea of heads he could make out Summers, the midshipman, at the roulette wheel stationed nearest the door. The lad was also concerned, and made to abandon his place, despite instant protests from the throng of players.

For a moment true fear grabbed Holby as he roughly pushed his way through the crowd but, as he approached the staircase, reason took its place. There was surely no need for anxiety; respectable men of business did not fluster and panic but behaved in a calm and measured manner. If one of the gamblers was causing a problem it would be solved. Even if the *gendarmes* had decided to return, they could also be dealt with, while he had a purse of gold in his waistcoat pocket that was large enough to dazzle the eyes of even the most myopic official who might decide against his right to run a business. Summers turned towards him at that moment, and gave a look of relief.

"There were a bunch of guards trying to enter, and this time with an officer," the lad told him in a shrill voice. "Adams ordered the entrance bolted, but they won't go away."

"An officer?" Holby asked aghast, as he pushed the boy to one side. He could see up the staircase now and, sure enough, Adams was with the seaman employed to guard the door. And the fool was doing exactly that; standing with his hand placed firmly against the heavy oak as if it was his weight alone that kept it shut. "What are you about there?" Holby demanded, as he bounded up the stairs.

"Armed men, and they mean business," Adams told him seriously.

"They tried to get past, but I were able to stop them," Cranston added with an element of pride.

"Never mind that, if an officer wishes to see me, he should be admitted," Holby snapped as he reached for his purse. "Open the door at once, I shall deal with this."

"I'm not sure you'd want that, Mr Holby," Cranston warned.

"Do not tell me what I want," the older man snarled, and was about to add more when there was a loud thud. All three turned to stare at the door, which seemed unchanged. Then the noise was repeated and the blade of an axehead appeared through the thick wood, showering them in splinters.

\* \* \*

Lewis had begun to pace the brig's tiny quarterdeck. A short time ago he had been thoroughly out of sorts and finding it hard to control his growing anger, but now it was as if a dam had been

166

breached, allowing the pent-up emotions to flow out.

It seemed obvious that much of what he objected to in Reid's behaviour was not the man's fault. He had an unfortunate manner that was almost guaranteed to annoy, but this was outweighed by a greater knowledge of seamanship than Lewis had suspected. And the recent revelation had revealed far more than mistreatment by the India Company; Lewis felt he knew the lad a little better now, and might be able to cope with his nettlesome ways. He approached the taffrail and paused in his pacing to look back to what was a far more important irritation, and one to which he would do well to give his full attention.

The cutter they had sighted earlier was still with them. At first, simple chance could have dictated their courses to coincide but now it seemed otherwise. Currently she was off their larboard quarter and making every effort to forereach. The revenue vessel's single mast seemed to be bowing slightly under the pressure of the excessive amount of canvas she carried and, even at such a distance, Lewis could make out the cloud of spray that was being thrown up from her bows.

And her efforts were not in vain; the cutter was also close-hauled but, unlike *Narcis*, lay on the starboard tack, so not only was she coming up at a considerable rate, but also closing to larboard. If the situation did not alter she would catch them for certain, yet Lewis was unsure how to change matters without inviting yet more suspicion. Then a movement to his right distracted him for a moment, and Reid approached.

"There's the pennant, sir," he said, and Lewis wondered exactly what it was that made the young man so annoying.

"Pennant?" he asked, vaguely.

"What we were discussing earlier," Reid seemed to suppress a sigh as he pointed to the oncoming cutter. "You will see that flag at her masthead – it's what the revenue fly when they mean business. By rights we're supposed to heave to on seeing it, an' I should not be surprised if a shot or two don't come our way afore long. We really should prepare to meet with them."

Lewis pointedly waited until the lad had muttered a guilty 'sir', then turned back to regard the cutter once more. But he was right; *Narcis* might be reasonably fast for her class but was no match for a cutter. For a moment it all seemed too much; they were less than two days into their first run which was already looking as if it might become their last. Perhaps the best thing to do would be to spill their wind and throw themselves on the mercy of the revenue men? But even as he considered the terrible option, all irritation began to clear, and was replaced with something far more constructive.

Glancing over to larboard, the shore was starting to disappear into the dusk and there was no other shipping in sight; nothing to witness the plan that was steadily forming in his mind. It might not be exactly what he would choose, but Lewis had known he could not last a year without some action against his homeland being called for. It was just a shame it must happen on his first trip.

"There's still a chance," Reid was continuing. "The normal procedure is to heave to, and they may not bother to search: if we carry on as we are, she'll rummage us for certain."

But Lewis was not listening; a myriad of thoughts tumbled through his brain. If only he had a little more time to consider each in detail.

"Shall I order us to heave to?" Reid chanced.

"No," Lewis told him. "I have another idea."

The younger man went to speak, before thinking better of it.

"We shall be taking more positive action," Lewis continued. "You and Mr Masters will oblige me by seeing our guns are cleared away."

\* \* \*

The remains of the front door had all but dissolved and those standing at the top of the stairs found themselves being swept to one side as the stream of *gendarmes* entered.

"All stay still and no one will be harmed." It was a commanding voice and belonged to a surprisingly young *Capitaine* who strode confidently after his men. Holby and Adams were roughly pushed down the staircase and towards the scene of confusion that had been created below. Girls screamed, men shouted and there was the crash of dropped bottles and breaking furniture. Adams noticed Summers, who looked pale and confused.

"We shall be taking names," the young officer continued, "then most will be allowed to leave. However, those in charge of

168

this establishment must remain and face the consequences of their actions." The words may have been spoken through a thick accent, but they carried authority, and order was soon established. Summers looked anxiously to Adams; the two had been driven against the back wall of the cellar and now faced a line of blank-faced *gendarmes* wielding drawn cutlasses.

"Does he mean us?" he hissed anxiously.

"I believe so," Adams confirmed.

"But we weren't running the place," the younger man protested, and Adams raised his eyes to heaven.

"I think you'll find we were," he sighed.

* * *

The revenue cutter was closing on them fast, although that, Lewis decided, might almost be an advantage. Darkness was now complete and every mile made on their current heading would have to be won back later if they were to reach their rendezvous by midnight. And there was another reason not to delay; Lewis had resigned himself to what must be done, but would prefer to get it over with as swiftly as possible.

Masters and Reid were standing at the taffrail, and he came up behind them. There was still no moon, but the stars were bright, making the cutter's massive sails easy to spot.

"Sails sweetly, don't she?" Reid, unaware of his presence, murmured to Masters, and Lewis could only agree. He had been aboard a cutter once, but that was in harbour. Since then he had thought of them as beamy little craft that made scant provision for their crew and stank abominably. But now he was seeing a different side to the class, and could appreciate their true merits.

It was generally accepted that a well handled cutter was the fastest seagoing vessel afloat, and what he was currently witnessing confirmed it. The distance between them was diminishing even as they watched; in no time *Narcis* would be in range of the craft's popgun broadside and not much longer before the first of the customs officers attempted to board.

"Mr Masters, you will oblige me by attending the gun crews; Mr Reid, stand by to assist as we wear ship."

Both men started at the sound of his voice. Lewis noticed the youngster's eyes were unusually bright in the poor light; the lad had never seen action before and would be nervous. Reid on the other hand appeared rather too confident as he strode forward to take up position next to the binnacle, and Lewis wondered for a moment which emotion he preferred.

"I'm expecting to take them to larboard," he added to the boy. "See your shots are trained at the tophamper, and call any man you require to assist in reloading." If the battle was to be won, it would be by cannon fire rather than sail, and there was no danger in letting everyone know it.

Masters mumbled an assent, and then Lewis was left alone. He looked back to the cutter once more. She was far clearer now; small details of her rig could be picked out and then, even as he looked, a flash of yellow marked the firing of a warning shot.

"Ready about: upon my word..." he called, as the dull sound of the discharge reached them. It would have been a blank, but that did not alter the fact they were officially under fire. And the cutter was a government vessel, with little legal difference between it and the many Royal Navy craft Lewis had served aboard. If what he intended took place, there would soon be actual shot flying between them and he might add treachery to his list of crimes. There was little choice, however; *Narcis* was not fast enough to out-run it and, with no way of concealing her cargo, he and all her crew, would be taken for certain.

"Stations for wearing ship!" Reid called out eagerly and Lewis paused, but for only a second.

"Main clewgarnets and buntlines," he ordered, although with less enthusiasm than the mate. "Bring her about and be ready larboard battery!"

# Chapter Fifteen

*Narcis* staggered violently at the brutal handling; they were now presenting their broadside to the oncoming cutter but, however tempting the prospect, Lewis rejected the idea of firing immediately. The revenue vessel had not slowed, if anything her speed was increasing, although that might be an illusion. But if he expected his gunners to lay their pieces correctly, the brig must be as stable as he could make her.

He waited while *Narcis* continued the turn, his eyes never leaving the cutter's prow, nor the cloud of spray that steamed from it. Slowly, oh so slowly, *Narcis* came back, the wind began to find her canvas, and then she was returning on what was very nearly the reciprocal to her previous course.

"Ready, Mr Masters!"

The lad looked back from the waist, then addressed the servers grouped about their weapons. One raised a hand as if in confirmation and Lewis wondered how they would fare. To date they had held three dumb show exercises and all had been in harbour. The one time he authorised a live firing was a week back, during one of the brig's working up forays. Many were former service men and the evolution had gone reasonably well, except for one supposedly seasoned gun captain who was clumsy enough to break his foot. The difference between exercise and firing in anger was vast, however, and the crew of the cutter was bound to be more accustomed to their weapons. Then, just as Lewis was considering his opponent, an additional worry occurred. He had no idea how the British amongst his crew would feel about firing on their own countrymen. None would wish to face the noose, which might be the alternative for any deserters amongst them, but the odd cloud of conscience could make aiming more difficult.

They would be passing the speeding cutter a cable or so off; an ideal distance if Masters was to target the tophamper. The brig's guns were already loaded with round shot, and there had not been time to replace this with chain or bar, but even a six-pound ball could do damage to a fragile rig if properly placed.

"Upon my word!" Lewis called out, his hand instinctively rising. A ripple of flame spread down the cutter's larboard side as he paused; she too was firing. It would probably only be four-pound balls, and *Narcis* had a heavier frame, but wise to discharge his own shots before the enemy's arrived.

"Fire!" he ordered, bringing his hand down, and the larboard battery erupted in a ragged broadside that spanned several seconds.

Lewis never did discover where the cutter's shots landed; some might have fallen short, or passed harmlessly overhead, but there was no doubt about the damage his own cannon wreaked. The cutter's huge mainsail billowed dramatically in the starlight, then appeared to fly off into the night as, robbed of the mast's support, the hull rolled violently. Her main spar began to tumble as the entire craft slewed slightly and soon she was little more than a parody of her former, elegant, self.

*Narcis* was passed in no time; from his position on the quarterdeck, Lewis looked back and noticed how his adversary was already starting to founder. Some degree of wallowing was to be expected, but the cutter's freeboard seemed remarkably low, and soon the decks were undoubtedly awash. He swallowed dryly; the brig's shots had been aimed high, his only intention had been to wound: knock out a few sails and possibly take down the mast, although it appeared *Narcis'* meagre broadside had been far more efficient.

Now the darkness was taking the wreck from him, but he could see enough to know they had caused something far more significant than a simple dismasting. What had been a frail but lovely thing barely moments before was now utterly destroyed, and it had been of his making. Lives may have already been lost, with others to follow; they would also be directly attributable to him. Although there was one stark fact that seemed to echo about his brain as he strived for cognitive thought: he had fired upon a government vessel. More than that, he had almost certainly sunk her.

* * *

Early the following day, Banks headed a small group that filed in to the Commandant's office. Wirion was present and in his customary position at a huge and ornate walnut desk. It was truly a substantial affair and came with a matching throne-like chair although, rather than make him appear important, the furniture only emphasised their owner's lack of stature. He sat back to survey his British visitors and Banks wondered briefly if the Commandant's feet were actually touching the floor.

The new arrivals were not greeted in any way other than an airy wave to a row of far more serviceable chairs opposite. The Reverend Wolfe cast a glance at Banks as they seated themselves, and Captain Brenton pointedly scraped his seat noisily on the wooden floor, but still nothing was said. Then Wirion broke the silence.

"You will be aware of my reason for calling this extraordinary meeting," he told them. "Several of your men have disgraced themselves, as well as the service they represent. This is not the first time such a thing has happened, and you cannot expect me to allow such liberties to be taken without punishment."

"Mr Holby was a purser, and his business had no connection with his Britannic Majesty's Navy," Banks began. "He was also unaware of any restrictions to running a gaming room. Now that the position has been made clear, I am certain he will accept any reasonable fine, and nothing more need be said of the incident."

Wirion snorted. "I think not, Captain. To begin with, the man concerned clearly knew what he was about and is already on his way to Bitche. He will remain there for a considerable period; time enough for him to reflect on his shameful behaviour." Wirion leant forward and began to play with the blotter on his desk. "But we are not here to discuss his future; it is that of the others who were part of his scheme that concerns me," he continued. "Some are also King's officers I might add, and equally guilty."

Banks was careful to keep his face free of emotion. It was a familiar scenario; if Wirion was determined for those assisting Holby to share the horrors of Bitche, they would have been sent at the same time. This was simply a ploy; a device to extract money and possibly prestige from the British, along with as much unpleasantness as was possible.

"The men you speak of were employed by Mr Holby,"

Captain Brenton broke in with his customary low-pitched drawl. "One was an ordinary seaman, who considered himself acting under orders. None had any hand in planning the casino and neither were they to benefit from the profits."

"So they were not to be paid?" Wirion asked with a look of feigned surprise. "No, I disagree. I think they were as much responsible for the whole *épouvantable* affair as the purser and should be made to share his disgrace. I have been lenient in the past, some would say too much so. You and your countrymen are here as guests and lead lives that are luxurious, compared with those of Frenchmen in England. And yet still you take advantage of my better nature, while cheating your own, as well as the lawful inhabitants of the town that gives you shelter."

There was a pause; so accustomed were the British to stand-offs such as this that neither felt like going further, and it was only with effort that Wolfe raised the customary argument.

"*Général*, do I have to remind you that many of what you are pleased to call 'guests' are being held here illegally? And, though English prisons may not be so comfortable as Verdun, your countrymen held there are granted a full *Parole d'Honneur*, without the need for frequent *appels*. Besides, many have been returned to France in the hope of exchange, even though your Emperor has not seen fit to recognise the gesture by reciprocating."

"Pah – it is an old argument, and one we shall not resolve this morning," Wirion told them contemptuously. "If you have nothing more constructive to offer, I have no alternative other than to send your men to Bitche."

"You are clearly touting for a bribe," Brenton grunted, and was rewarded by a slight hiss from Wolfe.

"Not a bribe, Captain," Wirion replied coldly. "I do not approve of such things and neither do my men. I merely wish to continue offering what services I am able. These do not come cheaply and, when my tolerance is tried in instances such as last night, I am less willing to provide them. Take the recent provision of horse racing; you wish for that to continue, I presume?"

"If that is your example, *Général*, I fear you have chosen a bad one," Wolfe huffed. "I for one should not care a jot if the whole horrible business were done away with."

"But I think we are aware of what the Commandant is

174

suggesting," Banks interrupted. "You wish for some monetary contribution to be made that will guarantee future events," he continued, looking directly at Wirion, and ignoring Brenton's low rumble of protest.

"Some recognition of our efforts would indeed be acceptable," Wirion confirmed smoothly. "And might mean your junior officers can remain, although any contribution would have to be generous were I to allow them to continue living in their current quarters."

"We may have funds sufficient to keep them out of Bitche," Brenton grunted. "For anything extra, you will have to approach the men directly. Now exactly how much do you require?"

\* \* \*

"I don't think you understand quite what will be involved," King told Aimée firmly. "It won't be like a simple journey – there shall be danger and probably much discomfort."

"*Au contraire*, Commander!" she replied, a mischievous glint in her eye. "It is you who do not know what you are talking of. This is my country: *Monsieur* Brehaut speaks the language well I admit, but not as a true Frenchman. And neither does he know the complexities of living in France. Why, you should not last long without being able to buy bread and not cause suspicion. Or knowing who is likely to belong to the old regime, and so be trusted."

King was silent for a moment; what she said made perfect sense and part of him would have liked nothing better than for Aimée to return to England with him. Return, and live there together as husband and wife and let the war, the Royal Navy and all the world's troubles go hang. But there was something else that bothered him beyond the difficulties of escaping through France: something that blocked such a utopian future far more effectively. And that something was his wife.

King and Aimée had only been together a matter of weeks and there were many things each would have failed to tell the other, although King's lack of information about his marital status was not due to oversight or simple want of time. He supposed he simply loved too easily, and without considering the consequences; certainly his romance with Juliana and their subsequent marriage had been in haste. They had met while he was a prisoner of war in the Texel; at the time the two seemed perfectly suited but, when his situation changed and she was able to flee to England, they could not have been less compatible. And there had been another woman in his life since then, one that King had loved almost as deeply as he now did Aimée and he supposed it was hardly surprising she had not taken to the idea of becoming a mistress.

But being with Aimée meant so much that he was even fostering private thoughts about abandoning any attempt to escape in order to remain with her in Verdun. The fact of Juliana's existence would not go away, though; sooner or later the truth must come out, if not from his own lips, then through some wicked twist of fate. When it did, he would far rather be in England than France, for the prospect of living in the same town as a spurned lover would be too terrible to bear.

They were lying beneath a fine oak tree. The sun, though not hot, was very bright, and made the canopy a welcome shelter, although King's eyes were slightly closed.

"We have only to reach Valenciennes," he protested softly. "Once we meet up with your brother, all will be fine."

"Antoine will still have to see you to the coast," Aimée responded. "You are to be disguised as bargemen and such workers usually take their wives with them; so many bachelors might arouse suspicion, especially when only one speaks French."

That was hardly fair; when Aimée talked of wives, King's mind became totally distracted.

"Besides, how do you intend to get to Valenciennes?" she continued. "Wander through the woods and live on acorns? Ah, but I was forgetting, it is only a few hundred kilometres, there should be no difficulty."

King rolled on to one side and smiled at her. "And you will protect us?" he asked.

"I shall keep you from danger." She seemed suddenly serious. "And see that you do not behave too much like the fools."

The two considered this for a moment, and the pause was only broken by Aimée kissing him quickly on the lips.

King lay back and sighed. Having her come with them did seem entirely logical, and truly there was nothing he would have liked better. Besides, if he was so certain she would find out about

Juliana eventually, would it be so terribly wrong to enjoy a little time together first?

"You are not sure," she said at last. "And I will not force you. We have hardly known each other long and perhaps I am assuming too much."

His eyes opened in an instance and he reached out for her. "Do not think that – never think that. I want to be with you; nothing is more important to me than that. But I feel it will be dangerous."

"It is a danger I am prepared to accept, to be with you," she told him simply. "We should be together, we belong together, and there is no obstacle too large to stop that from happening."

He closed his eyes again and smiled. If only that were true.

* * *

"I was aware the fellow is not altogether sound," Wolfe grumbled, "but in this he has gone too far."

Once more the officers were meeting in Captain Brenton's house, and once more the Commandant was the subject of their discussion.

"Maybe so," Brenton agreed, "but you have to admit a certain logic to his thinking."

"Logic?" the cleric demanded. "I see no logic in demanding such a sum; especially when the men concerned have done nothing wrong in themselves."

Banks said nothing, although he could hardly concur. In any other prison, establishing gambling rooms would have been considered a major misdemeanour, and one where all involved could expect the harshest of punishments. It was just the apparent laxity of Verdun that made the junior officers' involvement seem relatively blameless. But be they guilty or innocent, twenty thousand francs was a high sum, merely to allow them to remain in the town.

"Do we have such funds?" Brenton asked, only to receive a savage shake of the head from Wolfe.

"No we do not," he stated firmly.

"We might apply to Lloyd's?" Banks suggested, but Wolfe was not to be shaken.

"To what end? The best we may achieve is the relative

freedom of youngsters who should have known better, while there would be the very real risk of finding ourselves faced with a sum twice as high on the next occasion."

There was certainly no arguing with that. Even in the year or so that Banks had been a resident of Verdun, he had watched the Commandant's fines creep ever higher. All assumed that little, if any, of the money collected was forwarded to the French government; it was simply an artifice that allowed Wirion an apparently endless source of income, and there was a measure of satisfaction in realising the bottom had been reached.

But that in no way compensated for the fact that four young officers and a seaman were to be sent to Bitche, a place where they would be subjected to conditions that disgraced those of a common slaver.

"Well, we have stated our case," Brenton declared. "I don't think the *Général* can be in any doubt of our opinion in the matter."

"And quite right too," Wolfe agreed. "I think you put it very eloquently, Sir Richard."

Banks bowed his head slightly but made no comment. He had certainly stated their position plainly, although that had mainly been due to anger caused by the colossal sum involved. But now he was able to consider the matter more carefully little had changed; it was still an obscene amount of money, even if Banks was soft-hearted enough to allow feelings for the men concerned to alter his thoughts.

"Perhaps if we made a counter offer?" he suggested at last.

"How do you mean, sir?" Wolfe asked and Banks could tell this would not be well received.

"I would say offer maybe ten thousand; or even five, perhaps with the promise of more when it became available."

"Do you think he would accept such a sum?" Brenton was clearly unsure, and Banks was forced to agree with him.

"It would be better than nothing," he supposed. "Which is what he will get if not."

"Whatever the amount, I feel we have been bobbed for long enough," Wolfe grunted, and it was proof of his emotion that he should use such a low term. "Whether the officers were employed or not, they must have been aware of the risk they ran. The funds we have are for the welfare of prisoners, both civilian and military; to use them in such a way goes against the grain. I might have been tempted to release a few hundred, but what the Commandant speaks of is totally outrageous."

"It is a shame the surgeon's cure is not pacifying him sufficiently," Brenton mused, although Wolfe did not appear to hear.

"If we give in now we shall only make ourselves liable for further exorbitant claims in the future," the cleric continued. "And frankly I should be against paying him even so much as a penny."

* * *

It was undoubtedly the largest group of musicians Lovemore had ever played with, and he could not have been more delighted. A proper band: there was another flautist, maybe not as gifted as him, but an affable cove for a Frenchman and also proficient on the *flageolet*. And two fiddlers, in addition to his friend from the dances, including one who had what Lovemore thought must be some form of bass viol. Then there was a dour looking fellow with a pockmarked face who played any number of brass instruments, a particularly worthy drummer and a comely young wench who everyone considered welcome company, even if she was not so talented when it came to playing her harp.

And, for probably the first time in his life, Lovemore fitted perfectly. He had always considered himself a seaman foremost and musician a long way second, but never had he felt so at home amid a crew as he did in that small band.

He had also been especially lucky in other ways; the engagement could not have come at a more opportune time. Both he and Cranston had assumed jobs for the working man would be ten a penny in Verdun, but that was not the case. With roughly ten thousand French inhabitants, the town provided more than enough home-grown labourers for its needs, and the two of them had been lucky to secure what work they could in Mr Holby's doomed casino.

Lovemore had sensed danger in the place from the off and, when he and Cranston were invited to stay on to work at guarding the door, had politely declined. It was a shame Cranston ignored his warning and now lay imprisoned in the Citadel, although his friend was of the type that usually made the best of a situation, and Lovemore was not unduly concerned.

And playing in the band paid far better than anything the miserly purser was prepared to pay, while the time already spent with the theatre group had been as exciting as it was lucrative: from the first night, Lovemore sensed he had found a home.

He threw himself into the music, spending most of the day in practice to ensure his place, while the evenings became a blur of hot lights, dancing feet and rapturous applause. Lovemore had no illusions; the whole affair was nothing more than a Penny Gaff. Some of the songs were undeniably coarse, and a good few of the female performers made up for what they lacked in talent by exposing rather too much flesh, but still he was captivated by the magic of it all. In fact so engrossed had he become that those premonitions which had haunted him in the past were all but forgotten. Lovemore had sailed on many seas, seen every form of weather the gods were capable of and even survived more than a few violent actions, but this was undoubtedly the best adventure ever.

The group of travelling players numbered twenty-three in all; in addition to the core of musicians, there were a number who spent two hours of every day upon a stage. Between them they seemed to encompass most, if not all, of the entertainment arts, and Lovemore had never encountered such a concentration of talent before. Some sang, others juggled and there was a magician who carried a mildly haunted look that the seaman found strangely familiar. But all shared the same ability to perform and seemed willing to do anything that might entertain an audience.

The pity of it all was that soon it must end. It was something Lovemore had tried hard not to think about although, on the rare occasions when his mind wandered to the fact, an odd feeling of reassurance quickly appeared to comfort him and he could not take the concept of finishing seriously. Something must come up: the Commandant would order them to stay an extra week, or another way must appear for him to remain with his new-found friends.

And at times the concept of escape occurred to him; the group were a tight bunch, but he had already been admitted into their fold. Knowing their language was an obvious bonus and it wasn't long before some were better friends than the mess mates he had sailed with for many years. At least two, including his fellow flautist, were conscripts on the run from Bonaparte's army, and another, one of the young men who danced so delicately and could sing like a nightingale, was wanted throughout France for a series of perverse crimes. He sensed that, if chance presented, he would be welcomed as a permanent member, but was unsure how to go about making an escape, and it was not something he could afford to try, without being sure of a successful outcome.

As a regular seaman, Lovemore was not bound by any of the honourable strictures that seemed to tie his officers to Verdun: no signed paper had been required of him and, as he was undoubtedly a commoner, neither was he asked to give his word. But there could be no doubt that, should he be caught trying to leave with the players, he would be punished. That might mean simply being shot dead by a *gendarme* – an act considered so commendable that it often led to promotion for the officer concerned – or simply a one-way trip to Bitche.

And there was another consideration; he may be welcomed into the fold, and even able to make his escape from Verdun, but could he really leave Cranston behind? Had he retained his liberty, the seaman could have proved his worth as a stage hand and might have stood in for the drummer on occasions but, for as long as his friend remained in the mighty stone tower, there was little point in thinking further.

The worry of what he should do grew with each successive night and seemed to fill much of his waking thoughts. On several occasions he had considered speaking to *Monsieur* Lamar, the players' leader. He was a remote and strangely private man who rarely attended rehearsals and never performances, preferring to spend much of his time in a small and windowless carriage that served as both office and bed place. To consult him would be the obvious solution: Lovemore could discover his exact position and whether a permanent place would be found for him. Although there was something about their enigmatic leader that discouraged contact, and he was not the only member of the company who thought so.

Lamar made all the negotiations, paid their wages and handled the group's list of engagements with supreme efficiency while never appearing anything other than courteous and well mannered. But he also carried a strange authority that did not promote casual conversation, or the asking of favours. Lovemore supposed a strong and remote character was needed to control the eclectic bunch of performers and took his lead from the others by keeping his distance.

And then there was the final option. He knew that, if he concentrated upon them hard enough, his premonitions would tell him all he needed to know; whether Lamar could be trusted and what exactly was the best means of escape. This was yet another route he was not prepared to take, however. Even without encouragement, Lovemore's awareness of the future was growing steadily and, however useful it threatened to become, he would never be comfortable with it.

So, although he sensed he would get a good reception, he did not broach the subject with anyone. Instead he stayed silent, thinking only of the music, and the last few performances he would be giving, while stubbornly ignoring the inner feelings that were ready and able to tell him all he wanted to know.

* * *

"There is little I can do for you if you do not take the medicine I prescribe." Manning spoke with professional authority and, to his credit, Wirion appeared to take notice.

"It is the tablets," he whined, not meeting the surgeon's glance. "They make me feel more ill than I am. I find I sleep most of the time and when I do wake, my wife complains that I become irritable."

Manning made no comment. Wirion's wife was something of a legend in Verdun, and one who used her authority, albeit referred, to its full extent. Anyone who organised a social gathering where her name was not on the guest list was playing a dangerous game, and she frequently shocked both British and French by riding along the *Rue Moselle* with her legs completely bare.

"Are you taking any of my medication?" he asked, only to receive a sullen shake of the head from the Commandant. "Then there is nothing I can do." Manning slapped his notes down on the desk and bent to collect his medical bag.

182

"I am incurable?" Wirion still seemed to be looking into the middle distance as he spoke, and Manning realised he had not actually exchanged eye contact throughout the examination. He stopped and considered his patient, the small man who hid behind an inordinately large desk.

"Yes, quite incurable," he confirmed. "But then I made it perfectly clear that the condition could not be healed when we first met. I can offer you some relief and, almost certainly, an extension of life, though nothing can be done unless you agree to take the treatment I prescribe."

"Very well," the man agreed sullenly. "I shall try with it again."

"I'm glad," Manning sighed, and placed the bag on the floor once more.

"You should be, *Docteur*, because my terms remain the same." Wirion spoke softly and finally looked at him, although it was with a belligerent gaze. "If my condition is not markedly improved by the summer, I shall have no hesitation in sending you to Bitche."

# Chapter Sixteen

It had taken just over a week to make the journey and Holby felt he could remember every moment of it. The days had not been so bad; a simple matter of trudging along a road once more and he was thoroughly used to that. It was the nights that were especially terrible.

Not for him a comfortable bed in some auberge or roadside inn, luxury that had been customary during the long walk to Verdun, instead he had been chained in some godforsaken stable, with straw for warmth and a solid roof only if his luck was in. And now they had finally arrived, and what was rumoured to be the strongest fortification in France hung heavy on the horizon, there would still be no relief. Holby had been accompanied through the journey by the same three *gendarmes* who were given the duty as a form of penance. Consequently, they were not particularly keen to see to his comfort and the only one who had any command of English filled the quieter moments by explaining the niceties of his new home. Bitche, it seemed, was no Verdun: far more than eight days' march separated the two. If the truth be known, the distance was more like several centuries.

The place housed several specific types of prisoner. The top grade were those being held for diplomatic reasons. They were the most fortunate and lived in conditions that might be described as tolerable, although nothing like the kind Holby had so foolishly relinquished at Verdun. The second grade was for men who had previously tried to escape from other depots, but since seen the error of their ways. The horror of time already spent at Bitche had worn away at their minds; many were little more than imbeciles and prone to either interminable moaning or silent tears, and were not regarded as too great a risk. They were allowed cells of a sort, all be they horribly overcrowded, but at least most were set above ground level, with some even benefiting from beds and natural light.

Then there were two other grades, one of which seemed likely to fit Holby. They were the ones his guard was best acquainted with, so much of his description focussed on them. Holby would be housed below ground with months passing without the hint of sun or a breath of fresh air. And there would be no demarcations, just wide open dungeons for all to share and any difference in rank conveniently forgotten. All would have to struggle to survive, with constant fighting over the meagre rations. These would be similar in content to food given to wild animals in captivity, and served in the same manner.

But competition for such quarters was surprisingly fierce, as the alternative, that given to the lowest form of prisoner, was even worse. Raw rock formed the walls of the lowest dungeons, while the floors were of bare earth which, owing to the lack of sanitation, were constantly awash.

Holby had listened without comment, closing his mind to what was to come, and thinking only of the mistakes he had made in the past – mistakes that would not be repeated when the chance came again. Which he was sure it would: for all that Bitche and its horrors appalled him, he remained a survivor. There had been several in Verdun who had endured such punishment; they might have been damaged by the experience, but it was obviously possible to survive and he would also.

Or he would escape; it was an idea that had never occurred to him before as Verdun apparently offered everything he needed as well as the security to enjoy it. And though Bitche was a magnificent fortress, there would still be a way to break free, with one of his cunning being the most likely to find it. The thought comforted him during the cold nights and long, description-filled, days. And then, on the last evening, his guard had remembered something else: there was another category of prisoner.

This was reserved for persistent insurgents; those who had the temerity to rise up against the guards, or committed similar acts of rebellion expected of men when pushed to the limit. A few could even have been foolish enough to attempt escape from Bitche, and for these there was the punishment dungeon.

Holby hadn't wanted to hear anything of that, but his guard had obliged him with a full description and, when it was finally over, he knew there would be no attempts to leave for him, and he would become a model prisoner in Bitche for as long as was necessary.

"The start of the last week, my friend."

Lovemore had been trying to fix the annoying leak from the long F key on his flute and looked around in annoyance. He had seen the slight figure that stood before him on a number of occasions: he was one of the players, older than most though not elderly and undoubtedly gifted when it came to the magic tricks that were part of his act. But, out of all the performers who made up the small troop, he was one Lovemore had rarely addressed directly; in fact he had gone out of his way to avoid the man.

There was a certain presence about him: a personal atmosphere that was ever constant and instilled an element of concern, almost fear, within the seaman. And now – now that he was being forced into conversation – Lovemore felt no less cautious.

"Aye, last week it is," he confirmed in a determinedly neutral manner, before returning his attention to the flute.

"Forgive me, we have not been introduced," the man persisted, while proffering his hand. "My name is Marcel Garrett."

Lovemore placed the small screwdriver down and took the stranger's hand, mumbled his own name, then immediately collected the tool once more and returned to his work.

"You have enjoyed your time with us." It was not a question, and Lovemore felt a chill of foreboding.

"I have," he admitted.

"Perhaps you wish to stay longer." Again, this came across as more of a statement, and the seaman paused.

"But perhaps also you are worried that we might not accept you in our little theatre?"

Lovemore now regarded the magician full in the face. "You seem to know a lot about me, Mr Garrett," he said.

"Oh, but I know a good deal about many things." The man's smile was actually quite beguiling, although Lovemore felt no inclination to relax. "As would you, if your powers were put to good use."

"Powers?" Now Lovemore was feeling decidedly uncomfortable. He had never discussed such things before, yet this anonymous Frenchman seemed to know all about them, as well as his future plans.

"You need not worry, we are loyal," Garrett continued. "And I am not meaning the actors, though they can also be trusted." He smiled again, and this time it caused the pale-coloured paste covering his face to crack and Lovemore realised the magician must be far older than he appeared. "No, I am speaking about those who share such abilities. I am one, and it would have been strange if you had not met others during the course of your life."

"I don't know what you are talking of," Lovemore maintained stoically, and the man appeared to lose patience.

"I am talking of your capacity to see the future," he stated quickly. "Gain impressions of things you have no right to understand. You probably began some years before, and the ability will have increased, even though you may not have wished it. Such powers will grow further, if allowed, or they can be stifled, as you are doing now since you choose to deny their existence. But I can see the power inside you, Mr Lovemore, just as easily as you can see it within me."

\* \* \*

On *Narcis'* lower deck, opinions differed, and nowhere was the argument stronger than in Laidlaw's mess. All present had served in several Royal Navy ships and, although a customs cutter was hardly the same, were aware they had been responsible for the sinking. But it was not the loss of one of His Majesty's vessels that caused the controversy. Ships might always be rebuilt: men's lives could not. It was possible that some, even all of those aboard the frail craft had escaped with their lives – possible, but unlikely. And though most in *Narcis* had seen action before and were doubtless accountable for the deaths of many, it was a different matter despatching a recognised enemy to someone who could have come from their own home town.

"I don't see that there were any choice," Clinton maintained yet again. "If we had stopped and fished a few out, we would only have had to knock 'em on the head straight after. Wouldn't do to let any go free, not if they could peach on us later."

"We could have taken them back to 'olland," Judy, a particularly heavily set seaman, suggested. "Handed them in, then they could have sat out the war in some prison."

Judy was similar to Laidlaw, being a former R.N. hand and also a deserter, although his means of defection had been more spectacular than most. Judy's ship had already spent three long months in harbour under the wedding garland when he had the ingenious idea of swapping his clothes with one of the doxie's. Once suitably attired, and with a face covered in paint that had been enthusiastically applied by the girls, he had passed right under the first lieutenant's nose before leaving in a shore boat.

But on reaching land he found his problems were only just beginning: with all his coin spent on closing the deal and no clothes other than those bartered for, the port was suddenly an unsafe place. He spent three days dodging the press as well as the attention of several groups of seamen who viewed his predicament in diverse ways before finally escaping to the nearby countryside. But news of his exploits soon spread, and the nickname became established.

"And what if they were exchanged?" Clinton replied.

"French don't exchange seamen as a rule," Judy again.

"Not *Navy* seaman," Jones chipped in. "But these weren't Navy, these would have been customs men, and we're dealing with the Dutch, remember?"

"Frogs and Square-Heads? Makes no difference; both want us to carry on running booty, otherwise we wouldn't have been given that snug little berth in Flushing. Gobblers are just as much the enemy to them, and they ain't going to let them go."

"But it don't change matters," another chipped it. "Fact remains, we sunk a King's ship, an' that sort of thing don't get forgotten."

\* \* \*

Much of what the magician told him made sense, although Lovemore was still digesting some of it. And it didn't help that, despite what appeared to be a common bond, he was no nearer to liking the man. But Garrett seemed to know what he was talking about, while there could be no doubt that he was every bit as gifted as Lovemore.

And, despite what the man had said, this was the first time he had come across someone with a similar talent. Although that might not be quite true, Lovemore realised, there could have been others: brief acquaintances who may have held related powers. But he had sensed as much and always avoided their company. Apparently Garrett was more fortunate, or perhaps brave.

For fifteen years he had been the personal servant to a French nobleman, the *Marquis* de Puységur who was equally talented, and also had the time, money and interest to fully investigate the phenomenon. After offering a suitably generous reward, a stream of seemingly like-minded souls were attracted to the house and Garrett often sat in when they related their experiences. They came from differing backgrounds and their abilities were equally diverse. Some made predictions, which the magician would record and afterwards check, others used trances to become proficient in skills supposedly foreign to them. Once more, Garrett's job was to investigate these and, although there were a number of charlatans who only wished to rob his employer, a sizeable proportion proved genuine.

De Puységur's investigations came to an end with the Revolution and Garrett was forced to find an alternative source of employment. With a servant's skills being in poor demand, he had turned to the magic tricks learned as a child and, in what would usually have been a precarious life, found he could survive remarkably well by developing his powers. For the past twenty years or so he had been doing exactly that, while amassing a considerable sum in the process, and now Garrett was keen for Lovemore to follow his example.

But the seaman was uncertain: Garrett was encouraging him to look deeper into his premonitions, and offered to show how small instances of foresight could be expanded and become more reliable. And Garrett had plans, plans that Lovemore knew he could see only too clearly in the future. The two might work together: join forces and turn their combined talents into an act, something that would make the seaman a far more valued addition to the troop than any simple musician, as well as earning them both a considerable amount of money.

It was a path Lovemore was prepared to consider, although he already sensed his eventual decision. Despite the reassurance of knowing he was not alone in his talents, he felt no desire to expand them further and even the prospect of financial security was unlikely to sway him.

But that was for the future; his current dilemma was far more immediate and might even have been solved. As far as being accepted into the group was concerned, he had little to worry over: meeting with the magician had altered everything. The man was obviously keen for him to join them, and would be a certain ally in any escape attempt. And once they were clear of Verdun, he could consider the proposal again. For all he knew a little time spent with Garrett could change his mind completely and, if not, he may still be welcomed as a permanent member of the band. However, of one thing Lovemore was quite certain: that week might be the end of the company's engagement in Verdun, but he would play with them again, and often.

# Chapter Seventeen

"First time I have been to the theatre in an age," Timothy admitted as they walked through the wide doorway and into the foyer.

"Well I doubt you will find much in the way of culture," Manning told him stiffly. "This shall be more of a circus, if I am any judge, and even then not of the standard of Astley's."

"Still, a change to go out of an evening," Brehaut added.

"And to wear civilian duds." Manning brushed down the nap of his new woollen overcoat self-consciously. It was the first of such purchases; all had started to assemble a wardrobe for when the time came to make their escape. The wearing of such things was permitted within town, although any officer caught out of uniform in the countryside risked a one-way trip to Bitche.

"Frankly, I am amazed that Verdun should possess a theatre," Timothy muttered as they queued to buy their tickets.

"Oh, but there are two," Brehaut told him. "One is used as a church on a Sunday."

"I must admit to not having attended," the lieutenant confessed.

"Best entertainment of the week," Brehaut added cheerfully. "There's a proper English preacher: full Anglican service. They even position *gendarmes* at the door.

"To keep the crowds away?" Manning enquired.

"No, the Catholics," Brehaut grinned. "We can't have any trouble this side of heaven."

"So what can we expect?" Timothy asked when they were making their way through to the auditorium.

"Oh, usual nonsense, no doubt," Brehaut chuckled. "There might be an element of drama to give the thing a measure of class I suppose; otherwise it will be sentimental ballads, a few lame japes and, if we are especially fortunate, the occasional glimpse of a woman's thigh."

"I suppose there are worse ways to spend an evening," Timothy mused.

If there were, Banks had yet to hear of them. He had also come to the theatre that night as an alternative to his usual diet of meetings with Brenton and the others, but quickly regretted his decision. The players had done much to make the entertainment spectacular, and all could be heard, even above the constant hubbub of conversation from their audience. But even powerful stage lighting and the exaggerated face paints and powders of the performers could not disguise the banality of their material. He felt his mind begin to wander and soon his thoughts turned to Sarah, his wife, and their young family. It was so long since he had last seen her, while one of their children would be a stranger to him when they did finally meet. And then he realised Verdun had already been his home for over a year. The war still had some way to go before being decided either way and, if Bonaparte was determined to ignore the usual courtesies, it would be far, far longer before he could even think of returning to England.

Since his conversation with King, thoughts of escape had occurred to him more often but always to be immediately rejected. He was a senior captain, a common enough rank in England, but not so many had been captured by the French. Consequently, there was more than enough to see him occupied: keeping track of British prisoners and co-ordinating with the authorities to ensure all were treated fairly. It was not the duty he envisaged when first applying for the Royal Navy but one he was capable of and would undertake. Besides, with little alternative the distraction was almost welcome. Sarah might still join him in the future, but privately he thought not. That would be a distraction too far; to be with his family, yet not at home, and them all prisoners was not a cheerful prospect. And then there was something else, something he could only admit to in private, or the crowded isolation of a cheap theatre.

Since the loss of *Prometheus*, and even slightly before, Banks had been aware of a wanting in personal confidence. It might have been caused by nothing more than old age, or perhaps the result of becoming a family man, but the verve and determination he enjoyed when younger – when captaining a frigate and such things were vital – was now lacking. He was no longer in charge of a ship, so had no opportunity to test himself, but was secretly sure that, were the chance to come his way again, it must be declined. For he had the uncomfortable feeling that his days of being a commanding officer were over.

The pockmarked young man who had been singing of his unrequited love for a dairymaid finally came to some form of conclusion, and the band struck up with a lively tune. Soon the stage was filled with a dozen dancing bodies and almost twice that number of feminine legs – almost because one pair must surely belong to a man. But Banks was no longer in the mood to be amused. Instead he settled deeper in his seat while his mind played on the problems of the past, and waited for the entertainment to cease.

* * *

"It is not exactly as I had anticipated," King admitted awkwardly as the curtains closed on the end of the first half. He turned to look at Aimée, who was eyeing him uncertainly.

"You do not approve of our form of entertainment?" she pouted.

"Why, no," King spluttered. "It is in the best of traditions," he told her hastily. "We have the same in England, and it is extremely popular." For a moment he struggled for more words, then realised he was being made fun of, and the two relaxed into mutual laughter.

"Oh, *mon cher*, do not concern yourself," she told him when able. "This may not be the height of French culture, but you will rarely get closer in Verdun."

"Then it is indeed an encouragement to escape," he added dryly.

In the next row he could see Timothy and the others who shared his accommodation while, even further forward, that was surely Captain Banks. Apart from them, there were few commissioned officers, the rest of the house being made up of junior men, and what were either French civilians or off-duty *gendarmes*. And there was no doubting most of the audience were enjoying themselves immensely. The last act had been a stage magician who, assisted by a saucy young girl, had performed a variety of tricks that left most spellbound. The wench was yet to quit the stage, however, and continued to mine every last ounce of applause with a series of provocative poses that were keeping certain sections of the audience in raptures.

"I wonder what we might expect for the next half," King mused.

"Oh, I believe there is to be a short drama," Aimée told him.

\* \* \*

Banks had seen enough. The magician's assistant was still hogging the stage and doing so to the extent that he was starting to wish she really had been sawn in half. But as soon as she left, he would be going as well. He reached for the watch in his waistcoat pocket and strained to see the time. It was certainly late enough to go straight home and, even though it would be to an empty house and a lonely bed, the prospect was unusually appealing. The next morning he had an interview with Manning, his former surgeon. The man had been making poor progress with Wirion and was concerned that the Commandant might be seeking medical advice elsewhere, in which case his subsequent removal to Bitche seemed likely. Banks had never cared much for Manning, but would not wish such a fate on anyone, and an early night would ensure he was at his best when they met.

The girl had finished at last and, with one last kick from a shapely leg, deserted the stage. Banks went to move just as the curtains parted yet again, revealing a large oil painting depicting the buffoon who had the cheek to call himself Emperor of France. The band, such as it was, started playing a particularly raucous tune and all about him began to stand.

But stand was all they did; Banks had a short, tubby man to one side, and an equally rotund woman on the other, while the rest of the row was completely filled with tightly packed humanity. The noxious fumes from so many foot lamps was starting to annoy him; it clashed horribly with the stink of cheap perfume and rancid flesh, making him crave the crisp, clean wind that could only be found at sea. But even such fresh air as Verdun could provide would be preferable and suddenly he was desperate to be free of the place. He glanced about; all remained standing and he was as trapped as ever. Then he noticed that two seats behind, the row was more than half empty.

Such an obstacle was nothing to a man who had boarded small boats during a storm as well as the occasional enemy warship. The chairs were fixed to the floor, and it was little effort to clamber up upon his own, then swing himself over. He quickly repeated the process until he was standing in a near empty row, but there were crowds clustering at either end whereas, another five rows back, he would have a clear run to the exit.

No one had objected to his moving the first time, and he had actually rather enjoyed the exercise, so Banks did not hesitate in continuing and soon was climbing over yet another row of seats. He had nearly reached his goal and was starting to look for the quickest way out when he heard the first whistle. It was quickly joined by a second, and soon the entire theatre seemed to be echoing with high-pitched screams, while a low rumble of protest began to erupt from those about him.

But Banks was not concerned. His behaviour might not have been particularly elegant, but he had always been a resourceful man and not afraid of putting himself out physically. There was certainly no need for anyone to protest, and could that really be a line of uniformed gendarmes heading in to the auditorium? Surely they weren't coming for him?

* * *

"That man!" Aimée said suddenly as she and King were standing for the French national anthem. "What does he think he is doing?"

King glanced across and was horrified to see Banks apparently treating the auditorium like some form of obstacle course.

"It's Sir Richard," he said, as if in explanation.

"Well he plays the dangerous game," she muttered.

"What, by climbing over a few chairs?" King was surprised; it wasn't as if this was the ballet, or serious theatre, and the audience were hardly sophisticated.

"No, by turning his back on the Emperor." She looked directly at him, and King could tell Aimée was speaking in deadly seriousness. "That is the painting of him, and such a thing is considered a crime," she explained. "He will be lucky to escape punishment."

* * *

"The frogs have snaffled the Captain!" Manning cried out in surprise as he watched Banks being grabbed and roughly dragged down the rest of the empty row.

"The hell they have!" Brehaut roared in protest, and immediately began to mount the seating himself.

"Hey, have a care!" Timothy protested, but it seemed the sailing master was equally intent on intervening and both were clambering over the backs of the seats as if competing in some form of steeplechase. Apart from the briefest of times when he had been a temporary officer aboard one of his frigates, Timothy had not served under Sir Richard Banks and neither was he particularly acquainted with the man. But barely fifteen feet in front of him a senior British naval officer was being manhandled by a bunch of enemy *gendarmes*, and that was too much for him to take. Besides, Manning and Brehaut, two men he did know well and respected even more, were about to join the fight, and he was not to be left out.

* * *

"Thomas, where are you going?" Aimée shouted, but she was too late. King had already left her side and was pushing past the crowd of interested onlookers, clearly intent on joining some sort of brawl that had broken out near the end of their row. She sighed, and began to make her way more sedately towards the fracas; the second half was supposed to start with a drama, but she had expected something different.

* * *

"Ahoy the cooper!"

Lewis supposed the cry would soon become common place, this being the third time *Narcis* had made a delivery to the English coast. But to him a cooper would always be one who built and maintained casks; why such an appellation should refer to a smuggler's supply vessel was beyond him.

"We'll take you to larboard," Reid roared out with authority, and received an acknowledgement from the first lugger.

Lewis watched while the smaller vessel came alongside, was secured, and the booty began to be unloaded from the brig's two holds. They were using whips rigged from the yardarms, which were exclusively manned by *Narcis*' own men, Lewis having deemed such a precaution necessary. Contraband or not, they were dealing with a valuable cargo and he now knew his men well enough to trust them. Those aboard the lugger were a different matter, however. They would be part-time smugglers and the very fact they had chosen such an occupation, presumably as a boost to their regular wages, said much about them.

And it might be the third time, but Reid was handling the procedure well. Since the incident with the revenue cutter much of his previous arrogance had vanished, to be replaced by something far more mature and professional. It was equally obvious others were finding him less obnoxious, there was less tension aboard the brig in general and Lewis was starting to think of him as a friend.

"That last were a touch light!" the lugger's master complained in a snarling whine, and Lewis stepped forward to answer, although Reid was ahead of him.

"Eighty tubs of over-proof Crowlink," he announced, before referring to a list once more. "That's all you're due; you want more, take it up with your venturers."

The man gave a growl of complaint, but the lugger was released smartly enough and another came to take her place.

Lewis glanced round the dark horizon. It was almost midnight and there was still no moon, but the sky was clear and he could see for several miles in every direction. Two further luggers were beating steadily towards them and he could see the last as she prepared to take the wind and run for home. But, apart from them, the sea was empty.

Which was how he liked it, and how he hoped it would always

197

be although, if they were to meet any further trouble from the revenue, he now felt more able to cope. It was as if a major obstacle had been encountered, assessed and soundly dealt with. Any qualms he may have felt about firing on his fellow countrymen were now more than quashed: not only had there been action, but it was decisive.

The news had been ready to meet him as soon as he returned to Flushing with van Gent himself being there to pass it on as the brig moored. A twelve gun cutter, comprehensively destroyed by a single broadside – incredible indeed. Within hours the entire port was agog with gossip and speculation. There were no further details and, although Lewis might have learned more later, he did not attempt to. No vessel can be sunk in action without some loss of life, and if it had been one or twenty, the nett result would be the same.

But what had made a difference was the kudos they instantly attracted. Peppercorn moorage fees and exemplary help from the government dockyards meant over seventy British smuggling craft now called Flushing their home port, and few of their crews did not know what *Narcis*, and her devilish commander, had achieved. Such notoriety was perhaps useful – it certainly encouraged van Gent in his efforts to keep them well supplied – and most of the hands had discovered that mentioning their vessel's name practically guaranteed the best attention ashore. There was a less savoury side though; Lewis was not blind to the fact that the revenue service, and perhaps even the Royal Navy, would be equally aware of the brig's identity. Britain was on her knees with an invasion expected almost imminently, yet there would still be room for individual wrongs to be addressed.

But in one area he had no doubts: *Narcis'* gunners had proved their worth. He was quietly confident that no further customs vessel would get the better of them although, were the Navy to be brought in, it might be a different matter. The North Sea was a wide and relatively quiet place – certainly when compared with the Channel – yet his weekly crossings would soon become expected. Any dedicated warship of the same tonnage as *Narcis* might carry up to four times his crew and be better armed, while a sloop, or even the smallest of frigates, could take her without clearing for action.

And, were they to be captured, there could be no clemency for a man who had so blatantly turned against his country. He could have expected the noose for the simple act of smuggling but to have sunk an armed government vessel was tantamount to treason: a crime that could still see him hanged, drawn and quartered.

He turned his mind away from the unsavoury subject and concentrated instead on the second lugger. She was taking several bolts of lace, a regular cargo, and destined to trim the dresses of countless worthy ladies, while the brandy, hair powder and tobacco they also carried might go to their husbands. Most would be pillars of society, with some being members of parliament, or officers in the Navy or Army. Not for the first time, Lewis considered the dichotomy of so many influential people openly benefiting from a crime they were ostensibly trying to suppress.

Such things were not for the minds of him or his like though. The last two luggers were drawing close now, and they should almost empty the brig. Then there would be one more brief rendezvous off Deal, and they could return to Flushing; another trip completed and slightly more in his own coffers. In less than a year he would be both comfortable and able to look back on this period of his life with relief and gratitude. And for Lewis that time could not come quickly enough.

* * *

Whether it was the medicine Robert Manning had prescribed, the half bottle of Cognac taken on top of his wine at supper, or just plain bad temper, but Louis Wirion did not appear approachable that evening. He glared at the group of officers before him with a look that left little doubt of his intentions. Were it in his power, all would be dealt with in the harshest manner possible. And the officers stared back, fully aware it was well within his power.

"Not content with showing disrespect to an image of the Emperor," he told one in particular in a voice hot with emotion, "you then proceeded to resist my officers in the execution of their duty."

His eyes fell away from Banks, and he addressed the group more generally.

"Then you all joined and made an exhibition of yourselves by rioting in a public place." He began to walk up and down in front of the sorry group until King started to feel like a naughty schoolboy. But this was hardly the time for humour; not even the most evil of headmasters could deal out the punishments Wirion was capable of.

"Is this the way that British officers behave?" he asked, stopping again in front of Sir Richard. Banks wore full naval uniform under his cloak, which made the bruise to his right eye seem even more incongruous. "Do you perhaps engage in such — such *pitreries* when you are in your own country? Or is this a special behaviour, reserved for only when guests of the French?"

Banks swallowed dryly. He supposed it was understandable that the man should behave so. Rumour had it he was from common stock, which was hardly a crime in itself: Banks knew a couple of true gentlemen who had come from the lower classes. But to his mind Wirion had retained every coarse and vulgar feature of his origin, without absorbing any of the sophistication available to one in his new position.

And Manning was equally unimpressed. He, too, was judging the Commandant, although in his case it was using the criteria of a surgeon assessing a patient. The pupils were darkened, indicating the considerable use of drugs that might not have been prescribed by him, while erratic movement and an apparent inability to concentrate made him wonder if the Frenchman were on the verge of insanity.

"I cannot conceive why supposedly respectable officers should choose to behave in such a disgraceful way," the *Général* continued. "To turn one's back on the Emperor can only be regarded as *mauvais sujet*, and one for which you would have been severely punished," he continued, staring directly at Banks. "But for the rest of you to support such an act is inconceivable, and will not be tolerated."

King was actually a little ashamed. However much he hated the man, there was an element of truth in what he said. Sir Richard might not have intended insulting the Emperor, but was clambering over the seats in a theatre really the way a Peer of the Realm should behave? And quite what good he himself had thought he might do by joining in was another matter. With one arm he could barely look after himself in a brawl, let alone rescue anyone else from what was probably lawful arrest, while the fact that all had happened in front of Aimée hardly put matters in a better light.

Even if his behaviour had not soured matters with her, the incident probably signalled the end of their relationship. For the likelihood was strong they would be shipped away, possibly to Sedan or Sarrelibre; places far worse than Verdun, and a good way from Aimée and her family. And if they were especially unlucky, they might even find themselves in Bitche, in which case the lack of her company would be the last thing he would have to worry about.

But one thing was clear; the little performance that was being acted out before them now was purely for the Commandant to vent his spleen on Captain Banks, a man who had been a thorn in his side for some while.

Wirion continued to rant as King scoured his mind for more positive thoughts. If Bitche were to be their destination, and what he had heard about the place was true, it might not be the absolute end, although near enough to make no difference. There were three men currently in Verdun who had returned from a relatively brief spell in the depot: all lifeblood had been bled from them, and they were now mere shells of humanity. Timothy and Brehaut were sound enough and might withstand what was to come, while Manning could be relied upon to keep himself healthy in the poorest of circumstances. But Captain Banks was hardly at his fittest and, neither was he, even though it pained him to admit the fact.

"You will all be taken from this place with the next convoy." The Commandant was obviously tiring now and would be coming to the point. "I will be sending a message to *Général* Maisonneuve in the morning so he might prepare an appropriate welcome; there are facilities at his depot which you may find more to your taste."

And that was it, King decided. Maisonneuve was the Commandant of Bitche, and every bit as renowned for his vile ways as Wirion. He also hated the British with a passion that extended to a regular public burning of anything made in the country. His second in command was a Jerseyman known as Big Williams, a man rumoured to be wanted for murder in his native land, while the rest of the guards were made up from the very worst rejects from the French army; men known for taking positive pleasure in the ill treatment of prisoners and, as the place was designated as a punishment depot, little control was placed on their actions.

They would have just a few more nights in Verdun, and those were to be spent in the Citadel. It was a place where civilians were rarely admitted without good reason, which pretty much ruled out any chance of meeting with Aimée again.

And it was as King realised this that all the terrors of his eventual destination were dismissed by one, overpowering thought: whatever might lie ahead, it was the end of what they had shared. He was now quite sure he would never see her again, never be able to explain, to say goodbye properly, or express exactly how much he loved her.

* * *

The cell that they took them to was vast; it must have covered half of one of the higher floors in the Citadel, and already contained a few familiar faces. Adams was one and along with the other midshipmen he rose to meet them when they were driven up the stone stairs. A *gendarme* opened the only gate in the wall of bars that separated it from the rest of the room, and the officers filed through.

With the clank of chains and the turning of a large lock the cell was secured once more, and the *Capitaine* gave a snort of satisfaction before turning and leading his men back down the steps.

"Belike they feel able to trust us on our own," King told Adams by way of greeting.

The younger man pulled a wry face. "Aye, sir; it is the order of things," he replied. "But at least we are left in relative privacy."

"Excuse me, sir, but are you bound for Bitche?"

This was Summers, the midshipman, and King was disconcerted to note there was a look of hope on his young face.

"Aye, Mr Summers, I fear we are joining you," he said.

"But that may not be," Summers continued with what might have been enthusiasm. "One of the guards told us we are up for ransom; the senior officers are to pay a contribution which would allow us to remain in Verdun." The lad's words slowed as he realised that at least one of the officers concerned was in the cell with him, and looked likely to be sharing his fate.

"I should not put too much faith in that, young man," Sir Richard told him bluntly, before settling himself down alone against the far wall and closing his eyes.

Banks supposed it was possible that now he and the other officers had been added to the equation, Wirion's offer might be reconsidered, although he did not hold out much hope. Wolfe's resolution against paying any more bribes had been strong, and Banks was one of those who had championed it, so the odds against a change of heart were long. And, in truth, he would not have wanted one. Despite his current situation, he knew the only way to counter bullies such as the Commandant was to stand up to them. The price would undoubtedly have risen further now he was also being held: how would it appear to the other captured officers if the Verdun Relief Committee was prepared to pay for the release of one of their own, after having refused to do so for more junior men?

He opened his eyes and glanced about the dismal place. The others were talking in small groups, and doubtless there were worse places – as he would probably discover upon reaching Bitche. But by rights, he should have been snug in his bed, while his fellow officers might still be enjoying the second half of the performance. As it was, they could only look forward to being pinned up in this bare room to await the time when they would be taken somewhere far worse. And there was something else, something that made what was about to happen a thousand times more awful: the only person that could be blamed was himself.

A series of oil lamps burned in a line on the other side of the bars and well out of reach. It was the only light they were allowed but by it he could see their accommodation clearly enough. There were no beds, although several pallets – hard mattresses densely packed with straw – were laid out in neat lines and appeared clean, while a small lidded pail would take care of their personal requirements. There were also two heavily barred windows that looked out onto the dark night, as well as giving an indication that, even this high up, the Citadel's stone walls were quite substantial.

"You mean, we will all be going to Bitche?" From across the cell, Summers was continuing in a voice now void of hope.

"I'm afraid so," King confirmed. "But at least we shall have company."

"If you will excuse me, sir, there may be an alternative."

This was Adams, the midshipman King had promoted to acting lieutenant whilst aboard *Kestrel*, and all eyes went to him. For a moment he returned their looks with one of pleased anticipation, then turned and called back to the darkest corner of the cell.

"Cranston? A moment, if you please."

The seaman, who none of the new arrivals had noticed, eased himself up and made his way towards them. In his hand he held a short length of what appeared to be rope.

"In the devil's name, where did you find that?" Timothy demanded. Cranston wilted slightly under the stare of so many officers and indicated the mattresses provided for their bedding.

"I made it from what were in them there pallets," he replied simply. "We all have."

"He is quite correct," Adams confirmed, before turning to the nearest mattress and reaching inside. After a pause he brought out a handful of tightly twisted cord, each length being about a fathom long. "Cranston here is a dab hand at laying rope, as well as a fair teacher," he continued. "We've been whiling away the time by making yarn from straw, and there is plenty to make more."

King glanced round as Banks eased himself up from the ground and made his way over. "Enterprising," he conceded, taking hold of a length and stretching it experimentally in his fingers. "Though I hardly think it will carry any weight; that is ignoring the fact we have yet to get past those bars," he added, glancing up at the two windows.

"Beggin' your pardon, your honour, but these are just the strands; I intend to twist them into a proper hawser once we have enough."

Banks raised his eyebrows; that seemed reasonable, although it hardly dealt with the next problem. The Citadel was several hundred feet high and their open cell must be pretty close to the top. Below them a squad of *gendarmes* patrolled the base, while a squadron of mounted cavalry was constantly on hand and ready to pursue any who ventured beyond the town walls.

"Then we can splice the lengths together," Cranston, who had instinctively stepped back in the presence of a senior captain, continued.

"The guards tend to leave us alone; our meal times are predictable, and they make enough noise on the staircase to wake the dead." Adams continued. "We were reckoning on three more days to get a sizeable length, and Cranston believes it will take the weight of any man present, or possibly two, if pushed."

"And, if you will excuse me, sir," Summers butted in, "we've had precious little to do. Even if it is never used, making rope is better than staring at the walls."

Banks nodded: a good point and well made. The young men had showed initiative, although nothing altered the fact that a rope with no means of using it was little more than useless. But then he could think of nothing else for them to do, and if this last chance of escape were really to come to naught, it might even be better to say so now. Then at least every man would have the time to reconcile themselves to the fate that undoubtedly awaited them.

# Chapter Eighteen

Despite being utterly certain of never seeing her again, King had a visit from Aimée the following morning. He had been asleep and was roused by her soft voice calling. For a moment it was as if all that happened the night before was some terrible dream, and he found himself smiling into her eyes. And then reality returned; there were bars between them and, rather than a dream, he had woken to a living nightmare.

"Aimée, however did you get here?" he asked, clambering to his feet.

"It is not so very difficult," she told him simply. "The *gendarmes* know you are held securely, so what does it matter if a visitor is allowed?"

For a moment King's mind began to race. If Aimée were permitted to visit, she might bring in any amount of tools to help them escape. They had rope after all, a saw, or even a decent file would soon account for the bars on those windows. And then he remembered the height; they must be all of one hundred feet above the ground, with mounted troops and guards on constant patrol in the courtyard below. And even if they were to be able to cross undetected, there were still two substantial inner walls to scale before they reached the town's outer ramparts. No, he had to resign himself to the fact that escape was impossible, although it was still good to see Aimée one last time.

"Thank you so much for coming," he began. "And I am so sorry, so sorry for..."

"Never mind that now," she snapped, "we have things to consider, and it is better you listen to me than talk."

And this was now a very different Aimée: her face had lost none of its beauty, but she was regarding him crossly, as if he were nothing other than a minor irritation she had been forced to address. He opened his mouth to complain, then noticed the two guards standing not ten feet behind her. Neither would be likely to speak English, and he guessed Aimée was trying to fool them into thinking she was telling him off. At least he hoped so...

"I understand from James that you have access to rope." She almost spat the words, and King found himself recoiling from their vehemence.

"Indeed," he replied, in a tone that was suitably apologetic.

"That is good. All convoys to Bitche leave on a Monday morning," she continued. "It is customary to move Citadel prisoners to St Vannes the night before."

King repeated the name softly, and Aimée treated him to a look filled with contempt and disdain.

"That is the Convent Chapel used before the Revolution," she told him, and King nodded dumbly in reply. "Next to it is the storeroom, where you will probably be held, though the two are connected. And beyond there is a garden which is hidden from the courtyard and any of the guards. I can not give you details now it will look suspicious," her voice was softening, and King detected a note of tenderness which was quickly suppressed. "But I will try to come back tomorrow and tell you more," she huffed, before turning away in a flounce.

"Aimée, wait," King pleaded. She glanced back and the façade of a wronged partner slipped for a moment.

"I'm not sure," he began. "I'm not sure I can do this."

"But you will have to," she informed him, drawing closer once more. "That is, if we are to be together."

"I don't understand..."

"You see now I shall definitely be coming with you." Her voice had become harsh again, and to any onlooker who did not speak English, he was still being soundly chastised.

"But you can't..." This time King had no difficultly in making his tone pathetic. "It will be dangerous..."

"Then it is a danger we shall share," she snapped back, before hitching up her skirts and bustling towards the door.

* * *

"We figured it best to give you both a little privacy," Timothy told King once Aimée had gone.

"There were no need," he replied, now even more confused. Manning was approaching and seemed equally conciliatory; King

207

had the uncomfortable impression his friend was about to place a comforting hand upon his shoulder while even Sir Richard was giving him a sympathetic look from the other side of the cell. After Aimée's strange behaviour this was almost too much and King wondered quite what kind of world he had woken up to when realisation struck. On the opposite side of the bars, their two gaolers were regarding him with blatant grins; clearly the sight of a French woman berating an English officer appealed to them and King immediately took to the part of a humiliated lover and adopted a suitably glum expression that came relatively easy.

But the performance did not have to last long, which was fortunate, as he was truly no actor and all the British prisoners were simply bursting to talk. With a final comment that only Brehaut understood, the guards slunk out of the cell and went in search of comfort elsewhere.

"Well, that were quite a development," Timothy chuckled when they were alone once more.

"Aye, Tom, when it comes to picking women, you seem to have quite a knack," Manning agreed.

"If what she says is true, we had better start making plans," Brehaut added. "Cranston, how far are we with the rope?"

"Hold fast there," Banks spoke softly but with the voice of authority and all paid attention. "Mr King's friend made no mention of anyone else escaping."

"Well, I cannot see myself going far on my own," King replied. "Even though the Chapel might not be so high as this place, there is still a measure of physical work, and with but a single arm I am less than useless."

"And if one is needed to assist, we may as well all go," Timothy supposed. "There being safety in numbers."

"Aye," Adams agreed less enthusiastically. "If pursued, we may not all be taken, and there will be a wider selection to shoot at."

"I think it better no one dwells on the likelihood of being taken, or shot," Brehaut stated hurriedly. "And yes, you may get clear of the town. But there is still a good fifty miles before reaching the German border, while the French coast is nearer two hundred from here. Both distances would be better covered in groups of two or three, rather than a crowd."

"Besides, even in Germany the chance of capture remains strong," Timothy again. "And if we went west, there would still be the problem of crossing to England."

"We might signal a blockading fleet," Adams suggested.

"To what end?" Banks demanded, turning on the young man. "You think an inshore squadron will send a boat? You shall still be in occupied territory, remember."

There was silence for a moment as all considered this, and the mood of the group dropped significantly. Then King spoke.

"We need only to get as far as Valenciennes," he stated gently. "It is still a considerable distance, and there may not be much to eat, but Aimée's brother is there, and will provide for us."

"Will he indeed?" Banks grunted.

"He has a business ferrying coal by barge," King explained. "The entire family is no friend of the Emperor, as you may have guessed – I understand such a feat has been carried out before, though have not enquired deeply."

"Then it is settled," Banks spoke with the edge of command, something that had been missing in his voice for a while. "All must make an inventory of what civilian clothing is available. I suggest every man retains at least one piece of uniform in case of capture – that way there is a chance of avoiding being considered a spy. Greatcoats and the like will be invaluable; there are at least three with which to start and I shall add my cloak. Perchance more can be acquired along the way; you will have to trust that to luck."

"You speak as if we shall be travelling without you, sir," King said, looking directly at the senior man.

"I fear so," Banks agreed. "I know not what assurances any gentlemen here have made, and neither would I insist they comply with them. But I have given my word of honour not to escape and have no intention of breaking such a solemn oath."

Now the mood had definitely altered, and there were several deep sighs from the small group before Robert Manning spoke.

"I think I have heard enough about this so-called *Parole d'Honneur*," he said. "And frankly it makes me sick." There was a sharp intake of breath from some, but Manning was into his stride, and continued. "As if we did not have enough to contend with, being held by the French with the likelihood – no, the certainty – of spending our next years in a veritable hell hole, some are content to allow what they are pleased to call a gentlemanly commitment to bind them that much tighter."

"It is for each man to reach such a decision..." Banks began, but Manning would have nothing of it and spoke over his former captain – something that truly caught the attention of all.

"The daily *appel* is still insisted upon for most officers; that in itself contravenes any international agreement regarding *Parole*, while you seem equally keen to ignore the fact that the majority of those held in Verdun are here entirely illegally."

"Thank you, Mr Manning," Banks said with more force. "You will forgive me, but I repeat, it is every man's right to decide and..."

"M-maybe you are right, sir," Manning was red-faced although he spoke with passion and was not to be dissuaded. "Maybe foolish and outdated notions of honour should override thoughts of being at home with our wives and families. But you would be wise to remember this..."

All waited while the surgeon gathered breath.

"...It is universally agreed that the *Parole d'Honneur* only applies when a man has been granted some degree of freedom. As soon as he is held by force, be it by rope, chain or cell, all restrictions – lawful or imagined – cease to exist. In brief, gentlemen, there is nothing to stop us from leaving this foul place without any loss of so-called honour. And I suggest we do so, as a body, and as efficiently as can be arranged."

* * *

"Aye, that's *Swift*, sure enough," Laidlaw confirmed to Judy. They were on the brig's tiny forecastle, and the Navy sloop – his previous ship – was in plain sight and less than three miles off.

This was one of the perils of the North Sea crossing. It was roughly eighty nautical miles from their berth in Flushing to the first of their rendezvous points off the Suffolk coast. The distance could be covered in under a day if the winds were favourable, but such things could never be relied upon. Consequently, Lewis was in the habit of allowing twice that to make the passage, which often meant an entire day must be wasted, with the brig sailing idly in open water and under a clear sky. In such conditions they could run from any suspicious sighting as soon as her mastheads appeared over the horizon, but at night or in bad weather, another vessel might close to within hailing distance before she were spotted.

On that particular trip they had left harbour during the evening and in the midst of a storm which continued throughout the night. The wind stayed in their favour, however, and with the occasional change of sail *Narcis* made good progress, although Laidlaw and his mates were thoroughly soaked as a consequence. But now it was dawn, a time when the first strands of daylight revealed exactly what danger they could be in, and there was no mistaking the Royal Navy warship sailing to cross their bows, nor the fact that *Narcis* was less than a mile beyond the range of her broadside.

"And she's your old ship," Judy mused. "Fair captain, is he?"

Laidlaw shook his head. "As green as they come; if it is up to him, we ain't got nothing to worry over. But the first luff won't take no nonsense, and my guess is it'll be him what gives the orders."

Judy glanced back to their own quarterdeck where Lewis and Reid were also studying the warship. It was possible that *Swift* was simply passing by and would maintain the same course, allowing them to continue to their rendezvous without delay. The alternative, and it was one all aboard the brig silently dreaded, was for the sloop to attempt to inspect them and, considering the amount of booty carried, they would be smoked even before the first man boarded.

"Well, I don't rate our mate too highly, but the master's a seaman at least," Judy muttered as he returned to consider the sloop. "Though I don't see seamanship making a lot of difference."

"How's that?" Laidlaw queried.

"Laden as we are, a ship like that will run us down however badly she's sailed," he muttered. "An' even if she don't forereach, it won't take much to bring us into range."

"Aye," Laidlaw agreed. "And if we run, that'll be the first thing she'll try to do."

"An' the weather ain't gonna help none," Judy added, looking up at the dark sky. The rain had stopped but it could only be a temporary postponement; soon the heavy cloud would be sending down stair rods once more, although the wind, that had been strong for most of the night, was starting to fade.

"You know what they say," Judy added philosophically, "a lot can happen in the hour after dawn."

"They do," Laidlaw agreed. "And I think they may be right."

* * *

"Well, you didn't take any prisoners," King told Manning later in a hushed voice. They had moved away from the tight circle of men making rope and were about as alone as was possible in the open cell. "I don't think Sir Richard has been spoken to in such a manner for some while."

"Then it was time someone did," the surgeon hissed in return. He still appeared agitated after the encounter but was equally unrepentant, and there was something else in his manner: a slight edge that had become all too common of late when speaking with King.

The pair had been friends for many years and were used to trusting each other in all matters although King sensed this was no longer the case. He might be imagining things; confinement did much to change a man's attitude, while Manning also had the added pressure of a growing family, and one which he could do little to help or influence. But the cooling in their relationship was not something that could be blamed on their current situation: it had actually started before *Kestrel* was taken.

"You are certain about the conditions of *Parole*?" he asked, while noting Manning did not bother to look him in the eye.

"Quite certain," the surgeon confirmed. "I have a copy of my written agreement which Brehaut was kind enough to translate, though I should go if it were not the case. To be frank, Tom, the only things that keep me from Kate are physical; I do not care a jot about what I may, or may not, have said, or any signature on a foolish piece of paper."

"Some might not consider such things foolish," King replied, adding, "Indeed, a good deal treat their word as sacrosanct and you should not judge them for it."

"Is that so?" His friend finally turned to him and the dim light of the cell was sufficient to show the anger in his eyes. "And I suppose you class yourself amongst such worthies?"

"I would strive to keep my word, if that's what you mean," King admitted, blushing slightly. "Though freely confess what you say comes as a relief, as all may now leave whilst retaining their honour."

The surgeon leant back against the stone wall of the cell and considered King for a moment, then his face relaxed into a sardonic smile.

"Coming from you, Tom, that is rich indeed," he said, before looking away.

"But why?" King asked, the hurt in his voice evident. "Do you not regard me as a man of honour?"

"Oh I did," Manning told him flatly, while centring his attention on the bars before them. "That is, were I to consider such things at all. In fact there was probably no one I would have trusted more fully."

"And what brought the change?" King was now more confused than upset, even though he sensed this was at the heart of any chill in their relationship.

"It was Lesro," Manning stated firmly.

"Nik?" Now a feeling of disquiet came over King. Nikola Lesro had been a close friend of both men while they were stationed on Malta. He was killed in the saddest of circumstances: shot by a brother officer who imagined himself cuckolded. And yes, King supposed he had not been entirely honourable in his handling of the situation. But that had been after the event; Nik was already dead. If his behaviour was in any way dishonourable, it had been entirely to defend another; one whom he regarded as equally innocent.

"B-but I was protecting Tony Hunt," King stammered, before realising he had attracted attention from the group of rope makers, and lowered his voice to its previous whisper. "It would have done little good handing him over to the authorities," he hissed. "The man would have hanged, sure as a gun."

"Maybe so," Manning agreed more calmly. "But you organised his escape," he continued before looking King full in the face once more. "Is that what you would term as honourable?" he asked. "What half-truths or downright falsities were used to achieve such an outcome? There might not have been any formal agreements or solemn oaths in force, but many would judge your behaviour to be anything but worthy, and definitely surpassing the minor crime of a breach of *Parole*."

* * *

"We might add the t'gallants, sir?" Reid chanced.

Such suggestions had become rarer of late, but still Lewis found them annoying. *Narcis* was sailing sweetly enough under topsails with the wind, which had finally started to rise, on her beam. The warship, and the vessel that lay before them was undoubtedly that, ran before it and would soon be passing across their bows. If nothing altered for fifteen minutes it would be clear she had no intention of inspecting them; they only had to bide their time. And he was equally aware that, were they not patient and if the brig turned more than a point from her current course or added even a stitch of canvas, it would attract attention and almost guarantee a rummage.

"Additional sail would only bring us down upon them the sooner," Lewis told him levelly. "And I have no intention of manoeuvring, if that was in your mind."

Reid made no response, but Lewis knew the mild reprimand had been taken on board.

"Hands to breakfast, sir?"

This was Masters; the youngster approached his captain with a hesitant expression. But it was a sensible request and he was obviously learning quickly.

"Very good, Mr Masters; see to it, will you?"

The sloop might heave to at any time, although the hands could be called away from their meal smartly enough. And, if it came to a sailing contest, he would be relying on them, so preferred they had full bellies than empty.

"We should be on time to make Orford by nightfall." It was Reid again, and Lewis had to suppress a sigh. So much had improved of late, why the man felt the need to make conversation

214

at that moment he could not imagine. And then he did understand: Reid was tense, in the same way they all were, except his manner of showing it was to be annoying. Once he realised this, the mate's behaviour became easier to bear.

Despite the fact that rain was falling once more, Masters was showing good sense in feeding the men on deck. *Narcis* had been blessed with a cook of sorts; a Dutchman, happy to boil up burgoo, duff and other English dishes to please the majority of his clientele. The men were forming up with their wooden bowls before them, and seemed oblivious to the weather. A few might be complaining amongst themselves, but at least all were well paid and, on such short trips, there was little of the underlying tension Lewis was used to when serving His Majesty. Then, just as he was contemplating killing time by taking breakfast himself, a cry came from the maintop that caused all on board the brig to freeze.

"Sighting's hauling in her wind!"

"Dear God!" There was a rumble of discontent from the hands although Reid's comment was about the only intelligible words spoken. All eyes turned towards the sloop, and someone dropped a full bowl of porridge as the awful truth dawned. It was just as the lookout had reported; the sloop was undoubtedly slowing. And the only reason for doing so on such an empty sea was that she intended to speak with them.

\* \* \*

Aimée returned the following morning, and seemed just as angry with King as before. This was noted by the guards, who greeted her initial salvo with knowing grins, before retreating to the far side of the room to allow the girl full vent to her feelings.

"I have more details of how to escape from the Convent Chapel," she growled from her side of the bars, while King nodded meekly back from his.

"You will have to find your own way past any guards, and disable them as you think fit," she hissed. "But make for the altar; behind the cloth you will find an unbarred window. It might open, otherwise must be broken, that will also be down to you, but once

215

through, the Convent garden is outside."

King went to say something, but she stopped him with her hand, before giving a sly wink, and launching into another apparent diatribe.

"From the Convent there are two walls but I do not know how large. And you must pass through the Commandant's garden; this is set by the main town rampart, which will appear low, but there is a long drop of perhaps ten meters on the other side.

"We have a rope," King reminded her, and she gave a quick nod of understanding before gathering herself for a final volley.

"At all times you must be alert for guards, but I have checked and there will be very little moon on Sunday night."

"Sunday," King repeated to himself; it was less than two days away. By this time next week he could be fighting his way through the French countryside, or nothing more than a stiffening corpse in an unmarked grave.

"It will need a large convoy to take so many to Bitche; such things usually set off first thing on a Monday morning," Aimée told them briskly. "Now I must go, is there anything you need?"

There was; they did not have sufficient civilian clothes for the entire party and some form of tool, a hammer, or small saw would doubtless come in useful when breaking out of the Chapel. And, probably most importantly, he would have given anything for a soft word from her, but all of that must wait.

"No, there is nothing," he told her in a miserable tone that required little forcing.

"Then I will see you all again, you pigs!" she added to the room in general. The statement was taken in the correct manner and greeted by a derisory rumble from the younger members of the party, who found it easy to fall in with such a charade.

Aimée turned away without so much as a second look at King, and his last sight of her was as she flounced towards the door, with the guards lazily following down the staircase.

His last sight of her – although that might not be the case. The escape would be hazardous, but not impossible. And she could still be there to meet them when they finally made it beyond the town walls. But that would only be the start of matters; there remained many miles of French countryside to cover before they met up with her brother. And even then, the journey in his coal barges would not be without risk. King had hardly begun to consider how they would take the final trip across to England, but even if that were achieved, the original problem must remain. Juliana would still be there, and how would Aimée react to discovering she had been helping a married man return to his wife?

* * *

As far as Lewis could see, he had two choices: he could turn back, and make for the Dutch coast, or continue bearing down in the general direction of England, their goal, and the heavily armed Navy sloop that lay waiting in their path.

Before then he had never regarded himself as anything other than cautious, and knew most would have no hesitation in ordering the brig about. After all, *Narcis* was still a mile or so beyond the likely range of any cannon the enemy might be carrying. And it was a margin they would probably maintain when the sloop gave chase, as she inevitably must.

But even if he were able to make an escape, it would be the end of any thoughts of a rendezvous that evening, and might spell the finish of his entire smuggling career. He had not been captain of the brig for long but, even in that time, competition for positions such as his had become fierce. And no one would be likely to re-employ a man they could not depend upon. Besides, he would be banking on them maintaining their lead; *Narcis* was relatively well set and he was certain of her crew, but the materials provided by the Dutch shipyard were not of the highest standard. With a gathering wind, he would be forced to test his command to the very limit, and it might only need one line to part, a single spar to spring, or any of the sails to tear and they would be snapped up by the more powerful vessel.

Nevertheless, once the thought of turning back had been discounted, matters became relatively simple. The wind was undoubtedly growing, making any addition to his current sail unnecessary, while the enemy lay broadside on and dead in the water. Heading to larboard might buy them a measure of space as his opponent would have to turn before she gave chase. But he could only manage a point or two into the wind, and *Narcis* was not so comfortable on a bowline. Steering several points to starboard would bring the wind firmly on his quarter; heavily laden as she was, *Narcis* would give of her best that way, and every sense in his body was urging him to do so without delay. But it would do little good laying the helm across now; such a move would only give the enemy warning, and must surely end with them sailing straight into her guns. No, it remained a waiting game, and one he must continue playing for a while longer. And, if he was to win, it would only be with cunning.

# Chapter Nineteen

But there was no reason why he should not enjoy playing, Lewis decided, as he turned towards the waiting Reid.

"Rouse out the American flag and have it bent and raised to the gaff," he told him.

Reid, clearly eager for something more warlike, gave the order with obvious reluctance. *Narcis* had no need for a specialist signals officer, but Masters served when the role was required and Lewis watched as the young lad made for the flag locker. Since the incident with the revenue cutter, they had made extensive changes to the brig's appearance. Her whales were now picked out in an elegant dark green and, while they had not been able to exchange their shortened topmast for something more conventional, van Gent had found them a fresh main topsail. The original had been of a distinctive, light colour and its replacement blended far better with the other sails.

These were not the only changes Lewis had in mind; for as long as he held command his crew would have to get used to the frequent re-painting of various fittings. And, if a full length main topmast was really out of the question, he hoped at least to replace the main course with a more conventional brigsail. The latter might even be loose-footed, as in a snow, and was one of several other alterations he was considering. But the best defence he had against inspection was currently being hoisted: the American flag gave him licence to sail the North Sea almost at a whim and, possibly more importantly, every reason to avoid a British warship.

The Royal Navy's habit of pressing American seamen had become notorious of late; admittedly the vast majority of those taken were British born and had a nationalised status that was, at best, questionable but resentment remained and was growing. Consequently, short of actually firing on the sloop, anything he did to avoid the British boarding them would be understood for as long as that flag was flying.

Now he had come to a decision, Lewis felt easier. The stakes remained undeniably high and much would depend on him; they could still be trapped and boarded, in which case all subterfuge would be useless, but strangely that was not discouraging. In fact, he felt more energetic and alive than he had for some time, while the knowledge that next to him Reid was stewing with doubt and worry was a positive tonic.

Perhaps this was what other men felt? Those he had known in the past: men he had watched going into action with every appearance of thriving on the excitement. And not just battle: it was considered nothing for a seaman to stake several year's wages on a single game of pitch and toss, while the more gentrified would risk as much in speculative business deals and alliances. Surely it could not be just the prospect of winning that encouraged such behaviour?

"We might clear for action, sir?" Reid suggested and Lewis gave a deep sigh.

"There is little point," he said, in a voice that was as soft as the wind would allow. "A ship that size must be carrying twenty cannon; we are hardly likely to be exchanging broadsides with them."

Reid nodded, although Lewis could tell he was still unsure.

"I'm sorry, John but this is one occasion when we shall be relying on guile as much as firepower." Lewis noticed how the unexpected use of Reid's Christian name had sparked a reaction. "We have the Yankee duster," he continued, indicating the flag that was now flying above their heads, "while, if this storm continues, we should be able to lead our Navy friends on a merry chase and still be on time for the rendezvous."

Now Reid was looking more hopeful; as if something of his captain's confidence had been transferred to him.

"Very good, sir," he replied, and Lewis knew the man was wholeheartedly behind him.

* * *

"Well, I suppose tonight is the last night," Garrett pondered and Lovemore found himself looking away from that quizzical smile which was both disagreeable and compelling. "What is it that you have chosen to do?" he persisted.

"I have not decided yet," Lovemore temporised.

Garrett raised an eyebrow in apparent wonder.

"There is much to consider," the seaman continued. "If I am caught, it will be an end to all of this." He waved his hand vaguely to the band who were currently setting up about him. "I would be in a far worse prison, with no means of playing an instrument; at least if I stay in Verdun I have the evening dances."

"And, perhaps, the occasional theatre party," Garrett finished for him. "You never know when a group of travelling players may come along and offer to change your life..."

Lovemore went to speak but somehow the words would not come.

"Well, I will not press you further." Garrett's smile was perhaps a little warmer now. "I still say you will be welcome, and safe; things that I know have concerned you in the past. And there would be a future for you with me; combined, there is little our powers of perception might not achieve. But in the end, it is you that has to decide," he added, with a gentle tap to his shoulder.

Lovemore nodded, and the magician mercifully left him in peace.

Garrett was correct though, he conceded while continuing to assemble his flute. In the past few days Lovemore had learned a good deal and, though it had not made him like the man any more, at least he had a better appreciation of his powers.

The magician could almost be an example of what he might be capable of in a few years' time, although that was hardly a recommendation. But after talking with Garrett in depth he now knew that, though the powers of heightened intuition and prophecy were undoubtedly strong, they could not alter the future, only predict it. And neither were they infallible – that was something he had discovered for himself.

When Hobbs died during their ill-fated attempt to escape on the way to Verdun it had come as a shock. Lovemore was already harbouring misgivings about the whole venture, but there had been no specific warning such as that which accompanied Harris' death. And neither had Hobbs come back to haunt him, like his former messmate.

Then there was the other instance. It was some weeks back, when he had been playing for the dance. He had seen the death's head image as plain as day on one of the officer's faces, and knew exactly what it foretold. But, unlike Harris, the man had not died; he was still fit and healthy, with every prospect of remaining so for as long as he stayed within the protective enclave of Verdun.

Not that either example proved much; Lovemore also accepted the powers within him had been correct on far too many occasions to be seriously questioned, and meeting with Garrett only confirmed both their existence and potential. But as to whether or not he should go with the group, he was still, genuinely, uncertain. To do so must inevitably mean developing his talents further, yet he did enjoy playing his flute, and being part of a proper band.

Garrett clearly thought him to be prevaricating, and probably knew exactly what the seaman intended. But if so then he was lucky because, for once in his life, Lovemore did not have a clue.

\* \* \*

The Captain had ordered their turn to starboard some fifteen minutes before, and *Narcis* was now blasting through the sea with all the elegance of a charging heifer. The brig's heavy hull seemed to be thumping each wave individually, sending spray and spume as far back as the mainmast and regularly soaking all on the upper deck. The rain was holding off, but there was more breeze and it felt as if every inch of the vessel's frame was under pressure as she pounded the dark waters. But despite the wind, the strain and the fact that her topsails should really have taken a reef, *Narcis* was not travelling fast. Her cargo, the crates and casks that filled every available space from her kelson to the upper deck, kept her low in the water and the sloop was gaining steadily.

"Maybe it'll take an hour, and maybe longer," Laidlaw pondered philosophically as he rested one foot on the gun carriage. "But the Navy'll be up with us by noon, there can be no doubting of that."

"And they could do it sooner if there were the wish," Judy grumbled. "I never seen a King's ship handled so sloppily." A rumble of agreement greeted his words; be they friend or enemy, no regular Jack respected poor seamanship, and it was something the sloop was exhibiting in spades.

"It's her captain," Laidlaw informed them knowingly. "He's

nowt more than a lad with an admiral for a father. First luff's got more of an idea, which is probably why they put him there, though he's too much of a slave-driver to get the best from the people."

"Once they gets in close, it'll be a different matter," Compton snorted. "Lubbers or not, they'll swarm over our little lot with sheer numbers."

Laidlaw said nothing; whatever the situation, Compton always wore a Friday face, although on this occasion there was little to fault his logic. Even ignoring her firepower, a Navy sloop carried up to three times their complement and would easily overpower *Narcis* given half the chance.

And he was not the only deserter on board; probably half the brig's seamen would have been marked down as runners. The rest might get away with nothing more than being pressed into the next available warship but Laidlaw, and his fellow renegades, would face a far less pleasant outcome.

"Well he ain't got in close yet," Judy told them firmly. "And still might not, judging by the mess they made of settin' that t'gallant."

"An' without bow chasers, he'll have to come a darn sight nearer afore he can get a broadside gun to bear," Laidlaw agreed.

"You don't reckon she'll yaw, then?" Compton asked, and all eyes turned to Laidlaw as their resident expert on the subject.

"They might wish to," he replied steadily, "but I somehow doubt it. When I were aboard she didn't have the discipline for heavy weather manoeuvres. It were one of the reasons I jumped ship; no proper exercises and with the first luff treating us like a bunch of whipping boys, I'd had enough."

"And, it's a stiff breeze for fancy sailin'," Judy remarked, and even Compton seemed to agree. Minutes passed with no change and the men began to relax slightly. There was even a measure of laughter from another gun and Judy started to hum tunelessly. Then a call from the masthead turned them all to stone once more.

"Sightin's haulin' in her wind – no wait, she's turnin'!"

"He's right!" Compton was almost triumphant as he pointed excitedly over the top rail, although all could see plainly enough what was about.

"Well, will you look at that?" Judy sighed. It had begun with a flutter of canvas, but now the sloop was undoubtedly yawing. Even as they watched, her bows were being thrust savagely to larboard and soon her starboard broadside was being presented. Then they could see the open ports, along with a neat line of grinning cannon that were already run out and ready to do business. The sloop was less than a mile off and with ten broadside guns she was almost certain of scoring one hit at such a range. And possibly considerably more.

\* \* \*

Lewis watched his opponent manoeuvre in silence. It was hardly an elegant procedure; the sloop laboured in the swell like an ancient third rate, but it was done in time. He could not guess whether the American ensign had been noticed or simply ignored, but evidently *Narcis* was not to be treated to the customary shot across the bows; they may not be a seaman, but whoever commanded that sloop meant business.

"They're going to fire upon us," Reid stood next to him at the taffrail and seemed as fascinated by the Navy vessel as a rabbit might be by a fox.

"Then we must make every provision," Lewis snapped as he tore his glance away and turned to address his own command. "Stand to there! Secure yourselves!"

*Narcis* was in no position to reply and, even if she could, lacked the firepower to make a discernible impression on a proper warship. At such a distance the sloop's shots could have done a deal of mischief, but there was still the strong wind to consider, and Lewis doubted a broadside could be laid with any accuracy.

The men had obviously been ready for his order and all who could threw themselves down, gaining easy shelter on the cluttered deck. The quartermaster still gripped the wheel, but did so from a kneeling position, while the rest of the crew apparently vanished, with only the occasional head peeping up above the crates and packing cases that littered the brig's topsides. Lewis turned back to Reid, who was still gazing aft and apparently transfixed.

"You as well, John," he told him.

The younger man appeared uncertain at first, but eventually crouched down behind the timbers of the ship. Then Lewis looked up to face the enemy once more and, standing firmly as every captain should, noticed with apparent interest when a thin red line flowed along the sloop's side as her broadside was released.

\* \* \*

Considering the atrocious conditions, the shots fell with amazing accuracy, and *Narcis* was comprehensively bracketed. But their fortune had two faces: despite the inordinately good shooting, the brig only suffered minimal damage. A smack from aloft told the end of her main topgallant mast, although, as she was sailing under topsails alone, that made no immediate difference to her trim. But the debris still rained down on the deck, causing a split head here and a bruised shoulder there, if no fatal injuries. Lewis looked back from his examination of the brig, and viewed the Navy sloop anew. Little had changed, she still lay broadside on, and was being buffeted by the wind that blew across her beam.

"It must have been fortunate timing," Reid grunted as he clambered up from his hiding position and glanced about. "Not even service gunners can be that well disciplined."

"See to the wounded," Lewis told him briskly, while he continued to consider the sloop.

What Reid said might well be true, it being easier to train gun crews than topmen. That being the case, the enemy might stay as they were and chance another broadside, but every second the sloop lay wallowing in the swell would be one that must be made up in the coming chase. *Narcis* was continuing to add to her lead although one thing was clear: there would be little relaxation for him for as long as the warship lay on their tail.

Then there was a further complication; the wind was starting to die. Not significantly so at that moment, but in an hour or less he guessed they would have to set more canvas. Topgallants were the obvious choice, had not the recent damage to their main ruled out anything other than the fore. He could still turn, take the wind more on the beam, and add staysails and jibs, but such a course would be a greater advantage to his enemy, and capture now seemed even more likely.

Or they might ditch some of the cargo; that which lay on deck could be easily jettisoned, while there would be little difficulty in reaching the top tier of casks in the holds. Now they were under fire, there was little point in maintaining any pretence of what *Narcis* was about and, however Lewis looked at the situation, she seemed to be doomed. The sloop must surely catch her, in which case his only option was to strike.

It would undoubtedly be the ethical way to end matters; some might even say honourable. No lives would be lost, and the fact of his surrender might even count for him in a future trial. Although Lewis thought not; no officer who had first betrayed his word, then his country, could expect mercy and there was little point in thinking further.

However, it seemed no more broadsides were intended; instead the sloop was coming back to the wind and the chase would begin again. Once more the manoeuvre was clumsy, and Lewis was gratified to note *Narcis* had added a considerable distance to her lead. For the moment the breeze was holding strong and might continue to do so, although there was a tendency for it to gust. There may even be a return of the rain, in which case they could hide within a squall, and stretch the time out until darkness.

And then, even as he looked, the impossible happened.

* * *

Laidlaw was feeling groggy; a lump of tophamper had struck him on the crown, his vision was blurred and he had difficultly in moving. But all about him men were active; some dealing with their fellow seamen, roughly bandaging open wounds with strips of yellowed canvas, while others had set to ditching wreckage over the side. He held a hand to his head as the pain surged, then made for the bulwark as a feeling of nausea rose up inside him. The brass top rail felt cold and firm, a small segment of solidity in a world that was ever moving and, as he gripped it, he naturally looked back to his former home; the ship that had caused their damage.

She was turning. It was not an elegant manoeuvre, but one that would see her round in time, when, presumably, the chase would begin once more. He, too, was of the opinion the wind would drop; it had been growing fluky for a while, although the sky remained as dark as ever and rain might easily return.

Then he noticed the change. The sloop had been halfway through her turn, with the sails just beginning to fill, when a particularly heavy gust hit her. The entire ship dipped slightly as the wind pressed her down, and she faltered. Then, just as the hull was righting itself, there came a billowing of canvas, and her outline changed.

"The enemy!" he wheezed. "She's dismasted!"

Only those close to him heard, but soon others picked up on the fact and a ragged cheer began to echo about the brig. Laidlaw was not entirely right; the sloop had only lost her fore-topmast and main topgallant, but it was close enough; she would carry far less sail, and it was the end of any more chases for her that day.

Judy arrived next to Laidlaw at the rail and slapped him on the back in a way that made the Cornishman's body ring like a bell.

"How did that happen?" he asked and Laidlaw shrugged.

"Never were much of a ship," he muttered. "Poorly led, and poorly manned. Bad provisions an' her last refit weren't up to much. With no one botherin' enough to complain, that's the sort of result you can expect," he added indicating the stricken vessel that even now was disappearing with their wake.

"Well, that'll learn 'em!" Judy grinned, and Laidlaw nodded in agreement. It certainly would; there were those he had liked aboard that ship, but they were just the Jacks. Any of her officers could go hang, as far as he was concerned, and that included the boatswain, who was almost as evil as the first luff. All would have their work cut out getting the ship back into reasonable shape and seeing her safely to harbour. With a bit of luck she would have to wait for repairs, which meant those he cared for would get a bit of a break, even if there was no chance of shore leave. So, all in all, he supposed it was a good ending; he just wished his head did not hurt so.

# Chapter Twenty

Aimée had been spot on with her prediction. On the following Sunday evening Banks, King and the rest of those held in the Citadel were marched out of their cell and down the narrow stone steps that led to the world beyond. Outside it was dusk and raining heavily; those with coats pulled them tightly against their already cold bodies as the group splashed over the granite flags of the courtyard. The town below seemed quiet, even for a Sunday, although few would have gone out in such weather unless forced to do so. The guards wore long, wax-coated capes that almost met their full-brimmed hats but, despite being so prepared, were equally keen to be moving and guided them briskly towards the old Convent Chapel that stood opposite the Citadel. The derelict building looked large and forbidding; it would also be cold although, if it truly were to be their means of escape, the British trusted they would not have to suffer it long.

"We don't seem to be making for the Chapel itself," Banks muttered as they drew closer and passed by the large and heavily padlocked front door.

"No; the storehouse," King reminded him, over the noise of the rain. "Aimée said there would be a way through."

The smaller structure was made of a similar stone and set to one side of the Chapel. Its no less solid door was soon opened and the prisoners were hurried through.

Inside there was only one room, and it was relatively bare; no beds or pallets had been provided, just a couple of wooden benches, while the single window was set high in the wall. It looked out to the opposite side of the Chapel and was heavily barred. But at least they had a modicum of privacy: the guards did not follow them inside and, as soon as the outer door was heaved shut, the British were left alone.

Those who had coats took them off and shook away what water they could, while the rest merely rubbed at their limbs in an effort to get warm and dry. The room carried a vault-like chill and smelt of damp earth, although all had been waiting for this moment for some time and hardly noticed.

"There should be a door through to the Chapel itself," King muttered, as he glanced about. They had been left with one rush dip and the meagre light cast huge shadows over the bare, stone room.

"Nothing stands out." Banks was glaring suspiciously at the adjoining wall. Apart from a fireplace that had been planked over, it was without feature and seemed to stare back, solid, sound and impenetrable.

"It must be through here," King mused, as he collected the rush dip from its mounting and examined the fireplace more carefully.

"Can't see us getting very far up a chimney," Banks snorted, but King made no reply. The fireplace itself was sealed up, and he could feel his disappointment increase: yet Aimée had been certain of a way through...

He prised at one of the planks with his fingers; it had been securely fixed but another might give way, if only he had some form of tool. He glanced back and about the room.

"The pail," he said, pointing at the necessary bucket in one corner. "Can someone see if the handle will come free?"

Two of the lads made for the enamelled vessel and, between them, wrenched the curved metal handle off. One handed it to King, who was not the best equipped to use a lever, and passed it in turn to Cranston. Soon the seaman had persuaded one of the planks free; the others were then more easy to dislodge and within five minutes the old fireplace was revealed.

"It is shared by next door," Cranston announced, peering through the hole. "Though the other side is planked in as well."

"Can you deal with that?" Banks asked as he bent down to look also.

The seaman collected the light from King and crawled halfway into the fireplace.

"It's a thorough job, your honour," he muttered. "But I reckons I can kick it down, though will make a clutter doing so."

"Leave it for now," Banks told him. "We had better look to the rope."

They had been fed in their cell at the Citadel, so the next time they expected to see any guards was when they were collected at first light. Even so, it still felt unsafe to remove their shirts and openly reveal the lengths of laid straw that had been wrapped about their bare chests.

"See to it, Cranston," Banks said, turning to the seaman once more. "Splice them if you can, otherwise knots will be acceptable. And I need not remind you, it is vital they hold."

Cranston gave an ironic grin as he placed the light in front of him and settled down to work.

"When do we go?" It felt natural for King to whisper the question, even though there were no French in the room and, considering the weather, unlikely to be any immediately outside.

"I'd say the sooner the better," Banks replied. His voice was equally low, but carried the edge of command. "Each of you check your provisions," he continued more loudly. "Anything not vital must be left behind: we shall have to travel light."

They had been expecting nothing less, and were pretty much ready, although all the preparations in the world could not allow some of them to pass as civilians.

Robert Manning had a woollen coat, while Brehaut wore a master's jacket, which might have belonged to any form of mariner. Thankfully, King was wearing his overcoat when arrested and Banks had a generous velvet cloak; it was currently sodden, but would still serve as a disguise. But Timothy, along with Adams and the rest, only had their dark blue broadcloth tunics and even a hint of light would reveal them for what they were.

"You had better take this," Manning said, handing his overcoat to Timothy. "My surgeon's uniform will hardly attract attention."

"We still haven't fully solved the problem of getting into the Chapel," King pointed out, as the lieutenant gratefully tried the coat on. "If only it weren't so damned dark."

"I could break up a bench," Adams suggested as he peered at the fireplace. "It would make a longer lever."

"I still says I can kick it down," Cranston volunteered from his place on the floor. After his recent string of successes he felt able to speak out, even in such august company. "But you might want to find a way to muffle the sound."

"Kick it through a greatcoat," Soames suggested, and they

were beginning to consider this when a strange and low noise began.

It was not so much a note as a rumble, and came from the seaman splicing rope in front of the rush dip. For a moment no one moved, and King even went to order him silent. Then he saw the wisdom in the seaman's actions.

"*We'll rant and we'll roar, like true British sailors, We'll rant and we'll roar across the salt seas...*"

The lads were the first to join in, and did so with gusto; soon the senior men were following until the stone walls echoed to the sound of raw male voices singing in an approximation of harmony. A midshipman began to slap out a steady rhythm against his leg and Timothy, seated on one of the wooden benches, started stamping on the floor.

Banks was not a great one for singing, although he was quick to see the point in this instance. Cranston would be a while yet with the rope, but it made sense to start early; that way if there were any guards in the vicinity they would get used to their prisoners' strange behaviour. Of course, the noise would have to end as soon as they made it through to the Chapel, but there was no avoiding that; it was yet another chance they would have to take.

The opportunity came as their shared repertoire was being repeated for the third time; Cranston eased himself up from the floor and held the coil of line aloft in triumph. King looked enquiringly at Banks, who collected his cloak and walked over to the fireplace. By then the singers were firmly established in *Heart of Oak*, which leant itself to percussion accompaniment and this was soon augmented by Cranston's bare feet thumping in time against the wooden panels. The seaman had removed his shoes, presumably in an effort to reduce the noise and, even though he knew the soles would be as hard as iron, King still winced slightly as he watched. But at the fifth stamp the first splinter appeared and, just as they had finished the song, it was possible to press the rest of the planks out from the fireplace.

"Shall we go?" King asked, as Cranston cleared the debris away.

Banks gave a wry smile. "Unless you have a better idea," he replied.

They clambered through the fireplace, then gathered cautiously in the small room beyond.

"Must be some form of vestry," Timothy supposed as he held the light aloft. There were several pieces of furniture scattered about but every surface contained nothing but dust, while a quick check of the cupboards and drawers revealed them to be empty.

"Best try the door," Banks said as he walked towards it, and there was a collective sigh of relief when it opened easily.

Beyond was the vast, open space of the Chapel itself. Light from their single rush dip did not go far, and it was quite dark now outside; the large, and probably highly decorated, stained glass windows could only just be made out, while the constant trickle of water finding its way through the old roof told them that rain still fell.

"We're to make for the altar," King announced, remembering Aimée's instructions. They appeared to be at the head of the nave, which meant the chancel must be to their left. He stepped forward cautiously, but Banks was ahead of him, and began to stride over the stone floor as if it were broad daylight. King had been promoted to commander about a year before and was used to leading, but happily followed his old captain while Timothy, who still carried the precious light, tagged along behind.

"This must be about the place!" he said, as they reached the centre of the building. Sure enough, to one side they could make out an ornate statue set in front of a large window that was far higher than they had hoped. Timothy held the light up, and for a moment no one spoke. Then Banks broke the silence.

"Even if we could reach it, such a thing would be hard to break," he said, his voice betraying his disappointment. King said nothing; to have come so far, yet still be thwarted, was worse than making no progress at all. He could not blame Aimée; the plan had been proposed with the best of intentions, it was simply a shame she had misjudged either the window, or their capabilities.

Banks and Timothy went forward to examine the altar more closely, but King did not follow. He supposed they might return to their cell and get what sleep they could. The guards would be coming at first light and were bound to discover that wrecked fireplace. Well what of it? They were to be punished anyhow.

"Come on, there is a way."

King looked up to see the vague shape of Sir Richard who was standing on the altar and seemed to be climbing onto the statue itself.

"There's some form of curtain here," Banks told him when he drew nearer. "I would judge that..." there was a pause as he strained, then the rumble of falling cloth. King peered up. Something had fallen away: the wall behind the altar was now lighter and, more importantly, a small rectangle had been revealed.

"It must be some sort of casement," Banks muttered. "Get Cranston up here!"

The others had followed and soon the seaman was clambering up next to Banks, and examining the wall.

"It's a wooden hatch, but boarded up – like them fireplaces," he announced. "Let's see if we can't persuade it open, like we did them. What happened to that bucket handle?"

The bent piece of metal was passed up and the seaman began worrying at the wooden planking. All below waited in a silence that was soon broken by a gentle groan, followed by a sharp snap. Then Cranston ducked down.

"Kill that light!" It was an odd instruction for a regular Jack to address to a group of officers, but Timothy did not hesitate in obeying. The flame spluttered out, and there was no means of reigniting it, although all sensed Cranston had done something to make the rush dip redundant.

\* \* \*

"Blasted weather!" Timothy grumbled, as the three officers peered out of the small opening, but both King and Banks said nothing. It might not make their escape easier, but at least the driving rain should discourage onlookers, and any guards stationed nearby would be more inclined to take shelter than maintain a dutiful watch. There was no moon and the cloud was heavy, but still the town below them was visible, as was the small, formal garden directly beneath their vantage point.

"I'd assumed we would be coming out on the courtyard," King whispered. "This is unknown territory."

233

"But at least we are beyond sight of the guards," Banks pointed out. "We just have to get through this, then make for the outer wall."

"Would that be a fire?" Timothy asked, pointing to one side. King and Banks had to strain to see, but yes, there were definitely flames visible in the lower part of the town.

"Mainly storehouses in that area," Banks grunted. "Unless it is one of the shops – difficult to tell from this distance."

King said nothing, his mind was set on more immediate problems. It had already taken three men and quite a bit of effort to heave him onto the altar, and there was now a gap between that and the wall which must be all of three feet. How he would get across, manoeuvre out of the small space, then down to the ground he had no idea. The drop could be no more than fifteen feet and there would be obstacles far higher that must be negotiated later. Admittedly little actual climbing would be required, but even being lowered on a rope did not seem exactly feasible. However, Banks was not so pessimistic.

"Come, Tom," he said firmly. "We may as well start with you."

"Me first?" King asked, momentarily aghast.

"No reason why not," Banks told him briskly. "Leave it any longer and you will only concern yourself." Even in the poor light, King could see the look of amused understanding on the senior man's face as he called for the rope to be sent up and realised Sir Richard must know him better than he had thought.

Standing on the altar, King allowed the line to be secured about his chest before clambering to the edge and reaching tentatively for the opening. Then, with his good arm pulling, and Banks and Timothy supporting from behind, he heaved his upper body over the gap and onto the small ledge. Peering outside, he could now get a better view. There was definitely some sort of blaze in the lower town: he could see lanterns in the streets and what appeared to be a crowd heading in that direction. From such a distance it was impossible to tell what was going on, but if it took attention away from men escaping from an old Convent Chapel, he would be satisfied. He glanced down to the ground immediately below; the drop was not great, but looked so from that angle. Someone was still pressing his feet from behind and he kicked them away; if he was going to launch himself off into the darkness he would do so in his own time.

Easing out further, he reached the stage when his body was at the very edge of falling, then bent back and turned onto his side as he hung tightly to what seemed to be a stupidly narrow sill. All fears of being spotted were now forgotten as he clung on; the one thing on his mind was to get himself clear and be able to drop down to the ground below as quietly as possible.

Slowly, and with great care, he began to ease his legs down. His arm ached and, even though the night was sharp with cold, rain washed sweat from his face. For a moment he tottered on the slim piece of wood before giving the dimly seen group on the altar a nod. The rope grew taught as they braced up, then he kicked himself free and, gripping onto the wood with his only hand, King slipped silently out of the window.

He managed to maintain his hold while his body straightened out; then it slipped, and he knew himself to be falling. He dropped for no more than three feet before the rope pulled tightly against his chest; there was a moment of intense pain when the line rode up under his armpits and he had to suppress a cry as he began to sway slightly. Then the rope broke, and King fell the rest of the way to the ground.

# Chapter Twenty-One

He could not have travelled far, probably less than five feet, but the shock, combined with a physical jolt from landing flat on his feet, seemed to run through his entire body. For a moment he stood quite still, then glanced up to where the dim shape of Timothy's head could be seen looking down from above.

He was holding the other end of the line in his hand; seeing this, King examined his own piece. The thing had only been made from straw, and it was with little surprise that he noticed the fibres had simply parted. Throughout their time in the Citadel, it had never been possible to test the strength in any reliable fashion, and now it looked as if the line was not sufficient to hold the weight of a single man.

The rain still fell heavily and all was quiet in the immediate vicinity; he may not have been spotted but there were several hundred yards to cover and at least three further walls to descend. Without a reliable rope it would be impossible; they may as well wake up the guard now and hand themselves in.

But, even as he thought, the line snaked down beside him, and was soon supporting Timothy's body as it slithered down.

"Were you hurt, Tom?" he asked upon landing.

"Not a bit," King replied. "But we cannot trust the rope."

"I'm not so sure," Timothy whispered and he was looking up to where Adams was starting his descent. "You did give it quite a tug, and I managed fine. I'd figure it worth persevering a while longer."

King said nothing; his initial fall had been checked rather sharply although such an incident hardly inspired confidence.

"So where next?" he asked, when Banks joined their small group.

"We're to cross the Convent garden," the captain replied as he looked about. It was all very different to the courtyard. Across a patch of level grass there was a small stone wall, but beyond that lay mystery.

The others soon assembled with Cranston, the last down, flipping the rope back after him, and reeling it in.

"I take it we are happy to trust the line." Banks' words were murmured in a voice both low and intense and not phrased as a question. Yet it was clear all remained game, and they set off towards the first wall.

"That will be Wirion's garden," King whispered as they reached it and peered over.

"And those, his quarters," Manning added. Sure enough a lamp at a bare window revealed an empty kitchen, while several further rooms which were lightly curtained would probably be the living area.

"Never mind about that," Banks hissed, "we have to keep moving."

"Shall I be first again?" King asked dubiously.

"No, Tom, we'll send someone to catch you this time," Banks told him. "Summers, get yourself over and report."

The midshipman vaulted onto the top of the wall, payed out the line, and soon disappeared over the other side.

"It held," Soames reported. He had also mounted the wall, and was looking down at the drop below. "I'd say it were no more than twenty foot."

"That's longer than before," Banks grunted. "We'll send Mr King next; he can be lowered more carefully this time, then the rest can follow."

King stepped forward rather tentatively but it was easier. Several hands were able to help him up and over the wall, the line held, and in no time he was standing on the sodden grass below with Summers. He could see Banks directing from above; once more the line was looped about an obstruction, allowing the rest to clamber down on twice its thickness, before one end was pulled back when the last was safely down.

"There should be another like that," King told them. "Then we reach the outer rampart, which might not be so easy."

"Well it certainly won't be as low," Manning agreed.

Banks said nothing, he had been living in Verdun longer than anyone, although all were now familiar with its silhouette; in no place were the town walls less than seventy feet high and sometimes towered to more than twice that. Their rope could not measure more than eighty; anything taller would mean their jumping the remainder, and what they would do about King was another matter entirely.

And then he faltered. So far all had been going relatively smoothly; he felt he had led the group well, and they were following, almost as when he was a true ship's captain commanding his crew. But suddenly he began to have doubts. The relative freedom enjoyed in Verdun had almost fooled him into believing himself invulnerable, yet now they were outside their prison cell, in the dark and the rain, and no one could be in any doubt about what they were intending. Luck had been with them that far, but it would only take one guard to sound the alarm and armed *gendarmes* would come pouring out of every doorway. In the next thirty seconds any one of those under his command might be shot without warning while he, as their leader, could expect nothing less the following morning.

But the moment of doubt was only that; even as he acknowledged his uncertainty another feeling, one that owed much to age and experience, came to replace it. This might be the smallest crew he had commanded in ages, while the prospect of getting them out of the town did not seem hopeful, but he would carry it through, as he had with so many apparently impossible ventures in the past. And there was no sense in standing still and worrying; they might as well carry on and meet their demons head on.

* * *

The first half had ended, and Lovemore was just deciding whether to abandon his chair and go in search of a drink, when he became aware that something was not quite right. It was the last of so many nights in the theatre that he had become immune to the combined stink of lamp oil, tobacco fumes and humanity, but now there was a different cast to the air, and it did not take him long to realise what it was.

Smoke, though hardly the kind that came from even the cheapest cigar; this was a good old-fashioned fireside aroma. And not from wood either, although the scent was just as familiar. Most of the other musicians had fled in search of refreshment; only

238

Chiara, the girl with the harp, remained. Lovemore's French was improving all the time, but he still felt disinclined to ask if she could smell burning. For even as he sat there the fumes became stronger, and then he knew for certain the smell was from a coal fire.

* * *

They had crossed Wirion's garden and descended the next wall without incident but, now their final obstacle lay before them, Banks drew the group into the shelter of a large elm to take stock. There would be a brief climb to reach the ramparts from that side, but nothing more than seven feet and he felt they might lift King up that much. Then they would be on the walkway, with only what appeared to be a small wall to separate them from freedom. But the drop on the other side was his main concern, that and, while they were on the ramparts, his men would be horribly exposed. The sky was still dark, and rain fell so continuously that he, for one, had almost ceased to notice it. But unless it were pitch dark, anyone standing on the town wall would be obvious from a distance, and a group the more so.

"There appears to be no guard," Timothy commented, and there was a murmur of agreement from the rest.

"Why should there be?" Summers asked. "Who would wish to break into a prison?"

A smattering of laughter greeted the question, which Banks took to be a good sign.

"Besides," he added, "all seem to be gainfully employed in the lower town."

That was certainly true. The small fire first seen when leaving the Convent Chapel had now grown into a mighty blaze which lit most of the industrial area of the town, and even lent light to them, sheltering under the tree.

"That will be someone's loss," Manning mused. "Though it could not have come at a better time for us."

"And we may as well make use of the diversion." Banks' voice once more carried a note of command and, even before he ordered them off, his men were preparing to go.

He had been right in his assumption; King was easily bunked

up to the rampart walkway and the rest soon followed. Then, while the others kept below the level of the outer wall, he and Banks glanced over the edge.

It was dark on the outer side, so much so that the ground immediately beneath could not be made out. But the land that stretched away from the town was more visible, and must be over a hundred feet below.

"It's beyond the reach of our line," Banks said softly, and King did not reply. With the rope only having been joined that evening, they merely had an approximation of its length, although Banks was undoubtedly correct: it would not be long enough.

"We could lower you on a bowline," the captain continued, looking to King. "If nothing else, you should be able to tell us how short it is and, if it be but a small distance, we may jump as far."

Still King remained silent; which was probably the best policy even if the idea appalled him. The rope had already proved unreliable, and he would be launching himself above unknown ground. Were it to snap as before, there would be a hard landing and, with no help at hand, one that might cost him his life.

"Or we could send Summers instead," Banks continued, sensing reluctance. "He is a mite lighter than yourself, even discounting the loss of your arm, and may have better eyesight."

"No, I shall go," King was speaking the words before he realised it. And once said, they were impossible to take back.

"Good man," Banks told him. "Cranston, be ready with that line."

* * *

King lay face down on the rampart top. To one side Timothy and Banks knelt close by while Cranston finished securing the line about his chest. To the other was a drop of perhaps a hundred feet, possibly more. But whatever the exact height, it might mean sudden death for him were he to fall; unless, that is, they were able to lessen the distance.

"I've set it so the hitch slips when you gives the end a tug," the seaman explained, indicating the knot tied under King's stump. "But only do that if you're sure of a safe landin'," Cranston warned. "I seen men twist an ankle from the smallest of falls, so you be careful, sir."

"Thank you, Cranston," King's tone was dubious.

"We shall not be able to communicate," Banks told him. "The end of the line will have been reached when you cease to move. At that point if it is feasible you may jump; otherwise we shall wait for perhaps thirty seconds and then retrieve you. Does that suit?"

"Yes, sir," King replied.

"Or, should you wish to come up sooner, you might always give a sharp tug," Timothy suggested with a grin that King did not return.

"If you're ready then?" Banks asked, and received a grunt in the affirmative.

Together the three of them eased King over, until his chest was resting on the stone capping while his legs hung above a sheer drop. Then, holding him by the shoulders, they allowed his body to scrape over the edge, while those stationed behind began to take the strain on the rope. Slowly, and with infinite care, King slid further, until only his head was above the parapet. There was a creaking of fibres as the line stretched under his weight and with a final glance at Banks, he was lowered out of sight.

So far, so good; the rope was holding, and King could make out the details in the rough stone wall as he gently tapped himself away from it with his one good arm. He dare not look down, but knew they were going a fair pace, which was probably sensible. The line had not been fully tested until this point. By its very nature, a hand-reeved straw rope was bound to give; it was just a question of whether that would be demonstrated by gently stretching, or another sudden break.

And then he seemed to be slowing and King guessed they were coming to the end. Looking down, he was relieved to see the ground was not so very far below. He continued to descend for perhaps another fathom; a brief pause, and an extra couple of feet were grudgingly allowed before he stopped, apparently for good.

The rain still fell and he had begun to sway in the cold breeze, but King hardly noticed either. The ground could not be more than ten feet off; a manageable jump, although he would have the added complication of releasing himself. He reached for the hitch and found the end, just where Cranston had promised. For a moment he simply gripped it while inwardly summoning the energy for action.

241

And then, at the same moment as the line began to move once more, he bore down hard on the rope. The hitch slipped easily and he felt himself twist slightly before he began to fall.

* * *

The theatre made a good return on food and drink served during the interval, so Lovemore reckoned he had time to investigate the strange aroma. He stepped through the stage door and, avoiding the lines of touting women, made for the main road.

It was crowded; along with those from the theatre, there were numerous *gendarmes* about, and a good number of civilians wearing heavy coats and hats who had clearly come prepared. The main excitement centred on a street two down from where he stood. It led to the very lowest part of the town, an area reserved for small industrial buildings and the very cheapest houses. He pushed his way through the throng and reached the road. Looking down, there was nothing to see but smoke at first, although, as he drew closer, the dull glow of a deeply embedded fire shone out from the ruins of one of the warehouses. It was freezing cold and Lovemore was already quite soaked, but the heat was enough to warm him, even though he stood some distance away.

The ringing of a bell made him look round, and he saw one of the town's three fire engines clattering along the street. It was pulled by two dark horses whose eyes glowed red in reflection from the blaze. He stepped to one side, and almost into a figure standing near by.

"A sad night, brother." It was Garrett, the magician; the man must have only come off stage a few minutes before, yet was there before him.

"Sad for whoever owned it," Lovemore agreed as he stared at the warehouse. Garrett still wore his stage costume of formal evening wear with no coat or cloak for protection, yet gave the impression of being perfectly warm and even dry.

"The building contained coal that belonged to the Silva family," the magician told him. "Your employers."

Lovemore looked round in incomprehension; the name meant nothing to him.

"They run the summer dances," Garret explained haughtily.

Now he understood. And the Silvas were nice folk, a husband and wife with three pretty daughters. He hoped none were injured, although the destruction of the warehouse would probably mean an end to their business. But quite what Garrett was doing here was another matter.

"Did you see this coming?" the magician asked his question first.

"See it?" Lovemore hesitated. "W-why should I?" He felt the flush of guilt rise in his face and was glad of the night to hide it.

"I recognised something was about during my performance," the Frenchman continued with his customary smugness. "As you would have, were your senses suitably primed."

"And do your senses tell if anyone was hurt?" Lovemore replied.

"No, but they do say this is not a normal fire," Garrett smiled. "Which is why I was drawn here."

"Not normal – in what way?"

The man gave a slight chuckle. "Much tonight is not normal," he replied enigmatically, before suddenly placing his arm through Lovemore's as if they were the very best of friends. "For a start, it is our last in Verdun," he continued, steering the seaman away. "But perhaps not the last together." He stopped and looked Lovemore full in the face once more. It was both darker and far colder away from the flames, while the rain continued to fall in sheets. But Lovemore felt his eyes lock on to the magician's as if they were drawn by an inner power. "And I personally hope not; though that is something I shall not openly predict," Garrett continued, with what might have been an element of threat. "Let us simply leave it to your own mind to decide," he said.

* * *

King landed on his feet but instinctively rolled onto one side. He was in thick cover; thorns and harsh prickles bit into his skin and tore at his clothes as he struggled up, but their scratches, like the rain and the chill of the night, meant nothing to him. The main thing – the only thing – that mattered was he had made it.

He staggered away from the bushes realising, just in time, that he was not on the ground proper but rather an earthen ridge, built

243

up to support the ramparts. To one side it dropped steeply away, and he could see a flat meadow beyond, about twenty feet lower. He retraced his steps to the stone wall itself and looked up. Now that he was outside the town it seemed darker, but still he could make out the straw rope as it was hauled back. At the top a series of small bumps showed where his friends were still gathered and, even as he watched, a figure rose up, and transferred itself to the line.

King guessed they had decided to lower the first few down in the same way as he had been; it would cause less strain to the delicate straw fibres and wear on the rope in general. He watched as the single figure drew steadily nearer then stopped abruptly. There was a slight pause before it dropped the last few feet, and King went to meet it.

"Tom, you are alright?" It was Manning, the surgeon; hardly the most agile of folk, which was probably another reason they had chosen to lower him down.

"I'm fine, Robert," King told him. "But surprised they chose to send you so soon."

Manning's teeth shone white in the gloom. "It's my belief they wanted a medic on hand should the rope break," he grinned.

Timothy was next, followed by Brehaut, then Banks himself, after which the midshipmen began to descend on their own while Cranston, probably the most capable climber, was the last man down.

"There is just the final hurdle," Banks informed them when they were all gathered together. "That slope is little more than a sheer drop," he continued. "And the pity is we cannot claim back our line."

Cranston's rope was still secured to the ramparts and would have to remain so as a testimony to their escape.

"There wasn't the length to allow me to loop it about, your honour," Cranston explained.

"No, of course not," Banks agreed. "The French may find it, and discover how we escaped but there is no changing that."

"So what next?" King asked. He had been on the ground longer than anyone and was eager to be off.

"I say we make a jump for it," Timothy was looking dubiously down at the slope. "With luck, we may be able to slide most of the way."

"And end with a turned ankle, I shouldn't wonder," Manning snorted.

"There are many of us, so the odds are for some to be injured," Banks agreed. "And even one not able to walk for himself will be a burden on the rest." His mind was racing; there had to be a solution, and it naturally fell to him to come up with it.

"Beggin' your pardon, sir, I have an idea." This was Cranston again and, despite his lowly status, all eyes turned to him.

"If three or four of us gather together in line of battle, we should slide down, and not tumble as a singleton might."

Brehaut pulled a face. "We shall get devilish muddy," he said.

"None of us are immaculate now," Timothy sighed.

"There is not the time to discuss matters fully – it will do," Banks snapped. "Tom, you have but one arm, so cannot hold fast; take the lead, I shall go second, Soames and Summers clap on behind."

King duly placed himself on the edge of the slope and felt Banks' boots thrust themselves deep under each armpit. He clutched the right one with his good arm, and tried to wedge the other under his stump, while feeling the captain's hands clamp his shoulders in a vice-like grip. In seconds they were ready, and then began to inch their way over the edge until the only thing stopping them from tumbling down was inertia. A moment's pause, then either someone gave a push, or the ground itself gave way, and they were slipping and sliding down the near vertical drop, with King's boots kicking up mud and water as they went.

The human train held until they were three-quarters of the way down, then its tail gathered speed and they began travelling sideways. This continued for no more than a few feet before the group broke up, and they rolled down the last few feet independently. But each landed in one piece and, muddy, wet and mildly bruised though they might be, none were injured.

"Well that is an experience I shall not forget lightly," Banks growled, while attempting to wipe the grime from his clothing. The light was poor, but still he could see the two mids. were equally filthy, although they appeared to be giggling softly in the manner of lads and even King had a slight grin on his face.

Banks considered them with a set and stern expression. They

were still by no means safe: at any moment their absence might be noticed – bells would be rung and armed guards with dogs sent out to recapture them. Any one of his small force could be shot simply for being where they were, so what the youngsters found amusing was totally beyond him.

"Mr Summers, kindly signal for the remainder to follow," he told one of the midshipmen who was still chuckling softly. The boy stood up straight and collected himself, before starting to wave both arms to the waiting group above.

"Well, at least they know what they're in for," Banks mused, any planned rebuke temporarily forgotten.

"Aye, sir," King agreed, although there was something in his voice that sounded mildly forced, and Banks wondered if the sight of a blacked midshipman gesticulating wildly in the pouring rain had anything to do with it.

"Are you all right, Mr King?" he asked stiffly.

"Oh yes, sir," King replied, but there was definitely a strain in his voice. "I were just thinking about what they were in for," he explained, his suppressed laughter now becoming evident. "Best mud bath they're ever likely to take, and there we were worrying over disguises."

There was a moment's pause as Banks considered this, and then he smiled also. "It's like the old times, ain't it Tom?" he said, his tone finally softening.

"Aye, sir," King confirmed. "It is."

# Chapter Twenty-Two

Three hours later the rain had stopped and, though dawn remained some way off, their walking had generated a degree of warmth. But they were still wet – horribly so. If anything, the constant, regular movement seemed to exaggerate the feeling and King, for one, would have given anything for a hot bath, a change of clothes and a warm bed.

But there were plenty of other thoughts to take his mind from such luxuries. For a start, he was becoming increasingly worried about where they were going. The speed of their capture and later incarceration in the Citadel meant no firm plans had been made for their escape; the very opposite in fact, while the last time he had spoken properly to Aimée he was almost reluctant to go, and dead against her coming with them. Since then, the British had been working on what she all had but screamed at him through the bars of the cell, but such a method of communication did not allow for important details to be covered.

For a start, he was only vaguely sure when and where they would meet with her brother. From what he could gather, Antoine had an extensive business transporting coal through the canals of France and the Low Countries, but even if that meant a massive fleet of vessels, how were they to know exactly where to locate the man himself? Were they to run into Aimée before then, there might not be a problem, but that was something else that had not been fully addressed.

He knew her well enough to accept such an independent spirit would not be put off, but how was he supposed to find her in the dark French countryside? The others in his group would have more than enough to do keeping themselves hidden from search parties and curious locals to waste time looking for a single girl who might or might not be there, and he could see no end of complications if he wished to seek her out, while the rest chose not to.

And finally, King was not certain they were heading in the

right direction. On leaving the town they had turned west as it seemed the obvious choice and must surely take them closer to the town where Aimée's brother was based. They had passed a small village shortly afterwards, along with several unsigned intersections and, without map or compass, could not be sure if the road they were on was still correct. The countryside had changed from the wide open meadows that surrounded the town, to far denser foliage, while the road they currently trudged along was passing through thick forest. For all anyone knew, they might equally be making south, north, or even back to the east and Verdun. If the low-lying cloud gave way and there was a break in the trees, things would alter; all they needed was a brief sight of the stars to confirm their direction. But failing that, there was little choice other than to wait for sunrise and accept that every soggy step they took might be leading them deeper into danger.

"What cheer, Tom?" This was Manning; King could see him in the dim light as he increased his pace to come alongside and gave his old friend an amicable nod. It seemed any bad feeling regarding their escape had been forgotten and King was glad.

"Well enough, thank you, Bob," he told him.

"Stump not giving you problems?" the surgeon persisted, and now King smiled.

"I believe that to be a question you shall be asking for as long as we know each other," he said.

"Is that so strange?" Manning shrugged. "It is my way: my calling, if you like. Sure, it is rare that I am able to follow up on past treatments although, considering the strain you have inflicted on a simple amputation, I suppose that is for the better." He sighed. "There are few patients who try my work to such a degree."

"At the moment there are a deal of problems bothering me," King confessed. "Yet happily a past wound is not amongst them."

"Belike, why we are not being pursued?" Manning chanced and King glanced sidelong at him. Surprisingly that had not been his chief concern although, now that his friend mentioned it, the fact grew in importance.

"I think we might thank the fire for that," the surgeon continued. "Such coincidences are rare, and is it not strange that your young lady's family are in the coal industry?"

"It is," King admitted, forcing his tired mind to focus. "And they have a warehouse in the lower town, as I recall."

"I think you might properly say they *had* a warehouse," Manning corrected. "And my guess would be the very building we saw ablaze."

"But why would they do such a thing?" King asked, before realising he already knew the answer.

"To protect their daughter," Manning's tone was definite. "If the lass was intending to meet with us, she must have left the town earlier. Her father would be concerned for her safety and, were she caught aiding prisoners to escape, a spell in Bitche might be considered one of the better options."

Images of Aimée amid the terrible conditions of a punishment depot swarmed, unbidden, into King's brain and he shivered.

"But a sound fire, like the one we witnessed..." The surgeon left his sentence unfinished; really there was no more to say.

"And you think *Monsieur* Silva would have burnt down his warehouse, just to save us?" he asked softly.

"No I don't," Manning replied. "I think he did it to save his daughter, which he may well have done. The number required to put out such a blaze would put a drain on the guard and frankly I doubt if our rope has yet been noticed, or we are even missed."

"Then I should gauge we owe the Silvas a considerable debt," King mused softly.

"And one you may only repay by caring for their daughter," Manning agreed. "Wherever she may be."

* * *

Actually, Aimée was far closer than anyone realised. After a conversation with her family that lasted most of the previous morning, she had finished packing and, with a story about visiting a neighbouring village for the *gendarmes* at the *Porte Chaussée*, left the town just after noon. She, too, had been unsure of what route to take; the British were aware of their ultimate destination and she trusted them to head west, but there were two roads they could have chosen.

One led directly to Valenciennes, while the other meandered through forests and open countryside before finally winding up at the town. Strangely the second was the better option; it passed through fewer villages so there was less chance of papers being demanded, and tended to be quieter. It might cost them a day or more in extra travel, but there was a far better chance of arriving safely. She took it herself in the hope they would also but it was little better than an even chance; the British were bound to know little of French roads and, other than she loved him, Aimée hardly knew a great deal more about King.

She twisted uncomfortably in her hiding place. It was in the lee of a fallen tree and gave a reasonable view of the route back to Verdun: a road that seemed doomed to be forever empty. Her shelter was less than ten miles from the town, and close enough to head north to the other road if she felt the wrong choice had been made. But what concerned her most was the lack of commotion. She hardly expected to hear alarm bells from such a distance but, if the British had made it out of the depot, the search parties with dogs and lights would surely have reached this far in the time. Yet the only sound other than her heavy breathing was the constant drip of water from the sodden trees, and her concerns were growing.

For all she knew the British might not even have broken out of the storeroom, or the Chapel itself. Alternatively, one of them could have fallen on their way down the ramparts, or been spotted earlier on the road, and were already back in custody. And finally they might have taken the other road, which she should be making for now, if she wanted to avoid missing them completely.

Of them all, the last option was the worst, as effort was required, either in staying put or running north for all she was worth, and it was a supreme act of will that kept her sitting in her miserable shelter. But whatever the odds, and however misguided she may be, Aimée would wait a while longer. It would take an hour or more to reach the other road; a time when there was no chance of meeting with King, so she may as well spend it where she was. Then, if he absolutely refused to show, she might still try to catch his group elsewhere, or even make enquires at the next village. But of one thing Aimée was certain, she was not going back to Verdun.

During a varied life she had experienced much of the good, and bad, the world had to offer and both had left their mark. She was nowhere near as gullible or careless as when a child although, even after so short a time, was already certain the slightly naïve British officer was the best thing to come her way. And she had no intention of letting him go without a fight.

But it was cold, dark, wet and, despite being a relatively short distance from her home, Aimée felt very alone. With her she had brought a large bag filled with assorted coats and jackets that had belonged to her father and brother. She opened it now and, feeling mildly guilty, brought out a particularly heavy *capote* that was far too big, but wrapped comfortably over her own coat. The added warmth was almost immediate and she snuggled down in her nest, while tired eyes focused on the dark road that she so hoped would soon be filled by the escaping British. She was hungry, and had also brought bread, meat and cheese, but that was definitely for King and his companions. Aimée pulled the cape tighter about her and found herself resting against the bag of clothing. There was no way of telling the time, but she knew it to be late. She had walked a long way, worried a great deal, and now was very, very tired.

* * *

Dawn was undoubtedly coming; the first inklings of light were showing in the east, confirming their direction and signalling the time when they should rest, but still King continued to walk. He knew they should find a place to hold up for the day; his legs felt weary and he was beginning to see double with exhaustion but, however attractive the prospect, his mind still rebelled against it. For to stop now meant leaving the road; there was thick forest to either side and it should not take long to find somewhere hidden and sheltered where they could sleep in relative safety. Even a few hours would restore the group for another punishing night, then a couple of the lads might be sent out in an attempt to find food. But to do so meant effectively abandoning Aimée as well, and that was something King was not prepared to do.

Admittedly he would have expected to have come across her by then, and part of him wondered if every step he took was actually taking them further apart. But, while the faintest chance she might appear remained, he was determined to cling to it, and that slight possibility would dwindle to nothing when they took shelter. Consequently, when Banks and Brehaut caught him up and appeared eager to talk, he was noncommittal.

"Ready for a rest, Tom?" the sailing master asked, but King gave a neutral grunt and dug his good arm deeper into the pocket of his sodden overcoat. He could tell the two had been discussing matters before approaching him: maybe something of his reluctance to stop had been noticed, and they were about to take turns in winning him over. Well they did not have his incentive and would just have to work a bit harder.

"Master reckons we've covered all of fifteen miles." This was Banks' attempt. "That's probably far enough to see us clear of the town and, now that daylight's with us..."

"There may be *gendarmes* in pursuit," King mumbled, although they all knew the answer to that one.

"There might," Banks agreed. "Fire or no fire, our absence must be noticed by now."

"But they would not know in which direction we were set," Brehaut pointed out. "And we have already travelled a fair distance. Wirion simply does not have the forces for a wide search; there must come a time when we can consider ourselves relatively safe, from his *gendarmes* at least."

Yes, that was all reasonable enough, but King gave no response and continued the steady pace as if his legs were doing so of their own volition.

"I know you were hoping to meet up with the girl," Banks soothed, "but think we have missed her, and should stop."

Now the words were spoken it was as if a spell had been broken; the entire misery of the night's walk became apparent and King finally acknowledged the pains in his body that had been ignored for far too long.

"We may still meet up," he muttered stubbornly, although his pace had already begun to slow and both officers knew they were making progress.

"Of course we might," Banks agreed, carefully matching his speed. "Though she may be astern of us and trying to forereach, in which case stopping would be a mercy."

That was something King had not considered and the solid rhythm that had been powering him on decreased further.

"We could station a couple of the lads beside the road," Brehaut this time. "They can sleep watch and watch about and spot her should she appear."

King gave no reaction to this, although it was clear Brehaut's words had been on target.

"I really think we have gone on long enough," Banks repeated, this time more forcefully, before slowing dramatically himself.

Almost against his wishes, King found himself following and soon the entire group was standing quite still under the shade of countless dripping branches. The road they were on had been remarkably free of both traffic and habitation; at a few points they passed individual farms and there had been one small hamlet that was negotiated in the darkest hours. But for the past thirty minutes they had been passing through thick woodland and, now that shards of light were starting to cut through the heavy canopies, they could see it extended for some distance to either side.

"We might go right or left," Banks mused, as the rest gathered about him.

"Little to choose, I'd say," King sulked. It was a shame, but they were correct: Aimée had either missed them or changed her mind and decided to stay in the town, but the fact she was not there could not be disputed. They might still continue in the hope of meeting with her brother, but little good could be served by simply exhausting themselves. Besides, in daylight they must become far more noticeable; a group of men wandering the country lanes – it would be no time before the authorities were notified and they found themselves heading back into captivity. And then they heard the noise.

It was the faintest rumble of axles that was soon joined by the splash of horses' hooves on damp ground; a melody so subtle it might have been growing for a while and could easily have been missed entirely had they continued to walk.

"Horses!" Timothy hissed, and they all instinctively looked back in the direction of the sound.

"Take cover," Banks ordered. "But do not go too deep." The noise was growing louder by the second; whoever was pursuing them could not be far behind and, with the light growing ever solid, they might give themselves away in their efforts to escape.

The group split into two and dissolved into the heavy undergrowth that lined either edge of the road, breaking through briars and thorn bushes in search of safety. King found himself on the northern side with Banks, Timothy and Manning. He knew himself to be breathing heavily, as were they all, and pressed his hand over his mouth in an effort to dispel the cloud of condensation that could so easily give them away.

Then there came the grumbling of wheels; whatever followed must contain several vehicles, which would be logical in a long-distance chase, and explained the slowness of their pursuers' approach. Of course, it might as easily be a series of carts on the way to market, except the absence of any sizeable town from that direction would seem to discount it. Then King braced himself as the first sign of their hunters came into sight.

But it was not the troop of *gendarmes* riding ahead of a couple of service carts he had expected. Instead, King could make out a series of small closed wagons that lacked the uniformity of a military convoy and were driven by dark figures swamped in blankets and tarpaulins. Each wagon was pulled by two horses, with more tied to the rear of some, but none of the animals were being ridden and the only dog in sight was a rather scrawny terrier seated next to one of the drivers.

"Gypsies," Manning hissed in King's ear. "They are no harm to us," he continued, "We can let them pass by."

The surgeon was correct but, so tense had he become, King did not dare reply. It seemed the travellers had different ideas however and, just as the convoy came fully into sight and its carriages could be counted, it came to a slow stop. There was no noise; even the trees had ceased to drip as those hiding in the undergrowth held a collective breath. Then a figure appeared at the mouth of the leading coach.

Pushing past the driver, it jumped easily down onto the damp earth and stood for a moment, apparently taking in the scenery. There was something familiar about the man, but the light was still growing and, in his exhaustion, King knew his senses were not to be trusted. Then a second person appeared and this one he knew well.

"What the..." he whispered, and there was the hiss of protest from his companions as he began to pull himself up. "But it's Lovemore!" he protested. "Though the Dear knows what he is he doing out here!"

"Whatever it is, it would seem to be by his own free will,"

Manning added rising also, as the first man began walking about the carriage and staring into the woods.

"Who is the other fellow?" Banks asked; his voice was firmer and he no longer detected a threat.

"Seaman from my old ship," King replied. "Sound enough hand, but there's no telling what he's about in the middle of the French countryside."

"He may say the same for us," Banks commented dryly. Then a third figure appeared at the mouth of the carriage.

And this one was also recognisable; she was heavily clad in what looked like a man's cloak, but the face was unmistakable and, thrusting himself fully upright, King began to stumble back through the undergrowth and towards her.

She turned on seeing him coming and a smile broke out.

"Tom? Is that you?"

Ignoring the stiffness in his legs, King urged himself forward until he was almost running. And then he was on the road; that was Lovemore right enough while the other man was the magician from the concert party. But he only had eyes for the third figure and she, it appeared, was equally transfixed.

"Aimée!" he cried as he fell into her arms. "Aimée it's you!"

"Aye," Lovemore confirmed softly as he watched the pair embrace. "T'ain't nobody else."

\* \* \*

Two hours later Banks, King and Brehaut were crammed into one of the carriages and rumbling along a far better road. They had been given a change of clothes, some being provided by Aimée, others by the travellers, and now were tolerably warm, even though there was no obvious form of heating in the small space. Apart from the hard wooden locker they sat on, a bulging bookcase and a small desk, there was little other furniture in the carriage. Its owner, a slight, balding man of middle years with deep-set eyes and a benign expression, was seated opposite on what appeared to be an unusually large chair, although King suspected it would convert into a basic bed when the occasion demanded.

"*Monsieur* Lamar has confirmed they collected Tom's young lady some miles back," Brehaut translated for Banks and King.

"Since then they had been looking for us."

King had already learned as much from Aimée, while they had also discovered a good deal about the group's leader from Lovemore. It seemed that, despite an obvious lack of anything theatrical about him, Lamar had been leading the travelling players for many years. The company spent its time criss-crossing the country, calling at a variety of small towns and institutions where they gave a run of performances that lasted anything from a few days to several weeks.

"But how did they know when to stop?" Banks asked. "We were well enough hid, yet it was as if they knew where to find us." All eyes turned to the gentle figure seated opposite and Brehaut had begun to translate when a knowing smile spread over the placid face.

"Forgive me gentlemen, but it is probably easier if we continue in your own language," he said.

"We had no idea you spoke English," Banks protested, while trying to recall all that had already been said in what he had considered confidence.

"My knowledge is not great," Lamar replied. "But there is much to say and any other way will be slow."

"We were wondering how you knew where to look for us," King reminded him.

"As this gentleman has said, we found a young lady asleep, and she told of your presence."

"But you knew where to stop," Banks insisted, and once more that placid smile returned to add to his exasperation.

"My fellow travellers are of mixed abilities," Lamar explained calmly. "Some are performers, some musicians, and some have other talents that I cannot explain so easily."

The British officers glanced uncertainly at each other, but the man was speaking again.

"One of our number was sure you were in the hedgerow," Lamar continued. "And I am happy he was correct."

Despite the strong accent and, even though his explanation left much to be desired, the man spoke with such authority no one felt able to question further.

"But you will be wondering what it is you have joined," Lamar went on to suppose. "And where we shall be taking you?"

All three nodded in silence, and he continued.

"Our group is small, and its people change often," Lamar explained. "Much of the time it contains those who have been unfortunate in some way. Some are what the world calls criminals, and others have run from their country's demand that they should fight a war. I offer them a home, safety, and a chance to better both their circumstances and themselves. And I can tell you, gentlemen, that I am no friend of the Revolution, or the Emperor that has come after it."

"So what are you, a Bourbon?" Banks supposed.

At this Lamar gave a deep throated chuckle. "No, my personal roots are less easy to say. I was serving the Lord at Caunes-Minervois when my vocation was interrupted. I left with several of my fellow worshippers, some of which are with me still; others have found homes elsewhere and one has gone to join the Father. We began with just three carriages but the enterprise grew, as such things are inclined to when God's will is involved. At first we would entertain by singing plainsongs, but soon attracted a wider range of theatrical talents. Becoming touring players proved to be doubly beneficial: not only does it provide entertainment and diversion in what has become a sad country, but also a reason for our travelling."

In a land devastated by war and uprising that was plausible enough and Lamar was not the only one to have gone through a change of career. But from what they had seen of the company's performance, Banks found it hard to believe the players were led by a man of God.

"But I don't understand," he persisted. "You appear to have a company made up of felons and deserters, yet seem free to roam the country unchallenged. Why, all were in Verdun for several weeks and surrounded by *gendarmes*: how so?"

Lamar did not answer immediately, instead he treated them all to another serene smile. "That I can not totally explain," he finally confessed. "Though it does not bother me greatly and, if I am forgiven, neither should it you."

As a lifelong naval officer, Banks was not accustomed to such vague explanations, although strangely he felt his curiosity subside rather than grow. Whatever he pretended to be, there was no doubt Lamar was a man of exceptional personal presence and, from the brief time he had spent in France, Banks guessed such authority could be enough to see him out of a deal of trouble. And the religious angle would be an added benefit when dealing with the superstitious types; those weak enough to be swayed by such bilge.

"Well, I can only thank you once more," he said eventually, and was amazed to note none of his previous ill temper remained.

"And do you wish to know where you are going?" the old man enquired.

Again the officers swapped glances. "If it would not trouble you to tell us," King replied.

"It is another depot, we are to give a series of similar performances to those we gave at Verdun," Lamar explained.

"You are transporting us to another French prison?" Banks asked slowly.

"Yes, Captain, but do not concern yourself; no one is held against their will and we shall continue to do all we can to see you return to your own country."

"And where is this prison?" Banks asked, every suspicion now reawakened.

"Valenciennes," Lamar replied.

# Chapter Twenty-Three

It had been the fastest turn around Lewis had known; no sooner had *Narcis* moored than the small amount of cargo collected from England was removed and fresh sent to replace it. After the incident with the sloop, he had hoped to make further changes to the brig's appearance; perhaps a different colour to her whales, or some not so subtle alteration to the rig: anything that might dissuade a potential investigation, but all that was forgotten in the rush to get her ready for sea once more.

Not that he minded: the more trips he took, the faster his current position and responsibilities could be shed. Lewis knew little of the cargo they had taken aboard off the Suffolk coast but the crates were too small to contain wool, as the rough manifest proclaimed. Consequently, he realised his command had reached the standard of trust necessary and was now carrying British bullion to the French forces.

With a premium of over thirty percent, this was not so very surprising and, on the face of it, no worse than any other item he might export from his home country. Nevertheless, there remained something about carrying gold – surely the lifeblood of any civilisation – that emphasised the treachery of his current calling, making it difficult, if not impossible, to justify.

But even if such a thing were beyond him, he could still dismiss it from his mind, a trick Lewis was fast acquiring and doubly easy when at sea. For now he was truly comfortable with the brig. She had proved herself well found and weatherly and the crew were working as efficiently as any he had known in the past. There was the inevitable friction between Dutch and British, although this only served to strengthen individual loyalty in each and he had not encountered any of the problems feared when taking on deserters, felons and other undesirables.

His officers had also settled down well. Price was developing into a first-rate warrant officer, one who had won the respect of the hands while accurately conveying the wishes of his superiors, and young Masters performed the duties of a second mate with growing competence. Reid, the first officer, who had been a major concern, was now showing fewer signs of the nervous energy that made him so hard to serve alongside. Instead he was taking a more measured view on matters and progressing to the stage that Lewis was starting to rely on him in certain areas; a state of affairs he could never have imagined when they first met.

And now they were halfway through yet another voyage. Lewis had long since ceased to count the exact number, but knew he was well on the way to achieving the financial independence he so craved. Of course, he could not guarantee being around long enough to reach that point; even in the short time he had been the brig's commander they had suffered a couple of close shaves, and the chances of *Narcis* eventually being caught would only increase as she became better known. But if they went on improving in the same manner he remained quietly confident of seeing out his time as a smuggler.

From what he had discovered from other masters, *Narcis* had been particularly unlucky; the vast majority of runs took place without interference or even the sighting of an official vessel. But when it did finally come to an end he would still be relieved and, however well the brig was sailing and however close he had become to her crew and officers, would then walk away and feel no inclination to look back.

"Looks to be the first now," Reid commented, and Lewis turned his thoughts to more immediate matters. Sure enough a particularly sturdy, two-masted, vessel could be seen putting out from the distant shoreline.

"Seems eager enough," he grunted, while reaching for the deck glass. Indeed, it was barely three in the afternoon, and would remain broad daylight for some hours yet. The sea was unusually placid, however, and Lewis had no objection to unloading in the afternoon, although how the ketch intended to creep back to her home port undetected was another matter. "And she's the only one," he added, as he raised the glass to view her properly. "Are we expecting her?"

Reid reached into his jacket pocket and retrieved a sheet of paper. "There're two large ketches on the list," he said, adding, "The *Good Fortune*, which is coming to us for brandy and lace, and *Sunflower*, delivering wool."

Lewis was still inspecting the sighting and might have found a clue. She was riding low in the water, so was either heavily laden or carrying an extraordinarily large crew. The latter was out of the question; it was usual for his customers to have barely enough men to manage their craft, with coopers, such as *Narcis*, providing all the hands and equipment necessary for the transfer of cargo. Which meant that either she did not require much, or was planning to send booty aboard. A fully-laden ship might also have other rendezvous to make, which probably explained her early appearance.

"I'd say she were *Sunflower* then," he grunted, mildly annoyed as he remembered *Narcis'* holds and lower decks were crammed full and even her topsides crowded.

"Can you make out a name, sir?" Reid asked, surprised.

Lewis gave a derisive snort; it was hard enough examining the vessel through the brig's tophamper without having to answer damn fool questions. "Too far off," he replied. "We might hoist this week's signal, but would prefer to wait a little yet." There had already been one misread code in *Narcis'* brief career, and he had resigned himself to the fact that not everything in the smuggling world was treated with the same seriousness as the Royal Navy. "How much is she proposing to deliver?"

Reid referred to his paper once more. "If it be *Sunflower*, five cases, sir," he replied.

Lewis said nothing although he took the information with a pinch of salt. Room could be found for such a small cargo but, whatever those cases contained, it would not be wool, which was invariably carried in bales. If the ketch were truly bound for them she would have gold on board, and five cases of the stuff must amount to a substantial sum; something that might also explain the early arrival, though not her laden state.

"Keep her as she is," he ordered at last. Despite the gentle breeze, *Narcis* was travelling under topsails alone as he was in no rush to close with the English coast. At such a rate, the two would not meet for at least an hour, which gave ample time for space to be made on deck, as well as bringing dusk that much closer. It would still be light when they met, of course, and there would be time enough to confirm the vessel's identity before they did. So really he should have few doubts about what was about to take place, although there was still something about that ketch that vaguely worried him.

* * *

The scenery was truly delightful. Seated next to Cranston, who had taken to driving the small carriage with the versatility of all seamen, Timothy found he could see over many of the small hedgerows and into the fields and pastures beyond. Summer was still several weeks away, yet the past few days had been gloriously hot and he didn't think he was alone in taking to the life of the nomadic players.

Their welcome certainly helped; the travellers might have been an eclectic mix of renegades, misfits and petty criminals but the introduction of a group of British naval officers was accepted with little more than mild curiosity. Some had been with the players a short time, others several years, yet all were bound together by similar needs and a mutual dependence on their enigmatic leader, a man who spent much of his time shut away in his closed carriage.

The nationalities were every bit as mixed, with Irish, Italians, Swedes and Germans numbering with the French and Spanish who were perhaps in the majority. And though many of their countries might be at war, there were no signs of animosity, but rather a general acceptance of all without regard to previous lives or origins.

This corporate cooperation meant the mixture of languages was not the problem it might have been; Timothy had picked up quite a bit of French during his time in captivity, but even that seemed unnecessary as English was spoken by many, while those who had no shared language were happy to communicate through signs or a helpful third party.

And the relaxed ethos of the society was noticed in other areas; Timothy berthed with King, Brehaut and Manning in a carriage given over to them for the purpose. At first he had regarded this to be incredibly generous of the former occupants; an ostensibly married couple who were prepared to find accommodation elsewhere, although it soon became obvious that most of the travellers were as used to changing abodes as they were partners. It was also apparent that little property was individually owned, while every task and domestic duty was shared out in a way that caused no resentment or comment.

All of this was beyond a simple soul like Timothy's, even if the poet within him appreciated many aspects of the relaxed community. He soon became used to viewing the various goings on with a detached interest and was happy for the strange ways to continue, just as long as they did not affect him. For that day, and as many more as it might take, he remained content to sit in the sunshine, admire the scenery and allow the wagon to rumble steadily down the road and bring him ever closer to freedom.

* * *

"Ace of diamonds," Lovemore said after a pause. Garrett gave a grudging nod and raised the next card, which also faced away from the seaman.

"Seven of spades." Again the nod, and another was selected.

"Five of hearts." This time the card remained and Lovemore drew breath.

"Concentrate," Garrett urged, although the instruction was uttered more as a threat.

"Five of diamonds?"

This time there was a snort from the magician and the card was lowered. "Same colour, but the suit was wrong," he told him. "It is always the same: you tire."

"I cannot help it," Lovemore muttered. "This is new to me."

"It will come, but you must work." Garrett had picked up the pack again and was starting to shuffle them; Lovemore had the uneasy feeling he was going to start from the top yet again, and searched his numb brain for something that would make the magician stop.

"So, how is this to benefit us?" he asked. "Are you planning on card sharping or the like?"

The Frenchman shook his head. "Nothing so coarse, my friend," he replied, his expression as set as always. "The cards are just a tool, a device that will help you extend your powers. You practice with me and are usually good, because I send a strong signal; in time you will be able to read the minds of those who are not so obliging."

"And that will be part of an act?" Lovemore persevered. Ever since he had met the magician, the man had been telling vague stories of how their powers could be used. But even now, when Lovemore had thrown in his lot and joined the travellers, he was no nearer to discovering exactly what Garrett planned.

And it hardly made it any easier having the other British joining them. What had begun as a lone bid for freedom and a complete change of his life had turned into a proper spree, with officers and former shipmates appearing as if from nowhere to tag along. There was even a senior post captain who always looked as if he had been sucking a lemon, as well as one of the lasses from the Silva family.

"There are many ways in which the powers can be used," Garrett was speaking in that same patronising manner that always made Lovemore feel about twelve. "Some are connected with the stage, although I do not intend to spend my life like the *gitans*."

Lovemore's knowledge of French was good and growing; he and Garrett communicated well in the magician's language, but he had no idea what *gitans* were, and the fact worried him further.

"When you are ready we can leave together," Garrett continued, and now his tone was almost softening. "Travel the world; there will be no end to what we might achieve with the talents you and I have been given."

Lovemore said nothing; however his skills were acquired they had not been requested, and developing them further still did not sit easily with him. The idea of the two of them effectively going into partnership was also abhorrent, and he was determined not to let it happen.

"But maybe you are not so keen to be with me, and share what we have?" The dark eyes were looking accusingly at him now, and Lovemore swallowed; this was another reason why he wanted to end matters.

"I'm hardly saying that; it's just not in my mind at the moment," he lied, and Garrett gave a knowing look. "I simply don't want to rush things."

"So we will not rush," Garrett conceded. "And maybe take matters more slowly. Besides, it will be easier when your friends have left us, and we will be able to concentrate more on our work with no distractions."

Lovemore said nothing; it would certainly be different, but he didn't think any easier. Then Garrett collected the cards and, after a brief shuffle, proceeded to hold one up once more.

"Nine of diamonds," Lovemore told him. Perhaps the magician was right, maybe he was only tired. Another card was produced, and that was also correctly named, and another after that. Before long Lovemore found his reply was almost mechanical, and Garrett's expression began to soften further. But Lovemore could not have cared much either way; whether Garrett realised it or not, his mind was elsewhere.

* * *

Now the ketch was less than a mile off and, taking the breeze firmly on her beam, clearly intending to come up on their starboard side. That was sensible enough, Lewis decided. *Narcis* was the larger vessel but would not steal the wind too much, and being so positioned would allow for the transfer of cargo to take place in her lee. But still he could not detect any name or marking on the craft, and there remained something about her that slightly worried him.

He turned to Reid. "We shall carry on as we are for now; though prepare to spill our wind on my command." *Narcis* was barely creeping forward in the gentle airs, but it made no sense to increase speed when they would be early at their official rendezvous as it was. Delaying to deal with this unexpected visitor might actually be to their advantage, although Lewis was unable to see it in that light.

The mate gave an offhand salute, and nodded to Masters and Price, who were standing next to the binnacle and on the main deck respectively. She was still too far off for hailing, but Lewis could now examine the approaching vessel in more detail and saw nothing obviously amiss aboard her. Six men were visible on deck, which was reasonable enough for such a craft, and there was little else that should cause him alarm. Except, perhaps, her very presence.

A recent law prohibited any British vessel of over two hundred tons burden from travelling more than three leagues from the coast; the ketch exceeded both, although *Narcis* remained the only witness. And the unknown craft was also armed; there were seven carriage guns to each broadside, with a far larger piece mounted on a swivel atop her forecastle. It was heavy artillery for a trader, but probably justified, although Lewis knew he need not fear her. If one man remained at the helm, the most she could muster was five to attend her guns; at worst, *Narcis* might suffer a single broadside, but he judged her solid enough to see that out, and there would be no possibility of much being reloaded by such a scant crew.

But what was he thinking of? Lewis sighed and lowered the glass for a second. He might be relatively new to his current trade but had surely learned enough not to concern himself unnecessarily. The ketch would be alongside within half an hour; in twice that time she should be heading away, her business done, and *Narcis* could continue to her appointed rendezvous with that much less to do before making for home.

"The men are ready?" he asked Reid, who was clearly eager to talk.

"All ready, sir," he confirmed. "We've stowed the cases of tobacco for'ard, to allow for what our friend has in store for us, and both hatches are clear in case they also wish to receive."

Lewis gave no reply, although it was interesting that Reid must also have noticed the ketch was riding low. For a moment he considered discussing the matter: was it entirely usual to be met so far from the coast, and did the mate have any doubts about the oncoming vessel? But the urge was quickly suppressed; despite his confident appearance, Reid was no more experienced than himself and to invite opinions would only encourage the young man's tendency to advise.

"Very well," he said instead, and took a turn up and down the small quarterdeck. It was still gloriously warm in the afternoon sun; an exceptionally good spring day, and not one he wanted to spoil in a hurry. "You may hoist the private signal."

Again Reid touched the rim of his hat while Masters made for the flag locker.

It was purely a formality; often, when boats approached that they recognised, Lewis did not even bother, especially if the light was starting to fade. But there was time, space and daylight enough to run up three coloured flags to a starboard yardarm and await the answering hoist which would dispel all doubt. When it came, he could truly begin to relax and concentrate on other matters. And there would be no more hysterical fears or unfounded doubts about mystery ketches.

* * *

"I did promise to assist *Madame* André," Aimée told him with false severity. "She will need help with peeling of the potatoes for tonight's meal."

King made a soft rumble of protest and snuggled closer. The carriage they occupied had been allocated to him and three other men in the group; Aimée berthed with some of the dancers in another wagon. But the two of them had found his to be empty earlier that afternoon and taken possession.

The clatter of hooves and rumble of wheels, together with a shared knowledge they were so very vulnerable had made an agreeable accompaniment to their love making and, now it was finished, the couple lay amid the muddle of King's unmade bed.

"I had never believed travelling through France could be so pleasant," he told her sleepily. Then, on considering further, added, "Or so easy."

"It is certainly not so usual to pass through towns without being stopped," Aimée agreed. "Of course *Monsieur* Lamar was given a passport for Valenciennes by the Commandant, although I have the feeling such things are not always needed. He is a former monk, and so carries authority, even in these unenlightened times."

"A monk, you say?" King murmured dreamily. "Yes, I do remember his saying."

"An Abbott, or so I have heard," Aimée added.

"Sure, it is a strange occupation for a man of the cloth; though I always took him for a rum cove."

"Thomas, that is an extraordinary expression," she told him, while raising her head to look at him more squarely. King opened his eyes.

"I meant no offence; though you have to admit it odd for a man to carry about such a group of..." he struggled for the words.

"Such shameless people?" she asked, smiling. "Surely you are not being the prude?"

He considered her, and their situation, and found he had to smile as well.

"Of course not," he agreed. "But if someone does not accept Wirion's passport and decides to search the carriages, we shall be noticed for sure," King continued.

"I do not think that will happen," she replied firmly before resting back once more, this time against his chest. "There is a name for it; *Polichinelle*'s secret."

King looked at her doubtfully and Aimée explained.

"It is something everyone accepts but does not discuss. In this case many will know or guess there are escaped soldiers amongst the players, but the will of the people is very much against conscription."

"But not the *gendarmes*," King pointed out.

"No, not officially," she conceded. "Although some are still likely to be sympathetic. There are few families in France who have not suffered a loss during these terrible wars, and the Emperor is not always as popular as he would like to maintain. Nor as powerful."

"And are there many deserters in the company?" King asked.

"Oh, a very large number," Aimée confirmed. "I do not know for sure how many exactly, but would guess that roughly half of the men have been in some form of service. Have you noticed how some have lost the first finger of their right hands?"

King nodded; he certainly had.

"It was a common way to avoid military duties in the past," she explained. "At first it was thought a man who could not fire a musket was of no use; since then necessity has found them other jobs, and those who did not want to fight must try different methods."

"But it does not explain everything," King maintained.

"Oh, I cannot do that," Aimée confessed. "And there are doubtless some things that are better left as the mystery. But I do feel we are safe, and shall be in Valenciennes by tomorrow afternoon."

King could not see how she could be so sure, but felt disinclined to question further. Besides, Aimée's mention of the next stage of their escape naturally turned his mind to his own particular problem. Being with her and having already travelled so far through France had convinced him that reaching England was now not quite so unlikely. But to mention his marriage, especially considering the present situation, might still not be diplomatic.

"You are tense," she stated, raising her head from his chest to look at him once more. "Why do you worry?"

King gave a weak smile – how to explain?

"You will not concern yourself over my brother," she continued, settling again. "I think he will understand we are together and shall accommodate us as man and wife."

That sounded more than agreeable to King, even if it did not solve his current dilemma.

"I owe your family a lot," he mused. "We would not have escaped without your help, and your brother providing transport from Valenciennes may be the only thing that eventually sees us free."

"It is nothing," she shrugged. "They like to indulge me."

"But the warehouse," he continued blindly, "That was surely an act of great kindness?"

"The warehouse?" She raised her head yet again, although this time the warmth in her expression was replaced by a look of concern.

"The one that burned," King blundered on. "It must have cost them a deal of stock, even if they did not own the building."

"I did not know of this," Aimée told him quickly, her face now deadly serious, and King began to realise his mistake.

"It caught alight," he told her innocently. "Just as we were making our escape from the Chapel. I thought you were aware."

"I was not," she answered coldly and her eyes became more distant.

"It was a terrible conflagration," King admitted, all sense of diplomacy now abandoned. "Most of the town was raised to fight it. But without such a distraction we might never have made it this far."

"They wanted to be sure we got away," Aimée stated slowly, her expression now completely blank. "And it was not a rented warehouse: my father spent all his savings on purchasing the building, and much of our store of coal for the winter would have been inside. Really I think there is nothing my family would not do for me."

King had genuinely expected Aimée to have been aware of the sacrifice, and was stunned into silence.

"I have not told you of this before," she continued, "but once I was married."

Now his head began to spin. "Married?" he asked softly.

The spell was broken; she rose up from her place and, turning, looked him full in the face. "It was terrible, a big mistake, and one I vowed never to make again."

"I am sorry," he said, although Aimée did not appear to hear, and her gaze drifted to somewhere far beyond him.

"The man turned out to be an animal," she continued, "and someone I will hate to my dying day. It was my family that helped me then, and for that reason we moved from Rennes to Verdun."

"But I thought you were accompanying those English nobles?" King questioned.

"Oh, that was just a good opportunity," she explained. "But if the Tweeddales had not wished to move, my father would have gone somewhere else. We just wanted a place where my husband would not find me."

"And I suppose a prison town is as good as any," King mused, although Aimée was not listening.

"From then on I mistrusted all men," she continued. "It was only on meeting with you that I began to change my mind."

For several seconds all that could be heard was the gentle rumble of the wheels and someone singing a long way off. King had almost ceased to breathe as he waited for her to begin again.

"And my parents were so pleased that I was finally happy," she said at last, tears now forming. "Otherwise they would not have done such a terrible thing."

"I am sorry," King repeated.

"No you must not be." Her eyes found his again and some of her usual vigour returned. "They did it for the best, and so that we could be together. And you must not think too badly of me."

She was now fixing him with her gaze and King found it hard not to look away.

"No," he said at last. "No, I do not think badly of you, Aimée. I never could."

270

# Chapter Twenty-Four

"You may heave her to, Mr Reid," Lewis told him.

There was no point in waiting any longer; the ketch was making reasonable speed and *Narcis* would need all her hands for when they began to transfer cargo.

The brig slowly lost way and her hull bore round in the gentle breeze. Their recognition signal had been answered to a point; the reply given was that for the previous week, but such things were close enough and Lewis decided to take the vessel at face value.

Masters had begun to organise the deck while Price ensured the brig was secure; all Lewis and Reid had to do was wait and watch the unloading. Apart from a distant fleet of trawlers heading for home, there was no other shipping in sight and the sun had already started its long downward plunge that would end in dusk and evening.

*Narcis'* slight change of orientation meant the ketch was no longer obscured by shrouds and stays and, when Lewis raised his glass to inspect her again, it was more out of boredom than concern. But his grip quickly tightened on the telescope and soon his hands began to shake.

"Bring her back to the wind and set t'gallants – then prepare to go about!" The command, which had been delivered in the form of a shout, caused all to freeze for a moment, before pandemonium broke out on the brig's decks.

Price and Masters began to bellow a stream of orders and men who had been in the act of shifting deck cargo abandoned their loads to make for the braces. Others, the more skilled amongst them, swarmed up the weather shrouds while the helmsman spun the wheel to catch what wind there was.

"Is there a problem, sir?" Reid asked innocently and Lewis lowered his glass.

"I believe so," he said, mildly shaken by the activity his words had caused. For, despite an inner feeling that would not be denied any longer, there was very little basis for his sudden change of heart. All he had noticed aboard the ketch was a couple of hands moving forward while perhaps a dozen more had begun to file up from below. Admittedly, a significant cannon was mounted on the forecastle although there could be any number of reasons why two seamen should position themselves in that area when approaching another vessel, and the transferring of cargo at sea was undoubtedly a task that called for all hands. But the next few seconds would tell him everything; *Narcis'* sudden change must soon be noticed and it would be interesting to see how the ketch responded.

The brig was already picking up speed: at a nod from him, Reid began to cautiously issue the orders that would take her hard to starboard. Lewis raised his glass once more and was forced to the conclusion those aboard the other vessel were as confused by his actions as his own crew. But, just as he began to accept the fool he had made of himself, they finally reacted, and the mystery ketch granted him terrible vindication.

* * *

With no warning other than the flash, her bow mounted cannon erupted into sudden life: smoke poured from the heavy muzzle and, just as the deep rumble of her discharge reached them, the high pitched scream of a shot passing overhead made all on the quarterdeck instinctively duck down.

"That would be bar," Lewis muttered in surprise; the distinctive sound was totally different to that of round shot. He glanced back at Reid, who was shaking visibly as he raised his head once more. Masters was babbling something incomprehensible in the waist but he could spare no time for either. A quick glance assured him no major damage had been received aloft, but *Narcis* was still only halfway through her manoeuvre and so remained incredibly vulnerable. And now the ketch was yawing to present her starboard broadside; even without the aid of his glass he could see her decks were positively crowded with men, while her main cannon were being run out and trained upon him.

"Larboard servers, to your pieces!" His order rang out amid the confusion of turning and quite probably slowed the manoeuvre but Lewis did not care. His precious command was about to take a pounding; something he had no intention of allowing without making at least a token gesture in reply.

On board the ketch what had suddenly become enemy gunners were now adjusting the elevations of their weapons and Lewis guessed the brig's tophamper was to be targeted once more. For a second he felt a surge of anger – this must have been planned, and he had been a fool not to listen to his instincts. Then he drew breath and allowed a more reasoned attitude to take control.

He had no way of knowing if they were facing an enemy made up of government forces or rival smugglers; each was as likely although the latter seemed more probable. No ensigns were being flown and neither had there been any attempt at mediation before his vessel was fired upon. But whatever foe he faced, they were clearly not looking for prisoners, while *Narcis* was now almost beam on and presenting as fine a target as the enemy could wish for.

Then, with timing that would have done credit to any navy, a union flag raced up the ketch's gaff barely seconds before she released her full broadside. It was hard to accurately estimate the power of her guns but, when the shot began to strike the brig's spars, Lewis knew they were heavier than he had anticipated.

Several lines parted with a series of loud snaps, and there was the sickening sound of tearing wood as their main topsail yard was struck and swiftly disintegrated. The deck about him was sprinkled with splinters, dust and torn canvas, debris that also covered most of his own gunners and made their eventual broadside a far more ragged and ill-aimed affair, and one that did no perceivable damage. *Narcis* was still coming round and soon collected the wind in her fore topsail. But with the ketch unharmed and undoubtedly the faster craft, she was bound to close on them and must then deliver another dose.

"Aloft there – attend them t'gallants!" Price was bellowing at the topmen to continue their work. The enemy's shot must have passed amongst those still working aloft; some may have been wounded while all would be shaken, although it had now become even more important that the extra canvas was set. Then Lewis realised his other officers were responding equally well; Reid had shown the sense to call a few of the redundant afterguard away to help tend their own cannon and Masters was moving about the main deck, yelling both inducements and threats like any seasoned warrant officer.

Some of the servers appeared clumsy and confused, and none were working to reload the pieces at anything like the speed of Navy gunners. But *Narcis* should at least be able to make another response before long, and was finally gathering speed on her new course.

It was not all good news, however: the ketch had straightened her course and was continuing to bear down. Her forecastle-mounted chase gun fired again, damaging several shrouds which would make the huge mast that much more vulnerable. Soon it became clear their pursuer was steering to board them and, as Lewis inspected her decks with his glass once more, he was forced to conclude she was carrying far more men. Some, the officers, wore what appeared to be naval uniforms, although there was no commissioning pennant and the only flag flying remained that single ensign. But whoever did command her would certainly take *Narcis* if he gave them the chance.

Their larboard guns were almost loaded but with round shot; Lewis wondered about switching to canister for the next broadside, before rejecting the idea. He already knew much could change in such a duel; canister was only for close action, while ball would remain potent if they managed to gain any distance, and must still cause death and destruction when fired into a body of men at close range.

"She's drawing nearer," Reid muttered as he joined him. "Shall I authorise small arms?"

"Do that," Lewis snapped. He still had no intention of allowing the ketch alongside, but the men would be that much braver with weapons to hand.

And there was one advantage to the enemy trying to board, rather than subject them to a long-range bombardment. They were closing on *Narcis'* larboard side; consequently neither vessel's broadside guns would bear and the only fire they were being subjected to was from the ketch's bow chaser. That might prove sufficient, though, as Lewis was well aware. Were they to receive a significant hit to either mast, the brig's speed would decrease further, making her capture inevitable.

"Mr Price, I'd like the main and fore stays'ls rigged!" Lewis bellowed as he finally tore his gaze from the oncoming enemy. Price was standing in the waist; he glanced up to the masts, then to *Narcis'* cannon and the meaning was obvious. Rigging extra canvas would take men from the guns and some might think them better placed letting off broadsides than adding sail. "Quick as you can, Mr Price," Lewis added firmly. The order, like the decision behind it, was not an easy one, but totally a captain's responsibility.

The larboard guns were now ready to fire but to do so he would have to yaw; the time for that may well come, though for now Lewis was more interested in putting as much distance between them and the enemy.

A shot passed overhead, it was yet another from the ketch's chase gun, but fortune remained with them and it passed through the cat's cradle of their tophamper without causing damage. However the enemy were still gaining on them. Looking back over the taffrail once more, Lewis could see actual faces of men on the ketch's deck; it would not be long before the vessel came alongside and sent a swarm of boarders over their top rail.

Then he noticed something even more terrible; clearly their superior speed was not enough for whoever commanded the ketch and, even as he watched, the craft began to turn.

"They're going to rake us!" Reid announced in horror as he too realised what was about.

But there could be no doubt about it; the ketch had begun to rock in the gentle seas as her helm was put across, and steadily her broadside was presented to their stern.

Lewis had already revised his estimation; the craft was heavily over-gunned, and must be carrying nine - if not twelve - pounders. What effect her round shot would make on *Narcis'* vulnerable stern was foolish to estimate, but even a nine-pound ball could be expected to pass through much of the vessel and do untold damage before being brought to a bloody halt.

"Not if I have anything to do with it," he murmured softly. And then, with an edge of defiance: "Bring her to larboard!"

* * *

The convoy was making a brief stop in a small village and it had been agreed that the band would set up in the market square. Such

275

things gave a good impression as well as raising funds for the troop in general and Lovemore, for one, always enjoyed playing in the open air. He and Cranston strolled down the line of wagons enjoying the sunshine, Lovemore had his precious flute under one arm and Cranston was looking with interest at the small row of shops that lay ahead. Both had become accustomed to the relative freedom; their country might be at war with France, but any locals who recognised them for what they were showed no surprise. And neither man paid particular attention to the phenomenon: England had not been so ravaged by the wars as France, nor was it recovering from a revolution, but each would probably have shown the same apathy towards a French civilian, were the situation reversed. Tales of King George, or Bonaparte, might be told to frighten naughty children and both countries' newspapers would rant about the evilness of the other, but most common people were inclined to take a more phlegmatic view of the war and were actually united by a mutual dislike of it.

Besides, Lovemore was looking forward to playing for the villagers as much as he would any audience, while the knowledge that this would be the measure of his life from then on gave him a pleasant feeling of fulfilment. It was just a shame that, to achieve such a goal, he had to mix with the likes of Garrett and, more to the point, increase the strange power within him – a power that was becoming more abhorrent as it grew.

During the course of their journey he had been studiously avoiding mixing with the British officers; such things were not expected, even in the relaxed atmosphere of the travelling company, although Lovemore had a stronger reason for keeping himself aloof. The death's head image noticed previously on one had returned and was now more prominent. His increased senses told him the wearer faced almost imminent death, and it was hard to mix with a man while carrying such knowledge.

But on that particular morning he was not worried; this was an official break from training with Garrett. He would spend the next hour or so in pleasant relaxation, doing what he enjoyed most. So when a strange voice speaking remarkably close to him caught his attention, Lovemore was taken by surprise.

"My friend – a word, if you please?"

Lovemore turned and looked about, but Cranston had already

noticed the familiar figure of Lamar, the troop leader, standing at the tail of the plain black carriage they had just passed.

"Reckon the skipper wants you," he said, nudging his mate in the side and pointing behind with his thumb. "I'll carry on and tell the band," he continued. "Don't seem as if I'm invited."

It certainly did not, the familiar bald-headed man only had eyes for Lovemore and was beckoning with one hand in the manner of a schoolmaster.

As the seaman turned towards him, his mind began to race. He had never addressed more than a couple of words to the company's enigmatic leader and could only be concerned by this dramatic summons. Supposing something had been said against him? Perhaps his talents were no longer required? It might mean this was as far as they went, and Lovemore was to be abandoned in the middle of France with all the perils an escaping prisoner of war should really expect.

But Lamar appeared to pose no immediate threat. "Come inside, do," he urged before following Lovemore up the steps and through to the darkness within. It had been such a fine day; the sun was shining and he had been looking forward to a spot of music, but as his eyes accustomed themselves to the dim light, Lovemore's fears grew. There was now no doubt in his mind that a significant change was about to occur to his life, and the strange thing was, he had received no warning.

\* \* \*

*Narcis* was now in a state of apparent confusion; the helm had been put across and canvas flapped as most of the hands attended her cannon with only a few left to manage sheets and braces. Lewis was not so much the fool, though; he might only have been captain of the brig a matter of weeks, but the time had not been wasted. He felt he knew almost every aspect of *Narcis*, from her fabric to her people, and all, including the officers, had improved beyond measure. By throwing them so suddenly into action was risking a lot, although the same inner feeling that had warned him the ketch was dangerous now spoke just as clearly, and told him his confidence was well placed.

And so it proved. They met the ketch broadside to broadside, with the two less than a cable apart. The brig might have the weaker armament, but her frame and scantlings were solid. However, she was already damaged aloft, whereas the ketch, a faster and more agile craft, also had the larger crew.

"Aim for the hull, lads!" Lewis bellowed, and there was a rumble of approval from those at the guns. He had no doubt the enemy would be training their pieces at his tophamper, and a sizeable hit on the spars of either vessel would almost guarantee victory for the other. But *Narcis'* guns were loaded with round shot. By targeting the hull he might not disable his enemy with a single broadside, but a tightly grouped broadside that swept crowded decks with heavy ball would weaken her almost as much.

*Narcis* was still rolling with the swell, although some of her braces had been hauled round and the movement was gradually decreasing. Lewis was glad to see that Reid, who had moved down to the main deck, was waiting for him to despatch the weapons, and that each gun captain was staring fixedly at the ketch, their outdated linstocks poised above the touch holes.

Then the ketch fired, and did so in a neat ripple that spread from bow to stern in less than five seconds. The first shots hit *Narcis* shortly afterwards; several lines parted and the freshly set main staysail was holed, but no more. If anything the enemy's action seemed to encourage those at the guns, and most seemed especially eager to return the compliment.

"Steady there!" Lewis warned, as he strode to the break of his tiny quarterdeck. "On my word, and make your shots count... Fire!"

The guns rattled off in a ragged broadside, and those that tended them went straight into reloading their charges. But others were free to witness the results, and soon a loud roar of approval rose up from them.

The ketch had been competently targeted, with only one shot straying mildly towards the stern. But the rest, those that peppered her centre with a series of irregular holes, had done damage.

"She's coming back to the wind!" Masters' call came as Lewis was reaching to the same conclusion. Damaged or not, the ketch was showing sail once more, and soon her slender hull began cutting through the water and heading directly for them.

He glanced down; the servers were still hard at work, although it would be several minutes before their cannon could be fired again. Meanwhile there were hardly enough men available to tend the braces and bring *Narcis* back to life. And all the time that elegant hull was cutting through the water as the enemy shot like a dart in their direction.

Price, Masters and now Reid were looking to him for direction, and it was with effort that Lewis focused his mind.

"We'll remain for one more broadside," he cried, coming to a decision. "Rake her prow, then prepare to meet any foolish enough to come across!"

That was expecting a lot; not only must the gunners have their pieces ready, they would need to train and fire them in a disciplined manner before the ketch punched into the brig's side. And those shots must also count, although there would be those – many probably – who would still try to board and take them whatever they did. Lewis could summon barely thirty men, about two thirds of whom would be skilled fighters; if only the same number boarded from the ketch, *Narcis* would be captured for sure.

\* \* \*

"I understand you have expressed a wish to join us," the bald-headed man told Lovemore. "All I have spoken with are in favour of such a move," he continued, "but others of your countrymen have also appeared and I wished to talk to you before coming to a final decision."

The seaman nodded mutely. This was indeed a shock; despite being joined by Cranston and the officers, Lovemore's escape from Verdun had been totally independent and he already regarded himself as one of the travelling players. There were certainly no thoughts in his mind of continuing to England.

"Mainly, I wanted to ask if you still wished to stay. And, if so, why?" *Monsieur* Lamar sat back in his chair and seemed quite comfortable while Lovemore, balancing on the hard wooden locker, was less so.

"I'd like to remain," he found himself speaking, almost without willing it. "You see I enjoy playing the flute."

As he spoke the band struck up from far away. Strains of familiar music filtered into the dark carriage and the seaman began

279

to relax.

"You may play your instrument anywhere," Lamar pointed out, and Lovemore was amazed by the warmth that now seemed to be filling the small space. "On board ship, where you are a sailor, I understand music is very common."

"Oh it is, sir," Lovemore confirmed. "But being with your theatre group is far better."

The band were playing one of Lovemore's favourite tunes, and his foot began to tap without his willing it.

"And it is just because you like music?" The man was clearly probing, yet his gentle countenance remained and the seaman felt he might say anything if the right question were asked.

"It is being in the band – with other musicians – it is as if we are able to communicate."

"But your French is very good; you need no help in that area."

"Music is different," Lovemore explained. "It goes beyond speech." The man was looking at him strangely and he hurried on. "And I like it when people sing, and dance together – it makes me feel as if I belong."

"And that is the only reason you wish to stay?"

The seaman shrugged; a habit he had acquired of late. "I have met with another in the company – Marcel Garrett," he admitted.

"Ah yes, our conjurer," Lamar gave a quiet chuckle, and did not seem surprised by the confession. "He is a friend, perhaps?"

"No, not a friend." It suddenly seemed very important that Lamar knew this. "In truth, I do not care for him greatly."

"Then why was he mentioned?" Lamar asked, but began speaking again before Lovemore could reply.

"We are indeed a mixed collection," he said. His words were soft, yet spoken with authority and Lovemore found himself transfixed. "Many are here to avoid the fighting, although some have other reasons. But all might be regarded as criminals – according to the laws of this world, at least," he continued. "Such things mean little to me, though, as you probably already know. There are those who men judge wicked that I consider good and, all too frequently, the other way about."

Lamar stopped then, and stared more intently at Lovemore. As with all bald men, the lack of hair gave him a mildly aggressive appearance but, now he could be considered more carefully,

Lovemore noticed the kindness in his eyes. And there was more; it might be due to his recent training with Garrett or simply basic intuition, but he sensed something inherently spiritual about the man, and felt drawn to him.

"I fear that Mr Garrett is one I do not consider to be good." The smile had gone, although Lovemore remained captivated and hung on every word. "Then why do I allow him to remain in my troop, you may ask? And I have to admit, it is not easy.

"You see, there is much that happens in our little company that I do not approve of," he continued. "Many of the young people do not stay with their partners for long; something that can lead to suspicion and jealousy, and most take too much wine. Yet I have to remind myself that this is not a monastery. It would be wrong to impose my own values on them: far better they learned for themselves. So in some instances I permit a certain amount of evil to continue, if only that I may watch and see how it develops."

"Keep the devil in the daylight and you will never be deceived." Lovemore only vaguely remembered his mother's little motto yet volunteered it without hesitation.

"You have it exactly, my son," Lamar told him. "Although Mr Garrett is actually very useful to me. Over the time he has been with us there have been several such as yourself that he has befriended. On every occasion I was able to help, as I hope I can now, but first I must ask exactly where you stand."

He leant forward slightly. "I am aware of the powers you and Mr Garrett possess and, as I have intimated, do not approve of them. But tell me honestly, what is your opinion?"

Lovemore had opened his mouth to reply even before he found the words. "I do not want it," he gushed. "I do not, and never have. What Garrett teaches is against my wishes." He added an embarrassed smile, yet knew Lamar understood exactly what he meant. "But it seemed to be necessary if I were to join your troop and become part of it."

"Oh my son." Lamar was shaking his head in amused sadness. "My son, how little you know. I might add that I wish you had spoken with me first, but that is probably my own fault for being too much the hermit." He smiled again, and the warmth in the tiny space became even more apparent. "But I am glad we have talked together now, and that you see fit to tell me everything."

"I am also glad, father," Lovemore replied, and the feeling of gentle peace grew stronger.

"So, it is a situation we can remedy very easily," Lamar announced, rising from his chair.

Lovemore considered the matter for a moment. "I would not wish to get Mr Garrett into any trouble," he said.

"Oh, you shall not do that." The old man had turned to his bookcase and was extracting a remarkably thick volume that appeared well thumbed. "As I have said, this has happened before and is the reason I allow such a person to remain in our company." Then he looked across to Lovemore and, though the kindly eyes seemed no less benevolent, they now held an additional deep and dangerous strength. "I am empowered to rid this talent from you," he declared, "as long as you are quite sincere in wishing for it to be gone. But it must be your decision; no one can make it for you."

* * *

The enemy came straight for them. Lewis had armed himself with an ordinary seaman's cutlass and, glancing down, could see all were ready. Each gun captain had his cannon trained on the oncoming target while those standing by to make last-minute adjustments to the aiming were ready with handspikes. The rest, or at least those on the main deck, stood between the guns waiting for any boarders to arrive while the forecastle and quarterdeck also seemed crowded with men. Lewis had reckoned no more than a third of the brig's crew would be prepared to fight for her, but that had been a major underestimation. As far as he could tell, not one was declining combat and, as the ketch came on, the raw energy from their constant cheering was almost tangible.

The enemy were now close enough for *Narcis'* cannon to make a better impression, and Lewis nodded to Masters, who was standing with the guns.

"Be ready..." the youngster warned, as musket balls began to whine overhead.

The gun crews stood to and each captain made minute alterations to their pieces. Then, at a shout from Lewis, all five cannon discharged almost simultaneously.

The noise was literally deafening, although its full effect

282

would only be noticed later. For now, the one thing that mattered was the result of their work and any that could began to peer through ports or over top rails.

The enemy ketch had been soundly smitten; her martingale stay was shattered and both jibs floated down like bedsheets from a broken washing line. One anchor fell away, and a mushroom-shaped cloud of splinters showed where deeper damage had been wreaked to her prow. And then, at the very last minute, the foremast began to tumble.

Lewis turned to Reid and the two exchanged looks of triumph. Without a foremast, the ketch could not sail efficiently; all they need do was creep away from her, and *Narcis* might yet go free.

Much would have to happen before then though, for the ketch still came straight for them. Wreckage from the fallen spar had slowed her considerably and there was no more small-arms fire coming from her tattered forecastle. But Lewis was not fooled; despite that broadside and the loss of the foremast, her men would be just as willing to fight – perhaps more so. And, by his estimation, they would start boarding in under a minute.

\* \* \*

Lovemore clambered down from the carriage. He felt peaceful and not a little sleepy, while a warm feeling within told him he had never been so spiritually healthy in his life. The travellers were preparing to get underway again and he knew he should make for Garrett's carriage and continue that day's training. Then the splendid realisation returned: what talent he had possessed was now gone and never again would he be imprisoned by its power, or those who shared it.

He walked down the line of assorted wagons in a dizzy haze. The band was still playing, although it was not a tune he knew, and for a moment Lovemore wondered how they had rehearsed it without his knowledge. But the mild worry was soon forgotten; Lamar had told him he was welcome to stay with the group, although he also made it plain that, should he wish to return home with his countrymen, that would also be acceptable.

But for once Lovemore was glad to know his future; his life now lay with the travelling players, and he would stay with them and play his flute for as long as he could. Thoughts of the instrument struck a chord in his mind, and he looked down at his empty hands in horror. Throughout his time in captivity the instrument had hardly left his side, yet now it was nowhere to be seen. A momentary panic threatened to dislodge the feeling of inner peace before realisation struck. The flute must still be in Lamar's carriage; somewhere he knew it would be safe. But though he remained as relaxed, the fact that he should have forgotten about it for even so short a time was disconcerting. It was almost as if the instrument were no longer important to him.

* * *

The remains of a tattered jib boom came over *Narcis'* forecastle, and the ketch slewed round to slam sideways against her hull. Almost at once a ragged broadside dug deep into the brig's innards, although the enemy's lower firing platform meant most of the shot hit only cargo, some feet below her main deck. And the superior freeboard helped in other ways; there was no rush of men tumbling down upon *Narcis'* decks, while a few of her own crew chanced their luck upon the gangways and began hacking down on any attempting to board.

Laidlaw was one of those designated to attend the cannon for the final broadside and, after the gun was secured, had collected a cutlass and swung himself up amidships. Jones was also nearby, as well as Judy and the three of them stood together as they fought back the stream of potential boarders. Some of the enemy were armed with pistols and Jones fell to an early shot, but the weapons were soon discharged and it became a fairer fight, with muscle and determination becoming the deciding factor.

At one point, one of *Narcis'* hands became carried away and launched himself down upon the enemy's deck. He was quickly, and publicly, despatched by the ketch's crew, and none followed the example. A blood chilling scream rang out as someone took a pistol bullet in the belly, and Masters, still standing by his precious guns, fell to a boarding pike thrust through a port that neatly skewered his upper arm. Then, as easily as the two hulls had come together, they began to drift apart. The brig was showing significantly more canvas and those manning her bulwarks found they had to reach further to cut down on the enemy. Soon all hand-to-hand fighting came to an end, and only defiant roars and the occasional pop from a musket could be heard.

"Gun crews to your pieces!" This was Reid bellowing and Lewis turned to see the young man standing proud at the break of the quarterdeck and brandishing his cutlass like something off the London stage. The enemy were yet to man their long guns and, if *Narcis* could despatch another broadside, it would do incalculable damage.

But though those who remained uninjured quickly presented themselves, it soon became clear the effort in reloading would be wasted. *Narcis'* sails had been brought into order; the canvas was filling properly, and soon she was making credible speed, leaving the stricken ketch to wallow in the swell. In no time there was half a cable separating the two, with both vessels considerably out of the other's arc of broadside fire.

"We could yaw, sir!" It was Reid again, although now he was addressing Lewis directly, and the fighting madness in his eyes was all too obvious. "Tack, and give the guns to starboard a chance? They'll be loaded, and we might finish her off nicely."

"To what end, Mr Reid?" Lewis sighed. He had seen enough of fighting that day, and did not wish for more. "Maybe take down another mast, and kill a few more of her crew?"

Reid looked confused for a moment, and then became defiant.

"But we could take her!" he insisted.

Lewis said nothing; he must have been every bit as foolish once, and certainly just as young. What Reid was not allowing for was the men still aboard the ketch. They may now be fewer but would still outnumber those aboard *Narcis*. Were they to risk closing, then presumably boarding, there remained every chance the ketch might still win the day.

Gunfire from astern broke into their thoughts: the two men turned to see the enemy had restored some form of order and her bow cannon was clear to fire upon them once more. The shot ran foolishly wild, but they would remain in range for several minutes and there was still the possibility of a hit injuring them further.

"No, John," Lewis said, as gently as his strained nerves would allow. "I thank you for your very able assistance, but feel we have done enough for one day. See that the fore t'gallant is squared up, and we will make for home."

"But the rendezvous?" Reid asked, aghast.

Lewis glanced about the battered brig. Wherever he looked there were splinters and shattered fittings, while wounded and dead still littered the deck. And *Narcis* had already sustained substantial damage below; some might be attended to, but he was several hands down, and a fair amount of her cargo would have been destroyed. It went against the grain to return early, his mission unfulfilled, although the recent battle was a good enough excuse if one were needed. But why was Reid looking at him expectantly? And then Lewis realised he had not answered his question.

"The rendezvous?" he replied, absent-mindedly, before shaking his head at the young man's enthusiasm. "I fear this is one we shall have to miss," he said.

# Chapter Twenty-Five

It wasn't that he didn't wish to return to England, the very reverse, in fact. But, now such a prospect was starting to appear possible, Sir Richard Banks was experiencing severe doubts.

He wanted to see Sarah again, of course, and his young family, one of whom he had yet to even meet. And there were bound to be a thousand issues to look to on the estate, despite his wife's letters keeping him relatively up to date. But the professional side of his life posed very different problems.

First, he would have to stand trial for the loss of his ship. A court martial was mandatory when any officer charged with a vessel gave her up, be it to the enemy or the elements. Though truly there was nothing to worry about on that score, he told himself for the tenth time that morning. *Prometheus* might be the first major warship lost during the current war, and she undoubtedly fell to enemy action without properly accounting for another vessel. But he had fought her to the end, despite being wounded himself, while the odds faced on that fateful winter's night had been considerable.

Even now, as he remembered the time, his palms grew moist. There had been the danger of a lee shore with an impenetrable wall of liners to windward edging him ever closer to it, and all the while pain from the wound to his head was denying any chance of logical thought. So were he to be condemned by a bunch of landlocked admirals it would be a travesty indeed and he should not choose to walk the deck of a British warship ever again.

But there was the rub: he may not get the chance, for even an exemplary verdict would leave him on the beach. There had been nothing so very heroic about the action: no spirited chances were taken, no audacious risks that handsomely paid off. *Prometheus* was simply worn down by a superior force, atrocious weather and – he may as well admit it – a wounded commander. And his subsequent escape from captivity had been unremarkable to date and mainly through the volition of more junior men, not to mention civilians who were nominal enemies. Banks was a senior captain of more than three years' standing, so deserving of a two-decker at least, while there were several of his rank with considerably less sea time who had already hoisted commodore's pennants and were leading their own squadrons. He told himself he would be happy with another seventy-four; possibly one of the newer types, as *Prometheus* had been a trifle antiquated, but in his heart he wondered if the energy remained to take on another large command.

It had been different in frigates – smaller ships with a crew you could get to know, and where the captain's position was not quite so remote. And the missions such craft were entrusted with, although ostensibly of less importance, were also more stimulating. But to start again with a battleship, a wardroom filled with fresh officers and a raw crew of several hundred unknown faces, was another matter entirely. They must be trained to a workable state, then supervised to ensure all continued to improve, while maintaining the fabric and provisions of such a monster was more suited to a bookkeeper's mind than that of a fighting officer. And he might go through it all only to be consigned to a distant blockading squadron, and then spend his middle years polishing an enemy coast; that or stuck in some distant harbour.

And all of which was assuming he received a command. Even now, with Britain boasting an unsurpassed number of ships in commission, there was a limited number of suitable vessels. He might wait months, years more likely, and by then the war could be over. His contemporaries would doubtless favour him with sympathetic looks and conciliatory words before going on to excel in their own careers while he was left with a position in the Impress Service, or pestering the Admiralty for the administration of a dockyard.

He might retire, of course; resign his commission and turn to managing the estate. Some might consider all senior captains to be old and mildly crusty, but there were a good few years in him yet and definitely time enough to begin a new career. But the idea of learning cow husbandry or the intricacies of cereal crop rotation was far worse than any prospect of stewing at anchor. No, Banks longed for something more, and he had the disquieting feeling it would not be found in the Royal Navy.

But all that would have to wait for now; he was still deep inside enemy territory and on the run for his life. They were due to reach Valenciennes by early evening; Tom King seemed confident of meeting up with his lass' brother by then, and that the transfer from the current convoy of wagons to a fleet of coal barges could be made without undue danger. The last point had yet to be proven, but Banks was prepared to risk everything in trying. To most people that meant his house, family and life in England although, despite his doubts, Banks was more considering his future as a sea officer. And when he thought of it in that way, there was very little to lose.

* * *

"Ace of diamonds?" Lovemore enquired, but the card was slammed back down on the pack with the rest and Garrett shook his head in frustration. They had only reverted to the device as a last resort, as the seaman's training had already extended beyond such simple measures. But that morning he was proving particularly dense and the magician was obviously losing patience.

"I'd have more luck with one of the ponies," he grumbled, while shuffling the pack expertly in his slim fingers.

"It might just be a set back?" Lovemore suggested, only to receive a look of pure hatred in return.

"Set back be damned!" Garrett snapped, then went to say more, before apparently thinking better of it. Lovemore had mentioned nothing of his meeting with Lamar, but remained sensitive enough to realise Garrett would know exactly what had gone on.

"What say we try again this afternoon?" Lovemore did not know quite why he made the suggestion, he had no wish to meet up with Garrett then, or ever again, if the truth be known. Besides, he was confident of being just as obtuse whenever they did. But there was something else on his mind at that moment; something far more important than wasting time with a second-rate conjurer who had remarkably bad breath.

"Very well, we shall gather again at two," Garrett grunted, and

Lovemore eased himself up from his chair. *Monsieur* Lamar's carriage was the one following theirs; whether that was by arrangement or not, Lovemore had no idea, but it would be relatively easy to drop down from Garrett's wagon and see if the old man would speak with him. There was an important matter he wished to discuss.

* * *

King had really taken a liking to driving a carriage; even with his physical limitations, he found it easy to control the horses. By grasping each rein so one ran over and the other under his fist, he could direct them with a simple twist of the wrist. He lacked a spare hand to attend to the whip of course, but the docile animals were experienced enough to need no such urging. And the gentle, if monotonous, rhythm of their hooves was conducive to thought. In reality, he had only to concentrate on the carriage in front and let the beasts do all the work. But even this lack of responsibility, combined with the beauty of the sun-blessed countryside did little to ease his disposition: the details of his current predicament kept rolling through his mind until he felt his head might burst.

Aimée had a husband. The fact should not have been a concern considering his own marital status, although it still haunted him with all the persistence of a dull toothache. From what she had told him, the man was an utter rake, and one who had deceived her with false promises and outright lies. When last heard of he had been fleeing from conscription, but that was two years ago; anything might have happened in the meantime. He may be sheltering in some neutral country, or even have made it to England, as he had a British mother and a reasonable command of the language. But until firmer news were received, they would be unable to marry, and that definitely removed any pressure from King to disclose his own spouse.

Of course, he had intended telling her of Juliana from the very beginning, and had only been waiting for a suitable time to do so although, now the need had passed, he privately admitted to a measure of relief. And really everything seemed set for the future; they could still travel to England and set up a home together.

Aimée's existence would have to be kept secret from Juliana, who might cause real trouble had she the mind, but that should prove no great hardship as they were unlikely to be moving in the same social circles.

He knew he was being a coward, and privately despised himself for it, especially when Aimée was obviously feeling guilty and trying to make up for her own deception. But if they all kept their heads down, King genuinely felt everything might be sorted without any effort from himself. It was close to a perfect solution in fact, and so doubly strange that he felt on edge and, despite the idyllic surroundings, unable to relax.

* * *

Lamar appeared unsurprised to see Lovemore, and helped him up the rear step of the moving carriage.

"Thank you, father," the seaman said, using the term unconsciously.

"Is there something more you were wanting?" the old man enquired, as he led him inside and took his customary seat.

"I wished to ask..." Lovemore stopped, as if suddenly uncertain. "I wished to ask about my flute."

"Surely that was returned to you?"

"Yes, and I am grateful. But the difficultly comes when I try to play." Lovemore could not think why it was suddenly so hard to talk; perhaps the presence of the driver made a difference – they were only separated from him by a sheet of canvas. Or maybe it was something to do with his shared history with the old man?

"I hope it is not damaged," Lamar told him and Lovemore shook his head.

"No, father, it is fine; but I cannot hold a tune in my head any more. I wondered if it was to do with..." Now the words truly failed him.

"I gave you healing," the old man replied pragmatically. "In the Bible it is often referred to as casting out devils." He angled his head slightly. "Perhaps that is misleading, but evil was certainly banished from your mind. And on some occasions a change is

291

noticed elsewhere, in which case it is possible the two are connected."

"Connected?" Lovemore pondered. "You mean my flute is an instrument of the devil?"

Lamar gave a quiet chuckle and it was a reassuring sound. "No, my son, that is unlikely, although perhaps the evil was entering through your talent for music," he added after a thought. "Tell me, are you reading the English Bible I provided?"

"I am, father, though some words are unfamiliar, and I am a poor scholar."

"You must persevere." Lamar's tone was gentle, yet carried authority. "Little of value is achieved without effort. Nature abhors a vacuum and, if you will forgive me, there may be a spiritual emptiness in your mind. It is important to fill the space with the word of the Lord."

"I understand, father." Lovemore bowed his head slightly.

"Allow a little time." Lamar's eyes rested on Lovemore as if he were a favoured child. "Right will always come through if given the chance."

\* \* \*

They arrived at the outskirts of Valenciennes as darkness was beginning to fall and the carriages held up in a small clearing set next to the edge of what appeared to be a large forest. It had been a warm day and the dry undergrowth was buzzing with small insects, but there was an energy in the air as the British came together, with Aimée locked proprietorially onto King's right arm.

"We should continue from here on foot," Banks declared. The officers were meeting together for the first time since joining the travellers and could speak in relative privacy. "As far as we can ascertain, Miss Silva's brother's yard is less than five miles down this road. The forest extends for most of that distance and should provide us with cover if needed. But the deciding factor is that Mr Lamar does not intend entering the town until tomorrow. I don't wish to wait that long, and would prefer we made for it on our own. That way, if we are discovered, it would not reflect so badly upon our hosts."

All present nodded in agreement; it would have been the

ultimate insult if their presence were noticed at this late stage, although Banks had another reason to leave early. The bohemian atmosphere of the convoy had started to annoy him; he was a King's officer with a force of fighting men at his command and the presence of a bunch of peripatetic performers was hardly conducive to the strict discipline he would be enforcing from then on. And they were on enemy territory, a fact that was too often ignored in the relaxed atmosphere of the players' carriages.

"Do you know your brother's premises, madam?" he asked, turning to Aimée.

"I have never been," she replied doubtfully. "But Antoine described it well, I am thinking."

"We shall find it, I have no doubt," Banks stated with a confidence he did not feel. "A yard so large cannot be so very difficult to locate. But are we certain someone will be there to meet with us?"

"Oh yes, he lives on the premises," Aimée explained. "And my father promised to send a message so he will be expecting us."

"Then we had better make a move while some light remains." Banks looked about. He could see a number of shadowed faces peering from behind the shutters of their carriages. Most would be entertainers of some type: a breed he knew little about and did not fully understand. In fact, he had yet to make up his mind about the company in general. If it truly were an altruistic enterprise he was prepared to give it every respect, although the cynic inside him still sought a better reason behind the venture. There could be little money to be made in what its enigmatic leader did, while the chances of detection must grow with each fresh case helped. And Lamar himself had not shed any of his mystery, despite their travelling in company for several days. In polite society it was customary for those of a similar status to socialise to some extent, yet he had remained shut inside a bare wagon like some sort of monk.

He turned back to his own group; men, in the main, and all but one a sea officer. They were people he could understand, while their current predicament was only too plain and comfortably within his control. "If you would all collect your possessions and take leave of our hosts," he said, his tone once more of command, "we shall reform here in ten minutes."

Cranston had not been invited to the officers' meeting; being a mere regular Jack, such things were not of his world, although he felt no resentment and would rather spend the last few minutes with his old tie mate.

"So you're dead set on staying?" he asked for what must have been the third time, and the curly-headed seaman sighed.

"Aye, I fear so," Lovemore said, the patience in his voice now noticeable.

Cranston was unperturbed; you didn't mess with a man for so long without seeing him in every mood. "So, you'll be giving up the sea..." he mused, and it was more a statement than a question. Lovemore said no more; there was little point, instead he turned his attention to his flute. He had the instrument in his hand and had ostensibly been mending the thing. But there was no fault with it; any defect lay within himself.

He was still grateful to *Monsieur* Lamar; the kindly old man had done him a huge favour. The constant premonitions and flashes of insight that had plagued his life for so long were now gone, and for what should be forever. Ever since their meeting, Lovemore had felt a better, fuller man: one who could sleep without risk of interruption or look his fellows full in the face, and not fear what might be seen. But there was no doubt that, despite the second visit, his musical ability had suffered. He could still make a noise on the instrument and might play any individual note he chose, but all memories of melodies previously learned had completely disappeared.

It was something that should come back, or so he assured himself, even if the prospect disconcerted Lovemore almost as much. For if one talent could return, why not another? He had avoided any current problems with the band by claiming to have hurt his lip, but such an excuse could not last for ever and, were his lack of ability permanent, he did not dare consider the implications.

And there was another matter, one that played on his mind until he could think of little else. There was that last premonition; the death's head skull he had seen on the officer's face. It had gone now, of course, but the memory remained. And, since reading Lamar's Bible, the fact worried him more than ever.

It was as if a responsibility had been passed to him; he had not caused the image to appear, and neither could he tell exactly what it meant. But the man would die, there was no doubt about that. And Lovemore felt obliged – compelled almost – to warn the officer concerned. That way any necessary arrangements could be made, along with peace with his Maker, should he so choose. But how could a regular hand approach someone holding the King's commission with such a vague and unlikely story? He would immediately be thought of as a fool, and Lovemore's natural inclination was to say nothing. Yet this was something that surpassed the bounds of rank; the two were fellow human beings. He felt a responsibility to tell all and in a few brief minutes his last chance would be gone.

All of which made Cranston's constant questioning the more annoying for, in truth, the temptation to quit the company was strong. Lovemore could not be certain his musical talents would return and, if they did not, he must surely go anyway. To do so now, while a way existed for him to reach England again, was surely tempting. On returning home he might ship before the mast as before: a far better prospect than starving on the streets of some miserable French town which was the only future a talentless escaped prisoner of war might expect. But he had so enjoyed being part of the travelling players, and a life making music without having to turn out at all hours and in every weather, did have its attractions.

"Well, I wish you luck, whatever," Cranston said at last. He could see his friend had made up his mind, although it seemed a shame to part now, when they had gone through so much together. And he was also concerned on another level; Lovemore had not been himself these last few days; there was something decidedly different about him which worried the seaman. Had there been others about, men of their own rank who knew Lovemore as he did, the problem could have been addressed, but with only the two of them they were denied the wisdom of the mess. Still, Cranston would continue to worry about the cove, there could be no doubt of that. And in the times to come, must surely miss him.

* * *

"Are all assembled, Mr King?" Banks asked, the more formal title coming naturally now they were about to leave the caravan.

"Yes, sir," King reported, from amongst the group of officers. "All present, apart from Lovemore, who has expressed a wish to remain."

"Very good," Banks grunted. If the fool wanted to throw in his lot with a bunch of performers that was of no concern to him, although he remained surprised that a regular Jack should make such a decision. He glanced over his men, an eclectic mixture of civilian clothing had been provided for them by both Miss Silva and the travellers, and they appeared anything other than a military force, with little discernible difference between the officers and Cranston, a lower deck hand. And the addition of a woman made the contrast even greater.

The players were to remain in the clearing for the night, and had set up camp; all about them buzzed the noise and bustle of domesticity while a scent of cooking drifted appetisingly on the breeze. But, if their information was correct, Banks' party should be at the barge docks in little more than an hour. Not for the first time he was experiencing doubts; their escape thus far had been aided, indeed facilitated, by Frenchmen, and it was still slightly galling to realise that whether they succeeded or failed would be entirely in the hands of one of his officer's concubine's brother. He knew it wrong to consider the woman in that way and accepted that, if they should be arrested, she must suffer as much as any under his command, but still could not suppress some doubts.

The elderly bald man who was in charge of the travellers had made a rare departure from his carriage, and now stood with a group of theatricals who had gathered to see them off.

"I have to thank you for your assistance, sir," Banks told him, as he stepped closer. "Your aid has helped us incalculably and I will make every effort to see those in authority in England are aware of the fact."

"Thank you, Captain, but I would prefer if nothing were said," Lamar replied softly.

Banks paused for a moment, before nodding his head. "As you

296

will, sir, though we shall not forget. Now, if you are ready?" he added, turning back to his men.

There were brief handshakes from the officers and far less reserved hugs from the women that seemed mainly to be aimed at the midshipmen. Then Banks cleared his throat, the British formed into a more regular body, and began to walk away from the clearing.

"Five miles," Brehaut muttered as they headed into the woods. "After the distances we have walked in the past, it will seem like nothing."

* * *

And the journey was completed in no time; it was a dense forest, but the path remained clear and, fortunately, empty. In little over an hour they had come to its end and were standing at the very edge of the town.

"There is no guard on the gates." Brehaut nodded towards the stone entrance. "Though I am not totally surprised; we are still many miles from the sea, and no one would expect a group of British as far inland."

"We must make for the river," Aimée said, stepping forward. "Antoine said his was the only large business in the town, and it could not be missed."

"Perchance we should split into small groups," King suggested, "so as not to attract attention?"

"No, we go as one body." This was Banks, he had been a little way behind and was only just catching them up. "Dividing us will only increase the chances of detection; better to put our disguises to the test." He glanced back; the group was almost together now, only one had yet to join them.

"As soon as Cranston appears we will strike out," he announced. "Where has the fool got to?"

* * *

Cranston had purposefully been at the end of the line; walking with so many officers had been awkward in the past, but then at least there had been Lovemore to accompany him. Now, on his own, and without even the French guards to dilute them, he felt decidedly out of place amongst such illustrious company. But he had not intended to delay; other matters caused that.

He strode on now, bounding along the earthen path in an effort to make up for time lost and, when the officers finally came in sight, turned to his companion.

"You'd better explain it were you what delayed us," he said. "Tie mate or not, I'm taking no responsibility."

"Don't worry," Lovemore replied phlegmatically. "I'll tell them."

# Chapter Twenty-Six

King's barge was slightly less than seventy feet in length, but wider than the similar vessels he had seen on British waterways. Her freeboard was also deeper, with a high, sweeping bow that might even see her across the Channel, or so Aimée's brother had assured them. But no such journey was in anyone's mind; Antoine had already made arrangements for their trip back to England and the barges would only be used to transport them as far as the coast. In theory this would be a perilous journey, with the might of Napoleon's army now gathered at a few strategic ports the chances of them being detected was surely great, although King was not unduly worried.

Indeed he had seldom felt more relaxed, and with the sun beating down from a cloudless sky, a slight wind filling the loose-footed gaff to perfection, and the prettiest woman ever accompanying him, it was hardly surprising. Once more he felt blessed, and it was a sensation he was almost coming to expect, which must surely make him one of the luckiest fugitives alive.

They had met up with Aimée's brother without undue complication; the town might have been another prison depot but run on more conventional lines to Verdun. At the time of their arrival the prisoners of war were tightly locked up within its fortress, leaving the town itself relatively unguarded. And the Silva yard was easy to find. King had only encountered the young man a handful of times before but they were soon like old friends, and everyone settled to the fine meal of cold meats and cheeses that had been saved for them.

Arrangements were then made for their travel; the four barges Antoine deemed necessary were almost ready to sail so the British only needed to spend three days and four nights hidden in one of his warehouses before they could depart, and much of that time was used in preparing for the journey.

None of them had sailed anything like the squat, heavy vessels before, yet it was important they were handled in a competent manner if their disguises were to be believed. Consequently, the men spent many hours furtively watching the busy traffic on the nearby river, noting how the barges were handled. Special attention was paid to managing the sails and mooring procedures so that, when their turn came, they could carry out similar manoeuvres in roughly the same manner.

It was customary to carry no more than three men in each vessel, although occasionally a woman might be added, or perhaps an apprentice, so the British were divided up, with Cranston joining King and Aimée on their barge. Brehaut, the only competent French speaker amongst the officers, took charge of another, with Adams and Summers as hands; Antoine, accompanied by Manning and Bremner, had the third and Banks commanded the fourth, assisted by Lovemore and Soames.

They were carrying cargo, of course, and the momentum created by up to fifty tons of coal in each made approaching quays or wharfs a daunting procedure. But once they were under way, with the wind filling their heavy gaff mainsails, and each blunt prow showing a credible bone in its teeth, the barges were a joy to conn, and King was struck, yet again, by the wonders of water transport.

With just one man to assist, he could carry a tremendous load at a fair and regular speed for all the daylight hours; a similar cargo moved by road would require several large wagons, a constant supply of horses, and upwards of twenty men to go half as far in twice the time, and that was not accounting for the inevitable snapped axle or broken wheel.

And they were being fortunate in their breeze; sailed close-hauled, with two massive leeboards rigged to either side, the barges could make progress remarkably close to the wind. But the nearest they had come to that was a broad reach; the rest of the time Cranston had been able to set the main to larboard, the jib to starboard and let the light airs carry them as smoothly as any bathtub yacht.

King currently had the helm, while a trail of smoke from the chimney showed how far Aimée had come with preparing the evening meal. He glanced back at Brehaut, who had the following vessel, and gave him a merry wave. But either the sailing master was not watching, or had other matters on his mind, for there was no reply. Antoine, in the leading vessel, was more forthcoming though, and King, settling his only hand back safely on the tiller, found he was beaming like a child at the sheer pleasure of it all.

Aimée appeared at the small hatch just forward of him and clambered up the two steps carrying a couple of tin mugs, her tongue just peeping between thin lips as she concentrated on not spilling the contents.

"It is coffee," she said in triumph, adding, "and I have sweetened it with some honey and added the cow's milk."

King beamed at her while she set the mug down next to him. He liked coffee, but actually preferred chocolate. Of course, such a delicacy would not be expected in the galley of a coal barge, but it made him realise how little each actually knew about the other. They had barely been together more than a couple of months, in fact, and yet it felt more like forever, and he wanted nothing else. And then he remembered the one, vital point he had been purposefully keeping from her, and suddenly the whole magic of that afternoon vanished.

\* \* \*

Watching the British depart – a group that included several former shipmates – had proved the last straw for Lovemore. He might have remained with the theatre company if he were still able to play his flute but, though several hours of private practice had produced at least one recognisable tune, he knew himself to be nowhere near proficient enough for professional performance. Besides, the hours of relative inaction in the coal depot had given him time for other studies; he had read a good deal of Lamar's Bible and actually begun to understand a fair amount, although it seemed even a limited knowledge was opening doors a simple seaman would never have believed existed.

During the time Lovemore had the talent of prophesy he became used to a certain superiority; he could usually tell how matters would pan out, even if precise details remained hidden. That ability was now gone, but had been replaced by something almost as omnipotent: he might not be able to foretell the future, but knew himself to be cared for by something just as powerful and to whom nothing was hidden or impossible. Even reading a few of

301

the chapters Lamar had indicated assured him of so much and he found he was learning more each day, although not every lesson was coming through the pages of scripture.

Speaking with the travellers, Cranston, and latterly some of the midshipmen, had opened his eyes to much that had been missing. For the first time in his life he had time to spare and, when practice and reading were at an end, was able to consider matters previously ignored. Almost immediately an understanding of his fellow man developed and began to grow; incidents in his past life took on greater importance and he recognised guilt for the first time. In the past such a thing was always connected with breaking the law but now he could understand more fully why certain acts had felt right and others wrong. Of the latter, one stood out in importance and had been the final tug that tore him away from the theatrical group and into the company of his fellow countrymen.

There was no longer a death's head scull on anyone's face; all such tomfoolery being long forgotten and he knew himself the better for it. But there remained a responsibility; one that no one had proclaimed but Lovemore felt must be honoured. He was the carrier of information: news almost. It might not have stemmed from a righteous source but, as his studies had already indicated, what came from evil could also be used for good. And this was important, possibly not to him but to his neighbour, which he now accepted as very much the same thing.

As soon as he saw the officer concerned make for the forest he had known his chance was departing with him, and it had taken only the time it took to snatch at his flute: bid a hasty farewell to Lamar, who seemed content to see him go, and ignore Garrett's less than friendly glare, before he was thundering up the path in hot pursuit. He had not known quite the reception he would receive, but was inwardly certain of doing the right thing. And it was a good feeling.

\* \* \*

Lewis walked down one of the wide, open roads of the port. It was early morning, the town was not yet busy, although in all the times he had been ashore in what he insisted on calling Flushing, he had

302

never known the place feel anything but spacious. His appointment with van Gent was at ten, and there was ample time to reach the large house overlooking Stranger's Quay.

*Narcis* had returned to port without major incident, although two more of her men died on the journey making the final total seven, with another nine wounded. That meant more hands to find, although the prospect did not worry Lewis greatly; he had learned there were always fresh men available. It was the loss of those he had come to know that remained in his thoughts. And, of course, there was Masters.

The lad had born his injury well, having put up with the wounded arm being roughly bound up with bandages that were enthusiastically, if not expertly, applied by Reid. To all appearance the bleeding stopped, and he was able to stand watches on the journey home. But Lewis made sure he sought more professional attention on reaching port, and was now in the town's military hospital where the medical staff were debating about removing the limb.

Lewis felt bad about the boy's injury on two counts; the obvious being that a bright young man had been badly injured while under his command. If Masters were to heal, further employment could be found for him, but he had the uneasy feeling an extended injury would not be financed by Crabtree and van Gent. Should that be so, Lewis would step in himself; he had already acquired a reasonable sum for his efforts, and if a chunk of it were used to secure a decent future for the lad rather than himself, it would not have been wasted.

But the more immediate problem of being one officer down was not so easily solved. There were several promising hands who might have stepped up to the position, but that would mean promoting them above Price; something that was bound to cause friction, while the man was far too good in his present role to risk giving him the post. With luck, van Gent would provide him with a suitable replacement, although that would not end Lewis' concern for Masters.

And it was the first action with him in command when men had fallen: something he was taking a good while to get used to. There had been no negligence on his part; perhaps he might have identified the ketch for what she was a little sooner, but had still been the first to do so. And not one decision made or order given during the action did he regret, even in retrospect. But still the fact appalled him; as did the damage caused to *Narcis*.

She had already been assessed and two weeks was the minimum needed to put her shattered timbers back to something approaching order. He supposed they had got off lightly; it wouldn't have taken many more shots from the ketch to cause really devastating damage that might have seen the brig scrapped, even assuming he could have made Flushing once more.

He had not been her captain long and smuggling was by no means his vocation, but already Lewis did not wish to imagine continuing the work without *Narcis*. She was merely a jobbing brig with a stunted main and a handful of guns added as an afterthought but Lewis had learned so many of her ways that he felt he knew her as well as some did their spouses, and probably loved her almost as much.

But the repairs were authorised without a second thought, and neither had he faced any reproval for returning home early. Actually the position was far worse than he had thought; no fewer than thirty-nine tubs of over-proof spirit had been ruined during the action, which had also destroyed several bolts of lace as well as a consignment of earthenware pots. But when he asked questions about their attacker, both van Gent and his assistants proved stubbornly evasive.

Lewis was not to be put off, though, and was determined to discover as much about the mystery vessel as possible. Clues were found in one of the popular hotels near the harbour, where he met with a group of masters who plied a similar trade. A couple claimed the ketch was a relatively new sight off Britain's eastern coast but had been spotted twice in the area where *Narcis* was most active. And it was their view that Lewis had been fortunate in his encounter with her.

The theory was she belonged to the Sea Fencibles, a form of waterborne militia but manned by professional seamen. These were either experienced fishermen or trained hands; men who benefited from regular pay, immunity from the press and the luxury of sleeping at home and in their own beds. Consequently, service in the Fencibles was considered a softer option than a Navy or revenue posting, although that did not explain the ketch's recent activities.

In the main, vessels employed by the force confined their activities to coastal defence in anticipation of invasion. Why one particular craft had taken on the role of vigilante and was waging their own private war against smugglers was anyone's guess. But Lewis was not in the mood for further mysteries; one brush with death had been enough, he had no wish to repeat the experience, nor watch any more wounded being unloaded from one of his commands.

If van Gent did not know of the ketch he would shortly enlighten him. They were meeting that morning to discuss the next voyage, but Lewis was determined to see that was not the only subject on the agenda. Not only did he want to know more about the mystery vessel, he would see to it that *Narcis* was in a better position to meet her in action. For, if what the other masters said was true, such a thing must be considered likely.

\* \* \*

"Permission to speak, sir?" the seaman's voice was full of respect and, though he was not clutching his hat before him and both men wore civilian clothing, it was the classic confrontation between officer and lower deck hand.

"What is it, Lovemore?" The man had not slept particularly well and needed his breakfast.

"It is sort of unofficial like," the seaman hesitated.

"Do you mean personal?" the officer asked. He supposed such a thing was not to be surprised at. The two ordinary seamen must find it odd living aboard the barges in such proximity to their betters and he was experienced enough to know such things created friction. Doubtless one of his colleagues had been a trifle high-handed and given the men more work than was reasonable.

"In a manner, sir," Lovemore agreed.

"Very well, we had better go somewhere more private." The others had wandered off to the nearby forest in search of firewood; only two of the midshipmen remained and they were stretched out aboard the nearest barge enjoying the early sun. "Come, Mr Silva's vessel appears unattended."

It was: all four barges had spent the night moored to a grassy bank in an otherwise deserted spot. The isolation had been welcome; it was several miles from any village as well as some way from the nearest road and they had all enjoyed their collective evening meal of boiled pork and potatoes eaten *al fresco* on the shore. It had been a particularly pleasant time and the memory remained with the officer as he led Lovemore into the small cabin to the stern of the barge.

"This suit you, will it?" he asked, indicating a pair of stools, and Lovemore nodded.

"Thank you, sir, it will be fine."

There was a silence that the senior man felt obliged to break. "Well?"

"It is difficult to explain, sir," the seaman began. "Only I was thinking you should be careful."

In all his seagoing experience this was the first time such an approach had been made, and the officer was taken aback.

"Do you mean I am in danger?" he questioned.

"Not exactly," Lovemore confessed, blushing slightly. "Least, not any more than the rest of us. But I used to get these feelings – hunches, if you like."

"I see. And what did this hunch tell you?"

The man was smiling, and Lovemore realised he was not being taken seriously.

"It told me you're going to die," he stated plainly, and had to admit to a little satisfaction at seeing the expression change.

"What are you talking of?" the officer demanded, his tone now more solemn.

"I used to have a skill," Lovemore continued at a rush, his eyes closed and face growing evermore rosy. "For some time I could see things in the future. Nothing definite," he assured, looking once more. "Least not always; just feelings."

The officer nodded; he had heard something of Lovemore's abilities from the other officers, most of whom attributed them to what they assumed to be a Romany background.

"Well all that is behind me now," the seaman continued. "I have found the Lord and turned away from all such ways. But I felt honour bound to pass on what I had seen in you."

"Seen?"

"Yes, sir," Lovemore confirmed, then paused. He was still not certain if the officer was truly listening and sensed that if he explained about the death's head image, he would think him a fool for sure. "I could see something of your future," he continued. "And it ain't good, sir. Ain't good at all."

The senior man swallowed; usually such things meant nothing to him. Like tales of ghosts and other foolish goings on, they were simply scuttlebutt: suitable only for wardroom conversation after a powerful meal and to be instantly disregarded. But Lovemore clearly believed what he said and, in the privacy of the cabin with no one else within sight, it was becoming easier to take him seriously.

Not that he was in any way religious. In a world where any who claimed a lack of faith were treated with contempt it was a fact kept to himself, but in private he regarded the scriptures to be nothing more than folk tales and superstition. He could tell Lovemore was in earnest however, and the fact worried him more than a little.

"So, you're saying I'm going to die?" he asked lightly, almost glorying in the drama of his words. "Why, the same can be said about any one of us; yourself included."

"Aye, sir," the seaman replied, and now there was a different light in his eyes. "Though the matter no longer troubles me greatly, I were merely thinking you would like a warning; so as to prepare yourself, as it were." Lovemore had noted certain Bible passages to use if the conversation had gone differently, but it was clear his words were falling on stony ground.

"Well, I'm obliged to you, Lovemore," the officer said, straightening himself on his stool. "And tell me, do your premonitions say how I should meet my end?" he asked, his tone still mildly frivolous.

"No, sir, I know no more. Just that it is likely."

"Likely?"

Lovemore lowered his eyes. "I've never been wrong in the past," he confessed.

307

# Chapter Twenty-Seven

"We will soon be in Anvers, and I shall leave you there," Antoine announced. "I cannot go further without attracting suspicion. But it is not far to Flessingue – what you will know as Flushing, though the Dutch are calling Vlissingen," he added with a wry look. "Commercial traffic is not welcome, due to the number of soldiers preparing to invade your country."

"That surely does not bode well," King mused, and the Frenchman gave a short laugh.

"Oh, you must not worry; our beloved Emperor makes many plans, but only some are carried out and often fail; especially those connected to the sea, or so I have noticed."

A smattering of polite laughter swept round the small group, even though all present were taking the matter seriously.

"No, but I think you will have few problems," Antoine continued. "I have details of a safe house where you will meet with a man who shall take you further. I regret, I cannot say his name for we have never met."

"I quite understand," Banks told him. "And where will he take us?"

"I have no idea," Antoine replied with a smile. "We do our own work and try not to interfere with anyone else's; that way all stay safe. But I know of several before who have reached their homes without trouble and you should do the same."

"And the journey to Flushing?" Brehaut this time. "You said it is not far, though I recall several navigational hazards."

"The passage is wide and tidal," Antoine explained. "But there is nothing to worry a small boat and only a few islands which are easily seen, even at night."

The sailing master nodded, as did the others while Banks sat back in his chair, clearly satisfied. So far it had been an uneventful journey through the canals and waterways of the Low Countries, and all were eager to believe the rest would be little different. There had been one nasty moment, when an over-officious *gendarme* on the French boarder had insisted on searching one of the barges. But Silva had chosen his cargo wisely; the coal they carried was of a low grade and exceptionally dusty. Once the first hold was opened a great cloud of fine grit flew up, coating all about and the convoy was hurried on without speaking further with its crew.

Apart from that, and the time Summers fell into the canal, there had been no real excitement; the trip might even have been considered boring, had not the warm weather and stunning scenery turned it more into a holiday jaunt. But now they were nearing the end, Banks, at least, was becoming pensive. Be it a short journey or long, they must still make Flushing; the place where a passage home had been promised. The port was a haven for smugglers, which would help to keep their presence unnoticed, while the Frenchman seemed sure of those who would be taking care of them. They had still to reach the port, however and, according to Brehaut, that would mean an estuary trip of roughly forty miles. He assumed they would be provided with a suitable craft, although still had a purse full of gold, and was quite prepared to spend it.

In fact, so close were they to their destination, a part of him wanted to throw in his lot with the escape team. They might continue independently, bargain for a small boat or even capture one where they were, and then find their own way to England. It was a foolish thought, of course; far better to remain in the hands of those who had done such things before. But still Banks was gratified to realise the old urge to command was returning.

"Do you have everything you need for the journey?" Antoine was asking, and Banks brought himself back to the conversation to glance about the table. Both King and Brehaut seemed content, only Timothy and Manning appeared eager to talk.

"Our disguises," the surgeon spoke first. "They have passed muster aboard the barges, but when we reach the town, how will people consider us?"

Antoine smiled. "They will probably think you have spent some time aboard a coal barge," he admitted, amid general laughter. "But do not concern yourselves. I think it better you appear so, and probably safer than being dressed smartly. The poor are present in every port; they do not attract attention and neither will you."

Manning rolled his eyes slightly at the last statement, but appeared generally content. Then it was Timothy's turn.

"Should we be caught," he began and continued determinedly, despite several jocular moans from his fellow officers. "I mean, I am not wishing for it of course, but there is a possibility..."

"*Bien sûr*," Antoine conceded.

"Well, they will ask us how we arrived, and it might not be easy to say nothing."

Now all humour had gone and Timothy's point was accepted. However hard they tried to resist, it would be strange if at least one of them did not break under interrogation. And once the French became aware of the little enterprise and, specifically, Silva's part in it, his entire family must surely be seized.

"It is indeed a risk," Antoine nodded slowly. "And one we are aware of. We may all work separately but, by the end of your journey, you will know each of us well and must surely be a danger, even when safely in England. But we must also be realistic; however honourable your intentions, any man can break his word without realising he has done so, and only a fool would blame him in such cases."

There was an awkward pause; some seemed to be struggling for the right words but none would come. Then Banks broke the silence.

"We shall forever be in your debt," he said simply.

"I know nothing of the *politique*," Antoine shook his head deprecatingly. "Though believe the current war is not favoured amongst many of my countrymen. And I do understand right from wrong. It is not right what is happening: the fighting, the dying," he waved his hands in the air in an attempt to express himself more fully. "But if men stand by and allow such things, it is not right either," he sighed. "I am not prepared to do so, and neither are my family."

"I think we understand that," Banks assured him gently, "and will do all we can to see your efforts are rewarded."

"Thank you," Antoine nodded seriously. "But perhaps you will say nothing for now – especially to the French..."

The ripple of laughter that flowed about the table owed much to relief. But Banks realised that, however long the rest of their journey might be, it should at least reach an end, while the Silva family would be living under the fear of capture for the foreseeable future.

"If there is nothing else, I suggest we all get a good night's sleep," Antoine said, rising from the table. "We should reach Anvers at about midday; by this time tomorrow evening you will be well on your way to Flessingue and freedom."

There were several grunts of approval from the British as they dispersed, but Antoine had more to say to one of them at least.

"Tom, I wonder if I might speak with you?"

King turned and allowed Timothy and Brehaut to pass him. "Of course, Antoine. What can I do for you?"

"It is not me, it is Aimée," the Frenchman said when they were alone, and King could sense the importance in his manner. "You will know of her arrangement, I assume?"

"Arrangement?"

"Her status." The man was blushing slightly now. "That she is..."

"Oh yes, I am aware," King assured him in a softer voice and with what he hoped was an air of understanding.

"It was that I am considering."

Now King's heart was truly starting to pump, and he felt his hand begin to shake. What fresh news was Aimée's brother about to impart? Apart from her revelation, their time together had been all but perfect. Then a terrible thought occurred; suppose someone had let slip about his own marital status. It might have only been in passing, but even a chance remark could cause as much damage as an all out confession. For the umpteenth time he cursed himself for being a coward, then looked the Frenchman in the eye and prepared to hear the worst. But when the news came it was not as he expected, although every bit as terrible.

* * *

Lewis felt a little more settled after his interview with van Gent. The man had been his usual conceited self, but finally accepted the Fencible ketch to be a potential problem. A larger crew was immediately promised, along with the possibility of uprating the brig's cannon although Lewis would far rather *Narcis'* cruising ground were simply changed. But at least van Gent had come through with a replacement main topmast; a suitable spar had been secured and would be set in place at the end of the brig's refit. Lewis did not know how such a thing had been found; all spars were in desperately short supply, with masts being the rarest. But at least with a standard main *Narcis* would no longer be so recognisable.

This was more than a comfort to Lewis: it altered his attitude completely. As a sea officer in the Royal Navy, he had fought a good many actions and was fortunate in none having left any lasting impression, although the few occasions when he had commanded the brig in battle had been very different. It was one thing to be a part of a battle, to look after a battery of cannon or head a boarding party, quite another when every element was totally under his control. And to knowingly sail a vessel so recognisable was at best irresponsible; at least he would now be able to lead his men knowing he had done as much as he could to keep them safe.

So he still had command of the brig, which was something he might easily have given up, while fresh cargo was being arranged for the next run. And soon he would be setting out on another trip, another foray across the North Sea, to cruise within touching distance of his homeland, but no closer. But it would be one more to add to the number needed to finally see him free of the trade forever. And that time was coming ever closer.

* * *

"It is Aimée's husband, Albert van Gent; he is in Flessingue."

King heard every word and understood exactly what the Frenchman meant but when he slumped down on his seat again, he could only think how foolish it was to have so many names for the same port.

"I'm not sure exactly what his official position is," Aimée's brother continued, "but he has a key role in the port and I think it unlikely you will get as far as England without his hearing of it."

"How long have you known?" King asked at last, and Antoine lowered his head.

"A little while, *mon ami*; I regret having kept his existence a secret from you both."

King delivered a sharp look, and the Frenchman explained.

"There seemed little point in raking up bad ground," he said. "Their marriage did not work and everyone thought van Gent to have simply disappeared."

Van Gent; so that was Aimée's true surname. Strange, despite King knowing her to be married he had never considered she must have another.

"We were all so sure he would never find her in Verdun," Antoine sighed. "And now it seems she has found him."

"And he has a position in the port?" King asked after a pause.

"Indeed, and is much respected," Antoine confirmed. "He does his work well, or so I understand. All matters concerning the smugglers come under his charge; he sees to it their vessels are well provided for and their crews have everything they need."

"Kind of him," King grunted.

"But there is more," the Frenchman added. "That is his official business; unofficially he has also helped many of your countrymen back to England. That is an especially dangerous activity, even in the Batavian Republic. The Dutch who have pledged allegiance to Bonaparte can be far more virulent than the Emperor's French officers; I suspect they would deal harshly with a countryman who is playing the traitor."

"Do you know why he helps the British?" King asked, and Antoine shook his head.

"I am not sure, though think his mother may be from your country. He definitely speaks the language well." He sat back in his chair and smiled. "These are strange times," he said. "Some Frenchmen love the Emperor, others hate him with the same strength, and it does not do to enquire too deeply into any man's loyalties as you are likely to get the nasty surprises. And the Dutch are far worse," he continued. "No one can be so sure on which side they play, so Albert may be essential to your plans. Certainly little can be done without his agreement and he will be aware by now that you are coming."

"And Aimée; does he know she is with us?"

At this Antoine's glance dropped and he shook his head. "I am so sorry, *mon ami,* but I think you must assume he does."

* * *

Aimée had all their possessions neatly piled when King returned and together they took no time in placing them in the canvas bags Antoine had provided. The barges were moored against a quay at the southern end of the small harbour, and would soon be taken for unloading at the coaling wharf.

"Sir Richard and Brehaut have gone to meet with our contact," he told her.

"And he will see us to our ship?" she asked brightly.

"Eventually, or so I believe," King answered. "He is a Dutchman living in the town, I don't know what arrangements have been made. There is nothing else?" he added, looking at the scant piles of luggage.

"No, that is everything," Aimée replied. "Except what we are standing in of course," she told him with a smile. He looked around the small cabin that had been their home for such a long time and where they had been so very happy. Banks had hardly approved of their living arrangements, although accepted such things were necessary, if only as part of their disguise. The cabin had been cold at night, with a stove that smoked abominably but, with Cranston berthing forward, it had been their own private space, and was especially hard to give up now. King even had the absurd desire to remain where they were, and live forever in the dusty coal barge. But then the knowledge that Aimée's husband remained nearby would only haunt him, and he wondered if he should speak further of the man now.

The pressure of holding two secrets was already starting to tell; in addition to the existence of his wife, there was now this latest news. King was still unsure why Antoine had not told his sister of her husband's presence in the port, even if he accepted it better kept from her. But that did not lessen his own responsibility and, while they were in the midst of an escape, he did not wish for more.

"Are you well, Tom?" she asked, and King realised something of his preoccupation must have been noticeable.

"I am fine," he said, forcing a smile. "But will feel better when we are on our way."

"Oh, I also, yet we have already made it so far," she continued. "I have never been beyond France before, and soon I will be in England, which will be even more exciting I have no

314

doubt."

King smiled; he supposed it would be better to set off although, after what Antoine had said, remained uncertain if he actually wanted to go to Flushing. And neither, he felt, would Aimée.

* * *

But the journey went smoothly enough. Antoine's contact turned out to be a middle-aged Dutchman with fine yellow hair named Jansen. He spoke reasonable English and it was with an accent King remembered from his past.

Before he had even met his wife, her brother, Wilhelm van Leiden, had been a good friend. Jansen bore no resemblance to the younger man, being somewhere in his fifties with a belly that slopped easily over his belt and round glasses which made his eyes appear unusually large. But the voice and manner of speaking was almost identical, so much so that King found the memories came flooding back without his willing them.

The British were ushered through Jansen's large house and eventually found themselves in a back room where tea was served before Jansen broke away to set about organising their transport. An hour later he was back with several loaves of freshly baked bread, which were promptly dropped on the floor, and news that they would be leaving that very evening.

"It is a journey of about fifty kilometres," he told them breathlessly. "Though not so very arduous, and we shall have the current in our favour."

"We?" Banks had questioned.

"Why yes, I shall be accompanying you," Jansen informed them with a self-important wriggle of his round nose. "Otherwise you may get lost, or decide to simply cross the sea in my boat, and it would be too small for such a journey."

"You have my word, we shall restrain ourselves," Banks assured him, but the man was determined and, three hours later, they were clambering into a tiny skiff.

The estuary was wide and, as they had been assured, the current ran with them. Even without a totally agreeable wind, they were able to make reasonable time and, as dawn began to break,

315

were nearing the island port.

"A big enough place," Banks muttered as the first shafts of light revealed a collection of jetties and wharfs.

"The French have been building here since taking it over," Jansen confirmed, his breath condensing in the cold morning air. "Already they have improved the shipyard, as well as adding an arsenal, sluices, a dry dock and a barracks."

"Ah yes, the barracks..." Banks pondered. "It is hard to conceive that the presence of soldiers will not present difficulties."

"But there are also a great number of British in the port," the Dutchman assured them. "Many of their boats are based here; you will have no problems, I am sure of it."

"And these would be smugglers, I'd chance?" Banks sighed.

"Mostly, yes," Jansen agreed. "The French welcome them like brothers, and make every provision for their comfort. Indeed, their trade is an important addition to the French economy," he chuckled.

Sir Richard made no reply, although most aboard the skiff could guess his thoughts.

"But we are to make for the Stranger's Quay," Jansen announced, changing the subject. "You will oblige me by keeping watch for a green lamp when we are a little nearer to the sea."

All settled to the task, although the growing light was providing distractions by the score as the skiff cruised past rows of static shipping. The sight of these, as well as mention of the sea, made most of the skiff's passengers thoughtful. After so many months in enemy territory, it now seemed escape was not only likely, but almost imminent; the same water that currently supported their little boat would soon be washing the shores of England, and they might easily be there before it. All they needed was to locate a suitable vessel and allow it to take them home. And, to the majority at least, it hardly mattered if she were a smuggler, for why should it? Even if they were intercepted, none of them would be committing a crime, and could expect a welcome fit for any returning hero.

Except for Banks and King, that is. Both would have to stand trial for the loss of their ships, while the latter had even more worries to occupy him.

Hearing the broad Dutch accent had awoken other memories;

once they were in England he would have to face Juliana. And that was strange: King realised then he would far rather confront his wife, with all the unpleasantness that must involve, than speak with the sweet and gentle creature seated next to him.

"I have it!" Timothy's voice cut through the silence as he pointed triumphantly to starboard.

The single green lamp stood out plainly and marked a simple quay where a variety of fishing and other small craft lay moored alongside. Jansen began to burble excitedly while Summers calmly eased the helm across and Cranston took in their sail.

"No one about," Banks muttered.

"And I can almost see the house from here," Jansen whispered eagerly, as King wriggled on his thwart.

"Are you alright?" Aimée whispered, and he gave her a reassuring smile.

"It's being aboard a small boat," he lied. "I had forgotten quite how uncomfortable they can be. But how is it with you?"

She beamed back in the growing light. "Oh I am fine, thank you; just happy to be on our way."

There was still no one in sight when the skiff silently neared the quay; Lovemore stood up in the bows, a painter in his hands. Within seconds they were alongside and safely secured.

"So who do we meet now we are here?" Banks asked after he and the Dutchman had clambered free of the craft.

"I have it written down, in case there were the problems, but I know the house well," Jansen said, passing a piece of paper across. Banks unfolded it and stared at the writing.

"The house of Albert van Gent," he recited thoughtfully.

Cranston, who had been stretching out to help Aimée from the skiff, gave a cry of surprise as her hand almost slipped from his grip.

"Steady there, miss," he warned. "I thought I were going to lose you then."

"I am so sorry," she said, finally stepping onto the stone quay.

"Are you alright, my dear?" King enquired, following her; he had missed hearing their destination, but certainly noticed Aimée's reaction.

"Yes, yes, Tom. I am fine," she replied, brushing herself down. "Though I am also not so used to small boats."

317

King took her hand and gave it a gentle squeeze. "It won't be long now," he reassured her. Really all he wanted to do was get her to a place of safety before there was any chance of meeting with her husband.

* * *

The house was indeed less than three hundred yards away; a sizeable, modern affair with three floors, nine large windows and a stepped roof. It stood amongst a line of similar buildings, all of which appeared comfortably asleep in the early morning light.

Brehaut, Manning and Jansen reached it first, and had heaved on the ornate bell pull before King, walking just ahead of a seemingly reluctant Aimée, arrived.

"There doesn't seem to be anyone at home," the sailing master told him as he joined them.

"Try knocking," Banks instructed from behind. It was barely dawn, but soon the streets could be expected to fill up, and a group of ill-dressed civilians might look suspicious in front of a well-to-do property.

"There will be someone about," Jansen told them importantly. "He uses the house as a place of work as well as his home, and has a large domestic staff."

"I don't think Aimée is well," King murmured, turning to her once again. His last few remarks had gone unanswered and she had a pallid expression that was noticeable, even in the poor light.

"What appears to be the trouble?" Manning asked, stepping across and placing a professional hand upon her forehead.

"It is nothing," she began, but said no more. For the door had finally opened, and a thickset man clad in a dressing gown stood before them.

For a moment he viewed the men with caution and what might have been hostility, then his eyes fell on the girl and instantly softened.

"*Aimée, ma chère,*" he said. "*Comme c'est bon de te voir!*"

# Chapter Twenty-Eight

It was an awkward and cold interview. Van Gent got rid of Jansen by despatching two of his servants to accompany him home, then showed his visitors through to a room at the front of the house. It was stark and uncomfortable; the windows were lightly covered with linen drapes, but there were few other soft furnishings and the plain wooden floor was bare and unforgiving.

"Rest yourselves if you will," he instructed while pulling the curtains back and permitting a little more light to enter. Aimée was shown to the only comfortable seat, a low *chaise longue,* the more senior British chose what hard upright wooden chairs there were and the youngsters and seamen simply stood.

"I did not expect so many," the Dutchman announced, addressing his visitors as a group. But his eyes continually flipped back to Aimée and, latterly, King, who was perched uncomfortably on the foot of the *chaise longue.*

"I was not aware of the figures you were provided with," Banks explained. "Our escape was unplanned and rather rushed."

"It is no matter," van Gent said, turning to Sir Richard and sensing importance. "I have access to many vessels and you will be provided for."

"We are grateful," Banks admitted. But the man shook his head.

"It is not through kindness to you that I do this," he replied firmly. "I am prepared to help any officer who will fight against the Emperor and may even see fit to transport your seamen," he added, looking pointedly at Cranston and Lovemore.

The pair stared back in frank surprise, although the discrimination was lost on Banks, who had other matters to consider.

"But we will have to take you in small groups," van Gent continued. "The boats I use are not large and too many travelling at once will attract attention."

"That is understandable. When might we begin?" Banks

asked.

"Not tonight," van Gent replied. "It is too soon. Tomorrow we can send the first three."

"Very well," Banks agreed, "though we have nowhere to stay."

"That will also be organised," van Gent snapped.

"Well, we expect to pay for your trouble," Banks again. "You must have expenses, and are doubtless taking a great risk. We have a small amount of gold, or I would be pleased to sign a promissory note – if you would honour such a thing."

"A note from an English gentleman is always acceptable," van Gent assured him. "But I do not require payment; as I have said, it is enough that you return to fight Napoleon."

"It is most generous of you; I am sure we are all grateful. And you mentioned accommodation," Banks reminded him. "Where might we stay?"

"You will remain in this house," the Dutchman informed him stiffly as he turned. "It will not be very comfortable as there are so many." He glanced back at the group and seemed to be assessing them. "I shall allow two rooms; you may be crowded at first, but that will ease as the numbers decrease. Perhaps the senior men in one?" he suggested, before making for the door.

"Thank you, that would suit us well," Banks replied. "Though we also have a young lady to consider."

Van Gent stopped and turned back once more. "I had not forgotten," he said, fixing Aimée with his eyes yet again and noticing how she turned away from his gaze. "And will be making special arrangements for her."

\* \* \*

"I must confess to never having known a fellow who can live such a complicated life," Brehaut told King as they walked slowly along the quay. Despite being a working day there was an air of Sunday about the place; few berths were clear, but much of the shipping appeared to have been laid up, and neither was the town in general particularly busy.

"Oh, Tom has always been an expert at such things," Manning added. "I recall that little filly on St Helena and, what was her name, Sara, in Valletta?"

"Sara should surely not count," Brehaut assured them with authority. "She were hardly Tom's for more than a day before setting course for the next, and had much of the Royal Navy in her sights as I recall."

King pressed his good arm firmly into his pocket. He could understand his friends finding fun in such a situation, but for him it was less than amusing.

"Though I must confess I thought you had landed a pearler with Aimée," the sailing master continued. "Only to find she already has a spouse!"

"Which hardly makes her so very unusual," Manning added more seriously. "Tell me, Tom, what does she think of Juliana?"

"She does not know of her," King admitted. "And I would thank you to keep such information to yourself, for the time at least."

There was a pause before Manning spoke again. "But I assume you intend..."

"Oh, yes," King interrupted. "I will certainly tell her and probably should have done so already. It just seemed unnecessary..."

"Well, I think you owe her that much at least, especially considering what the Silva family have risked for us," the surgeon continued in a softer tone. "But she will not hear it from me, and I think I can say the same for the others." He looked pointedly at Brehaut.

"Oh, I shall not say a word," the Jerseyman assured them.

"So, there is no guessing which are the famous smugglers," Manning said, breaking the conversation and all three paused to consider the line of two- and three-masted vessels that now faced them. Most were obviously abandoned and appeared ready to sink at their moorings, although a few stood out as being in prime condition.

"Aye," King agreed. "Trim little craft and well cared for by all accounts."

"That would be down to van Gent," Manning added. He had considered referring to the man as Aimée's husband, but sensed King had been teased enough for one afternoon.

"And manned by Englishmen in the main," Brehaut continued.

"Though I doubt Sir Richard would refer to them as such."

"Sure, it is a shame that we might not seek a passage home aboard one," King mused. Despite his friends' amusement, he was still reeling from the shock of meeting with Aimée's husband; the fact that he lay in the man's power made matters so much worse and, as the British force was to be steadily whittled away from the following night, he could imagine only too well who would be left towards the end of their stay.

"There would be little wrong in our making a private arrangement," Manning, who was also harbouring misgivings about the Dutchman, suggested. "We have made no commitment."

"But such a thing would be considered the height of rudeness," Brehaut protested. "Why, the fellow is risking much to keep us safe."

King said nothing; if the others had no wish to leave early, that was up to them, but they did not share his interests. The brig before him would make England in a couple of days, and might indeed be so bound; he had little experience of dealing with the kind who would cheerfully see their country ruined, but chanced that profit must be a motive, and there was still coin remaining in his pocket. Slowly the old sensations began to make themselves known: his heart started to race, and there was the prickling of sweat on his face and chest. A plan was surely forming but, even before it could be realised, he noticed something that both surprised him, and appeared to seal matters for certain.

* * *

Lovemore and Cranston had also been exploring the town, although their sights had been set slightly lower than the officers'. As seamen, they were more accustomed to the shadier areas of unknown ports and had quickly assessed the place. It differed little to many others visited in the past, with its share of taverns and cat houses, the only true distinction being Flushing was officially enemy territory. But even that was soon forgotten with the sound of brazenly spoken English echoing about the town's streets.

The reason for this was soon revealed; in addition to the number of smugglers who called the place home, several American traders were in port, with their crews given liberty to taste the

322

delights of the shore.

"Well, if they don't take us for runners, at least we may pass as a couple of Jonathans," Cranston muttered cautiously with an indirect glance at his friend. "But in any case, we're probably safe enough, wouldn't you say?"

Lovemore made no comment either way, and Cranston was mildly disappointed. In the past, his mate could have been counted on for some form of prediction, whether it be intentional or not. But since leaving the travellers he had stayed remarkably quiet on that front, and Cranston was starting to wonder if he were ailing from something.

"Well, safe or not, I'm glad to be free of that square-head cove," the seaman continued. "Might have had the officer's benefits in mind, but it were clear as a bell he cared nothing for your regular Jack."

"Aye, one law for the rich, and another for the poor," Lovemore agreed. "Whereas we are all equal in the sight of the Lord, and sinners every one."

Cranston treated his mate to a second sidelong glance; that was another change that had occurred since leaving the travellers.

"Well what say we goes for a wet?" he asked. "There's plenty of pot houses to choose from, and maybe we can squirrel out a bit of fresh soft tack when the stores open up once more?" Cranston had considered suggesting visiting somewhere less salubrious, but with the recent change in his mate's attitude, guessed such a thing would be rejected. In fact much of what Cranston would normally have looked for when ashore was being denied; Lovemore only seemed interested in reading his Bible and playing that damned flute, except he was nothing like as good at the latter as he had been. It seemed a drink or two was still within his mate's new found ethics though, and they pressed their way through the door of the next tavern.

Inside, the darkness was emphasised by a thick atmosphere. The scent of a wood fire came to meet them; it mingled oddly with that of tobacco smoke and unwashed bodies and was just the welcome Cranston had hoped for.

Some of the faces turned their way. The vast majority were obviously mariners and most lacked the beards and hangdog expressions of those awaiting employment. Cranston felt the memories stir as he glanced about for a vacant space. This was the first time he had been in company with true seamen since their failed escape attempt on the road to Verdun, and it was a good feeling. He moved across to a table where two sat behind dented tankards and settled himself comfortably on the bench opposite.

"What cheer, friend?" one asked, and Cranston was pleased to note a West Country accent.

"Right enough," he replied, as Lovemore joined them with their pots.

"You freshly in?" the stranger enquired, and Cranston glanced quickly at Lovemore before replying.

"You might say so," he temporised. "Leavin' in a few days, though."

"Runner?" the man persisted.

"No," Lovemore replied more coldly. "We fight for the King, not against 'im."

"Nowt wrong in being a runner," the Cornishman's friend stated easily as he picked up his own tankard.

"To some, maybe," Cranston allowed.

"But it ain't the way we choose to earn a living," Lovemore added more piously.

"It be ours," the second man said, laying down his pot. "Do you have issue with that?"

Cranston took a sip from his tankard and looked from one to the other. A decent brawl was one of the things he had been missing, and it seemed Lovemore had unwittingly walked straight into one.

"Well, I'm not so sure," he said, glancing at his friend. "What do you say, Curly? Do we have issue with that?"

* * *

When King and his fellow officers returned, van Gent was nowhere to be seen.

"I understand him to be working," Banks explained when they found him in a back room and seated at a plain table sipping coffee.

"Is Aimée still in upstairs?" King asked.

"I believe so; would you gentlemen care for coffee? There is plenty here and more if we ask."

Manning and Brehaut helped themselves to cups and set about draining the pot, but King was more concerned about Aimée. Before he left, van Gent had shown her to a small room near the top of the house. King had tried to follow but it was awkward with the other officers present. Besides, there was something about seeing Aimée with her husband; after all, the man held an official position in her life, and King felt decidedly out of place. He was well aware how much she hated van Gent, but that did not alter anything, and it was hard to accept those days spent together in the barge's cabin had meant nothing.

But as he whispered her name and tapped on the panelling he heard the lock turn back with a reassuring click, and his doubts were assuaged as the door opened. She reached up and wrapped an arm about his neck and, pulling down, kissed him full on the lips before breaking away, heaving him into the room, and closing the door behind them both.

"Are you alright?" King asked, feeling not a little foolish.

"Oh I am fine, and do not worry about Albert; he has behaved himself, so far."

"So far?" King didn't like the sound of that.

"He is an animal, Tom, but one I can handle. He has a position to uphold and besides, there is a strong lock on this door."

King looked about the room. It was high in the house and clearly intended as servant accommodation. The one small window looked out to the brick wall of a neighbouring building, and there was barely room for the single bed and night stand. But, as she said, the lock was substantial.

"That is all very fine for now," he supposed, "but when the rest of us start to be taken..."

"I know, and rather suspect you will be the first to leave," she agreed.

"Does he know about us?" King asked.

"I think he may have guessed," she sighed. "I said I was escorting officers from Verdun; but he is not so much the fool. Besides, if I were merely a guide, why would I wish to travel all the way to England?"

King shook his head. "It is an impossible position," he said. "We cannot stay here, yet equally cannot leave."

"Indeed, as if we were two kinds of prisoner," she agreed.

"I thought I might have found a solution earlier; ran in with a former shipmate who has command of a smuggling brig."

She said nothing, although he could see the hope rise in her eyes and it almost broke his heart.

"But it will not work," he added hastily. "He has commitments, so is not permitted to carry passengers. And I can not blame him."

She placed her hand upon his shoulder. "Never mind," she said. "Something will come up, it is bound to; it always has. And at least we are together: I can face much when you are by my side."

* * *

The fight barely lasted a minute, but in that short space of time much of the interior of the tavern was wrecked. Tables had been overturned and there were two broken chairs, while the plain earth floor was now generously sprinkled with broken glass, splinters and the occasional tooth. Cranston flexed his fists and glared down at the seaman beneath him.

"Had enough, matey?" he asked.

The Cornishman wriggled himself upright. "I have and so have you," he replied thickly, while feeling at his chin.

"He's right," his friend said joining them. "The French'll be here in no time and it would be best for us all if we weren't about."

Cranston glanced round; the woman who had served their drink was screaming hysterically in the corner while Lovemore stood near by with blood running freely down his cheek as he drained a tankard that was not his own.

"Hey, Curly; we'd better cut and run," he called out.

"You'll need a place to run to," the Cornishman's friend told him. "No good just turning out in the street, they'll round you up in no time. And if you is what I thinks you is, that'll be the end of any escape."

Cranston looked at him blankly; the Dutchman's house must be all of a mile away; they might make it, but to arrive with a file of *gendarmes* in pursuit might not be approved of.

"Better head back to the barky with us," the Cornishman muttered as he properly gained his feet. "She's not more than a cable or so off and can hide us all."

"You're sure?" Cranston asked; barely seconds ago the pair had been knocking seven kinds of hell out of the other, yet the man was prepared to help them.

"I'm sure," the Cornishman replied firmly. "Though the brig's a smuggler like the rest of us. You got an issue with that?"

* * *

It was a change to share a room again with his fellow officers, and King tried hard not to think of Aimée, lying alone and only one floor above. But he would make the best of it; Banks had already bagged one of the beds and Timothy the other, while Manning obviously intended sleeping on the large leather couch set beneath the window. Looking around, King decided to settle for a woollen rug that would at least be preferable to the bare boards of the floor, and probably provide a better bed than he had known on other nights. He slipped off the round jacket Antoine had provided and laid it to one side, then collected a blanket from the pile on the dresser and was glancing about for a pillow when he heard the noise.

At first he though it to be his imagination; his mind was still set on Aimée so it was probably natural he should think to hear her voice. But soon he realised this was no daydream: Aimée was shouting, and somewhere nearby.

"What the devil is that?" Banks demanded, but King did not stay to answer; dropping the blanket, he made for the door and, leaving it swinging open behind him, thundered up the staircase.

He was at the next level within three bounds, and almost collided with van Gent who stood at the top of the stairs and directly outside Aimée's door.

"What are you doing here?" the Dutchman demanded. "I have provided you all with rooms, why do you not use them?"

"Never mind me," King gasped. "What business have you with Aimée?"

The lock gave a loud click, although neither man noticed.

"This is hardly your concern," van Gent spluttered. "I have to speak with my wife, it is not of your business."

"What is it, Tom?" Manning's voice came from behind, but

King did not turn, instead he rounded on van Gent.

"She does not want to see you: leave her be," he cried.

Van Gent gave a slight smile. "Do not tell me what she wants, and neither should you attempt to intervene between a man and his possessions."

The door opened and Aimée's face appeared at the crack.

"It's all right, Tom," she told him. "Albert will leave."

"I go nowhere," the Dutchman shouted. "This is my house and you are my wife, now let me in!"

"Is this true, Tom?" It was Sir Richard's voice and King's spirits fell: why hadn't the old fool stayed abed?

"Only to a point, sir," he replied, although his eyes remained set on van Gent. "The cove walked out on her some years back, there is nothing between them now," he added, with a plaintive glance at Aimée.

"You will go!" van Gent roared, turning back on the group of Englishmen. "Go, and leave us be; this is not of your concern!"

"If Aimée is involved, I shall stay," King spat back. "And for as long as you remain."

He sensed, rather that saw the fist that was thrown at him, but the warning was enough to send him to one side, so dodging the blow by a good measure.

"Now steady there!" Banks' voice rang out with the full authority of a senior captain and all took notice. "I am not certain what is going on, but there will be no violence!" he boomed, before turning to King.

"Does this man speak the truth, Tom?" he asked. "Is Miss Silva his wife?"

"There is no Miss Silva," van Gent interrupted, but Banks silenced him with a single look.

"He is my husband," Aimée admitted. "Though in name only."

Once more van Gent went to speak, and once more the Captain's very presence brought quiet.

"If that is truly so, we should not be here," Banks announced, his eyes passing from King to Manning, and finally resting on van Gent. "But as for you, sir: you will think twice before attempting to strike a wounded man," he ordered. "And I expect to hear of no such violence against this young lady, whatever your marital arrangements."

All, bar Banks, began to speak at once but King was the only one to take action. Pushing the protesting body of van Gent to one side with his shoulder, he reached in and opened the door further.

"Come, Aimée, we are not staying in this house a moment longer."

The girl nodded silently, and stepped back into the room, only to return immediately with a bag.

"I can go now," she said, her eyes set on King, rather than the spluttering figure next to him.

"What are you thinking, Tom?" Manning demanded. "There is nowhere else. This is a French occupied town; you will be arrested!"

"We're leaving, and no one will stop us," King cried and he collected Aimée's bag adding, "Certainly not this beast," with a withering look at van Gent.

"You will go nowhere..." the Dutchman began, and extended a hand towards King's shoulder.

"I said, no violence," Banks snapped, and the arm fell away.

Seeing his chance, King threw himself down the stairs with Aimée close behind. Then, with no more than a dash into his room to collect his jacket, they were heading along the corridor towards the front stairs.

An elderly man in a shabby dressing gown and night cap appeared, but King brushed him aside and descended the larger staircase. Then they were in the hallway, and approaching the massive front door.

"Tom, come back you fool!"

King glanced round to see the worried face of Robert Manning following behind. But there was no time for talking, no time for anything. He knew what he must do, and was determined to do it; whatever the cost.

# Chapter Twenty-Nine

The cabin was smaller than most yet still intended to hold two men. King and Aimée fitted into it perfectly, however and, though they both lay in hammocks, each could feel the other resting softly against them.

King stirred first; he opened his eyes to see the vague features of a deckhead directly above and briefly luxuriated in the smell of damp wood, pitch and linseed oil that told him he was once more in his natural element. He yawned, stretched, then gently eased himself from his bed, trying hard not to wake the still sleeping body next to him. But some things were easier done with two sound arms; Aimée gave a faint moan of protest as his feet touched the deck and, when he took a step towards the narrow door, she called his name.

"Go back to sleep," he whispered foolishly, for there was no one else to hear. "I shall investigate breakfast and bring it to you."

"Don't be long," she warned. King said he would not, then slipped quietly out of the door.

Actually, food was the last thing on his mind; he had to seek out Lewis, and discover exactly what their position was. When he and his fellow officers sighted his friend the previous day it had been a tremendous stroke of good fortune. Not only were they all pleased to see the man, but the former lieutenant from *Prometheus* also happened to be in command of a tidy little brig that would seem ideal for the short trip back to England. Lewis had been less than enthusiastic, however. Though equally pleased at the meeting, he was even more awkward and reserved than King remembered, and it took some time before he relaxed in their company.

Lewis' attitude softened after telling his story though, especially when all three expressed their disgust at the way he had been dealt with. There then followed a brief inspection of the brig, and soon it was as if he had never left *Prometheus'* wardroom. The fact that *Narcis* was a runner was obvious to all, yet no mention was made of the fact, and when King asked Lewis outright if he would see them home, it had been with every expectation of his wish being granted.

But Lewis was reluctant. Whether this was due to learning that King and his fellow officers were staying with van Gent, or the fact that Sir Richard Banks, his former captain was amongst them King did not know. But he proved evasive and once more his mental shutters came down.

Despite most of her repairs being completed, the brig still awaited a fresh main topmast; one had been promised, and Lewis was loath to sail until it had been fitted. Had the original been sprung, King would have understood but, apart from being a few feet shorter, the present spar functioned perfectly well. So he had no option other than to regard this as an excuse; something to hide behind to avoid putting himself out to help old shipmates, and King had not expected such an attitude from a friend.

Consequently, when he and Aimée turned up late the previous night and woke the brig they had merely been looking for a temporary place of safety. Despite the earlier disappointment, the two men knew each other well enough to make complex explanations unnecessary. The brig's second mate was ashore; they had been given his cabin and could sleep knowing few would guess their hiding place. But this morning it was different. This morning they must face the consequences of the previous night, and make the best of it.

King had little doubt van Gent would effectively disown them, which was something he was quite prepared to accept. He would start by making enquires with the other smuggling craft but, even if they were unable to secure a passage to England, it was not far back to Antoine who would look after them for as long as was necessary. But King's main concern lay with Manning, Banks and the rest of the British. Should the Dutchman have taken against them as well, matters might not be so easy. A man and a woman travelling together attracted less attention than several men of military age and, after what he had already done for them, it would hardly be fair to lumber Aimée's brother with such a liability a second time.

He stood outside the small cabin and looked about. What open space there was appeared all but empty; only a few hammocks were filled with their inhabitants apparently asleep. There were two more narrow doorways that presumably led to other cabins or possibly store rooms as well as what appeared to be lockers that must hold light equipment or supplies. The vessel was far less well presented than a man-of-war, with an obvious absence of paint or polish although everything appeared clean and functional. He walked towards the nearby companionway and climbed up to the main deck. That was apparently empty, then he noticed a couple of seamen sitting on the forecastle, and there was the hint of wood smoke in the air to tell him somewhere, someone was cooking breakfast.

"Did you sleep well, Thomas?"

King swung round to see that Lewis had emerged from a far larger doorway set in the brig's stern. He was dressed well in smart civilian clothes and had obviously taken trouble over his appearance. But his face carried deep lines, and there was a reddish cast to his skin that made King wonder how his night had been spent.

"Indeed; very well, thank you," he replied. "And thank you once more for taking us in last night: I am not certain what we would have done if you had not."

"It were nothing." Lewis gave him the long-remembered smile. "I do recall a certain midshipman helping me in the past, and was happy to repay the favour. Come, join me in my quarters and I shall see if some coffee can be found." He paused in turning, "Though, now that I think of it, chocolate is surely more to your taste, is it not?"

\* \* \*

"We shall not presume upon your hospitality for much longer," King assured Lewis when they had settled in his small, but well kept, cabin. "Aimée is still abed, though should rise shortly; then we will be making our way back to Antwerp."

"Antwerp?" Lewis seemed surprised.

King looked about. He instinctively felt safe aboard Lewis' brig, and there was no one else apparently in earshot. But still he felt awkward about saying too much.

"We have a contact there who shall look after us," he explained. "Our only need is to secure a suitable boat to hire."

332

"But would you not rather sail for England?" Lewis asked.

"Why of course." King felt his heart begin to race, and forced himself to pause, "Though considered such a thing impossible. Were there not further repairs to be undertaken, while I also seem to recall your employers not allowing passengers?"

"Indeed, though the spar can wait," Lewis told him firmly. "And as to passengers, this would not be a standard run. Besides, I have been thinking much during the night, and not just about my own position here." He paused, then began again; more slowly and with a hint of sadness.

"We live in what appears to be an honourable society, Tom, though, in truth, it is little more than a game. And a game where a man's word may still be considered his bond, so much is taken on trust. But it remains a game nonetheless, and in such things there must be rules." He sipped at his drink before continuing. "They are unwritten maybe, but we are all expected to abide by them. And if we do not, if we deviate in any way, we are told we may not continue to play – as I myself can testify," he added with a wry smile.

King nodded silently; he had no idea where this was leading, but it clearly meant much to Lewis. And, as his friend held the key to the future, he was more than prepared to listen.

"The problems begin with the rules; sometimes they become too important and ruin the game they were established to protect. Pick up any newspaper and you will read of supposed criminals who have been punished, often severely, for crimes they had been forced to commit: the mother stealing food for her children, or a seaman who deserts his ship so he might care for his sick wife. These should not be considered crimes in the accepted sense, but must be punished as if they were, for fear of devaluing the law that defines them. And so we have the ludicrous situation where justice is denied on account of a rule that cannot be broken; a rule that was established to protect that very justice in the first place."

Again he paused, and again King said nothing. For there was more to come, of that he was certain.

"And so it is with honour," Lewis said at last. "Let us not be under any pretence; the work I choose to carry out aboard this brig is against the laws of our home country, yet I am still bound to do it by the will of my masters. They have imposed rules on me, one of which says I must not carry passengers, even if they be escaping prisoners of war, as they fear prying eyes should jeopardise their organisation. And I am expected to respect their rules, while breaking others; frankly Tom I see no sense in that, nor any of it."

Put in such a way, King could only agree, and the hope began to rise within him.

"So yes, I shall take you to England." Lewis sat back and smiled. "*Narcis* still has a few minor repairs to complete, but is more than capable of sailing as she is and the topmast was mainly for appearance. Her next voyage is not scheduled for at least a week, she should be back in time to meet it, and may be able to ship the spar then. I will explain the situation to all hands; no financial rewards will be offered, and none shall be penalised for failing to come with us. But they are a sound bunch in the main, and I'd predict a good few are becoming stale from staying so long in port. My second mate is currently indisposed and I do not expect him back for some time, but I am ably supported by my first who, I believe, will wish to come. And perhaps I might rely on you to support a former hand if need be?"

"To be sure!" King was grinning like a lad. "And never could I have wished for a finer captain!"

"Then so be it." Lewis' tired face also broke into a smile. "I shall address what men are available now, and put the word out to the rest. If we can assemble a suitable crew we might consider sailing tonight; would that be acceptable?"

King's answer was interrupted by a stout knock on the cabin door. Lewis called for the visitor to enter and a nervous young man dressed in a dark blue uniform entered.

"There is a deputation to see you, sir," he said, glancing sidelong at King.

"A deputation, Mr Reid?" Lewis questioned.

"Yes, sir. Three Englishmen, who claim to be sea officers and would have words with you."

"Then you had better see them aboard," Lewis said, with a knowing smile.

* * *

334

It was late afternoon, yet there were remarkably few about and no sign of a military presence as they stumbled along the hard.

"It's not far, sir," Brehaut said encouragingly as they passed yet another line of laid up vessels.

But Banks was still unsure if they were doing the right thing. The van Gent fellow certainly came across as abrupt, and last night's incident had not shown him in his best light, although Tom hardly came out of it smelling of roses. For King to have been carrying on with a woman for so long was bad enough, but attempting to come between a man and his lawful wife was another matter entirely. And then the young fool had made matters worse by rushing out into the night and dragging the child with him. Cranston and Lovemore, two trusted hands who really should have known better, had also failed to return the previous day, so he supposed the rest of the British departing without notice or explanation would not come as too much of a surprise to the Dutchman.

Although Banks had other reasons for apparently turning down van Gent's offer of escape. However safe it might appear, Flushing remained enemy territory. Were even one of the wanderers arrested, the rest would undoubtedly be at risk.

That last point was actually the one that finally persuaded him to join the others in their plan. Despite not greatly liking van Gent, he had been willing to trust him enough to see them safely home. But if the Dutchman were betrayed it would be the end of any help to future escaping prisoners, while the only trip Banks and his fellow officers would be making was to Bitche. After coming so far, he did not think he could face such a prospect; already the lure of home and images of his family were growing stronger and, though the craft they had found was a smuggler, he supposed he could repress his finer feelings for the short time it would take to fetch the English coast.

"That's her," the sailing master informed the group, and Banks slowed to examine the brig before them. She was tidy enough, and had obviously been freshly painted in places. But he didn't care for her curious rig, nor the ensign that drooped from the gaff.

"Appears sound," he muttered remembering the alternative. And sailing together aboard one vessel was probably a better way home than relying on the prickly Dutchman, so he supposed he should show a little more gratitude to his men for securing it. "She will sail for a hundred guineas, you say?"

Brehaut agreed; in fact Lewis required no payment, but they guessed Sir Richard would be more agreeable if some form of monetary inducement were involved.

"Very well then," he grunted. "We'd better step aboard."

* * *

Cranston had already decided it was a snug little berth, while the pair they had met up with in the tap house were proving remarkably straight, despite what was undoubtedly the worst of starts. On that front he had no doubt where the fault lay, and was suitably repentant, although how the fight had come about remained a mystery. Of course Cranston had been in similar brawls in the past but only when part of a mess and he supposed chancing upon the company of seamen after so long had awoken the desire. Certainly the last few months had been nothing like the life he was used to; since *Kestrel* was taken, the nearest he had come to his old trade was crewing on a coal barge and knew his body, which had been so prime and lithe, had suffered as a result. But now he was back aboard a proper vessel all that would change; he would become fit again, then find himself a true warship where he would return to his old life. Being with Lovemore was all very fine but, since leaving the travellers, the cove had spent so much time either reading his Bible or playing that wretched whistle that their friendship had started to fade. Besides, there was only one of him; Cranston longed for the close association of a mess almost as much as he did the routine aboard a man-of-war. The scrap in that pot house might even have been a symptom of his frustration, but the next time such a thing happened, he would be sure to have a bunch of mates by his side to support him.

And, despite his stance of the previous day, Laidlaw and Judy had intimated a permanent berth in the current brig might be found. It was something he would certainly consider although there were those that approved of smuggling and those that did not; and Cranston remained with the latter.

For many years, dodging the revenue had become generally accepted, with most considering it no more a crime than coin clipping or poaching. Those who benefited from cheap tobacco and Crowlink gin came from all social classes although every successful smuggling gang depended on seamen for its very existence. So, as a regular Jack, Cranston was probably unusual in his disapproval, but then he had seen the darker side of the trade.

Before leaving for the sea, his home village had been controlled by a particularly rough crowd who did not confine their activities to running the occasional illicit cargo. In addition to the considerable profits earned in that area, they made extra by exploiting the villagers themselves, forcing them to store booty or serve as tubmen. Their unchallenged power also allowed access to private possessions; his own family had lost two fine horses and a wagon that way, as well as untold amounts of feed, so he truly understood the pain an apparently harmless crime could cause.

And it seemed Lovemore shared his views although that hardly surprised Cranston: since finding religion, his friend seemed to disapprove of most things.

But, if what he had just found out were true, there shouldn't be any such nonsense on their trip home. Laidlaw, the Cornishman he had fought the previous day, had just brought him a mug of hot tea, along with the news they would be sailing that evening. More to the point, it sounded to be a simple trip, with no fooling about off lee shores awaiting boats from the land. Laidlaw seemed relatively certain the pair would be allowed to work a one-way passage and Lovemore had gone off with him to speak with the captain.

If the wind held true, they might be walking English streets by the end of the week, although the attraction for Cranston lay more in returning to his old life, than any mere patch of land.

* * *

"You?" Banks gasped as he looked on the face of his former officer.

"Good morning, Sir Richard," Lewis replied with more composure. He was equally appalled at the meeting, although had at least received some inkling of it.

"Good morning be damned, whatever are you doing here?"

"I am to conduct you to England," the younger man replied.

Banks turned back to King. "Did you know of this?"

"I knew Mr Lewis had charge of the brig," he admitted. "And that he agrees to see us home; which is noble of him, considering the way he has been treated."

"Noble?" Banks' face was now flushed and he appeared to choke on the word. "I see nothing noble in this rogue's antics. Why, you broke your word, sir!" he added, rounding on Lewis once more. "How do you dare walk the same deck as honourable men?"

"I dare because it is my deck," Lewis replied simply. "I am master of this brig and, for as long as you remain aboard her, you would do well to remember that."

Banks took a step back and glanced sideways at King. "Do you hear what the fellow says?" he demanded.

"I heard," King confirmed. "And it is the law of the sea, as you know well, sir."

Now the only sound that came from the senior officer was a vague spluttering hiss, followed by what might have been a cough.

"Perhaps we had better inspect our quarters?" King suggested.

"Indeed; our lack of junior officers allows a goodly amount of space," Lewis explained. "Though Captain Banks may have my cabin, should he so wish," he added with a glance towards the older man.

"Then perhaps I should lead the way?" King suggested. "Come, Sir Richard, let us see what accommodation has been provided.

\* \* \*

"Sure as night follows day," Lovemore assured him. "The whole lot, and filing into the captain's quarters like they owned the place."

"All of them?" Cranston questioned in disgust.

"Every one," Lovemore confirmed. "From Sir Dickie Bickie down to the youngest mid."

His friend shook his head. "I don't know, it seemed as if we'd shaken that lot off when we lost *Kestrel.* And then again on the road to Verdun."

"I thought the same when I hooked up with them travellers," Lovemore agreed. "But, like the bad penny, they just keep turning up."

# Chapter Thirty

"No fear of blockaders?" King questioned. *Narcis* had slipped her moorings before dusk and now with no moon, but stars bright enough to see by, she was clearing the mouth of the Westerschelde and setting her prow for England.

"Nearest squadron is several leagues off," Lewis replied. "We might sight the occasional ship, but few will have any truck with us," he continued. "Mostly they know where we comes from, where we're bound and the purpose we serve, but are rarely bothered. Mind, it would be a different matter were *Narcis* based in a French port."

King could understand that to some extent; despite Camperdown, the Dutch were considered by many to be closer to allies than enemies. But it didn't alter the fact that smuggling continued to erode Britain's economy, and at a time when it could least afford it. He supposed the families of naval officers would benefit from the cheaper goods as much as anyone, although was still surprised that Lewis and his like should be treated so casually.

"Mind, I have a host of ensigns to raise if they did show interest," Lewis added with a grin. "None are guaranteed to fool, but no captain wants for legal issues, especially in home waters, and the right flag can give them leave to turn a blind eye."

While he was speaking another figure had made his way up the aft companionway and, without turning, both men knew Banks had joined them on deck.

"When would you gauge we might raise England?" King asked, and it was as much for Sir Richard's benefit as himself.

Lewis sniffed the wind, which was coming over their larboard beam and blowing strong.

"If this breeze holds, a little before dawn," he replied. "I propose to come as close to Ramsgate as I might, and send you in aboard our cutter."

"That would suit well," King told him. "The prospect of breakfast ashore is most appealing."

340

"But that is depending on our wind," Lewis reminded him. "Were it to fail, we should have to remain at sea until night fall."

"I understand that," King conceded. "Do you know these waters well?"

Lewis gave him a sidelong glance. "This is not my usual cruising ground, if that's what you mean."

King inclined his head slightly; he had not meant to pry.

"But I am staying away from there," Lewis continued, adding, "Too many in those parts know my silhouette, and not all are fellow runners."

King had decided not to enquire further, although it was at that point that another voice broke into their conversation.

"Mr Lewis, I believe I owe you an apology."

The two men turned to see Banks was indeed standing behind them. He wore his civilian cloak that was now showing distinct signs of wear over an equally shabby uniform tunic. But despite his dishevelled appearance, he remained every inch a senior captain.

"There is nothing to apologise for, Sir Richard," Lewis replied evenly.

"No, I was in the wrong," Banks persisted. "I have since spoken with the other officers and realise my mistake. I gather you have gone out on a limb for us, and am grateful."

"As are we all," King agreed.

Lewis appeared lost for words, and merely nodded in acknowledgement.

"Mr Lewis was saying we might fetch England afore dawn." There was the possibility of an awkward pause, and King had no intention of allowing it to spoil the moment.

"That is good news indeed," Banks exclaimed.

"Sadly it can not be guaranteed, Sir Richard," Lewis added hurriedly. "We would need to keep this wind, and I am noticing signs of it failing."

"We shall be put ashore at Ramsgate; Mr Lewis will provide a boat."

"You would not consider sailing into harbour?" Banks chanced. "I am not without influence and would be happy to speak for you."

"Such a thing may mean your re-admittance into the Navy," King added, but Lewis was not to be convinced.

"I have been a runner a good while now," he replied firmly, "and believe my name to be truly blackened."

"But returning with so many officers..." Banks persisted. "And if you were prepared to speak against your former employers?"

"It is a kind thought and I thank you both." Lewis sighed, but said no more. However good their intentions his former colleagues had little understanding of the position he was in, while he lacked the inclination to explain. In the past few months he had clashed with nearly every government department apart from Trinity House and, however attractive the offer of influence might be, it would carry little weight against such a record.

"As you wish," Banks nodded. "But my proposal shall stand. If ever you decide different, I shall back you, be sure of it."

* * *

Timothy was certainly enjoying being back at sea. The sound of canvas flapping in an eager breeze combined with a moving deck beneath his feet and the clean, salt tang of the very air itself had awoken a dozen differing emotions inside him. It was as if while being held captive, and even as a fugitive, so much had been suppressed. But now he was drawing the deepest breaths for what felt like months while countless half-forgotten poems were creeping out of the shadows to amuse him once more. He took a turn about the small quarterdeck; it was not a man-of-war or even a British vessel yet he felt extremely comfortable aboard the brig. And that feeling could only grow, for soon they would sight the shores of England and then he would truly be home.

But it was always the way when returning from a long voyage; the place would have altered beyond measure and must contain a thousand surprises. It might take weeks, even months to fully adjust to the differences: what particular commodity was, or was not, available, as well as the latest fashions and changes in etiquette, while simply being able to walk the streets without fear of arrest would take some getting used to. Then there would be the inevitable trudge of seeking employment, although Timothy was not downhearted on that score. Actually being home would be so

342

much of a relief and, when he did feel the urge to set sail once more, he must surely have acquired enough experience to find a seagoing position of some kind. Besides, along with his love of poetry, another desire had been awakened that was equally welcome.

He cursed now the opportunities wasted at those country dances; had he been as diligent as Tom King there might be a comely wench beside him even now. But Timothy was determined to make up for lost time just as soon as his feet touched English soil.

For he would no longer be either prisoner or deserter, but a respectable serving officer; one who had already built a solid career and should have a rosy future ahead of him. There must be a measure of back pay awaiting and he had every intention of spending it in the most indulgent way possible. Perhaps not rush back to the sea, but take in a little social life instead. After so many years away, he was perhaps entitled to a period of rest: a time to take stock of his life. And Timothy could see no reason at all why he should not resume his search for a wife. It might be his last chance of domestic comfort, but one he was determined to take and use to its full potential, just as soon as the opportunity presented.

* * *

They did not keep the wind. By midnight it had dwindled to a gentle breeze and, when dawn began to break, *Narcis* was a good thirty miles from the English coast.

"I shall have to take her north," Lewis explained as the first shafts of light revealed a number of small vessels in the far distance. "None of these are men-of-war, but it would be prudent to lie low."

"As you will," King replied, while his friend stepped away to bellow the necessary orders. Neither of them had left the deck throughout the night although King, for one, was not feeling tired. Just to be aboard ship and at sea again had revitalised him greatly, and the knowledge that his home lay only a little way over the horizon added an extra stimulant.

343

Forward, the hands were being roused by a bullet-headed man with a loud voice. There was no attempt at holystoning the deck, but all else appeared remarkably familiar, and King had to remind himself he was travelling aboard a smuggler.

Before leaving Flushing, Lewis had put out a call to all hands. After an extended stay in harbour, most of the British were quick to choose a jaunt across the Channel over wasting yet more days ashore, and the extra men promised by van Gent and already recruited brought these up to a reasonable number. The second mate was still confined to hospital, but his duties were being shared amongst the midshipmen, while King noticed Cranston and Lovemore had magically reappeared as part of the brig's crew.

But even including the officers, they could raise little more than forty men, which was considerably less than the complement for a government vessel of their size. Lewis seemed remarkably calm about the numbers though, as he was the prospect of spending all day drifting aimlessly in the North Sea. King supposed such an attitude was born from habit; he had not enquired deeply although his friend must have carried out many similar trips and was hardened to the task. But for himself, he would only be happy when darkness fell and they could turn to raise the English coast once more.

A large metal caboose had been rigged on the forecastle and the men were now clutching at their wooden platters and forming a line for breakfast. Noticing this, Lewis walked across to rejoin King.

"I'm afraid I can offer little in the way of home comforts," he explained. "When at sea I tend to eat seamen's fare, though believe there to be soft tack in the officers' store."

King went to reply when a call from aloft brought all on deck to the alert.

"I've a sloop to windward," the lookout bellowed, his right arm pointing over the brig's transom. "Appears like the one we ran in with a while back."

King glanced enquiringly at Lewis, who looked a little crestfallen. "We did not engage," he explained. "Though she fired upon us."

"But you escaped?" King pointed out with a grin.

"We did, but more by luck than anything else," Lewis

allowed. "There were a storm blowing and I'm afraid our friend was partially dismasted."

"Was she indeed?" King laughed, while looking out over the taffrail in a vain attempt to spot the ship. "Then I expect she will recall you only too well."

* * *

King was right; not only did those aboard the sloop appear to remember *Narcis,* they were also set on a hot pursuit. By mid-morning the Navy ship had gained to the extent that she was in plain sight from the brig's quarterdeck.

Banks and the other officers were clustered in a group by the larboard bulwark while Lewis, who had yet to quit the deck, remained by the taffrail with his first mate, an excitable young man who seemed to treat his British passengers with a measure of caution.

"There's frustration," Timothy muttered, his eyes fixed on the oncoming sloop. "We spend months in France dreaming of a British man-of-war and, now one comes to hand, we must run from her."

"Lewis has to protect himself," King commented uneasily. It was still a good hour until noon and there would be eight more of daylight after that. With the rate at which the British ship was forereaching, they would be caught long before darkness. Such a fate might not concern him or his fellow officers; they were committing no crime, nor had they. But it was clear the sloop's captain recognised *Narcis*, and Lewis would have a deal of explaining to do.

And yet he remained apparently unmoved and King, who had commanded a more powerful vessel and for far longer, could not help but be impressed. He did not doubt the myriad worries the man must be concealing, yet he appeared happy to yarn with his second in command, a man whose nervous energy alone would have been enough to send most commanding officers into hysterics.

"Mastheads in sight to starboard," the lookout's laconic call did nothing to create excitement and Lewis called for clarification in a similar manner.

"She's a couple of points off the starboard bow," the hand went on to explain. "Heading to cross our bows, as far as I can see, but a good way off, and I'm only getting glimpses of topsails, so clearly ain't in no rush."

There could be a dozen reasons why a ship might be crossing the North Sea in either direction, although, in even such light winds, it was unusual for one to proceed quite so slowly. King noticed all his brother officers' attention had turned on Lewis who once more seemed unmoved by what he had heard.

"What say we go below and see if Aimée is about?" he suggested. "Belike there will be coffee to be had, and I for one would welcome the chance to rest for a spell."

"A capital idea, I think," Banks, the only other with experience of command agreed. "We shall leave you the deck, sir," he added, with a brief nod to Lewis before shepherding the remaining British officers towards the companionway.

"As you will, gentlemen," Lewis replied levelly, and few could guess the relief he felt.

\* \* \*

Lovemore and Cranston had settled down remarkably well. The brig's crew weren't a bad bunch on the whole; some had even served in service vessels the pair were familiar with, though not at the same time. And, as with the rest of the British escapees, they felt something especially thrilling about being at sea again, to smell the salt, fresh air and feel a living deck beneath their feet.

What had happened in the last few minutes was somewhat disconcerting, however. Usually the sighting of a British warship would be a welcome break in a dull watch: neither man had ever felt the need to run in the past. But both were fully aware of their own, rather fragile, position.

Despite two major mutinies and many long years of war, little had been done to regularise a lower deck hand's position. Officers joined the Navy, received a commission, half pay and a pension, providing their status warranted it, with their service time growing as they moved from one posting to another. But a seaman joined a ship and, though he was bound to her until the day she were paid off, sunk or taken, was then free to sell his talents elsewhere – or so the theory went. And though he might serve his country all his life, there would be little in the way of official entitlement at the end of it, except what was grudgingly allowed by a parsimonious government.

And now they could be counted amongst the crew of a smuggling brig; admittedly both were working their passage and had a whole host of officers to vouch for them. But such things could easily be forgotten: it would only need a moment of confusion, and they might find themselves pressed aboard a British ship before even reaching land. That or arrested as smugglers.

"Rum turn out, to be running from a Navy vessel," Cranston muttered. Once his friend might have made a constructive comment, although such things were now long in the past. But this time Lovemore did not disappoint; this time Cranston was suitably rewarded.

"There's no need to worry," the curly-haired seamen replied with confidence.

"You mean we'll come out of this safe?" his friend asked with a relieved smile.

"I'm certain of it," Lovemore assured him. "Have you not read, 'if God be for us, who can be against us'?"

"Oh yes, I were forgetting," Cranston replied while scratching at his belly and considering the oncoming sloop. "So that's alright then."

\* \* \*

"New sighting's a warship," the lookout sang out triumphantly. "Single-decker, small frigate or somethin' on those lines."

Lewis waited; there would be more, he was certain.

"Not showing no flag, but I'd say she were a Frenchie," the man obliged.

Coming from the east, that seemed likely, although the

347

lookout was experienced enough, and would be able to tell much from the vessel's rig.

As any other vessel would about *Narcis*, he remembered gloomily. If the sloop they had met before really was on their tail, he could blame the fact on that damned foreshortened maintop.

He had been a fool; his friends were safe enough in Flushing and could have waited the few days it would have taken to see the spar replaced. But then he remembered King had upset van Gent; for all he knew the man was denouncing the escaping British at that very moment, while it wouldn't take him long to notice the brig's empty berth and draw the obvious conclusion.

Which might mean the end of everything; Crabtree would rather lose a brig's captain than his all-important contact in Holland, and Lewis could easily end up having to take Banks' offer, and throw himself on the mercy of the British government.

He took a turn up and down his small quarterdeck to calm his nerves. But no, not yet; the time for desperate measures may well come, but there was much he could do first, and he still had command of a prime little brig.

Glancing forward, the topmasts of the fresh sighting were quite plainly in view as she lay fine on their starboard bow. *Narcis* must surely have also been spotted, although the British sloop coming up behind would remain out of sight.

"Take her three points to starboard," Lewis instructed, and Reid, ever by his side, called out the necessary order. The brig turned smoothly and began to take the wind more on her starboard quarter. They had all plain sail set and were cutting a decent feather of spray from the bows but then Lewis was equally sure the sloop astern was travelling faster.

And then he had yet another moment of doubt; supposing he had been right in his assessment of van Gent? The man was a wily creature, despite his professed hatred of the new regime, Lewis could imagine him taking umbrage over British prisoners rejecting his offer of escape. The ship ahead could have set sail last night with the specific intention of capturing *Narcis*. In which case he truly was between the devil and the deep blue sea. He swallowed dryly, before reason took control once more.

No, he was being fanciful; the French would not be so rash as to break the blockade, just to run down an errant smuggler, and one who must return to port herself eventually. Besides, he had committed no major crime, apart from not being present when his much requested topmast arrived. And, ironically, sighting a French warship had been a stroke of luck; until then he had been starting to despair of a plan. Now all he need do was close with her, and claim security. Much would depend on the ship's size, of course; were she a reasonable frigate, the British sloop would probably decline action. Lewis might then remain in the warship's protection until dark, when a quick dash for England would be followed by an equally fast return home. Come the day after tomorrow *Narcis* could be back in her old berth having her topmast fitted, with all unpleasantness between him and van Gent forgotten. And if the new sighting were not so large, if the pair of warships set to battle, he could simply make his excuses and leave them to it.

Of course that might not be so easy, considering his passengers. Should the pair really decide to fight, the officers he carried would be bound to want him to assist the British sloop. Well, they could wish all they liked, he had already risked much to see them safe. And as far as aiding a Royal Navy vessel was concerned, the chances of him being so foolish were slight indeed.

* * *

Two hours later the situation had changed. *Narcis* was closer to the French ship and her true size, that of a light corvette, had been assessed. With Masters absent, Summers and Bremner had raised that day's recognition signal, and so gloried in the unique experience of communicating with an active enemy warship. But their message was received successfully, and the brig passed peacefully behind the Frenchman's stern.

Cranston called out some crude witticism from the main deck and received an appropriate round of laughter from his new found friends although those of his former officers who heard were not so amused. They were still grouped at the break of the quarterdeck and staring in wonder at the oncoming British sloop. For she had gained on them significantly and now lay less than two miles off their transom. And it was clear the two warships were preparing to give battle.

"What do you know of them?" Banks asked Lewis, as the Frenchman began to take in her topgallants.

"Nothing of the French," Lewis admitted. "Not seen her in these parts at any time, though I'd say she were carrying at least twenty cannon."

Banks nodded; that had been his assessment although the corvette was not his chief concern. "And the sloop?" he asked.

Lewis paused. "I'd say roughly the same."

"But do you know anything of the ship herself?" Banks persisted. "Mr King mentioned you had encountered her before."

The use of King's surname indicated Banks meant business, and Lewis felt himself stiffen slightly.

"We have indeed met, Sir Richard, though I have never fired upon her," he added defensively.

"I'm not interested in that," Banks sighed in exasperation. "Who is her commander?"

"I would judge him to be inexperienced," Lewis admitted. "A better man would have taken us for sure."

"Beggin your pardon gentlemen, but Laidlaw knows more." All eyes turned to Cross, the Welshman, at the wheel.

"Is he a member of your crew?" Banks demanded.

"He is, sir; an' in my mess," the seaman confirmed. "He says she's *Swift*; a sloop, and the captain ain't no more than a child."

"I can send for him if you wish, Sir Richard," Lewis offered, but Banks shook his head.

"It is of no matter," he replied, while staring once more at the Frenchman. It was not so very unusual to give a young, well connected, officer command of something small in home waters. "I know nothing of the vessel, but if the captain truly is a child, let us hope him to be a gifted one."

\* \* \*

The action began less than half an hour later. By then, *Narcis* had rounded the corvette's stern and set her head to the west and the English coast that would soon be in sight. Meanwhile the British sloop, which had the windward gauge, was turning slightly to starboard and clearly intending to run down on the Frenchman with the wind on her quarter.

"Rather obvious tactics," Banks muttered softly to King, who stood near him by the larboard bulwark.

King pursed his lips. "Maybe so, but this is a clear playing field; darkness will not be for some hours, and there is no sign of intervention."

"If he leaves it too long, the French will claim the breeze," Timothy pointed out amid murmurs of agreement from the other officers. The corvette had certainly been edging to larboard for some time; she was now close-hauled and might tack at any moment.

But before she could, the sloop finally wore violently to larboard and seemed set to begin her run. It was not a smooth manoeuvre however; even when on her new course, several of her sails were slow to be trimmed. The professional witnesses on *Narcis'* quarterdeck let out a communal groan, while the corvette, which was still less than a mile off their larboard quarter, threw herself into an equally savage tack.

"Perfect timing," King muttered in grudging approval and there was little doubt that, in terms of seamanship and discipline, the French had the upper hand.

"They'll be at broadsides within minutes," Banks grunted, then turned and looked about. Lewis stood with his back to the taffrail, showing no interest in the action, although his young second in command was watching the Frenchman intently through a glass and appeared to be keeping his captain informed of the proceedings.

"I suppose there is little we can do?" Banks called out, and Lewis turned his attention from the western horizon.

"What would you suggest, Sir Richard?" he asked levelly, and there was a sympathetic murmuring from the other officers. What indeed? *Narcis* was armed with five light cannon a side; her current identity might allow her to come close and take on the corvette, but that would only create a minor annoyance. The French ship was not only larger, but far more soundly built; she could wipe them away with a single broadside, while still seeing off the sloop. And neither could they board; the only hope of tackling her was if both they and the brig came alongside simultaneously. A boarding action might then be successful, but

351

the Navy ship had already shown herself to be too poorly commanded for such coordination. Besides, why should the British consider such a thing with a feeble brig that was already firmly established as their enemy?

Banks came to the same conclusion, and turned back to watch the forthcoming action. *Narcis* was still solidly heading west on a broad reach, but remained close enough for them to witness every last detail of the British sloop's inevitable destruction. For men accustomed to being in the grip of battle it was strange to view combat so dispassionately. And on such a pleasant afternoon as well: the sun was shining painfully hot amid a rich and cloudless blue sky, while blank horizons lay clear of any sign of possible support. And then, even as they watched, the Frenchman fired the first broadside.

* * *

The sloop, which had been stoically sticking to her original course, was partially raked. Several holes appeared in her forecourse but all knew there would be unseen but far more deadly damage done to her hull. For a moment the British warship seemed to stagger and appeared likely to fall off the wind, but she soon righted, although there was no deviation in her heading.

"I'd say she's hoping to catch the frog as she passes," Timothy exclaimed. "Hit her stern with the same medicine."

King remained mute; the British ship must already have been soundly hit yet far more damage would shortly be caused by allowing the Frenchman to take the weather gauge. But Timothy was correct; if the two remained as they were, the sloop would be in an excellent position, although he sensed the corvette would not prove quite so obliging.

And so it turned out; before the Frenchman came within the British ship's ark of fire, she began to tack once more. And once more it was the smoothest, slickest of manoeuvres, with the entire vessel appearing to change course within her own length and soon began taking the wind to larboard.

"I'm not sure I wish to watch this," Banks said, looking away and noticing Lewis once more. "Can we not show more speed and be free of such a spectacle, Captain?"

"I should prefer not, Sir Richard," Lewis replied levelly. "This wind will surely grow and we are hardly blessed with men."

Banks heaved a sigh and glanced forward. Every hand aboard *Narcis* seemed to be craning to watch the action, with some even hanging in the larboard shrouds for a better view. A curly-haired fellow near the maintop looked familiar, and Banks realised it was one of the seamen who had accompanied them during their escape. He had no idea how the man had made it onto the brig, but he remained about the only thing Banks had left to command.

"You there, Lovemore," he bellowed. "Get down off those shrouds!"

The man turned to him briefly, then looked back to his mate, who Banks then realised was Cranston. But Lovemore did not climb down, he did not move a muscle, instead his eyes remained fixed and directed forward. Then, as he raised a hand and began pointing out across the brig's bows, he let out a mighty shout.

"Ship ahoy!"

For a moment there was silence and no one moved, then all appeared to talk at once.

"Sail in sight, fine on the larboard bow!" The masthead's hurried, though late, report overrode the various expressions of amazement.

"Good God," Banks, added as he focused on the two-masted vessel. She had been partially hidden by their forecourse, and was bearing down on the opposing tack.

"The bugger's hardly more than a mile off!" someone cried in disbelief.

"Take her to starboard," Lewis snapped and Reid called for hands at the braces.

"It's that bloody Fencible ketch!" Cross, at the wheel, exclaimed as the vessel came into clear sight from the deck. "The one what we fought a while back."

"What were you thinkin' of Dollins?" Price shouted up to the masthead. "Get your eyes out your arse and keep better watch!"

There was no response from the unhappy lookout and Lewis could spare no time to berate the man further; he had far more pressing matters to consider. The ketch was almost within accurate range, and was bound to start firing off that damned bow chaser at any moment.

"We shall have to continue turning; wear ship," he snapped at Reid, who nodded in agreement. *Narcis* was lying broadside on to the ketch and presenting a prime target, but if they could head back east they may yet find safety. This new enemy was the faster ship, although her captain may not be fully aware of the drama unfolding so very close by, and the distraction of a French corvette beating up a British sloop might be enough to save them.

"Another old friend?" King asked nonchalantly, and Lewis gave him a sidelong look.

"Sea Fencibles," he murmured.

"Not like them to be so far out," King mused.

"This one is commanded by a regular warrior," Lewis snorted. "All the verve of a militia officer, and with a crew equally sharp."

"Tis a pity such starch is lacking elsewhere," King murmured as he glanced across at the nearby combat. The British ship might be chasing the Frenchman, both being close-hauled and on the larboard tack, but what would come next was obvious to all.

"If our fellow don't back off, the frog will yaw and rake him once more," one of the midshipmen commented, and there was a rumble of agreement from the British officers. Lewis stifled a groan, if a youngster could spot the Frenchman's game, what was the sloop's captain thinking of?

Reid was still directing the brig through her turn; soon they would be picking up speed once more but the ketch was growing ever closer. Then a jet of smoke signalled she had opened fire, and the scream of a shot passing harmlessly to one side told of their escape.

"Captain's not happy," King observed as he noticed Banks catching Lewis' eye.

"That's as maybe," Lewis muttered. "Though he knew my trade when joining the brig."

"Well, I should go to Aimée," King announced as he went to leave the deck. "If there is to be shot flying it is best she stays clear of it." Lewis nodded and turned his attention to the ketch.

*Narcis* was nearly about now, and the bright sunshine gave the best view yet of his opponent. She was far more soundly built than most of her class, with a wide beam and solid stanchions while the guns that made up her main armament were only too obvious. But as he looked, he also noticed the vessel was turning. At first he had suspected she intended to present her broadside, in which case *Narcis* would have been lucky to survive without serious damage, but it appeared the more immediate problem of a French corvette had become apparent.

"Ketch's going after the Frenchie," Reid commented with a look of relief.

"And a good thing for us all," Lewis agreed. They could now turn back and make a run for the English coast. Darkness was not due for several hours but he was confident of keeping *Narcis* out of danger until then, while any passing warship was likely to come across the battle currently in process and not spare a thought for a lone trading brig.

But oddly Lewis was not reassured; the Frenchman was allowing herself to be overhauled, and would soon be delivering another raking to the hapless sloop. To abandon a British ship went against everything he had ever believed in and was almost more than he could bear. But it had to be done, at least if he wished to continue in his current trade.

# Chapter Thirty-One

"We are in action," King announced with his customary lack of tact.

"Action?" Aimée seemed bemused. "You mean we fight?"

He walked further into their tiny cabin and perched against the side of the washstand. "Well, we might try to, but are considerably outnumbered."

Aimée put down the book she had been reading and rose from the only chair. "Then I must come," she said.

"No, you must not," King laughed. "Bless you, but this is one problem you cannot solve. We have already been fired upon by a heavily armed Fencible ketch and there are two warships who are equally likely to join in."

"Then why are you here?" she asked.

"I came to see you safe," King explained. "Find a place beneath the waterline."

"So that I may drown more quickly?"

King clenched his fist in exasperation. "Aimée, you are not making this easy. I am needed on deck."

"Oh, so you are needed, yet I must be protected?" King went to protest before noticing the look in her eye, and knew he was in trouble.

"Let me tell you, Thomas, all the risks we have taken since leaving Verdun have been shared," she began. "And you may also remember that I had little need of escape, nor my family a reason to help."

He nodded mutely; she was right, yet again he had not thought matters through and wondered vaguely if he ever would.

"And now we are to go into what you call action I am expected to sit with the rats while you do brave things in the sunshine? I think not!"

He shook his head. "No," he said. "No, of course you are quite correct."

She seemed to relax, and rested her head against his chest. "I understand, and am grateful for your concern," she told him more softly.

"But you cannot be much help in the fighting," King reminded her. "Why not stay below and support Bob Manning? He would welcome your assistance I am certain."

She had been playing with his fingers as he spoke, and looked up quickly. "And you are going to be the brave fighter?" she questioned, still holding his hand.

King was lost for an answer and closed his eyes in frustration.

"Tom, I am sorry, that was not needed. Yes, I will help the doctor, and keep myself safe, and as you must also."

A wave of emotion swept over him and he wrapped her in his embrace. "I couldn't bear to lose you, Aimée," he admitted. "If that is hard to understand, I am sorry."

"No it is not," she replied, nestling closer. "It is something I can understand very easily."

"It has never been like this for me before," he persisted. "Not ever."

"Not ever?" she asked, drawing back, and he could see that wicked grin return. "Not even with your wife?"

* * *

King clambered up the aft hatchway, his mind a mass of confusion and doubt. There had been no time to say more, Aimée clearly knew all about Juliana, although the fact she didn't seem to care greatly was still to register. But even as it did, he could only feel contempt for himself, both for keeping his wife a secret, and effectively running away when it was finally revealed. He had good reason for the latter, of course; in fact, as he finally made it into the open air, he wondered if there could ever be a better one.

On deck, the British officers had also returned and were watching in tense silence. The ketch had continued to veer away from *Narcis*, and now lay close-hauled in full pursuit of both warships. And the wind was indeed strengthening, so there was now little to stop Lewis from ordering *Narcis* about once more, then making for the distant English coast.

"She's leaving us be," King remarked as he drew closer.

"It would seem so," Timothy agreed. "We dodged that one

shot before they noticed what were about further off."

King nodded, then went to join Lewis at the taffrail. His head still reeled from the recent conversation with Aimée, but this was of more immediate importance and he ruthlessly concentrated on the problem in hand.

"I don't suppose you would consider lending a hand?" he asked his friend, his voice purposefully low. "I realise you have not been treated well, but both craft are British and seem likely to be taken if we do not intervene."

"There is little I can do," Lewis replied, although he did not look King in the eye. "By rights we should have turned back already."

King understood. Ignoring the former lieutenant's chosen allegiance, the brig was hardly built for battle; even her armament, though large for a vessel of her type, dwindled to nothing when compared to that offered by a true warship. The French corvette was every bit as strong as *Kestrel*, his old command, and built to take punishment as well as dealing it out, with hefty timbers and strong bulwarks, to say nothing of a trained crew that would outnumber theirs several times over. Besides, for all that the brig carried enough Royal Navy officers to command a small frigate, *Narcis* was nominally on the same side as the Frenchman. He supposed they might make some difference were one of the British vessels to haul alongside, but that had already been discounted. Although Lewis had not gone about, and that fact gave King some clue to his friend's thoughts on the matter, as well as the barest glimmer of hope.

"She's turning!" The call came from an unknown seaman further forward, but all could see what he referred to.

The Frenchman had luffed up dramatically, and now lay broadside on to the annoying little sloop that had been chasing her. Either by order or instinct, the British helmsman had also turned away from the threat, but the move was not fast enough to avoid yet another broadside from the enemy. The shots came thundering down upon the small ship's prow and, just as the sound reached them in *Narcis*, the results became obvious.

The sloop's foremast had dissolved in a confusion of splinters, line and dust. Strips of canvas flew wildly about, and the hull turned further with the wind.

"That'll do it," Timothy muttered. "She'll strike now, sure as eggs is eggs."

"I wouldn't be so sure," Brehaut countered. "There's still the ketch, and she will be in range at any time."

His words were swiftly confirmed by a brief cloud of smoke from the smaller vessel's bows, and those aboard the brig watched as that hated bow chaser spoke out once more. But what could do damage to a commercial brig was far less of a threat when facing a minor warship. And, if the range was right for the ketch to let loose her single cannon, it should also suit the Frenchman, with a far heavier broadside.

"You had better turn back," King whispered at Lewis. "Witnessing such a sight will do no good; we may as well make for England and be done with it."

But Lewis' pale face gave no response. Like King, he had slept little, which probably accounted for the red rims to his eyes, but the firmly set jaw was caused by something else, and that stare, so intense and fixed, was almost frightening. King went to speak but the man had already begun to move and did not stop till he reached the break of the quarterdeck.

"Do you hear there?" he bellowed in a voice brittle with tension. The hands looked away from the unfolding drama and gave their full attention.

"There's a battle going down, and I gather some would wish to be a part of it."

They stared back in mute consideration as he continued.

"You all know our status, and that any intervention would jeopardise this brig and her future relations with our employers. But many of us were born British, and have a wish to help our country. Therefore I propose to draw closer, and see what comes about."

For a moment no word was spoken, then a faint cheer began to emanate from near the forecastle. It was picked up by others, until the main deck became alive with yelling seamen.

"And you, Mr Reid?" Lewis said, turning to his second in command. "Are you happy for us to close?"

"I am willing, sir," the lad replied formally.

"Then so be it." Lewis swung back and seemed to be examining his command in detail before glancing across to the

British officers. "If any of you gentlemen are carrying uniform, I suggest you locate it," he said. "And any assistance you wish to give would be welcomed. For if I am right in my thinking, we are about to come into close contact with some Frenchmen."

* * *

Lewis had ordered the brig closer to the wind, and she was now bearing down on both the ketch and the ferocious battle that was taking place beyond her. And it was exactly that action that currently drew everyone's attention, for it appeared the French captain had made his first mistake.

Rather than pulling away and keeping clear of the sloop, he had attempted to bear round and pass her close by, with the obvious intention of firing a second broadside into the stricken vessel's hull. But some clash of orders and intent had prevented this, and the two vessels collided. All aboard *Narcis* watched in horror as they became locked in a deadly embrace then, with a blaze of fire and smoke, the corvette finally fired off her broadside cannon.

At such range the effect would have been devastating, and actually torn the two hulls apart. However, the ketch was drawing nearer and, as she herself turned and delivered a barrage of shot into the corvette's prow, King felt hope stir within him.

But the Frenchman's last broadside must have caused the sloop true damage; there were now flames plainly visible about her forecastle, and her main mast – which had appeared unstable since the loss of the fore – suddenly crumbled, leaving the hull bedecked with its wreckage. The ketch was quick to resume her previous course and intended to engage the corvette's larboard side; if *Narcis* could only reach them before the Fencibles were overrun, there might still be a chance.

And they were not so very far behind: with bowlines tight and throbbing, every stitch of canvas was being strained to the limit, and the brig positively burst through the grey waves.

"Arm yourselves!" Price shouted from the main deck, and all those able snatched at cutlasses and pikes secured beneath the gangways and about each mast. "And if you would care to, sirs?" he added to the officers. "There's a small arms chest abaft the binnacle; Cross, see the gen'lmen are accommodated."

The helmsman nonchalantly indicated the box with his foot, although it seemed Price had more to say. "We could use a hand or two at the guns," he added with less certainty. "That is, if any of you has the desire."

The midshipmen dropped down to the main deck and joined the gun crews while Banks, Timothy and the other senior men helped themselves to cutlasses and began weighing them experimentally in their hands.

"We shall close her on our starboard bow!" This was Lewis, once more at the break of the quarterdeck. King glanced at him in disbelief; that side was surely blocked by the burning sloop. But no, now that he looked more carefully, Lewis was right; there was a path, small, admittedly, but the burning sloop was steadily drifting away and they might well burst through and claim a space.

"The enemy's starboard guns have been recently fired," Lewis explained more softly, "Whilst they shall not expect an attack from that quarter." That was true, but still it remained a dangerous option.

"I shall not be lingering forever," he continued, now addressing the men in his previous bellow. "We'll come alongside, deliver our shot, and be off. Any that wish to do so may board, but you will excuse me if I do not tarry to collect you afterwards."

All seemed to realise both the reasons and ramifications; Lewis must surely be in a hurry. With luck, it might even be touch and go, giving less chance of the French boarding *Narcis* in turn. But such a policy also meant the attackers must either take the Frenchman, or resign themselves to captivity; a difficult choice for the escaping prisoners who had already considered themselves as good as home. The whine of a musket shot passed overhead, and several turned to look for the source.

"It's the bloody Fencibles," Cranston cried out in dismay. "Don't they know what side we're on?"

A smattering of laughter greeted the remark, but King looked more seriously at Lewis.

"Do I have your permission to hoist an ensign?" he asked. "I did notice one had been provided earlier."

"I assume you would be meaning a British," Lewis smiled wryly. "By all means," he added. "May as well be hung for a sheep as a lamb. And Tom, shall you be going across?"

That was a hard one, every ounce of King's body wished to, but he knew well how clumsy a fighter the loss of his left arm had made him. And there was something else, something far more important that kept him back.

"I–I am not certain," he said. "Aimée is below; I cannot leave her."

"And I cannot wait for you," Lewis repeated. "Unless you take that Frenchman, my position will be in great jeopardy. But even then, our part in this will doubtless be discovered in time."

"Then remain," King urged. "We shall carry the ship together, then see her back to England in triumph. It would be a poor Admiralty that does not take note of your part in the proceedings. And if you were prepared to give evidence against those that employed you..."

"I am sure they would like nothing better," Lewis scoffed, "and would be more than happy for me to break my word in such a way."

King looked at him in hope, but Lewis shook his head.

"But no, it will not do, Tom," he stated firmly. "My pitch is already truly queered. I shall take *Narcis* back to Holland, but will probably beach her. My money is safe, and I may even find a way to England. Such things are not so very difficult," he added with a wink.

"Then we shall stay with you," King stated firmly. "Both me and Aimée. And later see that your efforts are properly recognised."

"Kind of you, Tom, though I fear it would be an upward struggle," Lewis replied, although now his face was void of humour. "And first we must deal with that Frenchman."

# Chapter Thirty-Two

The ketch was nearing the corvette now, which at least meant those aboard *Narcis* were spared the occasional musket shot passing over their prow; something that had continued even after an ensign had been crudely secured there. The French warship's bows were directly facing them and the space between her and the burning sloop was widening. There was now definitely room for the brig to come alongside, although King was doubtful if leaving again would be quite so easy. But there was no time to consider an alternative plan; already the ketch was falling under the shadow of the larger vessel and would be boarding in minutes.

"How many would you estimate our friend to be carrying?" King asked, indicating the Fencible craft, and Lewis shrugged.

"I should not care to guess," he replied, "though her decks seem well filled. Some, possibly all, will be experienced seamen, but I wonder how many have seen close action before."

King nodded, that was an important consideration. It was one thing to let off a cannon at a distant enemy, quite another to smell his breath as you fight him hand-to-hand. Below, on the main deck, the brig's starboard guns had been run out with their servers standing ready. There were several familiar faces amongst them, men which King knew to be battle hardened and he had the distinct impression many of the others were no strangers to combat. In each gun, canister had been added to the round shot, but five six-pounders would not make as great an impression as the ten long nines carried by the French. And, even as he looked, the corvette was beginning to tower over them.

"I'm hoping we can pass under her guns," Lewis, who had been following King's train of thought, commented. "Though still assume them yet to be reloaded."

King, who was doubtful on both points, made no reply.

"You won't be joining us, sir?" Timothy's voice took him by surprise, as did his formal tone and King turned to see the young man dressed in something close to a uniform. The tunic was decidedly shabby, and there was a tear in his white shirt, but Timothy was undoubtedly a naval officer once more.

"I should be of little use to you," King explained. "But will remain here and assist Mr Lewis."

"My first mate will be coming," Lewis announced and at that moment Reid himself appeared at the aft hatchway. He too was dressed in a naval uniform, although his was the blue and red of the East India Company. Noticing their glances, the young man blushed and turned away before collecting a cutlass from the arms chest and joining the boarders assembling on the starboard gangway.

"It seems there are others aboard who have not forsaken their roots," Lewis murmured.

Then the Fencibles' craft was almost alongside. The popping of musket fire between both vessels suddenly died away, only to be replaced by a deeper roar as the first of the ketch's broadside guns was despatched deep into the corvette's innards. Being set low, they should cause significant damage to the ship's hull, but would do little against the crowd of Frenchmen who stood ready to board or repel. Another gun fired and another after that, until smoke clouded the view for those aboard *Narcis*, although by then there were other problems for them to consider. They were coming up fast and nearing both the burning sloop, which lay less than a pistol's shot off their larboard bow, and the corvette that was considerably closer.

Timothy had joined those preparing to board and accepted one of the strips of canvas that was being handed out by a lad. The white bands were to be tied about their right arms and, in theory, should distinguish those of the brig from Frenchmen although, with Sea Fencibles liable to be on board, the chance of falling to a friend remained high. The only men left working the ship appeared to be Cross, at the wheel, a few hands tending the braces further forward and the gun captains standing by their pieces. Each gun was set with its quoin rammed home, so the barrel was depressed as far as possible. Such a low aim was intended to avoid hulling the corvette then striking the ketch to the other side. *Narcis* had a relatively high freeboard though and, with canister added to the mix, a few of the French would be cleared from their deck. Timothy wondered how many Fencibles would also be hit by their fire but quickly dismissed the notion; boarding an enemy ship was fraught with dangers and it didn't do to dwell on any one of them.

"Ready, Cranston?" he asked, spotting a well known face.

"Aye, sir," the seaman replied with an expectant grin.

"And you, Lovemore?" he enquired, noticing another.

"I'm ready." The second man's expression was far more solemn, and he seemed to be regarding Timothy in a curious manner.

"Well, keep your wits about you," Timothy added absent-mindedly. "We're heading for one hell of a rough house. If you can defend one of your own do so, but always look to yourself first. It don't do to be saving others only to fall in their place."

"Aye aye, sir," Cranston replied, and no one had any doubts where his loyalties would lie.

"And you be sure to take care of yourself an' all, sir," Lovemore added more seriously. "Don't go worrying about anyone else."

\* \* \*

Banks had teamed up with Adams, Brehaut and Reid, *Narcis'* first mate. The three were further forward and stood amid a mass of sweating servers who had left the final firing of their cannon to the gun captains. Glancing at the two younger men, Banks began to have doubts: it was several years since he had involved himself in any form of hand-to-hand fighting and, for all he knew, his reactions would be lacking, to say nothing of the stamina needed for even a brief action. He glanced back at King, standing firm on the quarterdeck, and found himself envying his obvious excuse to remain behind. Then guilt rose up to shame him and he turned his attention elsewhere.

"Have you been in action before?" he asked the mate.

"No, sir," Reid replied. "I were a John Company man before joining *Narcis*," he explained.

"The HEIC have their fair share of boarding actions," Banks mused. "Probably as many as the Royal Navy – in proportion, of course."

"Yes, sir, though one never came my way," the mate confessed.

"How long did you serve?" Banks enquired.

"Three years, then I were let go."

Banks eyed the young man. "Were you now? Well if you prove yourself today, I am sure they shall take you back," he told him. "I have associations with the India Company and would be glad to speak for you if it would help."

Reid considered this for a moment. "That's good of you, sir," he replied, "but Mr Lewis is a very fair master, and I should prefer to stay with him."

* * *

Lovemore was starting to know true fear, something that hardly made him unusual amongst those waiting to board the French warship, although his terrors were less immediate and far more personal. He was by no means unconcerned about going into action, but an even greater dread also occupied his mind.

The death's head image was back on Lieutenant Timothy's face, and that wasn't the worst of it. As men gathered about him on the narrow gangway, Lovemore could see more, seemingly randomly distributed amongst his fellows. And lower down, some of the gun captains on the main deck, one of the midshipmen, a topman on the forecastle... almost everywhere he looked that dreadful icon appeared to taunt him. And all the pleading, praying and muttering of half-remembered verses would do nothing to make them disappear.

He gripped his cutlass as the anger grew. Why had he listened to that old fool Lamar? Since speaking with him, he had spent as many hours reading the Bible as relearning the flute and this was his reward. If there had been as much progress with spiritual studies as music, those accursed images would have been consigned to history long before. As it was, there had also been the occasional glimpse of the future and he had the uneasy feeling that night-time encounters, such as that with the long dead Harris, were not so very far behind. And now those damned skulls were back: it was enough to test a saint.

* * *

"Port your helm," Lewis ordered as the brig grew closer to the Frenchman. All aboard were tense with anticipation, and there was now hardly a sound from the expectant boarders. Forward, he could see Price's bald head as he stood ready beside number two gun, and the starboard gangway was positively crammed with figures greedy for a scrap. Little could be seen of any action aboard the corvette, but there was enough noise from that direction to indicate a pitched battle still raged, while to larboard another fight was in progress between the crew of the British sloop and flames that were steadily claiming their vessel.

And now the brig's jib boom was reaching past the enemy's prow and a muttered growl rose up from those ready to board. The noise developed into a cheer that swelled further and was punctuated by *Narcis'* broadside guns being despatched with slow and considered care. The dull thud of a musket ball hit the deck next to him and Lewis instinctively looked up; there were sharpshooters in the corvette's tops. They must have finally identified the brig for the threat she was and were taking action. One of the British officers – Timothy it looked like – was raising his cutlass high in a defiant gesture, and the two vessels seemed destined to touch at any moment. Then, with a sudden lurch, they collided; several boarders fell back from the gangway and even Lewis had to steady himself, although both hulls drew apart almost at once. But not for very long, and not so very far: a short enough distance to leap when the fighting madness was in full throw.

He watched as the crowd began to swarm over the Frenchman's top rail. Another thump from a musket ball landing close by, but he paid it no heed. *Narcis* was all but empty now; only King stood next to Cross, at the wheel, while a couple who had been wounded when trying to board were lying where they fell on the main deck. King must have felt his eyes upon him and swung round.

"Quite a battle," he said, his face already blackened. Lewis went to reply, but a sudden sharp jolt to his shoulder interrupted him. For a moment he thought he must have been stabbed but there was no one close by. He glanced down, and noticed his white shirt now bore a red stain that was radiating out from a spot just hidden by his jacket. And then the pain began.

Timothy was one of the first across and hardly paused as his boots hit the Frenchman's deck. All was much clearer than he had expected; forward a mighty battle was being fought by the forecastle, and the half-deck was filled with struggling figures, some of whom were lacking weapons and seemed to be laying into each other with fists, handspikes and belaying pins. But there was space enough and he could see clear across the corvette's beam to the masts of the ketch that lay alongside. He turned aft, and almost instantly came across a bearded fellow in a dark red uniform that could never have been British. Cranston was beside him and the seaman had no hesitation in striking the man down with his cutlass.

And then they were into the fray. For several seconds all Timothy could see were strange faces; he did his best by parrying blows while striking out almost indiscriminately when he could, but the fight owed more to confusion than care and could never be considered scientific. Cranston remained beside him, as was Lovemore; the latter's head being a mass of ringlets as he swung his sword into the face of an unsuspecting officer.

"British!" Timothy yelled, and the cry was taken up by those about him as they forged deeper into the crowd. A bullet whined close by, someone was firing; someone desperate – or foolish – enough to risk hitting friend as well as foe. Then Timothy saw a uniformed man with a half-pike charging straight for him.

He tried to dodge but it was a blow from Cranston's cutlass that actually saved him. The thought occurred that the French must have received reinforcements as another came at him with a pistol. The thing must have been empty as he was brandishing it like a club and Timothy was able to despatch the man long before he grew close enough to use it.

A movement from further off caught his attention; it was another pikeman, but this time making for Lovemore. Timothy hacked down once again and managed to throw the man off balance. Lovemore looked his thanks but the danger was not ended, and Timothy stepped back to raise his sword for yet another strike.

And that was his mistake: he should have plunged forward with the blade extended which would have done the job just as well without the extravagance, and exposure, of a formal blow. As it was, another blade hacked into the flesh of his own arm and Timothy's cutlass clattered to the deck before it was less than halfway through its stroke. A searing pain erupted in his side and he glanced down in disbelief as the tip of yet another pike punctured the cloth of his shirt and was driven deep within. For a moment he remained motionless: was this truly how it would end, as a butchered corpse on the deck of a Frenchman? Hardly an unusual conclusion to a serving officer's career, but not the domestic bliss he had allowed himself to expect. In desperation his eyes fell on Lovemore, who was regarding him with a mixture of horror and remorse, and seemed to be saying something amid the carnage. Then the pain grew suddenly worse and the last thing Timothy registered was the deck as it rose up to claim him.

* * *

Strangely, the Frenchman's forecastle was where the main action seemed to have centred. Banks, assisted by Adams and Reid, made straight for the throng of fighting men, and soon all were in the thick of battle. Adams, who had followed, was one of the early fallers, succumbing to a brutal cutlass stroke that all but severed his right hand near to the wrist; the lad was forced to turn from the action and seek what shelter he could. Reid was more successful however; he had never been exposed to such brutality in the past but found his tense and overstrung temperament ideally suited to combat. In no time he had dealt with two Frenchmen, and was only stopped from despatching one of the Fencibles by a frantic shout from Banks.

Brehaut was faring less well: both by nature and physique, he could never have been regarded as a fighting man, although the present circumstances had been extreme enough to persuade him otherwise. But soon he was failing; the merest nick to his right ear caught him by surprise and it was all he could do to continue to parry blows from his moustachioed opponent, who remained unfairly intent on wounding him further. Taking a step back, he thrust his cutlass out before him in an attempt to hold the brute off, but his weapon was savagely swept to one side, and the man lunged forward, his own cutlass raised and poised to strike. From

369

nowhere, another blade appeared and countered the blow; Brehaut looked in surprise to see Reid, the young mate, as he thundered in with a series of barbarous slices that forced the sword from the Frenchman's grip.

Banks had accounted for himself credibly enough but was starting to tire when a uniform of a darker blue came into sight, and he automatically drew back. It was not a face he recognised, but the man was clearly Royal Navy.

"From the brig?" the unknown officer demanded.

"Indeed: we are British," Banks gasped, and the two separated, to continue the fight elsewhere.

* * *

"I'll get you below," King announced as he bent down to his fallen friend.

"I think not," Lewis replied, the words coming through teeth clenched in pain.

"Then I shall send for Bob Manning," King persisted, glancing over his shoulder for support. But the brig was all but empty; every man that could had gone. If the boarding attempt failed, the French might seize her with nothing more than the proverbial cook and ship's cat. No enemy was in sight, however as all remained heavily involved in the fight that still raged close by on the corvette's deck. But that didn't solve his current dilemma, and King returned to Lewis in desperation.

"I shall go myself," he said, coming to a decision, but Lewis shook his head.

"Don't go, Tom," he said, wincing at the foolishness of his appeal. "I do not wish to be alone."

"Very well," King assured him, and placed his hand on the man's shoulder. "Though I can do little for..." his words stopped as he realised the severity of the wound. But Lewis was shaking his head, and obviously trying to speak. King drew closer.

"I am sorry it should have come to this," he whispered. "It were never my intent."

"I know," King soothed, while wondering quite which part Lewis regretted.

"I should never have been a smuggler, Tom," he continued,

370

adding a slight smile. "Wasn't in my nature."

"Your nature is to be a fine Navy officer," King told him seriously. "As you were, and might be again, if only Manning would show."

But the smile remained on Lewis' face as the eyes closed and he slowly shook his head as the expression faded.

* * *

The action officially ended a few minutes later when the French tricolour was roughly torn down although not everyone registered the fact immediately. On board *Narcis*, King remained unaware of the victory until a loud voice began to make itself heard from the corvette and he realised the din of fighting had all but died. The voice was speaking in English and giving orders, but his muddled brain failed to distinguish any of the individual words, or rather it did not attempt to.

The owner made himself apparent shortly afterwards; he was a middle-aged man who wore a tailored full dress Royal Navy lieutenant's uniform and did so with obvious pride. King watched as the slightly portly figure clambered aboard the brig and, at the head of three armed seamen, strutted confidently towards the quarterdeck.

"And who might we have here?" he enquired, regarding King's shabby attire, only the tunic of which was at all recognisable. "Another runner with false ideas of grandeur?"

"I am a commander in the Royal Navy." King's words were spoken softly and more through habit than any wish to assert himself.

"We'll see about that," the lieutenant snorted. "And there is another who fancies himself a captain. But it don't allow for either coming from a known smuggler."

The man went on to say more, although King had ceased to listen. Aimée would be below with Manning; he should see to them both. And there would be others: King looked away from the garrulous lieutenant and across to the corvette that was undoubtedly in British hands. She was a fine ship, probably a little larger than *Kestrel*, but not less beautiful; the French had a way with lines that English designers could rarely emulate.

There was Cranston, one of his former hands; he appeared alive and well and was busy securing prisoners on the forecastle. Seeing the familiar face made King's thoughts return to the rest who had escaped with him. Most had gone across to board the Frenchman; from what he had just heard, Banks was also alive, but he should check on the rest.

Meanwhile flames still rose from the British sloop; a good many men would be needed to check that fire, with more to keep their French prisoners in order. For one who had experienced little of such work for a while, it appeared to be a lot of organisation, although King's main thoughts remained with Lewis, whose body still lay on the quarterdeck.

The two had met over ten years before. Since then King had always considered him a firm friend, even if quite how well he really knew the man had only become apparent in the last few hours. He wasn't even sure if Lewis had family or dependants of any kind, only that society had unfairly labelled him dishonourable with the nett result that he had fulfilled their judgement by becoming a smuggler.

And then such things seemed foolishly unimportant, as did the blustering fool in front of him, or any of the other minor irritations that had plagued him in the past. But suddenly there was one that stood out, and definitely could not be considered insignificant; even as King stood with the scent of battle still hanging in the air, it seemed to gather in importance until he knew he must take action without delay.

"Are you even listening to me?" the lieutenant was demanding, and King finally gave his full attention.

"You will call me sir," he told him bluntly. "As you will that captain you so rashly dismissed."

The man paused, swallowed, then prepared to resume, but King was too quick.

"Present yourself to him now for further instructions," he ordered. "I must go below to check on the wounded, but shall expect a report by the time I return."

Again the man went to speak, but King was already moving. There was no time to be lost; some matters had already been left for far too long.

* * *

Manning's temporary sick bay was remarkably similar to those found aboard the majority of King's ships when in action. He had cordoned off an area of the orlop deck which, though low – the deckhead being less than five feet – was not unusually so, and commandeered sea chests for an operating table, which was also quite in keeping. There had been no spare canvas to spread over the deck, and the place was just as poorly lit, with a selection of dips and glims gleaned from various cabins. And, once patients began to appear, it soon became an image of living hell, which was truly nothing different.

But he was not supported. Usually aboard *Narcis* the medical duties were taken care of by the cook and his young son. But as both were Dutch, the pair had not opted to sail, and Manning was reconciling himself to having to handle everything when Aimée appeared.

She was quickly detailed to assessing the wounded and making those requiring his attention – which were the majority – ready. But that soon changed as the need for a competent hand to attend dressings was realised. At first they were helped by the lack of manpower available to drag the injured below, so the only patients who arrived did so under their own volition. But when the guns ceased to fire they were faced with a positive torrent of tortured souls that were literally dumped into their care. Consequently, when King appeared he was hardly greeted warmly.

"If you ain't wounded, Tom, kindly leave us be," Manning barked, adding, "And if you are, you shall surely have to wait your turn."

King noticed his friend was currently stitching up a seaman's leg that had been torn open by an oak splinter and retreated into the shadows for a moment. But he did not leave. Instead, stepping carefully over the lines of prone bodies, he made his way to where Aimée was bandaging up the most recent of the surgeon's patients.

"Oh Tom, this is not the time," she protested upon noticing him.

"I shall go, I promise I shall go," King hurriedly assured her. "And I will come back with help – there must be further medical staff elsewhere. But I have to speak to you now, it is important."

373

She finished tying the bandage and wiped her hands on a piece of waste cloth before considering him again. "What is it?" she demanded.

"I-I wanted to make sure we were alright." In the heat and stench of that terrible place, he knew his words to be foolish, yet there was a pain in his chest that must surely equal any those about him were feeling.

"You surely are not speaking about your wife?" she exclaimed, and he gave a pathetic nod.

"Yes, we are 'alright' as you say it." Aimée's eyes left him for a moment as she watched for the surgeon to pass over the next patient into her care. "I was not so very pleased when I discovered, but then I am sure neither were you to learn of Albert. So perhaps we are even?"

"I suppose so," he replied, still feeling like a child.

"But if it helps, I should not have left Verdun, and travelled all this way if she bothered me so very greatly."

"Then you knew before?" King gasped.

"I knew from the very beginning," she replied. The surgeon looked to be finishing his stitching and she must prepare a space for the new patient.

King shook his head. "Who told you?" he asked. She looked sharply back at him.

"Who? Does it matter who? At least someone chose to. And after a while so many expected me to know already they let slip a dozen times."

"And you still want to be with me?"

The catgut from the last stitch had broken prematurely, causing a cursing Manning to pause and retie it. Aimée's attention returned to King in the interval.

"Yes, I still want to be with you," she said, with barely a trace of tenderness. "Tom, you are a fool in many ways, but you are my fool, and I wouldn't be without you for the world." A faint smile showed for a second, but was quickly dismissed. "Now will you go from here and allow me to continue my work?"

# Epilogue

It was several hours later when Lovemore made it back to the brig. By then a Navy frigate had spotted them and some measure of order was established. The fire that had continued to blaze aboard the sloop could finally be extinguished and the wounded transferred to the new arrival's medical department. There remained a good deal to be done, but Lovemore was able to slip away for a moment to attend to something more personal.

The lower deck resembled a shambles, but his meagre belongings still lay tucked in the recess where he had hidden them earlier. He seized the ditty bag and tipped out the contents; the largest fell to the deck with a clatter. It was his flute, still safe in the stiff leather pouch. Lovemore picked it up and held it for several seconds. The instrument had been with him for many years and, throughout that time, his skill in playing had undoubtedly increased. But that was not the only thing to improve; along with an ear for music, Lovemore's darker talents had also developed and it now seemed significant that Lamar's expulsion of these also removed that for music. He had indulged in many hours of practice since and they had definitely brought results. Although trivial compared to his previous proficiency, he could now play a number of tunes with reasonable accuracy and would doubtless continue to improve. But at the same time the other powers had also returned so he was forced to concede the two must somehow be linked.

And Lieutenant Timothy's death was the last straw; Lovemore had disliked his psychic abilities before, but now he hated them with an intensity that frightened even himself. He did not doubt that the knowledge Lamar had given him in return would keep them at bay, and from then on he would be putting time previously spent on music to that end.

He stuffed the rest of his possessions back into the bag and headed on deck once more. When he arrived, an officious officer was bellowing orders to anyone who would listen and he could see Cranston helping a boatswain repair the brig's shrouds. But

Lovemore closed his mind to it all and, with a purposeful stride that discouraged questioning, headed straight for the forecastle.

Once there, he had a clear view of the empty sea, and paused to draw breath. He had no foolish illusions about the instrument bringing bad luck, but Lovemore knew for certain he would never play the thing again and was oddly concerned that no one else should either. Reaching back, he hurled it over his shoulder and watched in silence as the polished leather case cartwheeled high into the air. The last rays of a dying sun caught it in flight, and he was able to follow the flute up to the moment it fell into the dark waters, then disappeared with barely a splash.

# Author's Note

**Verdun** was one of many prison depots in France during this period; others included Arras, Besançon, Givet, Sarrelibre and Valenciennes. Most were former frontier fortresses that had been made redundant following France's invasion of her neighbouring countries and some instigated broadly similar principles of detention which relied as much upon a word of honour as locks or chains. Such leniency was nominally only given to officers although ordinary seamen could be allowed a measure of freedom that would be considered strange today. However, Verdun stood apart as being unusually liberal; according to contemporary accounts, it was closer to a fashionable English town than any prison and provided every entertainment the upper classes could demand including horse racing, hunting, various forms of gambling and the theatre.

In addition to holding the majority of sea officers captured during the Napoleonic War, Verdun housed a large number of *détenus* – civilians illegally seized at the outbreak of hostilities – and both classes of prisoner benefited from its facilities. Permission was usually given for families, servants and, all too often, mistresses to join the captives while many British tradesmen and artisans set up businesses in the town. Brenton's school was eventually established and provided a sound education for children and the younger junior officers, while both Anglican and Methodist Churches were allowed with the former boasting appointed clergy and a regular congregation of over 300.

Such arrangements benefited both parties; the French government gained from a considerable income while their guests enjoyed a good standard of living which cost far less to maintain than in their home country, especially as there was little reason to keep up appearances. But there remained a darker side; spouses and dependants of prisoners were not officially detained and so allowed to return home should they wish although, while in confinement, remained under the strict discipline that lurked beneath the regime's sugar-coated surface.

Any who contemplated escape, either personally or by aiding others, were liable to summary execution and those who avoided this fate would almost certainly be sent to Bitche, the punishment depot where most were held underground and in truly dreadful conditions. Fines were also imposed for minor and often imagined infringements of the rules. These could be unusually harsh and were rarely declared to the French

378

government.

And while on the subject of escape it is interesting to note that, before this time, few Naval officers would need to contemplate the notion as the tradition of exchange had become entrenched in previous wars. Before Napoleon's refusal to continue the practice, the process could take a matter of days as it had become common to release prisoners of war after they made a simple declaration not to fight again until a formal agreement for exchange had been agreed. There was certainly no concept of an officer's duty being to escape but almost the reverse and, even late into the war, many preferred to remain in detention in the hope of what they regarded as an honourable trade. The younger and more junior officers were the first to adapt, although any that proved successful were afterwards interrogated and, if it was discovered they had broken their word of honour, ran the risk of being returned to the enemy.

Incidentally, the method of escape I have described is broadly similar to that practised by Ellison, Kirk and Alison in 1807. The three merchant officers were able to break out of the Convent Chapel of St. Vannes where they were being held prisoner and get clear of the town. They remained fugitives for eleven days before ultimately being recaptured.

**HMS** *Childers* was indeed commanded by a relative of Nelson; William Bolton married Catharine Bolton, daughter of Nelson's sister, Susannah in 1803. He was promoted to captain in 1805 and died in 1830.

**Jahleel Brenton** is yet another fascinating character that I have come to know a little better whilst researching the Fighting Sail series. The son of a rear admiral, Brenton was born in Rhode Island, the eldest of three brothers, all of whom opted for the Navy. In his case it was at the age of eleven, when he joined HMS *Queen*, a three-decked, second rate commanded by his father. He was later present as a lieutenant aboard HMS *Barfleur,* at the Battle of Cape St Vincent. Promoted to post rank in 1800, he first served as flag captain to Sir James Saumarez. In 1803, while in command of a frigate, his ship took ground off Cherbourg and he was captured. For many this would have been the end of a promising career, but Brenton rose to the challenge of being held prisoner and did much to see his fellow inmate's rights were respected by the French authorities. This involved many clashes that might easily have seen him sent to Bitche, although his efforts were not in vain. During his time at Verdun, Brenton successfully petitioned the French Minister of War for a reduction in the daily *appels*, pointing out that such restrictions went against the law and spirit of the *Parole d'Honneur,* and went on to promote the Verdun Relief Committee – all whilst suffering from a severe inflammation of the lungs. His wife, Isabella, was given permission to join him in captivity in 1806 and for a year they lived in a small village just beyond of the town. In 1807 Brenton was repatriated in exchange for a French prisoner of war. This was such an unusual event that it is tempting to believe the French were only too pleased to be rid of a troublesome guest. He went on to captain HMS *Spartan* in the Adriatic Campaign, raised his flag in 1830 and died a baronet in 1842. Brenton's personal motto was 'Reflect, Ponder and Resolve'.

**Reverend Robert Wolfe** was a *détenu* seized at the outbreak of the Napoleonic War. After successfully campaigning for prisoners' rights in Verdun, he asked to be transferred to Givet, a nearby depot which he regarded as more in need of his services. During his time there he undoubtedly did much to improve his fellow prisoners' lot, a fact openly acknowledged by the French, although conveniently ignored by his own government. It was only after his release in 1814, and following a minor public outcry, that the back pay due to a naval chaplain was grudgingly allowed.

**Louis Wirion** was born in 1764, the son of a pork butcher. He served as an attorney's clerk before the Revolution and hoped to become a lawyer. However, in 1789 he joined the National Guard of Paris as a cavalry lieutenant, a force that then became the 29th Police Division. Wirion was present at several notable actions including the Siege of Namur, and the Battles of Valmy and Aldenhoven; with his horse being shot from under him at the latter. During his tenure as Commandant of Verdun he became known for his corrupt ways, setting an example his staff were quick to follow and encourage. Few prisoners avoided his arbitrary 'fines' which steadily increased in both frequency and value until the Minister of War finally took action. Wirion was sent for but, rather than face an official investigation by the Council of State, committed suicide in 1810.

**Aimée du Buc de Rivéry** (the woman Aimée believed herself to have been named after) was a French noble famously lost at sea during the latter part of the eighteenth century. Legend has it she was captured by Barbary Pirates who later sold her into a harem. From there she was sent to Constantinople as a gift to the Ottoman Sultan by the Bey of Algiers and later emerged as Valide Sultan (Queen Mother) of the Ottoman Empire.

**Mrs Concannon** had been a popular London entertainer who was caught at the resumption of hostilities and founded *The Upper Club* at Verdun's Bishop's Palace. She was a large woman and much immortalised by the cartoons of Gillray. To celebrate the Prince of Wale's birthday in 1804, she sent out invitations to 120 people for entertainment and supper.

**Astley's Royal Amphitheatre** was a performance venue on Westminster

Road, Lambeth. It was opened by Philip Astley in 1773 and originally hosted horse shows to which light drama was soon added. After a series of fires, Astley's steadily evolved into one of the first permanent circuses, and is responsible for setting the standard size for a circus ring (at sixty-two feet in diameter) that has been in use ever since.

**Hanging, drawing and quartering**. This barbaric punishment was not repealed until the Treason Act of 1814, when it was replaced with death by hanging, followed by posthumous quartering; something that was to remain on the statute books until 1870 in England, and 1949 in Scotland.

**Armand-Marie-Jacques de Chastenet, Marquis de Puységur** (Garrett's mentor) is thought to be the earliest exponent of somnambulistic clairvoyance, which is now more commonly known as hypnosis. A pupil of Franz Mesmer, Puységur founded the *Société Harmonique des Amis Réunis*, which attracted a good deal of support until the Revolution when it was disbanded. Puységur then spent several years in prison but, following Bonaparte's downfall and a renewal of interest in the subject, later became accepted as the father of what some now regard as a science. Puységur preferred to divert all attention to his mentor however, and his contributions gradually lost prominence. In 1884 Charles Richet, the Nobel Prize winning physiologist, rediscovered his works and ensured Puységur's memory received the recognition it deserved.

**The Sea Fencibles**. This highly organised and efficient volunteer force was active during the Revolutionary and Napoleonic Wars. It was manned in the main by professional seamen, often fishermen or bargemen as well as former enlisted hands, and officially commanded by serving naval officers, although many would have been passed over or retired. The Fencibles' brief was to protect the shores of England during an invasion and, although partially land-based, they were equipped with various small craft which were always well armed and manned, and often used to seize enemy vessels in the Channel and North Sea. As membership of the Fencibles granted immunity from the press, they became a regular refuge for deserting seamen and active smugglers although, despite this, their duties were frequently carried out with every bit as much zeal as their regular counterparts.

Alaric Bond
Herstmonceux 2017

381

# Principal Characters

**The officers and men of HMS *Kestrel***

| | |
|---|---|
| Thomas King: | Commander |
| James Timothy: | First Lieutenant |
| Adams: | Acting Lieutenant |
| Brehaut: | Sailing Master |
| Kyle: | Master's Mate |
| Summers: | Midshipman |
| Soames: | Midshipman |
| Bremner: | Midshipman |
| Robert Manning: | Surgeon |
| Holby: | Purser |
| Curry: | Master-at-Arms |
| Crabbe: | Gunner |
| Thompson: | Captain's Steward |
| Lovemore | Seaman and Flautist |
| Raymond: | Seaman and Fiddler |
| Cranston: | Seaman |
| Hobbs: | Seaman |
| Kenton: | Seaman |
| Harris: | Seaman |
| Farmer: | Seaman |
| Beeney: | Seaman |
| Roberts: | Boy |
| Philby: | Marine Private and Drummer |

**Also**:

| | |
|---|---|
| Sir Alexander Ball: | R. N. Captain and Civil Commissioner, Malta |
| Sir Richard Banks: | R. N. Captain, formerly of HMS *Prometheus* |
| Corbett: | R. N. Lieutenant, formerly of HMS *Prometheus* |
| *Général* Louis Wirion: | Commandant of Verdun |
| Lewis: | Retired R. N. Lieutenant |
| Aimée Silva: | Breton woman living in Verdun |
| Antoine Silva: | Bargeman and brother of Aimée |
| Nikola Lesro: | Merchant in Valletta |
| Lamar: | Manager of the travelling players |
| Garrett: | Magician and psychic |
| Reid: | First Mate of *Narcis* |
| Masters: | Second Mate of *Narcis* |
| Price: | Boatswain of *Narcis* |
| Laidlaw: | Seaman in *Narcis* |
| Judy: | Seaman in *Narcis* |
| Compton: | Seaman in *Narcis* |
| Clinton: | Seaman in *Narcis* |
| Jones: | Seaman in *Narcis* |
| Crabtree: | Smuggler's venturer |
| van Gent: | Government official and supplier of contraband in Flushing |
| Jansen: | Dutchman living in Antwerp |

# Selected Glossary

| | |
|---|---|
| **Able Seaman** | One who can hand, reef and steer and is well acquainted with the duties of a seaman. |
| **Anvers** | British: Antwerp. |
| *Appel* | *(French)* Literally: call. |
| **Back** | Wind change; anticlockwise. |
| **Backed Sail** | One set in the direction for the opposite tack to slow a ship. |
| **Barky** | *(Slang)* A seaman's affectionate name for their vessel. |
| **Bean** | *(Slang)* Guinea. |
| **Belaying Pins** | Wooden pins set into racks at the side of a ship. Lines are secured about these, allowing instant release by their removal. |
| **Binnacle** | Cabinet on the quarterdeck that houses compasses, the deck log, traverse board, lead lines, telescope, speaking trumpet, etc. |
| **Bitts** | Stout horizontal pieces of timber, supported by strong verticals, that extend deep into the ship. These hold the anchor cable when the ship is at anchor. |
| **Blazes** | *(Slang)* A euphemism for hell (a word that was considered an obscenity). |
| **Block** | Article of rigging that allows pressure to be diverted or, when used with others, increased. Consists of a pulley wheel made of *lignum vitae* encased in a wooden shell. Blocks can be single, double (fiddle block), triple or quadruple. The main suppliers were Taylors of Southampton. |

| | |
|---|---|
| **Board** | Before being promoted to lieutenant, midshipmen would be tested for competence by a board of post captains. Should the applicant prove able they would be known as a passed midshipman, but could not assume the rank of lieutenant until appointed to such a position. |
| **Boatswain** | *(Pronounced Bosun)* The warrant officer superintending sails, rigging, canvas, colours, anchors, cables and cordage *etc.* committed to his charge. |
| **Bob/bobbed** | *(Slang)* To trick or be tricked. |
| **Boom** | Lower spar to which the bottom of a gaff sail is attached. |
| ***Bourrée*** | French dance in double quick time. |
| **Braces** | Lines used to adjust the angle between the yards and the fore and aft line of the ship. Mizzen braces and braces of a brig lead forward. |
| **Brig** | Two-masted vessel, square-rigged on both masts. |
| **Bulkhead** | A partition within the hull of a ship. |
| **Bumboat** | *(Slang)* Shore-based vessel used to convey small luxuries to those aboard ships at anchor. The name is a combination of the Dutch word for canoe and boat. |
| **Burgoo** | Meal made from oats, usually served cold, and occasionally sweetened with molasses. |
| **Bulwark** | The planking or woodwork about a vessel above her deck. |

| | |
|---|---|
| **Canister** | Type of anti-personnel shot: small iron balls packed into a cylindrical tin case. |
| **Cartwheel** | *(Slang)* Originally a two penny coin released in 1797 and the first to be minted by a steam press. The size was truly enormous; an inch and three quarters in diameter, a quarter inch thick and weighting two ounces. The term was sometimes used for the smaller penny piece. |
| **Catchpole** | *(Slang)* A sheriff's officer – also known as a Bum Bailiff. |
| *Capote* | A French hooded cape. |
| **Carronade** | Short cannon firing a heavy shot. Invented by Melville, Gascoigne and Miller in late 1770's and adopted from 1779. Often used on the upper deck of larger ships, or as the main armament of smaller. |
| **Cascabel** | Part of the breech of a cannon. |
| **Cat House** | *(Slang)* A brothel. Also, Nanny House. |
| *Chef de complot* | When the French authorities caught a group of deserters the senior, or oldest, amongst them might be shot, with the rest going unpunished. He would be known as the *chef de complot,* or ringleader. |
| **Close-Hauled** | Sailing as near as possible into the wind. |
| **Clutter** | *(Slang)* An unnecessary row or racket. |
| **Cogging** | *(Slang)* Cheating, especially with dice. |

| | |
|---|---|
| **Companionway** | A staircase or passageway. |
| **Counter** | The lower part of a vessel's stern. |
| **Course** | A large square lower sail, hung from a yard, with sheets controlling and securing it. |
| **Cove** | *(Slang)* A man, often a rogue. |
| **Crowlink Gin** | Illicit gin that was originally landed at Crowlink in Sussex (now Birling Gap). |
| **Cutter** | Fast, small, single-masted vessel with a sloop rig. Also, a seaworthy ship's boat. |
| **Dawb** | *(Slang)* A bribe. |
| ***Dgħajsa*** | A Maltese water taxi similar in appearance to a gondola, but powered by two oars that are used from the standing position. |
| **Ditty Bag** | *(Slang)* A seaman's bag. Derives its name from the dittis or 'Manchester stuff' of which it was originally made. |
| **Dogger** | *(Slang)* A two-masted fishing boat originally from the area about the Dogger Bank although the design was adopted throughout the English east and Dutch west coasts. |
| **Driver** | Large sail set on the mizzen. The foot is extended by means of a boom. |
| **Duds** | *(Slang)* Clothes. |
| **Fall** | The free end of a lifting tackle on which the men haul. |
| **Fat Head** | *(Slang)* Usually descriptive of a condition caused by sleeping in stuffy conditions, such as a crowded berth deck, but also for any headache or hangover. |

| | |
|---|---|
| **Fetch** | To arrive at, or reach a destination. Also, a measure of the wind when blowing across water. The longer the fetch the bigger the waves. |
| **Flushing** | British name for Vlissingen (or Flessingue). |
| **Forereach** | To gain upon, or pass by another ship when sailing in a similar direction. |
| **Forestay** | Stay supporting the masts running forward, serving the opposite function of the backstay. Runs from each mast at an angle of about 45 degrees to meet another mast, the deck or the bowsprit. |
| **Friday Face** | *(Slang)* Expression worn by one of a dismal countenance. For centuries Friday had become established as the day of abstinence. |
| ***Gavotte*** | Medium-paced French dance. |
| ***Gitans*** | *(French)* Gypsies. |
| **Glass** | Telescope. Also, an hourglass and hence, as slang, a period of time. Also, a barometer. |
| **Gun Room** | In a third rate and above, a mess for junior officers. For lower rates the gun room serves a similar purpose as a wardroom. |
| **Go About** | To alter course, changing from one tack to the other. |
| **Gobblers** | *(Slang)* Revenue men. |
| **Go Snacks** | *(Slang)* To offer, or accept, a share in something. |

| | |
|---|---|
| **Halyards** | Lines which raise yards, sails, signals etc. |
| **Hard Tack** | Ship's biscuit. |
| **Heave To** | Keeping a ship relatively stationary by backing certain sails in a seaway. |
| **High Life** | *(Slang)* The way of fashionable society. First recorded usage 1738. |
| **Jack Adams** | *(Slang)* A fool or simpleton (Jack Adams was a noted character in Clerkenwell during the rein of Charles II). |
| **Jack Tar** | The traditional name for a British seaman. |
| **Jib-Boom** | Spar run out from the extremity of the bowsprit, braced by means of a Martingale stay, which passes through the dolphin striker. |
| **John Company** | *(Slang)* The Honourable East India Company. |
| **Jonathan** | *(Slang)* American. |
| **Kelson** | A length of scarphed timbers stretching from bow to stern to which frames and plates may be secured. |
| **Larboard** | Left side of the ship when facing forward. Later replaced by 'port', which had previously been used for helm orders. |
| **Leeboard** | An additional blade set to either side of a hull. It can be lowered or raised in the same way as a centreboard and helps vessels maintain stability when sailing into the wind. |
| **Leeward** | The downwind side of a vessel. |

| | |
|---|---|
| **Lubber/Lubberly** | *(Slang)* Unseamanlike behaviour; as a landsman. |
| **Luff** | To sail too close to the wind, perhaps allowing work to be carried out aloft. Also, the flapping of sails when brought too close to the wind. Also, the side of a fore and aft sail laced to the mast. |
| **Lugger** | Craft with two or three masts and powered by lug sails. Varies in size from small (usually used for fishing and the like), to substantial vessels capable of carrying a number of cannon. |
| **Nanny House** | *(Slang)* A brothel. Also, Cat House. |
| **Mot** | *(Slang)* Term, usually derogatory, for a young girl. |
| **Orlop** | The lowest deck in a ship. |
| **Pallet** | A heavy straw mattress. |
| **Penny Gaff** | *(Slang)* A place offering cheap music and crude entertainment. |
| **Point Blank** | The range of a cannon when fired flat. (For a 32-pounder this would be roughly 1000 feet.) |
| **Polacre** | Small merchant ship common in the Mediterranean. |
| ***Polichinelle's* Secret** | *Polichinelle* is a character who first appeared in the *Commedia dell'arte* during the 17th Century. He became widely accepted throughout Europe and is the forerunner of Punch, in the British Punch & Judy. One of his many characteristics is to play dumb when being fully aware of a situation. |

| | |
|---|---|
| *Porte Chaussée* | The eastern gatehouse at Verdun. |
| **Pusser** | *(Slang)* Purser. |
| **Pusser's Pound** | Before the Great Mutinies, meat was issued at 14 ounces to the pound, allowing an eighth for wastage. This was later reduced to a tenth. |
| **Priddying** | *(Slang)* To make good, or beautify. Possibly from Priddy's Hard, the Ordinance Station in Gosport. |
| **Prigger** | *(Slang)* A criminal, usually a thief. |
| **Quarterdeck** | In larger ships, the deck forward of the poop, but at a lower level. The preserve of officers. |
| **Queue** | A pigtail. Often tied by a seaman's best friend (his tie mate). |
| **Quoin** | Triangular wooden block placed under the cascabel of a long gun to adjust the elevation. |
| **Rake** | *(Slang)* One who lives in an immoral manner, usually at the expense of others. Also the act of firing upon the bows, or stern, of an enemy vessel. |
| **Ramper** | *(Slang)* A strong guard. What would probably now be referred to as "hired muscle". |
| **Rattan** | A short cane carried by a boatswain partially as a badge of office, although it was often used on minor defaulters. |
| **Ratlines** | Lighter lines, untarred and tied horizontally across the shrouds at regular intervals, to act as rungs and allow men to climb aloft. |
| **Reef** | A portion of sail that can be taken in to reduce the size of the |

| | |
|---|---|
| **Rigging** | Tophamper; made up of standing (static) and running (moveable) rigging, blocks etc. Also *(Slang)* clothes. |
| **Rook** | *(Slang)* A cheat: probably from the thievish disposition of the bird. |
| **Running** | Sailing before the wind. |
| **Scarph** | A joint in wood where the edges are sloped off to maintain a constant thickness. |
| **Schooner** | Small craft with two or three masts. |
| **Scran** | *(Slang)* Food. |
| **Sheet** | A line that controls the foot of a sail. |
| **Shellback** | *(Slang)* And older seaman. |
| **Shrouds** | Lines supporting the masts athwart ship (from side to side) which run from the hounds (just below the top) to the channels on the side of the hull. |
| **Slop Goods** | *(Slang)* Items intended to be sold to the crew during a voyage. |
| **Smoke** | *(Slang)* To discover, or reveal something hidden. |
| **Snabbled** | *(Slang)* Killed, usually in battle. |
| **Soft Tack** | Bread. |
| **Spree** | *(Slang)* A spell of general drunkenness and debauchery for lower deck men, usually associated with shore leave. |
| **Starter** | *(Slang)* A short length of rope usually carried by a boatswain's mate and used to 'encourage' the hands. |
| **Stay Sail** | A quadrilateral or triangular sail with parallel lines hung from under a stay. Usually pronounced |

|  |  |
|---|---|
| | stays'l. |
| **Strumpet** | *(Slang)* A harlot or mistress. |
| **Swab** | *(Slang)* An epaulette. |
| **Tack** | To turn a ship, moving her bows through the wind. Also a leg of a journey relating to the direction of the wind – if from starboard, a ship is deemed to be on the starboard tack. Also the part of a fore and aft loose-footed sail where the sheet is attached, or a line leading forward on a square course to hold the lower part of the sail forward. |
| **Taffrail** | Rail around the stern of a vessel. |
| **Tatler** | *(Slang)* A watch. |
| **Tipping the Double** | *(Slang)* Cheating. |
| **Tophamper** | Literally any weight either on a ship's decks or about her tops and rigging, but often used broadly to refer to spars and rigging. |
| **Trick** | *(Slang)* A period of duty. |
| **Trinity House** | A corporation governed under Royal Charter responsible for lighthouses, pilots and navigational aids. |
| **Trumpery** | Showy but worthless finery (from 1610). |
| **Turk's Head** | An ornamental knot tied to the end of a line to form a stopper. There are many differing examples. |
| **Venturer** | *(Slang)* The financier of a smuggling operation. |
| **Veer** | Wind change, clockwise. |
| **Vlissingen** | Port to the south west of the Netherlands (English: Flushing). |
| **Waist** | Area of main deck between the quarterdeck and forecastle. |

| | |
|---|---|
| **Watch** | Period of four (or in case of a dog watch, two) hours of duty. Also describes the divisions of a ship's crew. |
| **Wear/Wearing** | To change the direction of a square-rigged ship across the wind by putting its stern through the eye of the wind. Also jibe – more common in a fore and aft rig. |
| **Wedding Garland** | An actual garland that would be raised when a ship was expected to remain at anchor for some while. It signified that the ship was not on active service and women were allowed aboard. This was considered a preferable alternative to granting shore leave, a concession that was bound to be abused. |
| **Windward** | The side of a ship exposed to the wind. |
| **Yankee** | *(Slang)* The term originally referred to any American. First recorded usage was in 1758 by General James Wolfe. |

# About the author

Alaric Bond was born in Surrey, and now lives in Herstmonceux, East Sussex. He has been writing professionally for over thirty years.

His interests include the British Navy, 1793-1815, and the RNVR during WWII. He is also a keen collector of old or unusual musical instruments, and 78 rpm records.

Alaric Bond is a member of various historical societies and regularly gives talks to groups and organisations.

**www.alaricbond.com**

# About Old Salt Press

Old Salt Press is an independent press catering to those who love books about ships and the sea. We are an association of writers working together to produce the very best of nautical and maritime fiction and non-fiction. We invite you to join us as we go down to the sea in books.

## More Great Reading from Old Salt Press

**Evening Grey Morning Red Rick Spilman**
In *Evening Gray Morning Red,* a young American sailor must escape his past and the clutches of the Royal Navy, in the turbulent years just before the American Revolutionary War.
In the spring of 1768, Thom Larkin, a 17-year-old sailor newly arrived in Boston, is caught by Royal Navy press gang and dragged off to HMS *Romney*, where he runs afoul of the cruel and corrupt First Lieutenant. Years later, after escaping the *Romney*, Thom again crosses paths with his old foe, now in command HMS *Gaspee*, cruising in Narragansett Bay. Thom must finally face his nemesis and the guns of the *Gaspee*, armed only with his wits, an unarmed packet boat, and a sand bar.
ISBN: 978-1-943404-19-3 978-1-943404-20-9

**Rhode Island Rendezvous**
Book Three, The Patricia MacPherson Nautical Adventures
by Linda Collison
Newport Rhode Island: 1765. The Seven Years War is over but unrest in the American colonies is just heating up…
Maintaining her disguise as a young man, Patricia is finding success as Patrick MacPherson. Formerly a surgeon's mate in His Majesty's Navy, Patrick has lately been employed aboard the colonial merchant schooner *Andromeda*, smuggling foreign molasses into Rhode Island. Late October, amidst riots against the newly imposed Stamp Act, she leaves Newport bound for the West Indies on her first run as *Andromeda's* master. In Havana a chance meeting with a former enemy presents unexpected opportunities while an encounter with a British frigate and an old lover threatens her liberty – and her life.
ISBN: 978-1-943404-12-4   978-1-943404-13-1

**The Money Ship by Joan Druett**
Oriental adventurer Captain Rochester spun an entrancing tale to
Jerusha, seafaring daughter of Captain Michael Gardiner — a story of a
money ship, hidden in the turquoise waters of the South China Sea,
which was nothing less than the lost trove of the pirate Hochman. As
Jerusha was to find, though, the clues that pointed the way to fabled
riches were strange indeed — a haunted islet on an estuary in Borneo,
an obelisk with a carving of a rampant dragon, a legend of kings and
native priests at war, and of magically triggered tempests that swept
warriors upriver. And even if the clues were solved, the route to riches
was tortuous, involving treachery, adultery, murder, labyrinthine
Malayan politics ... and, ultimately, Jerusha's own arranged marriage.
An epic drama of fortune-hunting in the South China Sea during the
first two decades of the nineteenth century, The Money Ship is a fast-
moving novel on a sprawling canvas that spans three oceans and a
myriad of exotic ports. As the pages turn, Jerusha voyages from the
smuggling and fishing port of Lewes, Sussex to Boston in its glittering
heyday, then back to newly settled Singapore, until her quest for love
and pirate treasure comes to a spine-chilling climax in the benighted
lands of Borneo.
ISBN 978-0994124647

**The Blackstrap Station by Alaric Bond**
Christmas 1803, although the group of shipwrecked Royal Navy seamen have
anything but festivities in mind as they pitch their wits against a French force
sent to catch them. And all the while rescue, in the shape of a British frigate, lies
temptingly close, yet just beyond their reach... Encompassing vicious sea
battles, spirited land action and treachery from friend as much as foe, *The
Blackstrap Station* tells a stirring tale of courage, honour and loyalty, set against
the backdrop of what becomes a broiling Mediterranean summer.
ISBN 978-1-943404-10-0 e.book 978-1-943404-11-7 paperback

**Blackwell's Paradise by V E Ulett**
The repercussions of a court martial and the ill-will of powerful men at the
Admiralty pursue Royal Navy Captain James Blackwell into the Pacific, where
danger lurks around every coral reef. Even if Captain Blackwell and Mercedes
survive the venture into the world of early nineteenth century exploration, can
they emerge unchanged with their love intact. The mission to the Great South
Sea will test their loyalties and strength, and define the characters of Captain
Blackwell and his lady in *Blackwell's Paradise.*
ISBN 978-0-9882360-5-9

**Britannia's Gamble by Antoine Vanner**
**The Dawlish Chronicles: March 1884 – February 1885**
1884 - a fanatical Islamist revolt is sweeping all before it in the vast wastes of the Sudan and establishing a rule of persecution and terror. Only the city of Khartoum holds out, its defence masterminded by a British national hero, General Charles Gordon. His position is weakening by the day and a relief force, crawling up the Nile from Egypt, may not reach him in time to avert disaster.
But there is one other way of reaching Gordon...
A boyhood memory leaves the ambitious Royal Navy officer Nicholas Dawlish no option but to attempt it. The obstacles are daunting – barren mountains and parched deserts, tribal rivalries and merciless enemies – and this even before reaching the river that is key to the mission. Dawlish knows that every mile will be contested and that the siege at Khartoum is quickly moving towards its bloody climax.
Outnumbered and isolated, with only ingenuity, courage and fierce allies to sustain them, with safety in Egypt far beyond the Nile's raging cataracts, Dawlish and his mixed force face brutal conflict on land and water as the Sudan descends into ever-worsening savagery.
And for Dawlish himself, one unexpected and tragic event will change his life forever.
*Britannia's Gamble* is a desperate one. The stakes are high, the odds heavily loaded against success. Has Dawlish accepted a mission that can only end in failure – and worse?
ISBN 978-1-943404-17-9  978-1-943404-18-6


**HMS Prometheus by Alaric Bond**
With Britain under the threat of invasion, HMS *Prometheus* is needed to reinforce Nelson's ships blockading the French off Toulon. But a major action has left her severely damaged and the Mediterranean fleet outnumbered. *Prometheus* must be brought back to fighting order without delay, yet the work required proves more complex than a simple refit.
Barbary pirates, shore batteries and the powerful French Navy are conventional opponents, although the men of *Prometheus* encounter additional enemies, within their own ranks. A story that combines vivid action with sensitive character portrayal.
ISBN  978-1943404063

**The Elephant Voyage by Joan Druett**

In the icy sub-Antarctic, six marooned seamen survive against unbelievable odds. Their rescue from remote, inhospitable, uninhabited Campbell Island is a sensation that rocks the world. But no one could have expected that the court hearings that follow would lead not just to the founding of modern search and rescue operations, but to the fall of a colonial government.

ISBN 978-0-9922588-4-9

**The Scent of Corruption by Alaric Bond**

Summer, 1803: the uneasy peace with France is over, and Britain has once more been plunged into the turmoil of war. After a spell on the beach, Sir Richard Banks is appointed to HMS *Prometheus*, a seventy-four gun line-of-battleship which an eager Admiralty loses no time in ordering to sea. The ship is fresh from a major re-fit, but Banks has spent the last year with his family: will he prove worthy of such a powerful vessel, and can he rely on his officers to support him?

With excitement both aboard ship and ashore, gripping sea battles, a daring rescue and intense personal intrigue, *The Scent of Corruption* is a non-stop nautical thriller in the best traditions of the genre. Number seven in the Fighting Sail series.

ISBN 978-1943404025

**Blackwell's Homecoming by V E Ulett**

In a multigenerational saga of love, war and betrayal, Captain Blackwell and Mercedes continue their voyage in Volume III of Blackwell's Adventures. The Blackwell family's eventful journey from England to Hawaii, by way of the new and tempestuous nations of Brazil and Chile, provides an intimate portrait of family conflicts and loyalties in the late Georgian Age. Blackwell's Homecoming is an evocation of the dangers and rewards of desire.

ISBN 978-0-9882360-7-3

**Britannia's Spartan by Antoine Vanner**

It's 1882 and Captain Nicholas Dawlish has taken command of the Royal Navy's newest cruiser, HMS *Leonidas*. Her voyage to the Far East is to be peaceful, a test of innovative engines and boilers. But a new balance of power is emerging there. Imperial China, weak and corrupt, is challenged by a rapidly modernising Japan, while Russia threatens from the north. They all need to control Korea, a kingdom frozen in time and reluctant to emerge from centuries of isolation. Dawlish has no forewarning of the nightmare of riot, treachery, massacre and battle that lies ahead and in this, the fourth of the Dawlish Chronicles, he will find himself stretched to his limits – and perhaps beyond.

ISBN 978-1943404049

**The Shantyman by Rick Spilman**
In 1870, on the clipper ship *Alahambra* in Sydney, the new crew comes aboard more or less sober, except for the last man, who is hoisted aboard in a cargo sling, paralytic drunk. The drunken sailor, Jack Barlow, will prove to be an able shantyman. On a ship with a dying captain and a murderous mate, Barlow will literally keep the crew pulling together. As he struggles with a tragic past, a troubled present and an uncertain future, Barlow will guide the *Alahambra* through Southern Ocean ice and the horror of an Atlantic hurricane. His one goal is bringing the ship and crew safely back to New York, where he hopes to start anew. Based on a true story, *The Shantyman* is a gripping tale of survival against all odds at sea and ashore, and the challenge of facing a past that can never be wholly left behind.
ISBN978-0-9941152-2-5

**Water Ghosts by Linda Collison**
Fifteen-year-old James McCafferty is an unwilling sailor aboard a traditional Chinese junk, operated as adventure-therapy for troubled teens. Once at sea, the ship is gradually taken over by the spirits of courtiers who fled the Imperial court during the Ming Dynasty, more than 600 years ago. One particular ghost wants what James has and is intent on trading places with him. But the teens themselves are their own worst enemies in the struggle for life in the middle of the Pacific Ocean. A psychological story set at sea, with historical and paranormal elements.
ISBN 978-1943404001

**Eleanor's Odyssey by Joan Druett**
It was 1799, and French privateers lurked in the Atlantic and the Bay of Bengal. Yet Eleanor Reid, newly married and just twenty-one years old, made up her mind to sail with her husband, Captain Hugh Reid, to the penal colony of New South Wales, the Spice Islands and India. Danger threatened not just from the barely charted seas they would be sailing, yet, confident in her love and her husband's seamanship, Eleanor insisted on going along. Joan Druett, writer of many books about the sea, including the bestseller Island of the Lost and the groundbreaking story of women under sail, Hen Frigates, embellishes Eleanor's journal with a commentary that illuminates the strange story of a remarkable young woman.
ISBN 978-0-9941152-1-8

**Captain Blackwell's Prize by V E Ulett**

A small, audacious British frigate does battle against a large but ungainly Spanish ship. British Captain James Blackwell intercepts the Spanish *La Trinidad*, outmaneuvers and outguns the treasure ship and boards her. Fighting alongside the Spanish captain, sword in hand, is a beautiful woman. The battle is quickly over. The Spanish captain is killed in the fray and his ship damaged beyond repair. Its survivors and treasure are taken aboard the British ship, *Inconstant*.

ISBN 978-0-9882360-6-6


**Britannia's Shark by Antione Vanner**

"Britannia's Shark" is the third of the Dawlish Chronicles novels. It's 1881 and a daring act of piracy draws the ambitious British naval officer, Nicholas Dawlish, into a deadly maelstrom of intrigue and revolution. Drawn in too is his wife Florence, for whom the glimpse of a half-forgotten face evokes memories of earlier tragedy. For both a nightmare lies ahead, amid the wealth and squalor of America's Gilded Age and on a fever-ridden island ruled by savage tyranny. Manipulated ruthlessly from London by the shadowy Admiral Topcliffe, Nicholas and Florence Dawlish must make some very strange alliances if they are to survive – and prevail.

ISBN 978-0992263690


**The Guinea Boat by Alaric Bond**

Set in Hastings, Sussex during the early part of 1803, *Guinea Boat* tells the story of two young lads, and the diverse paths they take to make a living on the water. Britain is still at an uneasy peace with France, but there is action and intrigue a plenty along the south-east coast. Private fights and family feuds abound; a hot press threatens the livelihoods of many, while the newly re-formed Sea Fencibles begin a careful watch on Bonaparte's ever growing invasion fleet. And to top it all, free trading has grown to the extent that it is now a major industry, and one barely kept in check by the efforts of the preventive men. Alaric Bond's eighth novel.

ISBN 978-0994115294


**The Beckoning Ice by Joan Druett**

The Beckoning Ice finds the U. S. Exploring Expedition off Cape Horn, a grim outpost made still more threatening by the report of a corpse on a drifting iceberg, closely followed by a gruesome death on board. Was it suicide, or a particularly brutal murder? Wiki investigates, only to find himself fighting desperately for his own life.

ISBN 978-0-9922588-3-2

**Lady Castaways by Joan Druett**
It was not just the men who lived on the brink of peril when under sail at sea. Lucretia Jansz, who was enslaved as a concubine in 1629, was just one woman who endured a castaway experience. Award-winning historian Joan Druett (*Island of the Lost, The Elephant Voyage*), relates the stories of women who survived remarkable challenges, from heroines like Mary Ann Jewell, the "governess" of Auckland Island in the icy sub-Antarctic, to Millie Jenkins, whose ship was sunk by a whale.
ISBN 978-0994115270

**Hell Around the Horn by Rick Spilman**
In 1905, a young ship's captain and his family set sail on the windjammer, *Lady Rebecca*, from Cardiff, Wales with a cargo of coal bound for Chile, by way of Cape Horn. Before they reach the Southern Ocean, the cargo catches fire, the mate threatens mutiny and one of the crew may be going mad. The greatest challenge, however, will prove to be surviving the vicious westerly winds and mountainous seas of the worst Cape Horn winter in memory. Told from the perspective of the Captain, his wife, a first year apprentice and an American sailor before the mast, *Hell Around the Horn* is a story of survival and the human spirit in the last days of the great age of sail.
ISBN 978-0-9882360-1-1

**Turn a Blind Eye by Alaric Bond**
Newly appointed to the local revenue cutter, Commander Griffin is determined to make his mark, and defeat a major gang of smugglers. But the country is still at war with France and it is an unequal struggle; can he depend on support from the local community, or are they yet another enemy for him to fight? With dramatic action on land and at sea, *Turn a Blind Eye* exposes the private war against the treasury with gripping fact and fascinating detail.
ISBN 978-0-9882360-3-5

**The Torrid Zone by Alaric Bond**
A tired ship with a worn out crew, but *HMS Scylla* has one more trip to make before her much postponed re-fit. Bound for St Helena, she is to deliver the island's next governor; a simple enough mission and, as peace looks likely to be declared, no one is expecting difficulties. Except, perhaps, the commander of a powerful French battle squadron, who has other ideas.
With conflict and intrigue at sea and ashore, *The Torrid Zone* is filled to the gunnels with action, excitement and fascinating historical detail; a truly engaging read.
ISBN 978-0988236097